THE QUEEN'S COMPANION

A novel of historical fiction

Maggi A. Petton

Dedication

For Peggy and Emma,
holders of my hope…

and for my mother…
always there.

Acknowledgments

If, indeed, it takes a village to raise a child, then I am of the belief that a global community is required to birth a book.

I am eternally grateful to the multitude of family, friends, associates, and even total strangers who encouraged me throughout the process of writing The Queen's Companion. Several people read or reread drafts and gave me valuable feedback. My heartfelt thanks go to Melanie Peterson, Alice Maechtlen, Cheri Stromberg, Susan Ellenwood, Peg Lahey, Dr. Helen D'Esposito, Loriel Weddington, Robin Howard, Carol Counelis, Gregory Hedges, Dr. Donald Clark, David Imbordino, Lori Upham, Charlene Killoran, Susan Stiger, Barbara Howington, Skip and Jackie Oddo, Celeste Tapia, and Peggy Counelis. Special thanks to Elisabeth Mulkern, whose initial response gave me the courage to open the door, letting loose the story. Author Jonathan Kirsch encouraged me to keep writing. (I haven't stopped.) And, to all of the wonderful people in Italy....grazie.

Thanks to Pam England, Midwife, Birthing From Within, for generously offering her time and resources to help me gain an understanding of childbirth in the Middle Ages.

Deep gratitude goes to Fran Lambros for giving my manuscript to book reviewer, Carol Haggas. Carol's feedback gave me the courage to keep putting the story out there.

Teresa Cutler-Broyles not only edited, but drew the story from me with skill, gentleness and humor. It was Terry who carted me off to Italy, setting in motion the discovery of the Palazzo Cervini. (Hey, Terry, I'm pretty sure Catherine and Bella would want me to thank you, too!)

My mother, Lucille Petton, generously gave her time and talent to a final proofreading. I am, as always, thankful for her support.

Ellen Novak has kept the fire lit to get The Queen's Companion in print. Without her, the story of Catherine and Bella might still lie in a box in my office. Bless you, Ellen.

Patti Brenneman and Joan Kavooras...where do I even begin to express my gratitude for your lifelong support and friendship? I would be a lesser person without you two.

The Reverend Brian C. Taylor of St. Michael and All Angels Episcopal Church in Albuquerque, New Mexico served as the inspiration for the character of Father Tim. Much of Brian Taylor found its way into the novel. Where I have quoted him, I have indicated so with a symbol of a cross †. If you are interested in learning more about Brian Taylor, or reading any of his books or sermons, feel free to visit St. Michael's website at www.all-angels.com.

Author's note:
During the 16th Century, I know that Italy was not yet "Italy." It is also true that Europe was not yet "Europe." That being said, I have called them that anyway. Trust me, it saves a tree.

Introduction

January 2010

A dream threatened to hold me in another consciousness on a February morning in 2008. I had to force myself from the altered state, but found that the images, the characters in the dream refused to dissolve as I went about my day. For weeks they pursued me, relentlessly. For eight months I was only able to sleep a few hours each night. The characters woke me at two o'clock every morning demanding that I tell their story.

It was like trying to take dictation from a movie that played itself out in my head. I found myself writing in every spare moment as the story, characters and the research consumed me.

During the process I became obsessed with everything sixteenth century. But, as the story revealed itself and my research deepened, I found details, things I could not possibly have known, to have actually existed. Each time I discovered one of these coincidences, I became less surprised.

I am forced to call this *historical fiction*. But, as you read the final coincidence in the Epilogue, you may decide otherwise. There, you will follow me as I journey to Italy where the characters finally release their hold on me. You may decide for yourself whether this story is fact or fiction or a little of both.

The Inquisition began in 1231. The last documented event was recorded in 1868. It was only in 1996 that Pope John Paul II allowed access to the secret archives of the Inquisition. He apologized for it in 2006.

Chapter One

August 1554

Five horses with riders made their way single file along a narrow path paralleling a high, rocky cliff. Few sounds accompanied the riders, as the creek normally gurgling through the canyon was dry. It was the end of a long, hot summer season. The sun seared everything it touched, drying and crisping all beneath its oven-like rays. Shimmering waves rose from the tops of baking boulders creating additional unwanted heat. Autumn was anticipated, but still too far away to provide any comfort. Nothing bothered to bloom.

Aside from the soft and steady clomp of the horses' hooves on the dry, powdered soil there was little noise. The tiny clouds of dust generated by the horses did not even have the energy to rise up to the fetlocks, but settled hurriedly as if anxious to avoid further drying. No breezes stirred the leaves. No creatures moved in the underbrush. The air was still.

The weary riders spoke not at all, keeping their mouths clamped shut, as if they might prevent the heat from scorching their insides. Perhaps their very surroundings had sapped them of the energy to speak. Maybe the disappointing journey from which they returned took too much out of them. Whatever the reason for their silent, unhurried amble, it was that very silence that caused the middle rider to stop. Instantly, the other riders halted and became alert, hands on their swords, eyes searching and scanning. Sounds. They all heard them now, muted echoes off the cliff. Human or animal, it was difficult to tell. Near enough to bounce off the rock wall, but not so near as to be visible. Grunting, like a wild pig rooting. No, too rhythmical. A moan, or was it more like a whimper? Definitely human.

The middle rider signaled the others to dismount and with hand gestures indicated that two of them circle around both to the right and the left, away from the rocky cliff. The remaining three began what could only have been a well rehearsed and stealthy approach toward the sounds. They did not have far to go. About a hundred yards from their horses, in a small, shaded clearing, they came upon a scene all too common in recent times.

Tied to a tree, lying face up on the ground was a woman. She was naked. What could be made of her face failed to reveal if she was young or old, for it was bloody, bruised and crusted with dirt, tears and mucus that looked days old. Her arms were stretched taut over her head, and her legs splayed outward and tied to makeshift wooden stakes at each ankle. It was from her that the moaning sounds issued, not of her own accord, but from the force of each violent thrust of the naked, grunting, filthy man on top of her.

The three waited for only a moment before the two circling soldiers arrived at either end of the clearing. At a subtle sign, all five stepped into the opening in the trees and laid their sword tips on a different part of the torturing party. The grunting ceased.

"Up, you vile swine," spat the soldier with his sword tip on the jugular vein of the now still man.

Slowly, attempting to save himself from the pierce of any of the five swords pressing into his flesh, the man pushed his torso up until his quickly shriveling penis emerged from the woman. Once he was standing upright, between the woman's stake-bound legs, the sword tips guided him backward without a sound. He reeked of alcohol.

"Bind his hands, but leave him naked," a female voice said. Its owner moved quickly to the bound woman. As she moved toward the body, she reached up to push back the light, cotton hood covering her head. Her long, dark hair was pulled back and tied with a ribbon at the nape of her neck. Though not beautiful, her face was striking with large, intense brown eyes that revealed her concern. She moved gracefully and with determination as she knelt next to the victim.

With swift, careful sword strokes she sliced the ropes from the tree and stakes. In a single action, she swung her cape around to cover the naked, nearly lifeless form on the ground. The battered victim seemed barely alive, but as her arms were untied and released she groaned and opened her swollen eyes. Through the minutest of slits she looked up.

"You are safe," whispered the rider. The woman slipped back into unconsciousness

The surroundings revealed a small camp that had clearly been in place for several days. Bones of small animals were strewn about. Ashes from a now dead fire lay in a ring of stones. An animal bladder reeked of some fermented brew.

One of the soldiers found the woman's garments, but they were useless, having been shredded.

Another of the men picked up pants and a filthy doublet, "These must belong to him".

"Shred those, as well, and leave them on the ashes", demanded a tall, dark man whose bearing suggested he held some authority.

"Yes, Captain."

Robert, Captain of the Queen's Guard walked to the now bound and naked man

"Your name," he demanded.

The prisoner spat at the ground near the Captain's feet and remained silent. At this, the soldier controlling the man's bindings drew his knife and placed it on the man's throat.

"I will make you answer, pig!"

Robert held up his hand, nodding to his soldier. "He may be more inclined to talk after his journey with us, Remy. For now, let us get her," he indicated the woman on the ground, "to a physician. She looks like she has been through a war." Captain Robert walked over to where his queen knelt, tending the unconscious woman. "Do you think she will live?" he whispered.

The queen took a dagger from a sheath in her belt and carefully sliced through the tight ropes around the woman's wrists. Fibers from the rough hemp rubbed into her skin leaving deep, blood encrusted sores that dried and caked themselves to the rope. "I don't know." She shook her head. "The journey alone may finish her. Will you be able to carry her? Is your horse able to manage you both after this arduous journey?" the queen reached out and gently peeled a strand of crusted hair from the puffy, unrecognizable face.

Robert nodded his assent as one of the soldiers appeared in the clearing leading their horses. The queen went to her horse and pulled a water bag from the pommel. She ripped a piece of cloth from the bottom of her garment and soaked it with water. When she knelt back down next to the unconscious woman, she placed the wet cloth on her lips. Reflexively, the mouth suckled, just a few drops, then stopped.

"You," the queen stood and walked over to the prisoner. "What do you know of her?" She indicated the near dead victim.

"She is a just a woman," he slurred. "Nothing more."

The Captain approached the prisoner and stood in front of him. With a raised eyebrow, he looked pointedly at the man's shrunken cock, then directed a cold glare into his prisoner's eyes.

"What of your mother?" asked the Captain. "Just a woman, as well, I suppose. You would likely be one of those who, in the name of all that is good, take the life of one you found defiling her."

Robert paused, started away, then turned back to the drunken sot.

"And what of your queen?" Robert continued. "Is your queen just another for men like you to defile?"

The man remained silent and sullen. As if to emphasize his disregard for life, he pissed where he stood, not caring that dirt and urine splashed up onto his own ankles.

The Captain turned in disgust and walked over to where his queen waited, again, next to the body on the ground.

With the aid of two of his soldiers, Robert was able to situate himself on his horse with the unconscious woman held as gently as possible in his arms.

"Remy, tie this blackguard to your horse," the queen instructed her soldier. "He will walk or be dragged to the castle."

"Yes, Majesty."

At the sound of her title, a flicker of fear shot through the eyes of the prisoner.

The queen mounted her horse, and the now six riders and one naked prisoner resumed their silent march toward Montalcino Castle.

Montalcino Castle could be seen from miles away. It was nestled high into the side of a mountain overlooking the town of Montalcino. The castle itself was ringed by two high, dark stone walls. The walls abutted the sides of the mountain itself, making the guard house the only port of entry to the castle.

The castle housed a center tower that was the tallest part of the structure. Angling out from the central tower were two wings of three stories each. The west wing housed the Great Hall, the Queen's office, the kitchens and sleeping quarters for the Queen and her family. The Queen's private quarters were on the third floor. The east wing held quarters for servants and castle staff. At the far end of the east wing was a second, smaller tower of the castle keep, the prison cells, which were mostly underground, and the torture chamber.

When they arrived at the castle, Robert dragged the exhausted prisoner to the cells. Because this man was caught in the very act of committing a crime, and by the queen, herself, Robert took him directly to the lowest of the chambers and chained him to the walls. There was no need to place him in the upper cell to await further interrogation.

"Your punishment will be delivered by the queen when she sees fit to deal with you," Robert spat at the man. "Meanwhile, you will be branded in such a way that all will know of your crime and be wary…should you live to see the outside of this cell."

The branding iron that Robert chose had never been used before. It held the queen's own mark, a crown encircling a one of a kind sword with an unusual cross guard. A fire burned in the corridor outside the prisoner's cell. Robert held the iron in the flames until it was red hot. When he returned to the prisoner, Robert grabbed him by his hair and held his head against the wall. The prisoner screamed in agony as the iron sizzled into his face on his left cheek. As Robert let go of him, he passed out. Robert left him dangling from his chains.

The nearly dead woman was carried up to the queen's quarters and the physician summoned.

By the time the queen made her way up the huge circular stone stairway to her quarters, the physician was already examining the patient who now lay on a pallet near the window. As he examined her, the queen's servants attempted to tend to Queen Catherine. She shooed them away with a wave, and turned to the physician, a short, graying man with a slight paunch.

"Will she live?"

"Difficult to say, Majesty. Were you to be lying here with these injuries, I would have no doubt, but she is unknown to me. How did she come to be in this condition?"

"Kidnapped, most likely, and held captive by a barbarian in the forest just south of the great granite cliff. He had obviously been having his way with her for some time. She was bound and naked when we came upon them. I don't know how long she was there, but she has remained as you see her since we found them." As she spoke, the queen moved closer and winced as the physician peeled back a swollen eyelid to peer into the woman's eye.

"I will not lie to you," he said, "her injuries are severe. She has been beaten, more than once, judging from the varying stages of her bruises. Although she doesn't appear to have any obvious broken bones, the swelling in so many areas of her body makes it difficult to make an accurate assessment. Her backside will need to be meticulously cleaned." He turned the woman onto her side as he spoke. "Her flesh is punctured with hundreds of thorns and small pebbles." The physician removed the covering and showed the queen the woman's back. It was a mass of cuts and tiny holes.

The queen's hand flew to her mouth, and she stifled a small gasp as her insides lurched. She already had difficulty imagining how the poor soul endured the torture of her ordeal without even considering the discomfort of this additional pain. She choked back her tears.

"If she regains her senses," the physician continued, "she will need much time to heal…and I must emphasize that she may not regain her senses at all, Majesty. Without her in a conscious state I cannot determine the extent to which she may have been damaged internally."

"I understand. My servants will keep vigil and tend to her wounds. We will call for you if she awakens."

"And you, my Queen, do you have need of anything from me? I have mixed a sleeping draught for the woman in case she awakens, and there is enough for you, as well."

"Thank you, no. I have need of a bath only. I guarantee that sleep will not be a problem." She managed a small smile.

Once the physician was gone, the queen directed her servants to draw her bath and then continue their ministrations to the injured woman. They were cleaning her body as gently as possible. As the dirt and blood were removed, more and more wounds were discovered. There was barely any part of her that was not injured.

A bath soothed the queen's aching body. The woman who tended her, a servant named Marie, washed her hair. Water was heated for a second bath, for the grime of many days was with the queen. When she felt sufficiently clean she allowed her body to be oiled. Following the extended camping of the past weeks, sleep came quickly and deeply in her own bed.

A commotion from her sitting room awakened the queen. Catherine had no idea if she had slept for minutes or days. She was disoriented, having spent weeks away from her castle, and had to shake her confusion away. She rose, put on a robe and rushed to the sitting room.

Three of her servants were pleading with the injured woman to be allowed to continue to tend to her wounds. Each time they attempted to approach her, the woman became more agitated and fearful. She could not speak or move easily for her injuries, but was trying to get up. She was sobbing and gasping for air. Her eyes, what could be seen of them through the swollen lids, were full of panic.

"Nooo. Nooo." That part was clear. The rest were just garbled sounds, not even recognizable as words.

"Stand back, all of you," ordered Queen Catherine, almost feeling the fear of the frightened woman. Instantly, all three servants retreated.

The crying woman tried to hold a coverlet to hide her nakedness. The queen did not make a move toward her, but waited without speaking. When she finally seemed to calm, the queen addressed her softly.

"You are among friends," she said. "We have no wish to harm you."

"I do not know you," cried the woman. It was difficult to understand what she was saying because of the swelling in her cheeks and jaw, but the queen understood.

"Nor I you, and so we are on equal ground. Leave us," she directed her servants.

The queen turned back, "I will not harm you. You are safe here."

Slowly, the woman looked at her. The queen saw the fear slowly leave her eyes. When she collapsed back onto the pallet, wincing in pain, the queen approached slowly and sat down next to her.

"Can you tell me your name?" asked the queen

"Isabella," was the garbled reply.

"Isabella," the queen repeated. "You have many wounds that need attending. Will you allow me to help you?"

Isabella nodded her assent. The queen helped to position her on her side, to allow the sunlight to illuminate the woman's badly injured backside. Sitting behind her, the queen continued what her servants had begun, carefully extracting some of the hundreds of tiny thorns and sharp stones that had burrowed their way into her skin. It was a tedious and time consuming ordeal. At times the queen's hand cramped as she worked the pincers and she stopped often to massage her hands and fingers. Eventually the sunlight abandoned her and torches were lit.

As the queen worked, Isabella drifted in and out of a troubled sleep. She'd accepted water and the sleeping draught, but she whimpered, sometimes jerking and yelling out. When this happened she attempted to get up, but her injuries prevented her. Each time, the queen's voice calmed her and she fell back to sleep.

Working to free every pebble and thorn from Isabella's body, the queen wondered at the softness of the other woman's skin. As princess and then queen, Catherine had always been tended to, she never had cause to observe or touch another body. She noticed the glistening of tiny blond hairs that covered Isabella's arms and legs. She became aware of Isabella's breath, how it labored in her sleep. She was astonished at the velvety feel of Isabella's skin and how warm and fragile it felt under her fingertips.

As she worked, the queen's mind wandered from prayer to silent meditation and back again to prayer. Her prayers were for her kingdom, her subjects, and the woman whose body lay broken before her. While her usual meditations centered on a phrase or two from the Psalms, as her eyes searched Isabella's body for tiny bits of grit and thorn, she lost all sense of herself, much as she did when her meditations took her outside of her own being. She never knew where she went at those times, only that time seemed to have passed without her participation. All she ever knew was that she returned as refreshed as if from a full night of sleep.

Catherine's spiritual life was the most important part of who she was. Being queen was the role she had been given by God, and a role she relied on God to help her fulfill. Although her kingdom, as most of Europe, was Catholic, Catherine realized that no longer could one tell who was faithful to the church because they truly believed and who appeared to be faithful out of fear. Her experiences with the religious leaders, and especially her own bishop, left a bad taste in her mouth.

Catherine's love of God did not come from the Church or the Church leaders, but from her parents. Both her parents believed in God, but from her mother she learned about the true teachings of Christ. Her mother was compassionate, accepting and kind. It was difficult to balance those traits as a ruling monarch, but Catherine attempted to emulate her mother's goodness in her role as queen. From her father, Catherine understood that being a monarch was more than just an inheritance; it was a calling. He never let Catherine forget that being queen was God-given and that she would answer to God for the ways in which she ruled. In times of difficulty, both of her parents often stole away to the church at night to pray. There she learned how to surrender her heart to God in the peace and solitude that was always absent when others were present in the church, especially the bishop.

When Isabella's back was free of the rubble, the queen had a bowl with warmed water and a cloth brought to her. In spite of the protestations of the servants, she did not allow them to perform this task for fear the woman would awaken again and become afraid.

Gently, changing the water often, she managed to clear Isabella's entire back of debris.

Once Isabella's body was cleaned, the queen ordered healing ointments. She attempted to count the number of wounds on Isabella's body as she applied the poultice, but quickly gave up. There were simply too many cuts.

When she was finally done, she covered Isabella and had the torches extinguished.

Isabella did not wake again, nor did she stir, for three days.

Chapter Two

When Isabella appeared to be emerging from her long sleep, the queen was notified. She did not want a repeat of the scene that so frightened the woman days before. As Isabella stirred more restlessly, the queen dismissed the servant she had ordered to sit watch, and took a seat near the pallet to read and wait.

It was not long before Isabella's puffed and discolored eyelids began to flutter and open. Her gaze fell on the queen who sat near her. At first, she stiffened and her expression was one of fear and suspicion, but as they held each others' gaze Isabella relaxed. She shifted her legs and grimaced, then looked down and raised the coverlet over her. She peered beneath. Her face filled with pain. Her eyes instantly darkened and filled with terror, her head shaking back and forth, back and forth.

"You remember," said the queen softly.

To this, Isabella only closed her eyes as if she could erase the memories by refusing to look at them.

"You need not speak of what you remember, but it may help you to talk about it."

A pitcher of water and a cup were on a stand near Isabella's pallet.

"Are you thirsty?" Catherine asked.

Isabella nodded.

Catherine stood and poured water. She aided Isabella gently to a sitting position and held the cup to her still swollen, cracked lips. Isabella drank her fill and the queen lay her back down on the pallet. Perhaps it was the remembering or just the act of drinking, but Isabella was exhausted. The queen said, "Go back to sleep, there will be time enough to talk when you are well." Isabella reached out for the queen's hand and did not release it until she was deep into sleep again.

It was late on the same day when Isabella, again, began to stir. The queen was in her quarters for the evening, her hair being brushed by Marie, and so was nearby when Isabella woke. In the reflection in her mirror, the queen saw the woman's eyes open.

Queen Catherine turned toward her, "Are you hungry?"

Isabella nodded.

"Bring some broth," she ordered Marie. The servant nodded and disappeared.

Catherine went over to the pallet where Isabella lay and sat next to her.

"You are beginning to look like you might live." She smiled.

Isabella opened her mouth and tried to speak. Her words did not come out right. "Ehre em I?" She lifted her hand to her mouth and felt the swelling around her face and lips.

"You are in my home, and you are safe." Catherine asked, "Are you in much pain?"

Isabella nodded.

"Truly," Catherine said, "it was much worse days ago. The swelling is coming down. Your body was a mass of cuts and bruises. Will you allow me to see how your back is healing?"

In answer, Isabella rolled carefully to her side to allow her back to be examined. Although it was still difficult for her to see through her badly swollen and purpled lids, she looked around, for the first time, at the room in which she lay. A round dining table was situated in the largest part of the room. It sat eight if necessary. Near to the table was a sitting area with comfortable chairs in front of a huge stone fireplace. On two opposite walls were massive, floor to ceiling bookcases, filled with leather-bound books. Apart from everything, in the farthest corner of the room was a five paneled, hand painted screen.

The queen pulled down the coverlet to reveal Isabella's back. After a careful inspection she said, "Your wounds appear to be closing and healing. It's also going to be difficult to wear regular clothing. A corset is out of the question for some time."

"Ooh ahr you?" mumbled Isabella.

At that moment the doors opened and the broth was delivered. When they were alone again the queen helped to prop Isabella up on the pallet and fed her. It was a slow and deliberate process to spoon, and swallowing was difficult for Isabella, but Catherine did not rush the task.

Again, the effort seemed to tire Isabella. Catherine removed some of the pillows and lay her back down. She was soon asleep and slept through the night.

As Catherine lay in her own bed she wondered about the woman, Isabella. What was it about Isabella that compelled her to care? This was not a task for a queen, and yet, Catherine found herself looking forward to it...both the caring for Isabella and the company. Her quarters seemed less lonely with the presence of another sharing them.

The next morning Isabella awakened as the queen was preparing to leave. Catherine found Isabella looking slightly better.

"I need to leave for the day, but will be near enough to call should you require me," Catherine explained. "This is Marie, in whom I have the utmost trust to care for you. She will not leave your side. I have requested porridge and some ale for breakfast. I am afraid you might not be able to chew anything yet, and the ale might ease your pain and help you to sleep easier," she continued. "I will be back. Rest well."

Marie, the daughter of the woman who had served Catherine's mother, had been with Catherine since she was a young princess. Although she was a loyal servant and doted on the queen, she spoke rarely, and never, ever gave her opinion.

The queen and Marie stood in the hallway just outside the queen's quarters. Catherine instructed Marie not to reveal her identity as queen to the injured woman.

"The physician is afraid that she might attempt to feign her recovery if she knows I am the queen. I don't want Isabella to know who I am. Is that understood, Marie?"

"Yes, Majesty, but..." Marie looked at the doors to the queen's quarters, "but what do I tell her if she asks?"

"Say as little as possible. Tell her that my name is Catherine. Tell her you are new to the position and only know that I am a lady of the castle. Don't reveal that this is Montalcino Castle."

"Yes, Majesty."

"And until further notice you must *not* refer to me as Majesty in Isabella's presence."

"Yes, Majesty."

21

"Marie," Catherine said with some exasperation, "it is imperative that you refrain from royal address. Please be aware."

"Yes, Ma'am."

"Keep all other persons out of my quarters except the physician. Stay with Isabella until I return."

For his part, the physician suggested that Isabella be moved to the infirmary so that "the queen need not trouble herself." But Catherine, having seen the torture this woman endured and still relived when she woke from her night terrors, would not agree to move the woman just yet.

In this way the identity of the queen remained secret.

And so it was that the Lady Isabella of Acquapendente proceeded to heal in the quarters of Catherine, the Queen of Montalcino. And Catherine, Queen of Montalcino, assumed the role of caretaker for a woman she had rescued from certain death.

Chapter Three

The days took on a routine, of sorts. Catherine left her quarters in the morning and attended to her duties. She returned in the evening where she had dinner brought up and she and Isabella ate together.

Catherine asked many questions of Isabella, as her ability to speak improved. Isabella, it seemed was the only child of the Earl of Acquapendente, who held much land in the southern part of the kingdom. Catherine knew of the Earl, but had never met him. She remembered her father speak of him and had a faint memory of the association being a positive one, but remembered little else. Isabella's family called her by the pet name, Bella.

Bella had married slightly over a year earlier. Her husband was considerably older than she, and an aristocrat. The marriage, though it was an arranged one, was pleasant enough. It was marriage that brought Isabella further north to her husband's castle and lands. Her parents came north to visit Bella following the miscarriage of her first child. Bella made attempts, over several days, to tell of the events that occurred during her parents' visit, but each time she tried it was as if a cloud enveloped her entire being in darkness. She became silent and withdrawn, her eyes unfocused. Catherine sensed that to speak those things aloud would give them the power to become real. She knew Isabella could not yet visit those memories.

At those times Catherine read until Bella gradually fell asleep.

As the weeks progressed the swelling in Isabella's face decreased. It became clear she was a woman of uncommon beauty. High cheekbones began to surface, and a high forehead. Her eyes were difficult to describe. They were of a color that changed with her surroundings...from blue to hazel, green to steel grey, depending on the light and the colors that surrounded her. Her hair fell to her breast line and was soft with golden waves. Although her lips were still swollen and discolored, they were beginning to return to their original shape, full and perfectly proportioned, with a slight downward turn. Her chin held a soft cleft at the bottom and it was evident that a scar would form to the right side of the cleft. She was twenty four years old.

"From the description, you could be this woman," Catherine commented one evening as she read aloud from a book about northern Europe. "You are much fairer than most women this side of Spain, or the Kingdom of Sardinia."

"Some of my ancestors were from the north. I favor them. And yes," she attempted a smile as she held up a strand of her hair, "my hair is the color of straw."

Catherine smiled as she looked at Bella. "You are lovely. And straw holds all of the hues of sunlight."

One night Catherine was awakened to the sound of Isabella screaming in terror.

"Paaapaaa! Nooo! Paapaaaaa!"

Catherine rushed to the outer room, and found Isabella reaching out and crying. She ran to grab Isabella's flailing arms and called out to her, "Isabella! Wake up" and finally, "Bella, please, Bella." Bella woke just as guards stormed in to the room.

"It's fine. She was merely having a bad dream. All is well." Catherine dismissed the soldiers quickly and turned her attention back to Bella who was drenched in sweat and shaking violently.

Bella clung to Catherine and cried, "I could do nothing...nothing!" Great heaving sobs wracked her body. "I was made to watch! There were so many of them...they wore huge crucifixes around their necks. I did not know who they were. They made me watch...they made me..."

"Watch who, Bella...watch what?" asked Catherine, although she could already have predicted what was to come. The Church had been trying to cleanse itself of heretics in the most unimaginable ways for hundreds of years. In the name of God the Church was responsible for the torture and murder of anyone suspected of being a heretic. All it took was for two people to make accusations of heresy and the likes of Bishop Capshaw could order execution or imprisonment. No matter that those two people may be criminals, or enemies or even a person's own children who were threatened by the Church. Catherine had been listening to the horrors of this Inquisition all her life.

"They came at night," Bella was still crying, "and tore us from our beds. They told us that we were accused of heresy against the Church!" At this Bella's face crumpled and she was unable to continue for some minutes as the weeping overtook her again. Finally, she went on, "My mother...oh, God, my mother. You cannot imagine."

Catherine held Bella patiently, rocking her gently and stroking her hair. Her heart ached as her thoughts swirled around and between the horror stories she grew up hearing. Knowing that Bella was a victim of such a crime made her angry. But she waited, silently, wanting Bella to be able to give voice to her torment in her own time.

"They would not even let us defend ourselves or profess our faith," Bella finally continued. "They dragged us outside in our nightclothes...my husband, my father and mother. The servants were already outside. They were told to observe what happens to heretics!"

Bella couldn't say more. When she tried to speak the only sounds that issued forth were whispered cries, "No...no...no!" She could not speak, and began to weep again. Her head shook back and forth as if she could shake the images from her mind.

Catherine held her until she cried herself to sleep.

In the morning, Catherine woke as she heard Marie enter the quarters. She was still on the pallet cradling Isabella. She gestured to Marie to come back later so that Bella might continue to sleep.

Over the course of the next many days Bella was mostly quiet. Periodically, Catherine saw her close her eyes and shake her head. The nights that followed were much the same, filled with restless sleep and nightmares, but gradually, the story of that night was revealed.

It was a sound that woke her. Shaking the sleep from her she wondered if it was a dream. Then there were shouts. She opened her eyes and saw the flicker of shadows on the wall of her bedroom.

"Daniel," she whispered, then shook him. "Daniel, wake up."

He was alert instantly. Light moved across the ceiling of their bedroom. Torchlight. Daniel was up in an instant and ran to the window. She was right beside him.

The servants were all in the courtyard surrounded by strangers, some on horseback, and some on foot. Nearly all of them held torches.

There were at least twenty men ordering the servants against the courtyard wall.

"Wait here," Daniel commanded. As he was grabbing his robe, the door of the bedroom burst open. Three men, two with swords drawn, and one with a torch, entered.

"What is the meaning of this?" Daniel demanded.

"Shut up!" One of the swordsmen shoved Daniel onto the floor and while he held his sword on her husband's neck, the other tied his hands behind him.

Isabella's hands were tied behind her, as well, and they were both pushed down the stairs and out into the courtyard.

"Here they are, Captain." Both Isabella and her husband were forced down onto their knees next to Isabella's parents.

Every time Daniel, or Isabella's father, James, attempted to ask a question, or protest, they were kicked, hard.

The man referred to as "Captain" by the others strolled over to where the servants remained lined up against the wall. Most of them were crying and clearly terrified.

As he sauntered back and forth in front of the staff, he said in a loud voice, "We have evidence proving that these nobles," he indicated Isabella and her husband and parents, "are heretics. You are about to bear witness to what happens to heretics!"

"Lies!" Daniel shouted. "We are not heretics. Who says such a thing?"

At a motion from their leader, one of the sword wielders walked over in front of Daniel and slapped him across the face. With his hands tied behind his back he was unable to keep his balance on his knees and fell against Isabella. They both collapsed onto the ground.

"We are defenders of the faith," the leader continued. "As such, we have the authority to review the evidence presented and act accordingly."

"Please," Bella pleaded from her position on the ground, "please, you must believe my husband, we are not heretics. Let us prove ourselves. There is some mistake!"

He walked to where she lay and stood over her. She looked up into a thin, stern face, an apparition of hate and evil. He glared at her with cold eyes, then threw his head back and began to laugh.

His laugh chilled her. Her anger turned to fear.

"We," he waved his arm to indicate his compatriots, "do not make mistakes. God has shown us everything we need to know. We act on God's word." He turned and nodded to a man who was standing and holding something in the flames of a fire.

"Bring him," He ordered a fellow standing near her husband.

Daniel was forced to his feet and dragged next to the fire. His nightshirt was ripped from him. Although he struggled to escape, he was held firmly with his arms behind his back. Another came to aid in holding him. Again, he was forced to his knees, his head held back by his hair.

As Isabella watched, a red hot branding iron with the letter "H" was pressed into her husband's chest. He howled in agony. When the iron was removed, he collapsed onto the ground.

Isabella's mother was crying. She and her husband were bound together next to Isabella. As her father was cut loose from her mother, Isabella tried to move closer to her. Someone, she could not see who, pulled her by her hair to prevent her moving.

There was a large tree in the courtyard. With sickening realization, Isabella saw two ropes dangling from it. Her father was led to the tree. His hands were still bound behind his back. One of the ropes was looped through her father's bound wrists and tightened. The other end of it was tied to the pommel of a horse. When the ropes were deemed secure, the horse was led away from the tree. Her father was lifted, arms behind him, into the air. Bella and her mother wept and looked away as they heard his shoulders pop from their sockets while he screamed.

The men watching her and her mother forced them to stand. "You will watch," he instructed, "or you will suffer a fate worse than that." He held up the branding iron and waved it in front of their faces. "I will burn your eyes from your heads unless you watch."

They forced themselves to watch as Daniel was led to the tree. Another horse was brought and Daniel forced upon it, hands still bound behind his back. As the noose was placed around his neck, Isabella realized that this was no show of punishment for heresy. This was an execution. She knew, in that moment, that none of them would survive.

The flat blade of a sword slapped against the hindquarters of the horse, which jumped and jolted forward. Isabella watched her husband writhe on the end of the rope. When he was finally still, her father's unconscious body was lowered to the ground.

As her father was dragged back to her and her mother, Isabella tried, again, to plead for mercy.

"I beg of you, let us go," she sobbed. "We are not heretics, but good, God-fearing Catholics."

Again, that hateful laugh filled her ears. "Bring her parents!"

A single pole, driven into the ground, stood in the center of the courtyard. James and Elizabeth of Aquapendente were tied to it. As the kindling was placed around them, Isabella screamed, "No! No! It is I," she cried, "I alone am the heretic! Please spare my parents, they are innocent."

Her cries were ignored. The kindling lit. As the flames caught and grew, the men in the courtyard seemed to feed off the fire and the fear. It was as if they were intoxicated by their own power and the pain they were able to inflict on others.

Suddenly, as the attention in the courtyard was focused on the fire beginning to consume her parents, Isabella felt herself pulled by the hair into the shadow of one of the outer buildings. At first, thinking that someone might be attempting to rescue her, she was silent. It was only after she found herself being rushed through the fields of her husband's land that she realized she was being kidnapped.

With the sounds of her parents' screams fading in the distance, Isabella was dragged barefoot through the forest for the remainder of the night. At dawn, her captor stopped in a small clearing and tied her arms to a tree and her ankles to makeshift stakes. Then he ripped her nightgown from her body and shredded it with his dagger.

The evening after the full story of Bella's ordeal was revealed, following a light supper and a bit of reading, Bella drifted off into sleep. Catherine went out onto the balcony where she paced. The sun was just setting on the western horizon. Catherine watched it glide slowly past the tree line as the clouds overhead transformed from a brilliant oranges to pinks in a sky of deep purple. She leaned on the wall of her balcony and sighed. Isabella's story was one that disturbed Catherine to her very core. The days of this kind of punishment for "heresy" were supposed to have been long passed and replaced by a more fair and objective process. But stories like this had begun to surface in the past year. The Bishop, Thomas Capshaw, claimed no knowledge of the rogue group instituting this "immediate justice." Worse than that, he did not seem to care.

Before finding Isabella, the queen had gone to Rome with a small detachment at the end of July. She went to see Pope Julius III to request that he solicit a small army to patrol the rural areas. Her subjects were more frightened now than they had been during the early years of the Inquisition.

The Pope agreed to an audience with Queen Catherine, but claimed, like her own Bishop, no knowledge of the rogue groups that were attacking many parts of Europe.

"We have had very few reports of this nature," the Pope looked to his advisors as he said this. "Cardinal, this is unusual, is it not?"

"Unusual, Holiness, but not unheard of. There have been a few such attacks in the Republic of Genoa. We have a report of one like this in the Republic of Lucca, just north of Montalcino. No others."

"The problem seems very isolated, then, Your Highness," the Pope said without much concern. "I would guess that this type of activity will not be able to sustain itself. Be patient."

He told the queen that he did not approve of fanaticism and asked to be apprised of any further incidents. The Pope assured the queen that he would make a formal request of her Bishop Capshaw to investigate the attacks, but it was unlikely that there was anything that could help. Catherine discovered, while in Rome, that Pope Julius was not inclined toward politics or ecclesiastical duties. His interests ran more to his untoward relationship with the young beggar boy he called his adoptive "nephew" who, it was said, shared his bedroom and his bed.

It was on their way back from Rome that Catherine and Robert found Isabella.

That the band of rebels that attacked Isabella's family had the audacity to strike so close to the castle only proved their arrogance. She would find them. She must find them. The Inquisition itself was already to blame for the torture and murder of thousands upon thousands of innocent lives. To think that the Church gave itself permission for such vile acts tormented Catherine. This had been going on for over two hundred years and she often despaired that it would never end. There were times when she became so angry that she shook her fist and screamed for God to intervene. Other times, when she learned of children being forced to watch the execution of their own parents, she fell to her knees and sobbed. And now, as if the Inquisition itself were not horrible enough, the sickest of sadists used the church for their own devious amusements.

As the sky darkened and Catherine paced, she determined to find out who directed this group and what they gained from the murders. Historically, the church gained the lands and properties of those convicted of heresy. If that was the intention of those behind the murder of Isabella's family, it should be easy enough to discover the culprits. She would address this matter with her Council. And given her Papal visit, and the assurances of the Pope himself, her Bishop would be required to support her investigation.

Chapter Four

Within a few weeks, Isabella was able to stand without assistance. Her strength began to return as she was able to take solid foods. Though bathing was suspected of washing away one's soul, and generally limited to once weekly, the warm water relieved the aching around her shoulders. The awkward angle in which her arms had been tied over her head for many days had left them painful. It was still difficult for her to lift her arms, but it always seemed easier following a hot soak. Bella had been delighted to find that behind the five paneled screen in the quarters was a large brass tub. The tub was embossed with reeds, cattails and heron. It flared up and out at the narrow ends, allowing the bather to lean back and rest her head.

The baths generally tired her and she often fell into a deep, more relaxed sleep following a bath. The water also seemed to soften the tissues around the crusted wounds, and this helped to make her more comfortable, as well. And so, an early evening bath became a ritual of healing and relaxation. Catherine assisted Isabella into the tub and steadied her as she emerged. While she was soaking, Catherine read to her. After, Catherine applied a variety of ointments to the healing sores, gently applying the salves to the worst of them. There were several deep sores, primarily around her wrists and ankles, from the bindings that held Isabella for so many days.

One evening while Isabella and Catherine were dining, Robert came to the queen's quarters and asked to have a word in private. Catherine excused herself and followed Robert.

"How is she healing?" he asked as they moved down the hall

"Well enough, given what she has been through," responded Catherine, "but you have not come just to inquire as to the health of our guest."

"No, Majesty," he paused and was clearly distressed by something. His forehead between his eyebrows pulled together in deep creases. He hesitated, and took a large breath.

"What is it?" Catherine indicated a stone bench in an alcove next to a window.

As they sat Robert said, "The prisoner escaped, Majesty," he said. "We have men and dogs out hunting, but I fear he may have had help and will not be found. I, alone, bear the responsibility and will accept any punishment you order."

Catherine felt her stomach clench. "Are we speaking of the prisoner brought in with Isabella?" she asked, "the one who did this to her?"

"Yes, Majesty." Robert bowed his head, his shoulders slumped momentarily, then he sat up straight.

"What are the circumstances surrounding the escape? Why do you suspect that he had help?" she asked.

"He remained chained in the lowest cells of the keep. He was fed only once daily at midday and was allowed contact with no one. The only person to see him was the guard who shoved his meal through an opening in the door. The guard claims there was nothing unusual when he was fed yesterday. This afternoon when the day guard arrived to give the prisoner his meal he found the cell empty, but the padlock was in place and remained locked. Majesty, the only way in or out of that cell is through the one door."

Catherine stood and walked away from Robert. Thoughts of what all this might mean tumbled through her head. Any hope of interrogating this man further was lost. That meant finding any connection to the murder of Isabella's family was going to be more difficult. But what angered her more than anything was the fact that he had help. Who was the traitor in their midst? She took a deep breath to focus her thoughts and keep her anger in check. When she turned and walked back to him, her face did not hide her concern. She sat back down next to him.

"I am more concerned with finding whoever it is that aided the prisoner's escape. I want the prisoner found, but he is the type who will eventually get himself killed, or caught again. Spend no more than a few days searching for him. If he is not found by then, do not waste more time. We have a larger problem. Find the culprit who helped him escape. Until we find the traitor, an enemy lives with us and we are not safe."

"Yes, Majesty." Robert stood, gently crossed his right fist over his chest, and walked Catherine back to the doors of her quarters.

"Who was that?" Bella asked.

"My cousin," replied Catherine honestly enough. "His name is Robert. We were raised together. My mother and his were sisters.

"He seems very fond of you," Isabella observed.

"And I of him. He is like a brother to me," Catherine smiled. "When we were young we were inseparable. We were born only a few months apart."

Catherine got up from the table and wandered over to the fireplace. After staring into the flames for a few moments, she turned back to Bella and laughed.

"Robert has always felt very protective of me. Once I remember, we could not have been more than seven or eight years old, we were playing 'queen of the castle' in the courtyard with other children. In the course of our game, I was the queen and a dragon attacked the castle. We were attempting to slay the dragon with wooden swords. I remember leaping onto a rock to join the fight and wielded my wooden sword dramatically. Suddenly Robert was on me yelling, 'Stop!' He was furious with me. 'You are the queen; you are supposed to let me save you!' I pushed him off me and shouted back, 'I can take care of myself! Queens are not such helpless creatures as you imagine!'"

Bella stood and carefully made her way over to the warmth of the fire. "What did he do?"

"He was so mad at me. He gritted his teeth and said, 'You don't know how to play!' Then he threw down his sword and left the courtyard."

Bella sat near the fire and Catherine covered her with a lap throw. Bella smiled, "I can tell by how he treated you today that he is still a wonderful protector, almost as if he were born to the role."

Catherine laughed. "Yes, indeed," she said. More than Bella would ever know.

As they grew into their true roles of queen and Captain of the Guard, Catherine often thought back on this day. One day last spring, as they walked the gardens, she reminded him of that afternoon.

"Do you remember," Catherine asked as they strolled, "the time we played queen of the castle?"

He stopped and turned red, "I remember being infuriated with you for not letting me slay the dragon."

"Why are you blushing?" she laughed.

"I threw a temper tantrum! Not a very soldierly thing to do!" He laughed.

She slipped her arm through his as they continued walking. "You know, cousin, I have often thought about your little tantrum," she teased. "I wonder how you perceive that episode now that you are a man."

He stopped and looked at her. "Actually, I have thought a lot about that day, too. When I stalked off I went and had a good pout about things. I believe I must have already felt my destiny tied with yours. I was born to my role of protecting you, just as you were born to be queen."

And she knew that she would be a lesser queen without him. Robert's loyalty and devotion allowed her the freedom to trust that he guarded her without susceptibility to enemy influences. As a rule, monarchs did not always have the luxury of such a certainty.

Isabella's voice brought her back, "There is a strong familial resemblance, especially around the eyes. He has very kind eyes."

Catherine smiled at this but said no more. Isabella did not pursue the conversation further and indicated the game table where a backgammon board awaited them. As with other times, questions about Catherine's family and her role in the castle were deflected or outright ignored, no matter how innocently Bella might ask. Catherine wanted desperately to tell Bella everything, to confess and be done with the matter, but fear held the queen's identity in check. Catherine hoped that Bella was content with the deflections about her life. The queen tried to be honest when she could, but she was grateful when Bella's questions seemed to fade. She hoped that Bella, as a guest, was content with limited information. Catherine knew that she could not hide her identity forever from this woman whose life had now become so much a part of her own, and she needed to think about how to broach the subject…but not now. Soon perhaps.

As Isabella grew stronger she spent her days reading and resting. Catherine's quarters were spacious and very comfortable. Just inside the large double entry doors was a long table against the wall. The room was fairly open beyond that, almost all the way to the balcony doors that looked out directly up the mountainside and down to the gardens outside Catherine's office. To the left of the balcony doors was a window. Under the window was where Isabella's pallet was placed. A screen was available to place in front of the pallet for Isabella's privacy, but she seldom requested it.

Bella availed herself of the many volumes of books. Sometimes, when she was too tired to read, Catherine read aloud from Dante. Sometimes they engaged in lively discussion over the readings. Some evenings, following the meal, they simply conversed.

"How did you come to your understanding of politics, Bella? It is very unusual for a woman." Catherine moved to one of the chairs near the fireplace. The stones surrounding the fireplace had grown warm from the fire and radiated heat. "Come, sit," she motioned for Bella to move to the chair closest to the fire.

Bella's face did not mask her smile or her sadness as her eyes drifted into memories of her past. "My father often entertained politicians in our home in Acquapendente. He encouraged me to learn by listening, so often after meals I sat in a corner of the room and worked quietly on my needlepoint and listened to their conversations."

"You must have been privy to some very interesting discussions." Catherine tucked a wrap around Bella's lap and walked back to the table.

"Quite. Invariably the discussions turned to the Inquisition."

"A dangerous subject. How did those conversations evolve?" Catherine poured them both cups of warmed wine and brought them over to where they had ensconced themselves by the fire.

"My father was cautious," Bella said. She smiled, "But there were times when I feared that his distaste for the way things were being handled in Rome might have been obvious. Do not misunderstand, my father was a devout and loyal Catholic," Bella added hurriedly.

"You need not fear any reprisal from me regarding Rome. And I do not mind sharing with you that I detest this whole Inquisition. If it were in my power I should dismantle the entire…" Catherine stopped short, knowing that she was heading into territory that she must avoid. "I am sorry. I must sound terribly heretical."

"You need not concern yourself with my thoughts either, my dear."

Catherine wanted to know more about Bella's father and his political friends. "Did you know the men who spent time with your father?" Catherine stood and moved closer to the fire, as she waited for Bella's response.

"Well enough to know which ones I trusted and which ones made me uncomfortable, I suppose. Well enough to hear the fear or the lie in certain voices without ever looking up from my needlework."

"Well enough," Catherine suggested, "to suspect any of them of betraying your family?"

Bella got up from her seat and wandered over to the doors leading to the balcony. She opened them and stepped out. It was unusually warm for the end of September. The sun was only partially visible as it dropped beyond the mountains in the distance, bathing the balcony in a soft, watermelon glow. Catherine followed Bella onto the balcony, wrapping the throw around Bella's shoulders. Her heart filled with tenderness for this woman who had been through so much.

"I've spent many days alone here wondering about those men and their views," Bella said. "It would be easy enough to blame any one of them for what happened. But I believe they were all cowards too afraid for their own lives to make trouble for anyone else. I suppose that if I suspect anyone, I suspect one of my husband's servants. There were several who made me nervous and who seemed discontent with their lives in servitude. My husband was often harsh, and I do not think that he realized how his treatment of servants may have resulted in revenge."

Catherine placed her arm around Bella's waist. Bella turned, resting her head on the queen's shoulder. Catherine felt the woman's body give in to fatigue, sadness and exhaustion. "Come, you are tired. Let's prepare you for bed."

Later that evening after she had helped Bella settle into bed, Catherine sat near the fire contemplating their talk. Periodically, Bella whimpered in her sleep and Catherine waited, holding her breath, hoping the whimper did not escalate into a full blown nightmare. It passed.

The closeness of the quarters and the intimacy of the care involved created an atmosphere of natural ease between the women. Their playfulness and affection, their ability to touch and laugh and talk increased. Catherine looked forward to returning in the evenings. On days when the kingdom did not require her presence, she was glad for the extra time to spend with Isabella.

Most days, however, Catherine spent dealing with issues of the kingdom. The lives of her subjects, the management of her lands, and production of paper in their tiny mill, generally consumed her mornings, but as of late, there were fewer visits from her subjects. Catherine noted how the visits decreased as the Inquisition tortures and deaths increased. When people did not know who to trust, they chose to trust no one.

Chapter Five

The season was changing. Days were shorter. The air was becoming cooler. It was one of Catherine's lighter duty days and she was enjoying the afternoon in her quarters with Isabella.

Catherine had recently brought needlepoint materials and a small lap harp for Isabella to enjoy while she continued her recovery. Bella was strumming on the harp, humming softly as Catherine sat near the fireplace and read.

On days when the cooler air combined with the dampness of the castle, Catherine noticed that Bella rubbed her shoulders more often.

"I think I might like an early bath." Bella said as she moved closer to the fire. "Would you mind terribly asking Marie to draw it for me now?"

Catherine saw the dark circles under Bella's eyes, a certain sign of increased pain as the weather changed.

"Is it your shoulders again?"

"Hmm," Bella nodded.

A bath was drawn and Marie dismissed. Catherine assisted Bella with her bath, carefully inspecting her back to ensure her sores were healing. The deeper cuts were taking longer, but most of the smaller wounds were nearly healed. She gently sponged Bella's back and then sat nearby while Bella soaked.

As Catherine helped Bella from the tub, she had a thought. "Your wounds seem to be healing. Do you think that you might be up to an outing soon?"

Isabella spun around and threw her arms around Catherine.

"Yes, oh, yes! I have been longing to go outdoors before it gets too cold!"

Catherine dropped the towel and wrapped her arms around Isabella, at first laughing and hugging Bella back, but then she became aware of Isabella's skin under her fingertips, her breasts pressing against her body, the scent of Isabella's hair in her nostrils. Then, more, a tightening and pulling at the very center of her being, and the realization that she did not want to let go. The innocence and pureness of what had been a simple gesture of happiness and affection was instantly replaced by a longing that Catherine had never felt before.

Catherine was on fire, suddenly consumed with desire to pull Bella into her very body, to run her hands along the course of her back, her hips, to bury her face in Bella's neck and kiss that mouth, those perfect lips. She wanted...she wanted...oh, dear God, what did she want?

Isabella's body continued to press into Catherine's. Catherine could feel her breasts pressing against her own, as her heart pounded fast, and faster. She wanted to take Bella's face in her hands and kiss her, kiss her without end, kiss and inhale and taste and touch and love.

The queen swallowed hard and slid her hands up to Bella's shoulders. Her breath came in short, shallow bursts. It took all of her will power, but she pushed Bella away and would not meet her eyes. Isabella reached out for her, but the queen bent to pick up the toweling, handed it to her and said, "I don't feel well. I need to go lie down."

"Catherine, what is it? Catherine!"

Catherine didn't respond and rushed from the room.

"Please, don't go, Catherine, please."

But Catherine quickly shut the doors to her private bedroom.

Catherine was terrified. She paced. She prayed. She tried, but could not sleep. Whenever she closed her eyes the memory of how Bella's body felt against hers threatened to overwhelm her. She felt her own body betraying her. It vibrated of its own accord. She was reminded of how it felt the first time her sword struck a boulder, how the force of the vibration worked up her arm and sped through her body, but this feeling emanated from her loins and spread its tremor outward. It was not tolerable. She must control this. She cracked open the door to her bedroom. Bella was asleep. While the moon was still in charge of the sky, she left her quarters and sought solace in the church.

Catherine relished the solitude of the church at night. She inhaled the lingering smell of the incense, allowed the soft glow of the candlelight to surround her, and watched the moonlight filter through the stained glass windows. There were times, in the stillness of night, she felt her parents with her as she sat to pray. And it was especially at times when she sat quietly that she was filled with the presence of God.

She needed that presence now. She would rather face a thousand foes with drawn swords than this unknown and unbidden feeling that flooded her.

She sat. The only candle glowing was the perpetual near the tabernacle. Her mind would not still. She waited for the comfort that usually sifted and settled around her within a few minutes of arriving. Never before had she felt so unsettled in this place. Her usual ability to slip into spiritual communion with God did not materialize. She thought that perhaps, because this struggle was more personal in nature that her approach may need to be different. She rose and approached the altar where she knelt. No matter how she tried to extinguish them, her thoughts returned again and again to Bella. Her face, her eyes, that exquisite mouth.

"Stop, stop!" she commanded the feelings. But visions of Bella persisted whenever she closed her eyes.

She rose and began to pace in front of the altar. The more she tried to shake her feelings loose, the more intense they became and the more she was afraid. Not only was she convinced that her feelings were sinful, she was certain that the feelings alone doomed her. She tried desperately to push them back down, but each time she remembered how Bella felt and smelled and looked, her body and soul rose up lighting fire to her senses and she felt as if she would die if she did not fulfill this desire. Never had she felt so alive and so doomed to death simultaneously.

"Remove this unholy desire from me, Lord," she begged. "I cannot bear this temptation. I do not want this," she prayed. As Bella's embrace flooded her thoughts again, she pulled out her rosary and attempted to focus on her prayers. It was no use. She could not banish thoughts of Isabella from her mind. Her thoughts took her back across the past weeks and her simple enjoyment of Bella's company. She tried to take herself back to those feelings. But even as she tried she knew that she might as well attempt to put an egg back into its shell. The feelings had escaped and there was no putting them back.

After hours of pacing and praying, Catherine prostrated herself on the marble floor before the altar. "Please, speak to me. I do not understand what is happening. My heart is open to you, oh, God. Help me," she pleaded. She wept and prayed until she fell asleep.

It was in this position that the Bishop discovered her in the church when he arrived for his own devotionals at dawn.

"Majesty," he whispered.

It took Catherine a moment to realize that she was in church. But the cold stone against her cheek helped bring it all back to her. She pushed herself to a kneeling position and looked to see who addressed her.

"Good morning, your Grace," she greeted him.

"Is all well?" he inquired.

"All is well," she responded as she stood.

"It is the tendency of those who are deeply troubled to spend the night in prayer," he continued solicitously. "Perhaps I can be of assistance in your search for spiritual enlightenment. Would you like me to hear your confession?"

"Thank you, your Grace. I simply became tired while I prayed, nothing more." She turned to leave, but his voice stopped her and she turned. He stepped to the altar and looked down his nose at her. His face, though not unpleasant, held the expression of someone who always has an ulterior motive. His eyes, deep brown, continually darted, as if he were always looking for someone, or something. His hair, brown with a touch of grey at the temples, fell just below his ears and was very straight. A goatee, that just a few short years ago had been brown, was now completely grey. It did give him the kind of distinguished look that she knew appealed to most people, but she thought it gave him a sharper, more evil appearance. She detested the man and found herself bracing for whatever he was about to say.

"How fares the woman who now lives in your chambers, Majesty?" His tone seemed to indicate that he was interested in far more than Isabella's spiritual well being.

"She continues to improve, albeit slowly," replied the queen. She offered nothing further.

"I will continue to keep your guest in my prayers," he went on. "I am sure you will be happy for her complete recovery so that you may have your own bed to yourself again."This time his tone left no doubt about his opinion in the matter.

Catherine did not rise to his bait, but feared that her feelings for Bella were somehow visible to the bishop. What did he see? How could he know? Her fear threatened to overwhelm her. Quickly, she expressed her thanks on behalf of Isabella. She crossed herself and left the church.

When she returned to her quarters Catherine found Isabella sitting on her pallet and staring out the window. A fire was burning and the table was set for breakfast. As Catherine entered, Bella rose and went to her. Catherine fought the urge to put her hands up to stop Bella from approaching her. She was briefly overcome by a wave of dizziness, and felt herself break out in a sweat. Swallowing hard, she forced herself to smile warmly as Bella approached.

"When I woke this morning and you were not here I was concerned. You left in such a rush last night. Are you better?" Bella asked.

"I was unable to sleep so I went to the church to pray," Catherine responded. "I am well. I simply have much on my mind."

She had hoped to avoid Bella, afraid to be in her presence, afraid that all she felt might be revealed in her eyes.

As she spoke she had difficulty looking Bella in the eyes…eyes that for some weeks now delighted her with their deep, changing moods and colors. Isabella reached out and took Catherine's arm, "I was hoping you would return and waited to breakfast with you. Come eat." Bella led Catherine by the hand to the table that was set with fruits, nuts and cheeses. Warm ale still steamed in a pitcher. They sat and Bella poured the ale and handed the cup to Catherine. As Catherine took the cup Bella reached up and lightly caressed her cheek, "Catherine, tell me what is wrong. You look tired and you seem worried. It is in your face."

The light touch on her cheek ignited her. Catherine looked up into Bella's eyes. She needed to know whether or not Bella felt any of this confusion, this desire. Her instincts, usually so attuned to danger, failed her. Bella's eyes revealed concern…but was there something else? Catherine was not sure.

"Perhaps I am just hungry," suggested Catherine.

"Let me serve you, dear heart, you have spent these past weeks caring for me, and I am gaining more and more strength daily." Isabella stood and filled a plate for Catherine. As she set it down in front of her, Bella let her free hand fall onto Catherine's shoulder. Catherine stiffened.

"What is it?" demanded Bella. "Something is wrong. Tell me."

Catherine ignored the question, "Please, let's eat. I'm just hungry."

Catherine ate little, however, and spoke little as well. The nearness of Bella, that yesterday had so delighted her, now confused her. How could such a thing be possible and so impossible at the same time?

Bella made several attempts to engage Catherine in conversation. Mostly, she made references to the outing that Catherine suggested.

"I am certain I'll be able to wear regular clothing in a few more days," Bella said excitedly. "Do you have anything that might be suitable for public wear? I will need to rely further on your generosity as I arrived here with no clothing."

"Finding clothes will not be a problem," said Catherine, who worked to block the image of assisting Bella into them…and out of them again.

"What kind of outing might we have?" Bella persisted.

"What would you like?" Catherine decided that perhaps the best approach was to try to pretend that nothing had changed. Isabella was still Isabella. She was still Catherine. Had anything truly changed or was it all in her imagination?

"I miss riding," Bella responded.

Catherine looked concerned. "I am not certain that your first excursion out of doors should be on a horse!"

"Please don't make me beg," Bella's face fell. "Riding is my favorite activity."

"Then riding is what we shall do," smiled Catherine, "and I have riding clothes that you may choose from. Come, let's search my wardrobe room."

At the last minute she asked Bella to wait while she brought some of her riding garments out to her. Bella sat on her bed. Catherine's royal attire, complete with crown, was quite visible in her wardrobe. She was glad she thought of it before bringing Bella in. While Catherine perused her clothing she wondered about the continued concealment of her royal title from Bella. What purpose did it serve now that Bella was well? The question was one she had been avoiding asking herself because she already knew the answer. Bella had been well enough for the past few days to leave Catherine's private quarters. Catherine was not willing to give up this one, private indulgence in anonymity. But it was more than that, Bella engaged Catherine in ways that no one but Robert had ever been able to do. At days' end, though, Robert had a home and a wife to return to, and who engaged him. Catherine relished Bella's companionship for pure pleasure. While royals had the authority to command entertainment for their own enjoyment, Catherine did not take to that particular benefit of being queen. There lacked a reciprocity in the very act of commanding entertainment. With Bella the conversations flowed, the expectation to respond "regally" was pleasantly absent. There was an easy give and take, an ebb and flow that was sometimes missing, even with Robert, because of her title. And Catherine knew that all of this could disappear if Bella knew that she was, in fact, the queen.

Catherine emerged from the wardrobe with three different outfits, each appropriate for an outing on horseback. Bella had spent her many weeks in simple, loose-fitting undergarments. Catherine saw that the thought of real clothes delighted her. She spread them out on the bed. Then, one by one, helped Bella try them on.

The first was a red silk gown with matching turn backs. It had a crimson and black two piece kirtle with jeweled fore sleeves. The smock was white with black-worked wrist frills, a black velvet French hood with jewels, pearls and gold-work.

The second outfit was made of green silk. The underside of the green was cream colored. It gathered from the floor to a point at the right side of the waist. The long, flared sleeves draped to a point from the gold braids at the shoulders. It, too, was lovely, but had a corset, and Bella desperately wished to avoid the discomfort of a corset just yet.

It was the third dress that nearly made Catherine gasp. The blue of the gown was rich, deep, nearly the color of the autumn sky. When Bella held it up, her eyes matched the color, impossibly blue. It was trimmed in silver with a low cut neck and a v-shaped lace partlet that stood up from the sides of the décolleté. A silver jeweled belt hung in a 'v' just below the waist and tiny beads of silver hung in long strands to the middle of her thighs. Long, lighter blue silk wings draped from the underarms. A loose hood flowed up from the shoulders to cover her head.

Catherine assisted Bella into it and thought she had never seen a vision so breathtaking. In fact, she had to work hard to keep her breath even and normal. Bella glowed with happiness and twirled in front of the mirror. Catherine knew that she must have grown tired of seeing herself in the drab, linen undergarments. The best part of this gown was that Bella could avoid wearing a corset.

As Catherine worked to help Bella into and out of the gowns, she struggled with having to push down the fear that bubbled up within her when she accidentally brushed her hand against Bella's skin. She found herself wishing for the easy, relaxed way that she and Bella related for the past many weeks. These new feelings cluttered what had previously been so simple, innocent and pure. Perhaps she needed to trust that easy intimacy would return. She took a deep breath.

"I like this one the best," Bella said of the blue silk, "and it fits the best."

Catherine could not take her eyes off of Bella. Finally, she said, "It is stunning on you. Please consider it yours. I never looked that good in it and I have rarely worn it."

Bella started toward Catherine to hug her in thanks, but Catherine turned and scooped up the other two gowns and made for the wardrobe. When she returned Bella was still admiring herself in the mirror.

"I was sorry that you did not feel well enough to apply the salves last night," Bella said as she looked at Catherine in the reflection. "It surprised me that they make such a difference."

The thought of rubbing the salves on Bella's wounds made Catherine's inside's lurch. To continue with that daily ritual would be a curse, and a blessing. "I hope the discomfort did not prevent you from your rest last night," she said softly.

"The discomfort caused by the absence of the salve was not what caused me to lose sleep." Bella reached for Catherine's hand. "I was concerned for you. You left so suddenly that I thought perhaps I had offended you."

Catherine jerked her hand out of Bella's. "You did no such thing. I simply was overcome by exhaustion and felt the need to lie down."

"Catherine, look at me," Bella implored as she reached again for Catherine's hand. "I know that something happened when we embraced. I felt it, too. Can you look at me and tell me that you felt nothing?"

Catherine looked into Bella's eyes and saw her own desire staring back at her. She saw, too, that Bella was not afraid. This fact terrified her even more. She shook her head.

"What frightens you so?" Bella asked.

Catherine did not know what to say…how to respond. There were no words for what she felt. She turned away, threw open the doors to the balcony and went out. As she stood with her head buried in her hands, Bella came and stood next to her, then reached out and placed her hand on Catherine's shoulder. "What frightens you?"

After a long silence Catherine said, "My very feelings frighten me, Bella. How can you not be frightened? I did not know it was possible to feel this way about a woman. I…this…we…" she stammered.

Bella sighed. "I didn't know it was possible either. But now I do know. Perhaps it is wrong for me to be unafraid." When Catherine did not respond, Bella dropped her hand from Catherine's shoulder and walked a few steps away, then turned back. "You stirred something deep within me. It has taken over. It is stronger than anything I have known. When you touch me I feel both the icy tingle of winter and the burn of flame licking my skin. I must fight not to grab hold of you and…"

Catherine whirled to face her. "Stop it! Do you not believe that these feelings are wrong?" she interrupted. "Have you no knowledge of God's laws?"

Bella took a large breath and exhaled slowly, sadly. "Ah, you believe that our feelings are sinful?" It was really more a statement than a question. "Catherine, have we done anything that you cannot live with?"

"I don't know how I can live with the feelings themselves!"

"Do your feelings for me torment you so much?" Bella asked.

Her feelings did torment Catherine. It took all of her willpower not to reach out and pull Bella to her. She wanted desperately to fill her face with Bella's hair, to touch her lips with her fingertips. Yet she believed that to do so would damn them both. It was not fair that she should want something so badly and have to deny herself. Knowing that she was denying Bella made it even worse. She would do anything for this woman. But all she said was, "I am confused by them. I have never felt this way about anyone before. I expected one day to feel this way about a man. Isn't that how it is supposed to be? I don't know how I can live with these feelings." Catherine paused, and added, "Yet I cannot imagine not having you here." Her eyes began to fill with tears as she struggled to sift her emotions into some sense of order.

"I have been aware of my feelings for you for some weeks now." Bella said. "They grew slowly, but grow they did. I have had much time to think about my feelings. Perhaps I am less afraid because I have already lost everything I hold dear." She walked back into the room and over to the window near her pallet. She was silent for a moment before turning back to Catherine, who had followed. "When you found me I had nothing left to lose. But now I have found you. I have never felt so alive. When you are away from me, my thoughts are consumed with you. When you are near I want you nearer, and nearer."

Tears fell from Catherine's eyes and she did not respond for some time. Bella went to her and reached for her hand. This time Catherine did not resist, but felt her heart breaking with the knowledge that she could never kiss, or hold Bella in the way that her body demanded. Catherine shook her head, "It is not right. It cannot be," she said softly.

Bella reached to place her hand on Catherine's face. "For now, then, let us just enjoy each other as we have these past weeks. We need do nothing about our feelings. I don't wish to cause you any discomfort." Catherine looked up and their eyes locked. They said nothing further, but for both of them, nothing demanded enormous effort.

Chapter Six

The days that followed were filled with temptation and desire. The women tried to resume their routine as they had fallen into it over the past weeks. They breakfasted together, and then Catherine left for a good part of the day. Evenings brought them back together for a simple supper. Bella's baths continued, though less frequent, since it was obvious she didn't require the ritual for wound comfort any longer.

Neither of them mentioned discontinuing the bath. Perhaps it was the temptation itself, or the act of resisting it, but they both looked forward to it.

Catherine never again neglected to apply the ointment to Bella's wounds, which were nearly healed now. But before, Catherine's fingers would gently dab the salve on each sore, now her hands massaged the oils into whole body parts...ankles up the legs, wrists up the arms, back, down to the roundness of buttocks. Sometimes Bella turned onto her back and reached for Catherine, but the queen resisted the urge to give in to an embrace. Catherine allowed her eyes to wander down to Bella's breasts, but there she always stopped herself, always managing to stop herself from acting. However, she could not stop herself from wanting. At times she wondered if she were designing her own temptation so that she could feel noble when she did not succumb.

Catherine no longer went to the church to pray. She had no desire for another confrontation with the Bishop. She found herself content to take her beads and her prayers elsewhere. Sometimes she prayed in her room, more often, however, it was the palace gardens that appealed to her. There she could walk in the midst of God's own beauty and search for her comfort...and her salvation. But in the matter of Bella, she found no solace, no answer to her prayers, and no elimination of her earthly, unbidden desire. God, it seemed, had abandoned her in this issue. Or so she thought.

If God had abandoned her, Robert, at least, had not. As faithful as ever, he met with her daily. Sometimes he went to her office, sometimes they walked the gardens. While mostly their talk revolved around matters of her safety and the kingdom, he always inquired about Isabella. During one of their meetings, as they strolled the gardens, Catherine was particularly on edge.

"I don't care what Lord Carfaggi thinks!" she fumed. "He's a bitter, hateful man. He and the Bishop both infuriate me. If Carfaggi is so concerned about securing the western border then let him supply troops from his own land. Let him feed and clothe the soldiers. I am pleased enough with the security supplied by Lord Giovanni."

"Yes, Majesty."

"Do not patronize me, Robert! I am in no state."

"I can see that. What has put you in such a foul state?"

"Nothing." Catherine shook her head irritably and sat on a stone bench. Just as quickly she stood again.

"What is it?" asked Robert.

"Nothing!" she practically shouted at him. Then softly, apologetically, "I am sorry, Robert. I do not mean to…" She stopped herself, turned to him and said, "Saddle our horses. Take me to the woods and let's practice with our swords!"

"Yes, Majesty!" Robert smiled. He thumped his chest happily with his fist and bowed.

When they were younger Robert was expected to learn all of the martial arts as part of his training. He was quick to learn and an excellent swordsman. It wasn't long before he was training the younger boys in sword technique. Whenever she could, Catherine watched him train. She was not permitted, as a princess, to train in any of the fighting arts. But swords always intrigued her. One afternoon when they were about thirteen years old she asked if he would take her on as a student.

"No," Robert answered.

"Why not?"

"You are forbidden to train with the sword and I am sworn to protect you."

"It's a stupid rule, and when I am queen I will abolish it. How could teaching me to defend myself be a bad thing?

"I did not make the rule, Princess," he replied, "I am only sworn to uphold it."

"Robert, please," she begged, "just for fun, then. It does look like such a great deal of fun! And it would be good practice for you, as well."

Robert adored his cousin, and always had difficulty saying no to her. "What if we are caught?" he asked, eyebrows raised.

"We won't be caught. We can go into the forest to practice. No one will find us if we're careful."

Robert shook his head, "I don't think it a good idea at all."

"Well, then, I shall simply have to command you. As your future queen I hereby command you to teach me the ways of the sword," she stated quite haughtily.

Robert laughed, "Well, then, your future Majesty, I am at your service."

Every opportunity following that afternoon Robert and Catherine escaped to the forest. He taught her everything he knew about swordsmanship. She was actually quite a good student and once the muscles in her sword arm strengthened sufficiently, she was able to spar with Robert well enough to feel that she actually could use a sword if need be. Once she became queen she did, in fact, abolish the rule forbidding royal women from training in any of the fighting arts. Whenever she traveled about the country she always had her sword with her.

She and Robert made for their old secret training ground. Robert dragged some fallen tree limbs from the clearing while Catherine put on her protective gear. She wore a shirt of chain mail and a helmet for practice because Robert insisted. Her sword had been a gift from Robert on her fifteenth birthday. He had worked with a blacksmith for several months to design something for her that would be functional and more protective than standard blade types. Ultimately, it had to be lighter than other swords, without compromising the strength. With

Robert's assistance, the smith finally created one that was very lightweight, the hilt of which was a complex twist of metal on the blade side of the grip. The twisting metal was designed to protect the hand of the holder and was much less dense and heavy than a regular cross guard. It had a dual protective quality in that if the blade of the opponent's sword tip moved into the coiled metal Catherine could disarm her opponent with a mere twist of her wrist. The grip was smaller than normal to accommodate her hand. The forte of the blade, the strongest portion from the hilt to the center of the blade, was thinner than most to lighten it even more, but it still needed to be strong enough to withstand and block blows. The forte also needed strength enough to add slightly more length to make up for Catherine's smaller stature. If she could not easily reach her opponents, they would have a distinct advantage over her in reach. Finally, he had her family coat of arms engraved on the pommel. All in all it was quite an elegant sword. Catherine was more excited about the sword than any gift she could ever remember receiving. She cherished it more than any crown or jewel that she possessed.

They moved to the clearing and crossed swords. At first the attacks and deflections were simple, standard, and allowed them some warm up to move in to more complicated moves.

Catherine had learned well from Robert how to fake some attacks in order to catch her opponent off guard so that she might take advantage while they were distracted. She faked a move toward his face. He was easily able to deflect her sword, but already knew that her real target was his femoral artery. He was ready and instantly swung his sword down. He swept her blade away in a circular motion.

The sounds of the swords striking against one another became more and more intense. With each blow Catherine's moves focused more on attacking. This was unusual for her during practice. Generally, Robert insisted that she focus on learning to protect herself.

Robert, aware of this dramatic change, found himself working harder than usual as she relentlessly attacked him from every angle. At one point she stepped back from him and then spun herself around with her sword in the air to avoid one of his lunges. She ended with her sword on his neck. If this had been for real, she could easily have beheaded him.

After about thirty minutes Catherine cried, "Enough! Enough, cousin! I am spent!" She collapsed onto a dead tree log on the edge of the clearing.

When they put their swords down both were breathing heavily. When he finally caught his breath Robert asked, "What battle were we waging, your Majesty?"

She smiled, exhausted, "What makes you think this was anything but a practice?"

"I saw your face as you fought, and I felt the force of your blows. Unless you're angry with me for some reason, you were battling an enemy," he looked questioningly at her.

Catherine sighed. "The enemy is myself only, dear cousin, and I don't wish to talk about it," she walked toward her horse to put up her sword and retrieve her water bag.

"I suspect," he said as he followed, "that this might have to do with a rumor about your Lady Isabella?"

"What have you heard?" She whirled toward him. "Tell me!" At once she was angry and fearful.

"Don't be upset," he pleaded. "You understand better than anyone the small minds and wagging tongues."

"Small though those minds may be, the Bishop has let me know that he suspects the rumors to be true," she said, "and that is no insignificant wagging tongue."

"True," said Robert with concern. "Who do you suspect of starting the rumors?"

"Isabella is tormented, as you might imagine. There are nights she cannot sleep for the terrible dreams. On occasion I have fallen asleep beside her while helping her back to sleep. Marie has found us together." She wondered if Robert could see through her, if he knew how she really felt about Isabella. She wanted to talk to someone about her feelings, and Robert was closer to her than anyone, but she did not trust that he would understand. So she lied to him. "I am sorely disappointed if it's Marie who is spreading an ugly lie that is, in fact, a kind gesture only."

"Don't worry about the likes of Marie," Robert soothed, "you know servants will always make up stories for their own entertainment…with or without your assistance. The Bishop, however, is a different story. That is a problem that needs to be addressed. With your permission I will see if I can find out what, exactly, the Bishop is saying about the matter."

They were mounting their horses to return to the castle. "Robert, you are so much more than my protector." Catherine truly felt that, with Robert watching out for her, she need not fear. "Your friendship is indispensible to me. Do whatever you like where the Bishop is concerned."

They returned to the castle sweaty, exhausted and in Catherine's case, more relaxed than she had been in days.

She was in sore need of a bath and ordered hot water brought to her quarters. When she entered her quarters Bella looked up from reading.

"What happened to you? You are a sight?"

"Robert and I went riding and decided to practice with our swords." Catherine did not see any need to hide this truth from Bella. "I have ordered Marie to bring bath water, I am disgustingly filthy. Will you help me out of this chain?"

By the time Catherine was out of her chain and clothing, Marie had filled the tub.

"Thank you, Marie. I can manage on my own. I just want to soak a bit. Would you just put up the screen?"

Marie put up the screen and left the quarters.

Catherine prepared herself to slip into her bath, trying hard to ignore the fact that Bella had followed her to the tub side of the screen and clearly had no intention of leaving. Bella drew up the stool that sat nearby and waited as Catherine submerged her body into the warm water.

"It seems strange to be sitting here as *you* bathe," Bella said after a few moments. "Marie is the one who has always ministered your baths. Are you certain you don't want me to call her back?"

It was a few moments before Catherine answered. Her mind screamed at her to answer, "Yes! Call Marie!" but her heart and her body wanted nothing more than to invite Bella to stay.

"No," she finally said. "I am content to sit and soak for a bit." Catherine leaned back, closed her eyes and sank down a bit into the tub.

"Let me wash your back," suggested Bella as she stood, and then knelt beside the tub. She encouraged Catherine to sit forward as she gently washed her back with the water and soap-soaked sponge.

Catherine's protests died before they even reached her tongue. She allowed the warm water to soothe her. But, eventually, Bella's hand came up from the water without the sponge. Her hand cupped water up to the base of Catherine's neck and her fingers tenderly slid down Catherine's back in long, sensuous strokes. Catherine was helpless to do anything but allow this sensation to continue. Finally, Bella reached around and pulled Catherine to lean back. Catherine resisted, but finally leaned back. As she did, Bella's face was fully enveloped in Catherine's hair; their faces drew alongside one another. Bella's breath was on Catherine's cheek, her nose and forehead lightly touched the side of Catherine's face. Neither moved. Bella's hand started a slow slide around to Catherine's middle...

Catherine gasped and stood. She grabbed for her toweling, wrapped herself in it and disappeared into her bedroom, closing the doors behind her. She was so close to giving in to the temptation that was Bella that she frightened herself. It would have been so easy to allow Bella to continue to touch her. "I must be more diligent," she thought angrily as she dried herself vigorously.

Bella stayed kneeling at the tub for some time, her heartbeat quick and strong. When, at last, her breath returned to normal, she went to her pallet and wept.

Chapter Seven

The tension between the two women was palpable the next day. Catherine spent as much time as possible away from her quarters. When they were together their conversation was strained and awkward. Neither Catherine nor Isabella brought up the subject of Bella's health, or her need to leave, but it hung heavy between them.

Two days after the incident in the tub, Catherine was preparing to leave the quarters to meet with Robert. Her hand was on the doorknob when Bella stopped her.

"Except for the riding clothes I have nothing to wear for travel…" Whatever else she intended to say remained unsaid.

If Catherine could have looked into Bella's face, she would have seen that it was washed in waves of grief. But Catherine did not turn around, for her own grief had overtaken her. She was afraid that if she looked into those eyes that had mesmerized her for all these weeks that she might lose her resolve, take Bella into her arms and never let her go.

"I will have Marie bring some things for you to try." Catherine was polite, but determinedly distant. She opened the door. As she started to step through, Bella's voice cut through her.

"I wish you had not found me. It would have been easier if you had left me to die!"

Catherine, hesitated, but forced herself to leave. Once on the other side she clutched at her heart with one hand while stifling a cry with the other. If she had turned and gone back through the doors of her quarters she would have found Bella tearing at her gown and weeping on the floor.

"Majesty," Robert addressed her and bowed as she entered the courtyard, "I was just preparing to come to your office."

The castle grounds had several courtyards. The one Catherine entered was the inner courtyard, located between the castle and the outer bailey. It contained a knot garden and hedges on the southern side, and fruit-bearing trees to the western edge. Stone benches were scattered at intervals. Catherine found Robert in the midst of the knot garden talking to one of his soldiers.

"I prefer to walk today, Robert." She turned almost absentmindedly toward the fruit trees.

He fell into step beside her. "We are no closer to finding the escaped prisoner. I've directed my men to abandon the search for now."

Robert waited for Catherine to respond, but she continued to walk as if she had not heard him.

"I believe that I may be close to finding the culprit who helped him escape, however."

When there was still no response from Catherine, Robert continued, "I have learned that a new, young soldier assigned to the keep may have befriended the prisoner. I intend to question him when he returns. His grandmother died and he was given leave to return home to bury her."

"Fine," was all Catherine managed.

Robert stopped. "What is it? I have never seen you so distracted?"

"What? Oh, nothing. I'm tired, that's all. Can we meet tomorrow?"

"Tomorrow is the day I have planned to take you and Lady Isabella to the flower fields. Have you forgotten?"

"Oh. Yes I did forget."

"Do you still wish to go?"

"Yes, of course," she said. "We'll be ready in the morning."

When Catherine returned to her quarters late that afternoon, she told Bella that she had arranged for Robert to take them riding.

"There is a meadow just on the other side of the forest. It will not be in bloom this time of year, but perhaps you can imagine it in all of its yellow and purple glory in the spring." Her voice was cool, detached. She did not meet Bella's eyes.

Equally distant in her reply, Bella responded. "It sounds lovely. I look forward to it."

They took their evening meal in near silence. Neither ate much. Following the meal, Catherine picked up a book and sat by the fire with the book in her lap.

Bella picked up a book as well and sat opposite Catherine. Periodically a page turned.

Catherine stood. "I neglected to take care of something. I shall return in a while. You need not wait up for me."

Bella merely nodded.

Catherine could not bear the distance and discomfort between them. She went down to the garden to be alone with her sadness. The garden was three stories beneath her quarters. She strolled among the dead and dying flowers, and finally sat on a bench near a favorite rosebush.

"I feel myself dying, too," she thought as she crushed the last of the dried rose petals in her hand. She fell to her knees. "I am lost," she prayed. "Show me the way, I beg You." As had been the case since the first night she realized her true feelings for Bella, she heard and felt nothing from God. Eventually, she pulled herself up again and lowered her head, holding it in her hands, and wept.

When, eventually, she looked up at the window of her quarters. Bella was on the balcony watching her.

By the time Catherine returned to her quarters Bella was already in bed, her back to the room. Catherine started over to her but stopped herself, deciding to let Bella sleep. She went into her bedroom and closed the doors. She did not see Bella's tears sliding down, creating a puddle on her pillow.

The morning of their outing dawned crisp and clear. It was a perfect October day.

As Catherine, Bella and Robert made their way through the forest on horseback, Robert made several attempts to converse.

"Lady Isabella, how does it feel to be outdoors after being confined for so long?"

"Quite refreshing, Robert. Thank you for making the arrangements."

As neither woman made any effort to speak with each other, or with him, Robert gave up and eventually rode along with them in silence. The leaves fell in great numbers, silently surrendering, shuddering toward their destiny. The air was cool as they made their way in and out of the shadows of the trees, but when the sun found its way through in small, open patches, it warmed and relaxed them a bit.

Emerging from the tree line of the forest lay a small rise. The horses made for the top. Spreading out before them a shimmering blanket of dying and dead wild flowers trembled in a soft breeze. As far as the eye could see the land seemed to billow with yellow-orange waves. In the near distance was a blue lake. The Apennines already snowed capped, rose up behind the lake. Isabella cried out as her horse stopped at the top of the hill.

"I have never seen anything so glorious!"

"You have been confined for too long," said Catherine with a smile. "In the spring, when the fields are in bloom, it becomes truly magical."

"I should like to …." Bella stopped short.

Robert led the way to a rocky area where they could sit. Once he settled the women with blankets and some refreshments, he took the horses away a bit to graze. When he returned, Isabella was wandering out toward the lake. Catherine was watching her, but her face was creased with pain and sadness.

"You admire her," he said to Catherine.

"She is a remarkable woman." Catherine leaned back against the large bolder that was behind her.

"She seems to be healing well. You have been good for her."

"Her body is healing, yes. But she remains tormented. That will take time."

Robert knelt beside Catherine. "Something torments you, as well, my queen." The way he said it, it was more an inquiry than a statement.

"Speak freely, Robert, you know I value your counsel." But as soon as the words left her mouth she felt her stomach rise up into her throat. She tried to ignore the fear.

It was a while before he spoke again. As if he were weighing what needed to be said.

"She has changed you."

"It's true. How can one be witness to such courage and strength and not be changed? She watched her family be brutally murdered…"

He interrupted her. "That is not what I mean."

"I know." Her response was only mildly irritated, but it did not hide the anguish she felt.

Robert looked at Bella wandering the field, and then turned to Catherine. "I have known you since we were babies together at our mother's breasts. You know I feel you are more sister than cousin." He reached up to push his hair back. Still watching Bella, he said, "I have long worried you would spend your life so devoted to your people that you would never find the comfort and happiness that another could bring." He paused and waited. Catherine did move while he spoke. She, too, continued to watch Bella walk through the field. Finally, he said, "When you are with her you are happy."

Working to disguise her true feelings, she replied, "I do not look forward to her leaving. She is well enough to return home."

"She has nothing to return to. And I see the way she looks at you. She is in no hurry to leave."

Catherine looked at him. "What are you saying?" she demanded as her fear rose up to meet her.

"Only that there is something special between you, something that goes beyond friendship."

"How can you even suggest such a thing?" Catherine stood and started pacing. "It cannot be! Why entertain such blasphemy?"

"Who is blasphemed by your feelings? Tell me." Robert continued to kneel, hoping she would calm and sit again.

"It is unnatural, and you know it is! How can I be an effective ruler if I cannot follow God's laws…if I allow sin to rule me?" Her feelings were beginning to jumble within her. The anger, so evident just a moment ago was mixing with her fear. Hearing her own words echo in her ears made them sound insipid.

"That is your bishop I hear coming out of your mouth," he scoffed. Now he stood and crossed his arms in front of his chest as he talked. "He is the last one to speak of what is natural and what is unnatural! Why there is barely a boy to be found in this kingdom not put upon to polish that enlarged sword beneath his robes! That pompous ass would twist scripture around to confuse his own mother if it gave him power over her. Since when do you allow someone like that to cloud your own thoughts?"

"My thoughts are clouded enough without the assistance of anyone else, I fear."

After a while, he continued, "You taught me the importance of finding my own clarity. You have always found yours in your own soul, a soul that more exemplifies the teachings of Christ than that Bishop of yours. You are strong and compassionate and you understand the importance of just and fair laws. You spend your life in sacrifice to your country and your people. And you have always done so by keeping God in your heart. What does your heart tell you now? There you will find your clarity."

"What if the devil has stolen my heart?" Even as she said this she knew how ridiculous it sounded. Her feelings were shifting, again, but she could not tell if she were winning, or losing the battle inside of her. Feeling almost beaten, she sat back down on the blanket.

"You think she is Satan?" he asked mockingly.

"No, of course not. But perhaps she has the power to bewitch."

He looked out at Isabella, then again at Catherine. Even as children he had played this role with her. Struggling to make sense of conflicts that warred within her, she often challenged him to arguments only to help herself eliminate those thoughts and feelings that did not quite set right with her. But always, the thoughts and feelings that discomfited her most, were the ones she defended most strongly. Finally, he said, "If she is a witch, her powers are sorely limited given the sorry state in which we found her. Tell me, my queen, has she requested items to create special concoctions in your quarters? Have you overheard her chanting words that have no meaning to you?" He chuckled.

A smile crept across her face. Still her eyes had not left Bella who seemed to float across the field.

"You love her," Robert continued softly, all the mocking gone from his voice. "And if I am any judge of these things, she has fallen in love with you, as well. Love itself is bewitching. That may help explain the unusual feelings that haunt you."

Her eyes began to glisten with tears.

"And that kind of love can only be a gift from God," he said.

As he finished speaking he looked up and saw Isabella making her way back toward them. He left and walked out to be with the horses.

"This place is special…it heals my spirit to be here," Bella said as she approached.

"Bella, sit with me." She took Bella's hand and together they sat. Catherine had her back propped against the flat edge of a rock, her knees bent before her. Isabella sat to the side of Catherine's bent legs and faced her. In a motion both fluid and natural, Bella rested her cheek on Catherine's knee and their eyes found each other. Her hand found Catherine's hand again and she held it gently in her own lap.

"You are nearly well," Catherine said.

Bella visibly paled and her free hand reached up to her stomach and she lowered her head. Catherine had to bend her own head down to see Bella's face. She could see that Bella was grimacing.

"What is it, Bella? Are you in pain?"

Bella opened her eyes and looked down at Catherine's hand in her own. She lifted the hand and tenderly kissed the back of it. "I am fine, dear one." The rustling of the dying leaves pulsating in the breeze was the only sound for some time. "And, yes, I am well enough, thanks to your generous ministrations."

"Have you given thought to what you will do when…?" Catherine's voice trailed off. Her eyes also fell on their hands resting in Bella's lap.

"When I am well enough and no longer need your care?"

"I…yes, I suppose that is what we need to consider."

Bella took Catherine's hand in both of hers now. "I no longer need your care, Catherine. I am strong enough to walk and travel. My bruises and wounds will soon only be painful memories." Catherine stopped breathing and Bella proceeded cautiously. "I may no longer need your care, but I find myself craving it, in spite of my healing." At this she raised Catherine's hand again and pressed her lips to the backs of Catherine's fingers. Both women looked up.

Bella searched Catherine's eyes. She turned Catherine's hand, placing the palm on her cheek. Slowly, tenderly, while she continued to hold that hand, Bella turned her head and kissed Catherine's palm. Her lips lingered there and felt no resistance. She kissed the palm again and again, then drew Catherine's arm toward her. Bella was kissing her wrist…and the soft, underside of her arm between her wrist and elbow.

Catherine could not move. Every sense betrayed her and she realized that she was dizzy and lightheaded. A moan escaped her. Bella stopped, raised her hand and placed it on Catherine's cheek. "I do not wish to leave," she whispered. Her eyes beseeched Catherine to understand.

In response, Catherine brought a trembling free hand up, cupping Bella's face gently. Slowly, her eyes never leaving Bella's, she leaned closer. Her lips sought Bella's and found them.

Catherine's breath quickened. Her entire body quivered. The strength that made her a force with which to be reckoned, that helped her to stand strong against her enemies, simply left her. She could feel, and hear, her own heart pounding in her ears. When she could, once again, open her eyes, she pulled away slightly from Bella. Bella looked into her eyes and smiled. Catherine was drawn into another kiss.

The pounding in Catherine's ears threatened to deafen her. Every sense now returned with heightened awareness. Bella's breath soft on her cheek, the feel of Bella's hair moving through her fingers, the touch of Bella's hands on her face, the taste of Bella's mouth on hers, the pounding, pounding in her ears. Then, another sound, more distant. The pounding of horses' hooves.

"Captain!" A cry from just over the rise. "Captain!" the cry even more urgent.

Robert, having heard the call first was already on his horse and heading toward the rider. Catherine was on her feet in an instant. She recognized Remy and could not imagine what crisis could cause the young man to be so urgent. The men spoke briefly then turned their horses and rode toward Catherine and Isabella.

When they were nearly upon the women, Remy leapt from his horse and knelt before her, "Majesty."

If the gasp that escaped from Bella distracted her, Catherine did not let it show. "Robert, what is it?" she demanded.

"My wife is in labor and is asking for me…Majesty," even in his hurry he was aware that the Queen's title was, at last, revealed to Isabella.

"Go to her," Catherine commanded.

As he wheeled his horse around, Robert shouted to the young soldier, "Stay and guard your queen. "

"Yes, Captain."

Robert was gone from sight and sound in a few seconds.

The queen directed the young soldier to retrieve the horses. She turned to speak...to no one. Bella was already nearing the horses. When she reached them, she mounted and rode away, disappearing in the same way Robert had gone.

Chapter Eight

When she arrived outside her private quarters, Catherine found Marie pacing. When asked, Marie informed her that Lady Isabella stormed into the quarters and demanded that she leave. Marie expressed her distress over this, but the queen reassured her and dismissed her for the remainder of the day.

She entered her quarters and closed the doors behind her. The day had been quite unusual so far, and she did not know what to expect next.

Bella was pacing near the pallet. She looked up as Catherine entered.

"Queen?" she spat. "Queen! When were you…?"

"I meant to tell you," Catherine interrupted. "It just never seemed the right time."

"The right time for who?" demanded Bella.

"At first, for you," Catherine ventured. "The physician was concerned that such knowledge would cause distress and prevent your healing."

Bella continued to pace. "And once my healing was certain and I was no longer in danger, then what? Was it a game for you then?" She stopped her pacing and turned to face Catherine. "Did it amuse you to pretend to be someone else with me? Have I entertained you adequately…Majesty?" The scorn in her tone remained in the room long after her voice had faded away.

Catherine started toward Bella but stopped when she saw the fire in her eyes. "I don't know why you're so angry. What's changed?" Even as she spoke the words, however, she knew that the newfound knowledge of who she was must feel like a betrayal to Bella.

"You are Queen!" Bella exploded. "How can that not change everything? If your royalty were not an issue why be concerned to conceal your title at all? You cannot have both ways in the matter. And what am I to do with this knowledge now?" Bella's hands flew to her hips as she glared at Catherine.

"I cannot answer that question for you." With that, Catherine turned and marched into the bedroom, leaving Bella in the sitting area.

She managed to stay upright until she reached her bed. There, she grasped the bedcovers and slid slowly to her knees. Whether from fear of losing Bella or the exhaustion of having dealt with a multitude of feelings she had never before experienced, it was an effort just to stand.

She had no sense of time, or how long she sat on the floor. But then, Bella was beside her, sitting in silence. After a while Bella said, "I need to know why you kept your identity from me."

A long sigh, filled with a lifetime of weariness escaped from Catherine. "By the time it was clear that you would recover I realized how much I enjoyed your company. Until you arrived, I had not known how empty my quarters had always seemed. I do not expect you to understand."

"That does not explain the deception," Bella prodded.

"Your company was unhindered by your perception of who I was. You don't know what it is to live with the kind of authority that comes with such a title! You don't know what it is to watch as people agree with you when you know they should not...to bend to your will when you want nothing more than for them to stand up to you... to watch the fear wash over their faces when they realize you approach!" She was near tears, but would not succumb. "I did not want that with you. I wanted...I want you free to be yourself with me. And I don't have the ability to imagine that freedom exists."

"Is it me, or yourself that you don't trust?" Bella queried.

"I don't know," Catherine responded.

They remained on the floor, leaning against the queen's bed. Finally, Bella broke the silence. "I can accept who you are. I can even accept that you may never wholly belong to any one person because of who you are. What I cannot abide is a fear that causes you to be dishonest with me. If you believe that your title will cause me to behave differently to you, then we are doomed. I won't spend a single moment trying to convince you otherwise. You must know it, or not." Bella stood and left the room.

Catherine remained sitting on the floor for some time. When she finally did get up, she walked to the sitting area. Although it was only mid-afternoon, Bella was sound asleep on her pallet.

Catherine stayed in her bedroom for the remainder of the day. Bella continued to sleep soundly. Catherine did not disturb her. Finally, weary from the days' events, Catherine prepared herself for bed. As tired as she was, sleep eluded her. She ruminated on the day. Her body would not still. Finally she rose and went out onto her balcony. She was watching a cloud pass across the face of the moon when she heard Bella cry out.

Although not with as much frequency, Bella still suffered from nightmares. Catherine stood over her and watched, waiting to see if Bella would slip back into a restful sleep on her own, but she cried out again. Bella's eyes flew open in terror and she did not know where she was. "Bella, Bella. I am here. You are safe," whispered Catherine as she enfolded Bella in her arms. Bella's heart was racing and her breath came in short, quick bursts. She clung to Catherine, until she calmed. When, finally, her breathing returned to normal she said, "Thank you, I am fine now." She lay back down.

Catherine took her words and action to mean that Bella wanted to be left alone. She rose and made her way back to her own bedroom.

With a sadness that threatened to crumble her, Catherine stood near her balcony doors, but did not venture out. The moon was uncovered and by its light the emptiness of her bed was all the more illuminated. The thought of a lifetime of sleeping in that bed alone was almost too much to bear. She shut her eyes tightly to keep out the vision, and to hold back the tears.

The feather light touch on her cheek brought her back to the moonlit room. Bella was there, in front of her, reaching out to her.

"I…" she began, but Bella's fingers moved to cover her mouth.

Wordlessly, Bella's fingers trailed down Catherine's face and neck, tracing the line of her collarbone. Her hand rested there, momentarily, and then tugged at the ribbon that closed the queen's night dressing. With both hands Bella pushed the gown off of Catherine's shoulders and let it fall to the floor. Neither of them breathed. Catherine's heart fluttered.

Bella's eyes hadn't left Catherine's, but now her gaze moved slowly downward to Catherine's lips. She reached up and placed her fingertips lightly on Catherine's mouth. Then her eyes and fingers drew a soft, tentative line down Catherine's neck. As they moved further down Catherine shivered and inhaled, sharply. When Bella's fingers drew softly over her nipples Catherine's mouth opened in surprise, her eyes closed and she was pulled, willingly and unwillingly toward her still warring thoughts. As Bella's hands and fingers continued their delicate descent down to Catherine's hips, the queen sought the will to resist. Her mind called out to God for help to battle this betrayal of her body. Then hands, softer than velvet, glided around her. Bella was behind her running her palms up her sides and back down to the gentle curve of Catherine's buttocks...around to the flat of her belly...back up to her breasts.

"Please God, give me the strength to do what needs to be done..." Catherine was praying, yet not wanting anything to extinguish the fire that burned within her. Part of her wanted to prove that she could resist anything, that she was more powerful than this temptation. But part of her wanted to be overcome, to give in...to give herself up to...

Bella remained behind her and her hands moved lightly, touching, yet not quite touching Catherine's body, and momentarily disappeared. Catherine opened her eyes. Her body was rigid with both fear and desire. She was about to step away, to try to regain command of her own senses, when Bella's hands were on her again, crossing around the front of her and sliding down her hipbones to the tops of her thighs.

Catherine stiffened and the breath that she had been holding in escaped her lungs in spite of her attempt to hold it in. Then Bella's naked body was against her...breasts pressing into her back...lips kissing the area just below Catherine's neck and between her shoulders. Bella's hands, those soft, velvety hands, the feathery touch of fingers were sliding back up past the tops of her thighs and back to belly...then down, down into the curl of black hair.

With a long, low groan, Catherine gave up her fight. Every muscle melted back into Bella and surrendered. Bella turned Catherine toward her. Hungrily, desperately, Catherine felt herself pulled against Bella and she pressed her lips to Bella's. No longer the tentative, unsure kisses of the meadow, these were the kisses of a passion held and awaiting release for what seemed like forever. Catherine's hands moved through Bella's long hair as she kissed and kissed her mouth, her face, her eyes, back to her mouth.

Bella guided Catherine backwards toward the bed and lay her down. Catherine pulled Bella on top of her. They were bathed in moonlight, and Catherine marveled at sight and feel of Bella's body. When Bella's mouth and tongue found Catherine's neck and then her nipples Catherine gasped and moaned with pleasure. Catherine found her body responding without even having to think. The feelings were new, but her sense was of having been waiting for them to be found, as if they lay buried just under the surface and only needed Bella to brush away the sand to reveal them. Breasts against breasts. Mouth against mouth. Legs intertwined. Hips pulsing, thighs rubbing against moist, unfolding, blooming lips.

Bella pushed herself up to her knees and her lips and tongue made their way down Catherine's body, tasting every sweet bit of flesh. She pushed Catherine's legs apart and her mouth found the tender skin inside her thighs. Bella lowered herself and buried her head in the soft fur between Catherine's legs. She inhaled deeply, and reached the fingertips of both hands to separate the outer flesh of Catherine's swelling folds. A perfect rosebud greeted her and she covered it with kisses. Catherine reached down and held Bella's head and as she groaned and lifted her hips.

Long after the moonlight slid off the queen's bed and both Catherine and Bella had sated themselves several times over, the lovers fell asleep locked within each other's embrace.

Chapter Nine

Catherine woke with the sun fell full upon her face. Bella's arm and leg were draped over her body, her breath soft and warm against her cheek. Gently, so as not to waken Bella, Catherine turned her body and rested her head in the crook of her own arm to watch Bella sleep. The memories of the night took hold of her. She had not known that her body was capable of such pleasure. She had not known that such pleasure even existed. She had not known that you could give yourself over and over and not lose, but gain yourself in the process. She watched Bella's eyelids flutter in dreams, and she wondered at how much her life had changed since she and Robert found her in the woods.

As Catherine remembered that day, her finger reached up and lightly, lovingly, caressed the scar on Bella's chin. Bella's eyes opened and Catherine looked into them.

"What are you thinking?" Bella asked sleepily.

"I am remembering finding you."

"Do you regret that day?"

Catherine's finger moved from Bella's scar to push a strand of hair off Bella's cheek. "How can you think that I would regret finding you?"

"Because I am afraid that you regret last night..."

"I have been lying here, watching you sleep for some time. I admit that I have tried to regret. I tried to imagine myself denying you. I have tried to tell myself that this must never happen again."

Bella's look was one of pain and mild panic. But Catherine continued with a smile.

"What I feel for you is more powerful than anything I have known. I know now that I could no more deny my love for you than I could deny my own existence. I am yours, plain and simple, and there is apparently nothing I can do about that, for God knows I have tried. I cannot fight my feelings for you. Trying to resist what I feel is like trying to stop my own breath. I cannot live without you. I will not live without you. If that damns me, then I am damned."

Bella's face relaxed into a smile. "When you fell asleep in my arms last night, I lay here wondering how you might torture yourself this morning. I worried that you might be so angry and full of regret that you might banish me from your sight. I was prepared for anything, but I knew that I did not regret a single kiss. I believe with my whole being that God brought you to me. I would be dead if not for you, but instead I am more alive than ever. If we are damned, we are damned together."

Catherine propped herself on her elbow and lowered her lips to Bella's. They made love in the full light of the sun. When they were done, Catherine pulled Bella on top of her and they lay quietly for some time.

"I love you, Bella. I think I have been falling in love with you from the first moment I looked into your eyes."

"I don't think it was my eyes you looked into, but my very soul. I am yours to love, my queen. I will love you with my dying breath…and, if possible, even after the breath is gone from me."

With a sense of overwhelming gratitude filling her entire being, Catherine enfolded Bella in her arms and they lay entwined, listening to the sound of each other's breath, happy just to be together.

Chapter Ten

Over the next several days Catherine feigned illness to her servants. She and Isabella did not leave the quarters. Meals were brought to them, but interruptions were for urgent royal matters only, and only to be delivered by the Captain of the Guard.

A few times, at the edge of her awareness, Catherine felt her doubt creep in. Was God angry? Would she be punished for giving in to her feelings for Bella? Each time she pushed the thoughts aside.

She did call for Robert at midday on the second day of her self-imposed confinement, anxious to know if his wife delivered safely.

His beaming face told her before he uttered a word, "Majesty, I am a father. He is the most beautiful son in the land. I could not be happier."

"I am glad, Robert. He is fortunate to be blessed with you as a father," she said as she took both of Robert's hands in congratulations and kissed him on both cheeks.

"And how is Petra after her ordeal?" asked the queen.

"Healing well and quickly," replied Robert. "She comes from sturdy stock."

Bella was sitting nearby and rose. "Congratulations, Robert."

As he thanked her, he made a small bow to her, a gesture of respect not lost on her or Catherine. He turned to Catherine and said with a small smile, "It is good to see you both looking so well."

Catherine took Robert's arm and escorted him to the door. "Robert, what's being said about my absence from the affairs of state?"

"Rumors are rife." He paused. "And creative. Some are concerned for your health. Others wonder that Lady Isabella remains here with you. It's the Bishop, I fear, who encourages the later speculation."

"My inclination is to resume my normal duties tomorrow. Please have my secretary arrange meetings in order of priority according to his discretion. I should like to meet with the nobles following the noon meal."

"Will you join them for the meal as usual, Your Highness?" He smiled slyly and raised his eyebrows as he asked.

"I think not," she returned his smile. "But I would, if possible, like to be privy to their conversation."

"I understand," Robert could not hide his amusement.

"Thank you, Robert." Just before she closed the doors behind him she turned and asked, "What have you named your son?"

Beaming, Robert answered, "Giovanni, after his grandfather."

Catherine was delighted that Robert named his son after his father-in-law. Lord Giovanni was the sweetest, most gentle man Catherine had ever known. And he was her most ardent supporter on the Privy Council. His nature was playful and endearing, although he was able to debate and make his points as well as any of the noblemen. Lord Giovanni was a big, round, soft man with a face as open and kind as a child's. Catherine found that nothing warmed her more than the man's hearty laugh. And, although it was not allowed to touch the queen, Lord Giovanni sometimes forgot himself in his affection for Catherine and spontaneously pulled her into a great hug. Someone present always pointed out the inappropriateness of his gesture and he would stop immediately and apologize, mortified with himself for the impropriety. Catherine always forgave him instantly and reassured him with a smile. The fact was that she loved when he hugged her. It was one of the few, spontaneous gestures of affection she had ever known.

Lord Giovanni informed Robert that talk during the meal continued to focus on speculation over the queen's absence.

Catherine swept regally through the double doors into the meeting room where the Privy Council had just finished their midday meal. The large rectangular table was cleared and they were, again, prepared to work. Two large southern facing windows allowed in light from the sun. The windows were opened, as the October day was one full of sun and warmth.

All members rose and bowed as she entered. She took her place at the head of the table. Her Privy Council was a small one, as Privy Councils go. But the kingdom was small, tucked away in the foothills of the Apennines, and not as wealthy as surrounding kingdoms. In general, monarchs relied heavily on their Privy Councils. While Catherine was no exception, she was very cautious of their advice.

"My Noble Lords, Your Grace, my apologies for neglecting to dine with you. I hope you enjoyed your meal." She gave thought to making an excuse, perhaps of feeling poorly, but in the end decided she need not make an excuse at all. If they wanted a reason for her absence, they would have to ask her for one. She doubted any of them would. Nevertheless, she worried that her happiness and the nature of her relationship with Bella was a truth that might show in her face. She made every effort to mask her feelings.

"As usual, Your Majesty, the meal was quite good," said Lord Navona coolly.

Lord Navona from Abbadia, in the central part of the kingdom was one of the Council who tended to go along with whatever Bishop Capshaw recommended. He was a slight fellow who had inherited a good deal of land from his father and grandfather. In spite of his small stature, he was an able administrator who hired even abler farmhands. As a result, his farms were some of the biggest growers of produce in all the Kingdom of Montalcino. Navona supplied a good part of northern Italy with produce. If he weren't so narrow-minded and intent on agreeing with everything the bishop said, Catherine might have even liked him. As it was, she tolerated him much the way one puts up with a relative whose views embarrass most everyone in the family, but whom, nonetheless, is family and, therefore, comes with the territory. Lord Navona was a distant cousin of King Edward, Catherine's father. She remembered how he used to support her father, even when everyone else disagreed. It was only since her father's death that Navona tended siding with the bishop.

"Very good, gentlemen," Catherine said, "then without haste I should like to deal with our most pressing issues only today. I am most concerned about the continuation of these rogue attacks upon our citizens by groups proclaiming to be acting on behalf of the Pope. Your Grace, have you any news for us? Have any of the perpetrators been identified?" she inquired.

"Not as yet, Your Majesty. I have, however, sent a delegate out to several districts to meet with the priests in each parish."

"A single delegate?" she asked with a raised eyebrow.

"Yes, Your Majesty. There have been no attacks in nearly a month," he said, referring to the attack on Bella's family. "I saw no need to hire more than one delegate. The attacks have been so random and widespread that, quite honestly, I fear we will never find the culprits," replied the Bishop with little concern.

"Never finding the culprits sounds like what we intend, Your Grace. One delegate out roaming the country will be an easy target. Are you not concerned for his safety?"

"He is a capable man, Your Highness, skilled and adept at handling himself. You needn't fear." The Bishop's disdain for his Queen's questioning of him was reflected in his response. He kept his eyes on his papers and did not look at her.

"What I fear is more attacks," said the queen. "What do the rest of you hear from your districts?" She looked around the table.

Lord Bagglioni was a man for himself. From Roccalbegna, he was ancient. He was invited to be on the Privy Council during the reign of Catherine's grandmother, Queen Anne. Roccalbegna was south of Abbadia and also had the fertile land of Abbadia. Although Bagglioni did not possess as much land as Lord Navona, he was wealthy from his family's years of good farming. Bagglioni was able to serve on the Council because his extended family continued to run the business and care for his land and home. It was he who responded first.

"Your Majesty, my lesser lords and nobles are afraid for themselves and their families. Especially since they heard what happened to Lord James and his family, who was from a greater house and not safe," he paused, and then added, "How does his daughter fare?"

At the mention of Isabella, Catherine felt herself flush. A vision of Bella's body shimmering in the moonlight swirled up and clouded her vision. Catherine's memories transported her to her bed and into Bella's arms. Her body responded to the memories of the past days distracting her until Lord Bagglioni's voice, insistent and concerned brought her back to the room.

"Majesty. Majesty?"

Catherine struggled to focus. "Yes. I am sorry, Lord Bagglioni. You asked?"

"I asked how Lord James' daughter was recovering."

Catherine shook the visions of Bella from her. Her fear took over as she worried that her love, and lovemaking, was evident to her Council, especially the bishop.

"Lady Isabella is finally nearing a full return to health," she responded with as much detachment as she could muster. "It is kind of you to inquire. But even her physical recovery will not banish the hideousness of the deeds done by these marauders. If we do not find them and bring them to justice I fear none of us are safe."

She turned to the Bishop, "Your Grace, I would like you to consult with General Moretti on this matter. I have ordered him to begin his own investigation into these illegal activities." Catherine noted and ignored how the bishop's eyes narrowed in anger. "While I appreciate your desire to be frugal in the matter," she continued, "we must place more resources at your disposal to conduct this investigation. And we must assume that since the attacks are so widespread this group is not recognized by the people they are attacking. Since they do not appear to limit themselves to a small area, I believe that the strategies of a military man like General Moretti would lend themselves to tracking them down. As General Moretti has oversight of the borders throughout the kingdom, he may be able to monitor the problem in ways we have not considered."

Lord Como, from Scansano, nearest the Mediterranean, was a large, loud, opinionated man who could easily dominate the Council if he had a mind to do so. Although he came across as quite uncouth, King Edward always appreciated his honesty. He was outspoken in his views. One day when Catherine complained to her father that she did not like Como, her father said, "My dear, the thing to remember about Lord Como, especially when he is at his loudest, is that you always know where he stands on an issue." Catherine was more observant of Como after that, finally realizing that her father was absolutely right. No one could ever accuse Lord Como of hiding his intentions or feelings about a topic. Como was neither supporter of the bishop, nor a supporter of the monarchy. Como was for himself. That was the clearest thing about him. He was the first to respond to Catherine's plan to put Moretti on the problem.

"That is a sound idea, Majesty. I will alert my vassals to cooperate with Moretti in any way possible."

There was a general consensus of agreement that made it unwise for the Bishop to disagree.

Lord Carfaggi cleared his throat. Catherine ignored him. Carfaggi was as hateful and deceitful a man as Catherine had ever known. Along with the Bishop, Carfaggi was an ardent detractor. A misogynist, like the bishop, he was recommended by Thomas Capshaw for the council position. At that time Catherine's father was still under the impression that he and Thomas Capshaw were fighting on the same side of the battle *against* Rome. Little did King Edward know that Carfaggi, cousin to Cardinal Carafa, had come at the insistence of Carafa in Rome. Carfaggi, like Cardinal Carafa, was in total support of the Inquisition as it had been conducted in Spain by King Ferdinand and Queen Isabella. Carfaggi believed that Spain's relentless purge of heretics was for the good of the Church. Humorless and stiff, with a drawn, pinched face, everything about Lord Carfaggi grated on Catherine's nerves.

Before she could bring up another agenda topic, Lord Carfaggi raised the issue of marriage.

"Your Majesty, please assure the Council that you have given thought, as we have requested on numerous occasions, to marriage."

The queen drew herself up, "My Lords, we have been over this time and again. While I appreciate your interest in my producing an heir, I have no inclination to marry at this time."

"Perhaps, your Majesty, it is a matter of finding a suitable match," said Lord Romeo.

Lord Romeo from Arcidosso was a treasure. He had only daughters, fifteen of them, and while he adored every one of them, he found them too much to handle after the death of his wife. Lord Romeo was of a more contemplative nature and the noise and bustle of a home with that many women was more than he was inclined toward without his wife. She had managed an orderly and quiet home for him. He could not bear being there without her. His daughters were old enough to manage the estate. The five older ones were married and able to care for the younger girls. The youngest was now thirteen. He visited them often enough, but was happy for his life and his role in the running of the kingdom. Lord Romeo was thoughtful and intelligent when considering all issues as a councilmember. Catherine was often inclined to listen carefully to what Romeo had to say. She knew he did not offer his advice without thoroughly having investigated all sides of a matter.

"With all due respect, Lord Romeo, there is no suitable match available, at least not that has been presented," Catherine was becoming irritated and had to work to control her feelings on this issue.

"Majesty," said Lord Novona, "while we understand that you are not inclined to marry for marriage sake, we beg you to consider your subjects. An heir is imperative to the people who rely on the continuation of your line. Your own father would advise you in this, I am convinced."

"The king," Catherine replied, "would encourage us all to consider my subjects, as he always did, but I am not inclined to pursue this issue at present." She did not like where this was leading.

"Majesty," the Bishop gave a slight nod, "we believe we have addressed your concerns about marrying."

Catherine hated this discussion. The whole idea of marriage had always infuriated her, as they well knew. Why could they not let the matter alone? She was still young, just nineteen, and knew that this was more about envisioning her successor than insuring the continuation of her line. They couldn't care less about her line, all they cared about was their own power and wealth and what would give them more control of that. She refused to let them bully her into marriage.

"The matter is closed, gentlemen." Catherine stood. "I will not discuss it again."

"Majesty, do you not even wish to know who we have found for you?" said Lord Carfaggi incredulously. He produced a list of acceptable candidates and proceeded to pass it to her.

She glared at Carfaggi. "The matter is closed. I will leave you to attend to your other affairs of state. I will expect a report on the current output of the paper mill by this afternoon."

Catherine left the room in a swirl of barely controlled anger.

When she arrived back at her quarters, Marie was rushing out of the room with a bucket of foul smelling vomit.

"Marie," she stopped the servant, "what is it?"

"Majesty, the Lady Isabella has taken ill. She has been vomiting since you left."

"Thank you, Marie, carry on," Catherine said as she rushed into the room.

She found Bella lying on her pallet, pale as a ghost. "Bella, what is it?" Catherine ran to her side. "What's wrong?"

"It's nothing," Bella said weakly, "please don't be overly concerned. "I am already feeling better. It's probably just something I ingested. It will pass."

All of Catherine's fears, all of her anguish regarding her relationship with Bella came rushing to the surface. In spite of her decision to accept her love for Bella as God's gift, regardless of the ability to push aside her anxiety, she continued to struggle with an inherent belief that her love for Bella was wrong and that, eventually, she and Bella would be punished for their sin.

"I will not leave your side until I am convinced," said Catherine as she moved to the pallet stroking Bella's hair until she fell asleep. But all the while her thoughts raced with fear of losing Bella.

Bella woke later that afternoon and looked considerably better. Catherine was reassured, but remained concerned as Bella had little appetite that evening. There were dark circles under her eyes, and she still looked tired.

Following a game of backgammon, Catherine called for a bath. Whatever questions or suspicions the servants had about the relationship between their queen and Bella, no one dared speak of it. Marie dutifully filled the bath and left the women alone for the evening.

The evening bath routine established during Bella's convalescence was reduced to twice weekly, with the exception that warm affection was replaced by sensual play. Bath time was no longer just for cleansing and comforting the body, it was prelude to physical exploration.

"You do look better this evening." Catherine said, still concerned.

"You worry too much, my love."

"Perhaps," said Catherine as she slipped into the tub opposite Bella, "but perhaps that's a response to your nonchalance."

"I promise if I am not better soon I will call for the physician myself." Bella smiled in such a way that Catherine just shook her head.

"I will hold you to that promise," Catherine insisted.

"What's on your agenda tomorrow?" asked Bella as she lifted Catherine's foot from the water and tenderly worked her thumbs into the arch.

"I ended today's Privy Council meeting fairly abruptly." Catherine told Bella about the pressure to marry and how the meeting ended. Bella furrowed her brow. Catherine continued, "I suppose I will attempt to meet with the bishop. He is sorely mistaken if he thinks I will simply allow him to delegate one man to hunt for an entire band of killers."

"I cannot imagine he will be open to further suggestions." Bella lifted Catherine's other foot.

"Mmmm. That feels nice. No, he will likely protest about the cost. If I pressure him and fund the search, he is more likely to make some effort. Also, tomorrow I will meet with Father Tim."

"He is the priest you like so much?"

"Mmm hmm." Catherine smiled as Bella's hands left her feet and worked their way up her leg.

Catherine pulled Bella toward her and drew the sponge over her shoulders and down her back. Bella turned in the tub and leaned back into Catherine. They sat quietly for a while, Catherine tracing a delicate finger down Bella's sternum and around her nipples until the nipples became erect and Bella moaned softly.

"Water's cooling...let's get out." Bella stood and pulled Catherine to standing. They stepped out of the tub and reached for towels. Catherine started to dry Bella's back, but Bella turned and grabbed Catherine playfully, pulling her, still dripping, against her.

"I will never tire of how miraculous your skin feels against mine," Catherine whispered hoarsely as she led Bella to the pallet. Bella seemed over her bout of illness, as evidenced by her energy as she made love to Catherine. They fell asleep on the pallet wrapped within one another.

The next morning when Bella woke, the vomiting returned. Alarmed, Catherine insisted that the physician be called. Bella begged her to wait.

"Catherine, please, it's nothing. I have struggled with this in the past. Give me today before you call for the physician. I promise that if I am not well by tomorrow I will allow you to call him."

"I do not like this, especially after all you have been through. Why are you so resistant? What if it's something serious? What if you're worse tomorrow?"

"I am tired only, and just wish to rest this morning, my love." But she ran for the bucket.

"Marie will stay with you this morning," Catherine insisted. "I'll return for the midday meal. Perhaps if you are not feeling better you will see reason in calling the physician."

Bella smiled weakly and went to lie down. The bucket remained at her side.

Chapter Eleven

One day each week Catherine met secretly with Father Timothy, a priest from Castiglione d' Orcia. Under the guise of a ride with her Captain of the Guard, she and Robert stole into the forest and met with Father Tim to discuss the latest rounds of accusations leveled at innocent subjects. Father Tim was as gentle a soul as Catherine had known. She learned of him when he arrived at the interrogation of one of her subjects by the bishop. Surprisingly, he affected a release of the innocent parishioner from the bishop's grasp. Father Tim was articulate and knew well his scripture. Catherine found in him an ally to fight the battle against the Inquisition.

Father Tim was slight in build with soft, gentle features. His hair was long, but did not quite reach his shoulders. He had warm, brown eyes that seemed to understand just about everything. His voice was as gentle as his manner, and she found him to be intelligent and thoughtful in all that he said.

The morning discussion revolved around concerns that the bishop had increased his hunt for witches.

Robert had a list of three women who were accused of witchcraft.

"On what grounds?" asked Father Tim.

"They carried herbs in leather pouches."

While these women were nothing more than healers, the bishop used the accusations to create even more fear than usual. Many villagers were now refusing to seek help for simple illnesses for fear of appearing to support witchcraft.

"The women are scheduled for interrogation by the bishop next week." Robert informed them.

"Then you will need to work quickly. Here are the names of two near the castle whom you can arrest on false charges. Can you get them into the same cells?" Tim asked.

"It shouldn't be a problem."

"I am always curious as to how you find these volunteers." Catherine said, intrigued.

"These particular women both came to me from elsewhere. Their lives were shattered by the murder of family members. Like most, Majesty, they feel they have little for which to live, so they have committed to this cause. Don't worry, they know what to expect."

Father Tim told Robert where to find the women to be arrested. He had already spent a considerable amount of time teaching the women how to prepare the poor souls accused of heresy and witchcraft. Much of his training centered on how to respond to the bishop's accusations and questions.

Robert arrested Father Tim's volunteers, who were imprisoned on minor false charges. During their imprisonment they coached the victims on how to respond during interrogations. Many of the accused were released with admonitions only. The others were mostly imprisoned for one year. The very unfortunate few who were executed lay heavy on the hearts of Queen Catherine, Father Tim and Captain Robert.

"As soon as possible, then," Catherine said, "have them brought before me so we can drop the charges against them." She did not want the volunteers to suffer longer than necessary.

Chapter Twelve

In truth, Bishop Thomas Capshaw had not always been a violent man. At one time, he was part of the underground rebellion fighting the Inquisition. But that time seemed long ago, and for Bishop Capshaw there was no turning back.

It was 1552, a scant two years earlier, when Thomas was called to Rome. King Edward had petitioned Rome to make Thomas Capshaw priest to the royal family. Rome granted the King's request in 1551, and then largely ignored both the King and Thomas until Thomas's Vatican visit.

Rome was different from anything Thomas ever expected or experienced. St. Peter's Basilica was more magnificent than he had imagined. The artwork and culture alone was enough to overwhelm a young priest from a small kingdom. He spent hours just wandering the art museums of the Vatican or sitting and staring at the ceiling in the Sistine Chapel. It was as if all of creation itself poured down from that ceiling and into his soul. He was filled with reverence and awe, and much to his dismay, found his sexual appetite stirred, as well.

By the time Thomas was actually called to meet with Pope Julius, he was certain he was going to be admonished for his alliance with King Edward, for it was known that the King was resistive to the harsher punishments of the Inquisition. Although the Inquisition had not fully encompassed the northern Duchies and Kingdoms as yet, there were those who were known to make reports to Rome.

With this in mind, Thomas entered the meeting with Pope Julius full of apprehension. And so he was surprised that Pope Julius did not even mention his King. Instead, the Pope chatted genially and invited Thomas to join him that evening at the Villa Giulia. He was even more surprised, at the end of their meeting, when the Pope invited him to stay as a guest at the Villa.

Pope Julius spent a great deal of his time at the Villa, which he had built on the edge of Rome, when he became Pope. Villa Guilia was large, lush and well appointed. There were many rooms filled with frescoes, statues and paintings. One room displayed a ceiling fresco depicting cherub-like putti playing with one another's genitals. The Villa was host to many in Rome, and was generally a bustling hive of activity.

Thomas entered the doors of Villa Guilia feeling slightly intimidated. He was unaccustomed to such decadence. The ceilings were high and marble everywhere shined. There was a gathering in the main hall when he arrived. As he was escorted up a stairway he looked down to see a host of young men surrounding a slovenly, bearded, older man. His escort stopped and whispered, "That is the famous painter and sculptor, Michelangelo. He's the one who painted the ceiling in the Chapel, you know."

Thomas stared in disbelief. How could this old, uncouth, ill-clothed being have created such overwhelming works of beauty? As Thomas stood looking down at the scene before him, Michelangelo shook himself loose from the gathering, threw his hand up in dismissal and walked away without a word, disappearing down a long corridor.

Thomas wasn't aware of the Pope's reputation prior to his arrival in Rome. At the villa, however, there was no doubt that the Pope was inclined to indulge himself at any expense. Thomas' first evening at the Villa found him guest at one of the Pope's luxurious dinner parties. Food and wine flowed, and following the dinner the Pope led everyone into the great hall for entertainment.

Once Thomas recovered from his initial discomfort, he began to relax. Musicians were the first to perform for the guests. The sounds of each instrument reverberated off the walls and high ceilings, and sent undulating waves of musical bliss up through the floor into Thomas' feet, up and up, until his entire body quivered with each note. He never felt music in such a profoundly intimate way.

The villa was full of young men, all of whom were clearly at ease in each others' company.

Several young men approached Thomas following the performances and engaged him in conversation. The music, the conversation, the wine relaxed Thomas and he began to enjoy himself.

As the evening wore on, he found himself in the company of two men. They were both younger. One was a local priest, the other one of the musicians whom Thomas noticed earlier in the evening. The priest flitted from group to group, and eventually left Thomas alone with the musician.

Thomas asked him about his violino piccolo and the young man lit up with delight.

"Let me show you how to play it!" the young man said enthusiastically. "Hold it here," the musician gave Thomas the neck of the instrument and showed him how to hold it. "Now place this part on your shoulder, just here."

Thomas did as he was instructed, but the young man stopped him and said, "Let me show you." He stepped behind Thomas and reached around him placing his hand over Thomas's on the neck of the violin. "Now, hold the other part here, under your chin." The young man put his face next to Thomas'. Thomas felt the roughness of stubble against his cheek as the musician held his cheek directly against Thomas'. "That's it. Now, take the bow in your other hand," the artist brought his right hand and arm around Thomas' other side and lifted it to draw across the strings. As he held Thomas's hand with the bow, he pressed himself into Thomas.

Thomas was highly aroused. Never before had he been so erotically charged.

"Is this alright?" whispered the violinist in his ear.

Thomas swallowed, hard. He could feel his face beginning to flush. "Yes…"

"I am glad. Here, try this," he said. He moved more to Thomas's side. As he moved around Thomas felt the unmistakable brush of the musician's erect penis draw across his buttocks.

Thomas felt himself going weak. He closed his eyes and locked his knees in order to remain upright.

The musician moved around to look at Thomas. He smiled as he locked eyes with the priest and said, "Come with me." He grabbed Thomas by the hand and led him to a small room down the corridor through which Michelangelo had disappeared earlier that day.

When they entered the room the violinist shut the door, put down his violin, turned and reached for Thomas. He clutched the robes at Thomas's chest, pulling him close.

"I am glad that you have such an appreciation for my talent. Allow me to demonstrate some of my other talents…"

He pressed his mouth against Thomas's. Thomas felt their mutual erections pressing against one another. They were both breathing heavily, almost frantically. As the musician began to grope him, he pushed Thomas back against the door they had just entered. The musician's mouth continued to explore him, pressing, biting, probing, while hands, the same hands that had just serenaded Thomas with such musical beauty, groped under his robes, introducing pleasures Thomas had only ever denied himself.

The hands drove Thomas to unimaginable heights of frenzy. He was new to this, but his body responded with a knowledge he did not know he possessed. Then the musician turned him, so that his face and chest pressed against the door. The hand resumed stroking his cock, slow, perfect strokes, and Thomas was certain he would die if it stopped. The musician's other hand raised the robes behind him. He felt the musician's hardness against him, pressing against him. Then his free hand moved to separate Thomas's buttocks. The tip of the musician's cock entered him and pressed urgently inward and up. A magnificent, exquisite pain tore into him and Thomas welcomed it with all of his being. The hand on his throbbing member continued its rhythmic stroking, blending with the thrusting of male to male joining that Thomas craved all of his life, but never knew existed in such splendor.

When Thomas cried out in ecstasy and pain as he climaxed, he would have collapsed onto the floor but for the musician holding him up, continuing his delicious pleasure from behind. When, at last, Thomas felt the violinist explode inside he cried out again and they slid down the door together, gasping for breath.

He never even knew the musician's name. It seemed there was a new face, a new pleasure open to him nearly every evening. As the faces changed, the sexual acts varied. Ultimately, the nameless, changing faces did not matter. Thomas both lost and found himself in his earthly pleasure. The sexual acts became his religion, his life, his obsession. He lived for every evening when the young men came calling at the Villa. He forgot about Montalcino. He forgot about his calling to God. He forgot about everything except experiencing different ways to satisfy his newfound, insatiable thirst for sexual pleasure.

Thomas stayed in Rome for two months. While there, the Villa Giulia was his home. The Pope saw to his comfort in the evenings. His days were sometimes spent meeting with different Cardinals, who *were* interested in knowing about his King and the Kingdom of Montalcino.

"How does your King support the church in the interrogation of heretics?" asked Cardinal Giovanni Carafa. They were meeting in one of the rooms of the Papal Apartments. Two other Cardinals were present, but neither of them spoke.

Thomas, still loyal to the King, and not yet under the control of anyone, protected Edward. "He is a good Catholic, and encourages me to follow the instructions of the Church in every way, Cardinal."

Thomas did not like Cardinal Carafa. Carafa was just the type of Catholic that he and Edward railed against. Carafa's push to cleanse Europe of heretics was just the thing that he and Edward worked against. He was glad that Carafa was only a Cardinal, and not the Pope.

Carafa stood and placed his fingertips together as he walked slowly around the room. "You seem quite comfortable at the Villa Giulia," Carafa said slyly. "How do you spend your time there?"

Thomas shot a questioning look at the two seated Cardinals, hoping to glean a hint of where this might be going. They sat stone faced. Finally, Thomas answered, "I am a guest. As such, I am invited to partake in meals and entertainment when there is entertainment. Otherwise, I roam the gardens, or read and pray in my room."

"Have you had opportunity to meet with the artist?"

"I have seen him there on several occasions, but have not spoken with him. No. We have not been introduced."

"There are rumors of lewd and lascivious conduct at the Villa. Have you heard of or partaken in any such conduct?" asked Carafa as he turned and looked directly at Thomas.

Thomas broke out in a sweat. He hoped it was concealed by his robes and hair. His legs were shaking. He was not accustomed to lying.

Although he tried to maintain eye contact, his gaze drifted. He felt himself begin to cower under the interrogation.

"I have heard or seen no such behavior, Cardinal," his voice trembled a bit as he answered.

"Really," Carafa continued as one eyebrow rose, "so in spite of the fact that many young men are seen entering the Villa almost nightly and do not leave until morning, you are not aware of such activity?"

Thomas swallowed hard, "No, Cardinal. As I have said, I spend much of my time in my private room. The Villa is quite large, so perhaps there are activities in parts of the Villa that are unknown to me. The Pope may be better able to answer your concerns."

"Father Capshaw," the Cardinal addressed him sternly, glaring at him through narrowed eyelids, "you may mistake my questions as a test of your loyalty to your King, the Pope, or both. I am not interested in your loyalty to people, but to your Church and your faith. Your very presence in the Villa for these past months has not gone unnoticed by me or the House of Cardinals, nor has your activity within those walls. I have enough evidence against you to burn you at the stake without hesitation. You are an abomination and a disgrace. If it were in my power I would see you, and that heathen artist burn. For now I must content myself with trying to cover the vulgar images he has painted in the Chapel...and send you back to your heathen King."

Thomas was terrified. His trembling was so bad he didn't know how the table remained still. He needed to get out of the room before he vomited. How had he let this happen to him, he who had always tried to be a good priest and a decent man? Carafa could destroy him and all because he gave in to temptation without even attempting to resist. His pallor gave him away. He thought he was about to faint when Carafa continued.

"Pope Julius will not always be in power. You would do well to remember that. Meanwhile, I think it wise for you to return to your little Kingdom of Montalcino. It has come to my attention that the Pope intends to make a Bishop of you. Very well, then *Bishop* Capshaw, I believe that we may have use for you there. Montalcino, like Venice and many other places, is succumbing to the teachings of that bastard Martin Luther. I will not have it. You are spared your life, but only so long as you ruthlessly work to cleanse the church of heretics. Just as I have my eyes in the Villa, they will be watching Montalcino…and you. I expect nothing less than your most rigorous efforts as an interrogator." Carafa paused, placed his hands on the table and leaned menacingly into Thomas's face. "It is time for you to return home."

Thomas stood, but nearly fell back into his seat on quivering legs. He managed to make it to the door. He did not look back. He was certain he would vomit, but he managed to get outside before he did so. He leaned against one of the large, stone pillars at the edge of St. Peter's square and heaved until he was empty. When he arrived back at the Villa, he could not remember how he got there.

Thomas sent word to Pope Julius that his presence was requested back in Montalcino. He wanted to leave immediately, but Pope Julius would not hear of it and pressed Thomas to stay another month.

"You are one of seven priests," Pope Julius informed him with a smile, "selected for a Bishopric."

Thomas bowed his head to conceal any possibility that he already knew. He hoped the Pope saw it as a gesture of humility.

"Holiness," Thomas said as he looked up, "I am deeply honored."

"We are planning the ceremony for one month from tomorrow. It would be a tragedy for you to miss such an occasion in your own honor."

"I agree, Holiness. It would pain me to miss such an event. But my King and my Church need me in Montalcino. I have already been gone too long. Please, forgive me."

"Well, then," the Pope relented, "we will have to make you Bishop in a private ceremony before you leave. When do you plan to return to Montalcino?"

"I had planned to do so this morning, Holiness."

"You will need to postpone your plan for a day or two while the arrangements are made for a private ceremony." The Pope turned to his assistant and said, "Please make arrangements tomorrow for Father Thomas' consecration in a private ceremony. Invite as many of the Cardinals from the College as are able to attend. If none are available, so be it, it is my presence only that is required." Pope Julius turned back to Thomas. "Your departure is untimely, Thomas, but I respect your desire to return to your duties. You will return to your Kingdom a Bishop."

"An unexpected and unworthy honor from the Holy See. I will work to serve Christ and the Church to the best of my abilities."

Thomas hid in his room at the Villa. At a time in his life when he should be celebrating his good fortune, he cowered alone, fearing to be seen in the company of anyone at the Villa.

Thomas was made Bishop in a small, private ceremony. Only one other bishop from the College of Bishops was in attendance. A small dinner was held that evening in Thomas's honor. Several other Bishops and a few Cardinals were present, but Thomas was so tense, so utterly unnerved by the presence of Cardinal Carafa, that he could not wait until the evening was over. He barely touched his food. As soon as he could, he left the party for his room, packed and tried to sleep. He left for Montalcino before dawn.

When Thomas first returned from Rome, the king attempted to find out what had happened to change him, to help him find his true vision again. As young men they spent hours in righteous indignation discussing how to fight the Inquisition. But once he returned from Rome, Thomas played his new part very well. In fact, he tried to convince the King that their beliefs as young men were childish and that they "should put away childish things" and act as responsible stewards of their Church and their faith.

As Edward pulled away from him he grieved. He missed Edward's companionship more than anyone could know. For in truth, Thomas loved Edward more than as a brother. When once, still young boys in the throes of physical games and youthful endeavors, Thomas lost himself and tried to kiss Edward. The young prince pushed him away.

"What are you doing?" Edward demanded. His look of confusion evident on his face.

"I am sorry, Edward, I don't know. I just...I thought that ..." Thomas sputtered.

"Don't ever try such a thing again." Edward said.

And he did not, but thoughts of Edward were never far from his mind...or his loins. Their friendship resumed. Edward forgot about

Thomas' momentary lapse, but for Thomas the unrequited love he felt for Edward continued to burn with soul searing intensity.

Thomas could see that his involvement in the Inquisition pushed Edward further away from him. He suffered quietly, and alone. There was nothing he could do to change what he had become…Rome had seen to that. But if his grief over losing Edward was intolerable in that first year he returned from Rome, it was insurmountable when the King died. Thomas was forced to abandon any hope that he would be able to make things right again with Edward. When Edward died, the Thomas that Edward knew died forever, as well. And Thomas, in his anger and his pain, became an ever more ruthless interrogator.

At first, he was uncomfortable with this role, finding his conscience troubled as he interrogated innocent victims, but Bishop Capshaw soon discovered that he was quite gifted in his ability to interrogate those suspected of heresy. He used the fear of those being questioned to his advantage, intimidating them into confusion. Confusion created responses that were inconsistent with responses they had already made. Inconsistencies were as good as confessions. Still, he sometimes waited for the tiny prick of conscience that connected him by an ever fraying thread to the beliefs of his youth. Those feelings rarely intruded on him anymore.

There were times he was glad that King Edward was no longer alive. The King was the one person who knew that his participation in the Inquisition was a complete reversal of his original beliefs.

Chapter Thirteen

When Catherine returned from her meeting with Father Tim, Bella did indeed look much better. Her appetite returned, along with her color, and they enjoyed a meal together.

When Catherine left the quarters again, Bella dressed to wander the grounds. She was feeling the need for some fresh air, but she had something else on her mind. She requested Marie to have the Captain of the Guard meet her in the palace gardens.

"Lady Isabella, it's good to see you out and enjoying the fresh air." Robert found Bella strolling through the garden.

"It must be beautiful during the spring and summer months," she replied as she reached out her hand to greet him.

"I understood that you were ill, I am glad to see that you are well enough now."

"I am fine, thank you," Bella responded.

They walked together in silence for a short while. Finally, Bella said, "Sit with me."

They found a bench.

She took a deep breath. "I wish to know what danger my presence poses to your queen."

Robert sighed and was quiet for several minutes, clearly giving his response thought. "Lady Isabella," he finally offered, "a queen is always in danger, but I think you know this. I understand why you ask, and I will answer you honestly. "

Bella nodded for him to continue.

"Our queen is more at risk because some suspect your relationship to be more than a woman's friendship."

He paused. Bella was not able to conceal her blush, but urged him to continue.

"As I am certain she has told you, our Bishop is no friend to her. He would like nothing more than to accuse her of heresy and replace her with a monarch more likely to rule under his own control. He suspects you and Catherine, but I don't believe he will do anything until he's certain that he can succeed in imprisoning her. He is far from being able to do so."

"What causes the enmity between them?" asked Bella

"That's a long and complicated story, but suffice it to say that she does not accept him as the final authority on the teachings of Christ and the Church, and he doesn't appreciate her independent nature or unwillingness to accept his authority as representative of Christ and the church."

"I see," Bella replied thoughtfully. "That must make the heretical threat all the more meaningful to his Grace."

Robert nodded.

"Do you believe she should marry?" Bella continued.

"It grieves me to say so, Lady Isabella, especially now that she is so..." he struggled with words, "now that I see her so happy. But, yes, I believe it is in her best interests to take a husband."

"You have had this conversation with her?

"Many times, Lady."

Bella stood and walked away from Robert a short way, then returned. She was quiet for some time, and then finally asked, "Why has she no ladies in waiting? It is very unusual for a queen, is it not?"

Robert laughed. "Unusual for a queen, yes, for our dear Catherine, no." He was hesitant to expound. He reached up and rubbed his face as if considering whether or not to continue.

Bella smiled. "You have no reason to trust me where your queen is involved," she said, "but I have a reason for asking these questions... and I ask that you search your heart to know that I, too, wish to protect her."

"Protecting Catherine is more than my sworn duty, Lady Isabella. She is a sister to my soul and I was born to serve her."

Bella reached for his hand. She raised it to her lips and kissed it fondly.

"I understand why Catherine adores you so, Captain. You are an unusual man." She waited to see if he would answer her query about the ladies in waiting. If he chose not to she would not press him.

He looked at her and smiled. "As children, Catherine and I tended to be each others' playmates. And as we grew, Catherine always eschewed the company of girls." He paused. "She found them tedious. Catherine was always more content with boy games. While this delighted her father, her mother attempted to rein in Catherine's swashbuckling endeavors with more sedate, 'princess-ly' activities. Catherine hated them. She hated the dress and formality of such 'mundane rituals' as she would call them. She was her father's daughter. They were very close."

"How did he feel about her 'swashbuckling'?" Bella asked.

"Catherine could do no wrong in her father's eyes. He adored her and encouraged her. I think he saw in her an inherent ability to succeed where he had failed."

"Where did he see his failure?"

"In his ability to protect his kingdom from his own Church. It tore him apart to watch his Bishop and his Church become something so hideously twisted from Christ's intention."

"Catherine shares this view," Bella offered.

"Wholeheartedly, but with less caution. That is another reason the Bishop so detests her."

"I see," she said. Bella was feeling sick again and needed to find a graceful way to end the conversation.

"As the expectations on Catherine grew, so did her resentment about the more feminine aspects of her future role. Her mother did, finally, insist on at least one formal lady in waiting."

"What happened to her?" She battled a rising wave of nausea.

"Once Catherine's parents were both dead she dispensed with the woman, whose ability to engage in intelligent conversation was limited, I fear. Catherine's mind was always more keen on military strategies. And her need to protect her subjects from the harsh realities of this Inquisition has always been her passion. Try engaging with your typical lady in waiting on those topics!" Robert laughed.

"Robert, I appreciate your candor," said Bella as she stood. "I believe we share the goal of protecting the queen. I may be able to convince her that certain things will be in her best interest."

Robert stood to take his leave, "Feel free to call on me, Lady Isabella. I am at your service as well...especially where the queen is involved." Robert bowed to Bella and turned to leave, but then turned back. "One last thing, my Lady, I feel I must caution you. Your continued presence here puts you in danger, as well. Your influence on the queen is being questioned by some. It would not be difficult to make a case for witchcraft against you. Please take care."

Robert bowed slightly again and took his leave. Bella turned and vomited into a dried up flower bed.

Chapter Fourteen

"Absolutely no! How can you even suggest such a thing?" Catherine fumed. "Is it not enough that I must be forced to endure such talk from my Privy Council? I will not have it with you!"

Bella expected such a response when she first brought up the idea that Catherine should consider marriage.

Catherine was pacing. Her face was red with anger. Bella expected her to bolt from the quarters, but to her surprise Catherine eventually calmed and knelt in front of her.

"Why? Who has put you up to this?"

Bella bent and kissed Catherine tenderly on the mouth. "I love you. Do you believe me?"

Catherine sat back on her heels. "I must confess I am not as certain of that fact as I was an hour ago!"

Bella smiled, "It is because I love you that I make such an outrageous suggestion."

"I don't understand."

"My love, can you not see how we are in danger?"

"I am accustomed to danger, it will pass. We need only to be cautious."

"How do you find cautionary admonitions to work with your subjects when dealing with Inquisitors?" asked Bella

A look of pained resignation passed over Catherine's face. She buried her head in Bella's lap.

Bella stroked Catherine's head. "Catherine, listen to me. We cannot continue to share your quarters without arousing suspicion. I am well enough to leave, and my staying only raises questions." She lifted Catherine's chin with her finger. "Think about this. If you marry, the Privy Council will be appeased...as will the bishop."

"The bishop will never be appeased by me." Catherine's voice was muffled by Bella's dress as she buried her head in Bella's lap again. Then she stood and turned, walking over to the balcony doors.

"Perhaps not," Bella said, "but he will be forced to rethink his accusations of heresy. Here is the part I want you to consider. If you marry we can use your marriage as the reason for your change of heart regarding a lady in waiting," Bella waited for Catherine to see the logic in her strategy.

Catherine slowly turned back and smiled, "And that would be you, my Lady?"

"Indeed, I would be honored, my queen."

"But that does not address the marriage! You do not know the men my Privy Council has paraded before me. One is as unappealing as the next!"

"You cannot possibly think that I would make such a plan without having given that consideration!" Bella was on her feet now and walked over to where Catherine stood. She reached for Catherine's arm and looked at her beseechingly. "Do you think I am willing to share you with just anyone? I am not inclined to share you at all... but, if I need to make this sacrifice to keep us safe and together," she emphasized, "then I have the perfect match. He is the third son of King Christopher of Perugia."

"I don't know him."

"At one time he was offered to my parents as a match for me. Fortunately, my father knew of him as a notorious womanizer and declined the offer. Even though it would have been a beneficial match for my father, he could not give me up to a life of such misery. He and my mother were very much in love. I was fortunate that he hoped the same for me."

"Did you love your husband, then?" Catherine asked, feeling a pang of jealousy.

"At first I found him acceptable only. I knew that the match would make my father happy, and I did not wish to continue to burden him with the task of finding me a husband. Daniel was a good enough man and I did grow fond of him. I suppose I did love him in a way," offered Bella. "But now that I know what real love feels like, I would call what I felt for him a great affection."

"Did you enjoy the marital bed?" asked Catherine cautiously.

Bella looked at Catherine, a smile slowly spreading across her face, "Why, Catherine, are you jealous?"

"It did not occur to me to be jealous, I was just sincerely interested to know whether you found the marriage bed pleasing!" protested Catherine, not able to mask her jealousy. It was difficult for her to imagine anyone else ever touching Bella's body...and giving her pleasure. Her concern must have shown on her face, for Bella laughed out loud and grabbed Catherine seductively, "Not close," she whispered, "to what I have with you." With that she kissed Catherine long and sensuously and led her to bed.

The marriage conversation was continued the next morning over breakfast.

"Prince Ambrose is also perceived to be a devout Catholic, so your Bishop cannot disapprove your choice," said Bella.

"I'm still not convinced, Bella. I do not know if I can stomach the thought of the marital bed with anyone."

"You seemed to enjoy your bed quite well enough last night," teased Bella.

"You know what I mean." Catherine did not like this idea, but the thought of her enjoyment of last night swept through her body, pulling on her loins.

"If this Ambrose is as my father spoke of him," Bella continued, "then you need rarely share a bed with him at all. Make it understood that this is a political marriage only, to produce an heir, and give him his freedom to continue his philandering. Perhaps, once you conceive a child, you can abandon the marriage bed altogether."

"That is placing an inordinate amount of trust in someone so untrustworthy." Although Catherine recognized the plan as one worth pursuing, she could not bring herself, yet, to accept marriage as a way to conceal her relationship with Bella.

"Perhaps Robert could convince him that his discretion is warranted."

"I am not entirely convinced, or comfortable, yet with this idea, perh...." Catherine stopped. Bella had grown pale and was searching for a bucket. Her vomiting began again.

When she finally stopped vomiting, Catherine was frantic and led her to the pallet to lay her down.

"Sometimes I am so fearful that God is punishing us for our sin," Catherine lamented. "I don't have the strength or the desire to resist you, so I fear God will take you from me. But sometimes I am utterly convinced that God has sent you to save me...I don't know what to believe..." Catherine knelt at Bella's side and held her through her sickness.

"Catherine..." Bella began.

"Now you will allow the physician," insisted Catherine as she stood. "I will call for him immediately."

"Catherine!" Bella managed. "It's not necessary. I know what's wrong."

"You are as stubborn as you are beautiful, I am calling..."

"Catherine!" shouted Bella, "I'm not ill, I am with child!"

Chapter Fifteen

The months that followed were agony for Bella. She felt the devil himself was growing inside her. This pregnancy was the result of being brutally raped for days without end. How could the offspring of such a union bear anything good? She didn't want this child. It would always remind her of those days. She was inconsolable.

"It will not be fair to the child to have me for a mother," she wept into Catherine's arms one night. "I will not love it...how can I?" She begged Catherine to help her find a way out of this intolerable situation.

"Are you certain you were not already with child when you were abducted?" Catherine asked, hoping there was a chance.

"It's not possible. We weren't together since my miscarriage," Bella answered shaking her head and fighting back her tears.

It tore Catherine apart to hear Bella like this. While she wanted to help Bella, she believed that this was an overreaction. She tried her best to respond with a voice of reason.

"Bella, please, let's wait and see what happens. We can deal with the child when the time comes," Catherine soothed. "Meanwhile, you must take care of yourself. You are allowing your fears to consume you. So much could happen between now and then. You miscarried your first child. This could cease to be a problem without help from anyone."

"I know there are herbs that can help eliminate the child."

"Stop! I will not have you talk like that. Are we not risking enough? We must not even consider such a thing. I could not live with myself. And I would never endanger any of my staff to involve them in such a sin! We will bear this together. That is final." Catherine refused to discuss the subject any further.

For her part, Catherine learned that she was powerless to do anything but allow Bella the tears and the emotions that seemed to dominate her. The only thing that took Bella's mind off of her pregnancy was helping to prepare for Catherine's wedding...yet another dreaded but necessary event in her future.

Chapter Sixteen

The Privy Council was astonished when Catherine informed them that she had decided to take a husband. Her presentation was such that after much thought and prayer, she felt that this was something that God wanted. The cavernous room exploded with animated discussion, angry and simultaneous. It seemed as if everyone was talking at once, voices echoing and bouncing off the walls, the high ceiling, the stone floor and the windows.

"What do you mean you have decided?"

"How dare you make this decision without speaking with us first!"

"Who is this man you have chosen? I hope you have not already made arrangements!"

Catherine was unable to understand or answer any of their questions because they all came at once. She raised her hand to silence them.

"My Lords, Your Grace, your concerns are noted and appreciated, but I have decided to accept Prince Ambrose of Perugia. His father has already been contacted and he and his family are traveling here from Perugia as we speak. Prince Ambrose is someone with whom I believe you will find no objection. He is from a noble line and his credentials are excellent. Your Grace, he is devoutly Catholic and is very much looking forward to meeting you.

Lord Carfaggi was the first to object. "Your Majesty, we know little about this man. Certainly you do not expect us to accept him without having knowledge about his politics or his personality?"

"It amuses me, my Lords," Catherine said, "that you had no such qualms when suggesting husbands for me about whom I had no prior knowledge." Catherine attempted to sound amused, but her anger was evident as she responded. "I know more about this man with whom I plan to spend my life, than any of the parade of misfits you have brought before me."

"Your Majesty," the Bishop said, "I believe I speak for the entire Council when I say that we have only your best interests at heart. We simply express our concern over whether this man will also have your interests at heart."

"Your Grace, let's not pretend to cover the real business here. It is not, nor has it ever been, my heart with which you are concerned." She allowed her gaze to circle the room and penetrate the eyes of every man present. Her detractors could not maintain eye contact. There was no doubt that she had made her point.

Chapter Seventeen

When the Bishop interrogated the poor victims who were accused of heresy, he had two or three persons present. One was his secretary, who kept written record of the questions and answers. The others were one or two guards who kept watch over the prisoner and the proceedings.

The interrogation room itself was tiny and unadorned, with a small fireplace for heat in the winter. A single, high window let in some sun, but even in the light of day torches and candles were necessary. A desk sat in front of the window in such a way that light from outside created a glare behind the bishop. In this way he could see every twitch and flicker of fear on the face of his victims, but his face remained unreadable to those he interrogated. There were several chairs; one for the bishop, one for the victim and two for witnesses. Very often Lord Carfaggi served in the role of witness.

"What is your name?" asked the Bishop.

"Mary DeMarco, Your Grace," answered the woman.

"You must take an oath to truthfully reveal everything you know," the bishop continued. He proceeded to administer the oath, to which the woman readily agreed.

"Do you understand why you are here?" he asked gently. He found that starting the questions in a friendly manner tended to impart a false sense of benevolence to the unsuspecting victim.

"I am not quite certain, Your Grace, as to my knowledge, I have done nothing wrong," answered the young woman sitting before him.

"You have been accused of witchcraft," the Bishop answered without malice. He looked up at the woman and raised his eyebrows in surprise. "How do you respond to this accusation?"

"Your Grace, it is not true." She looked truly horrified. "I am a God fearing woman! I know nothing of witchcraft!"

"How then," the Bishop proceeded, "do you account for these items found on your person when you were arrested?" He produced a leather pouch which he opened. Dried herbs and a powder were the contents of the pouch.

"Your Grace, they are herbs only....used for making tea to aid in digestion and sleep."

The Bishop knew that the powders were merely herbs. He almost wished he felt bad giving Mary DeMarco the impression that she had a prayer of saving herself, but he felt nothing. He was under pressure from Carfaggi to start making more examples, especially of the women in the village, to prove that he was sincere about his role as an interrogator.

"Are you a physician, then?" he asked.

"No, Your Grace, women are not able to become physicians. I am simply a woman who understands the use of herbs," she replied.

"I see. So you admit you are not a physician, but yet you take it upon yourself to mix potions for others," the Bishop continued. "From where do you acquire your herbs?"

"Some grow wild in the forest, Your Grace. Others I grow in my garden," the woman answered honestly enough.

"So, then, you admit to growing your own 'herbs' to create potions that you administer to others?" his questions began to take on an accusatory tone.

"Your Grace...I, make teas only, to aid in digestion. I am not a witch!"

"So say you!" he glared at her now. "You have been accused of using your potions to hold others in your power. What say you to that, witch?"

Her face registered her panic. "I don't know what you mean. I hold no power over anyone, Your Grace. I am a simple healer. Who has told you that I have power over them? It is not true. I am innocent!"

"Perhaps," the Bishop relaxed his tone again. "But your innocence is not supported by the evidence." This was almost too easy.

"Please, Your Grace, tell me what to say," the young woman pleaded. "I have small children."

"You should have given thought to your children before you engaged in such sinful behavior," the Bishop said sadly. But he did not feel sad, in fact, he felt nothing.

"I swear, Your Grace, I will stop practicing healing...I will tear up my herb garden...I will never make tea again...please..." the woman was sobbing now.

"So you freely admit that you have made potions for your neighbors...from herbs that you grew in your own secret garden?" Bishop Capshaw was on his feet now, looming over his prey.

"Yes...no!" she cried. "I grew herbs, yes...my garden is no secret. I only tried to help my neighbors with minor ailments." Mary DeMarco slid off her chair and onto her knees. She was weeping uncontrollably.

"Your accusers say that you lay your hands on those you treat for these minor ailments. They say that your lips move, but they cannot hear what you are saying. Miraculously, your 'patients' fall asleep after your administrations." He waited, and watched her crumble.

"Your Grace, my lips move," her reply was broken by great heaving sobs, "only because I.... pray for them.... sometimes they fall asleep.... but only because they are tired from whatever ailed them, and from the tea....nothing more." She could hardly breathe for gulping for air. Her body was nearly prostrate before him. "It is only by God's grace... that I know the herbs to use to help them. It is only God's prayers that I murmur." He could see that she was exhausted. "Please, Your Grace, I have had little to eat and no sleep. I am so afraid of the rats..." she cried. "I don't know what happened to my children. I am so tired." She looked up at him. "I have not ceased praying since I was arrested. Does that sound like something a witch would do?"

"Return to your chair and compose yourself, woman."

She pulled herself back up to her seat. It seemed to take all of her effort. Once Mary DeMarco was back in her chair he said, "It is a shame that your *prayers* could not be heard by others. That may have helped you here. As it is, your home has been searched. Among your things were found several vials of unknown powders," the bishop said sadly.

"Ground herbs only, Your Grace. Please, I beg you, send me home to my children."

"I cannot. No less than fourteen witnesses have heard you murmuring what they believed to be incantations while laying your hands on your subjects. Those same fourteen have confessed, under oath, that those same subjects fell to sleep and woke up cured…and believing that you performed some kind of miracle. Are you a miracle worker then? Has God seen fit to endow you with the power of miraculous healing?"

"Your Grace, please, how can simple herbs, made by God make me a worker of miracles?"

Bishop Capshaw was bored. It was time to end this charade of justice.

"Your neighbors have also accused you of inciting the carnal lusts of their husbands. It is widely known that all witchcraft comes from carnal lust."

Her jaw dropped open at this accusation. "Your Grace, I do not know what to say. I have never intentionally incited lust in anyone. I try to be a good neighbor and a good mother. That is all. You must believe that I am no witch!"

"You are fortunate, my child, that I do not plan to torture you for your confession. The implements of torture can be quite brutal. As to your denial, it is apparent that you do not intend to confess. The evidence against you is overwhelming. Therefore, you will be returned to your cell where you will await execution. You will be burned at the stake for witchcraft," the bishop stated without emotion.

Too tired and terrified to continue to protest in vain, she hung her head down and wept.

Chapter Eighteen

Catherine could see, from the bedroom window, the flags of the King of Christopher as he, his queen, and their son, Prince Ambrose made their way toward the castle. Although they were still quite a distance away it was clear that their entourage was extensive. They meant to make a good impression.

Her heart was heavy. It took all of her energy to feign happiness in front of the staff and residents of Montalcino Castle.

It was afternoon when the party finally entered the Castle grounds. They were greeted by cheers and much excitement. There was no way to keep the enthusiasm of her staff and subjects from their excitement over the wedding. There was little to celebrate the past many years. The king's illness and death, followed shortly by his wife's death had left a pall over the kingdom. And the Inquisition dominating all of Europe for so long created an atmosphere of gloom even on the best of days. That there was something to look forward to celebrating gave people hope. Catherine could see and feel the hope…and it gave her comfort.

A grand reception was planned for the guests, but Catherine wished a private audience with her future husband and in-laws. The reception was to take place on the day following their arrival so the party had time to settle and refresh after their long journey. The audience was scheduled for the morning meal in the private dining room of her quarters. Catherine was concerned there might be some discomfort to be overcome, given the circumstances of the king's prior pursuit of Bella's hand. She wanted to be able to handle any such discomfort with diplomacy…and privacy.

King Christopher, Queen Edith and Prince Ambrose were announced. Catherine rose to greet them. The king and queen entered first. It was clear King Christopher had been quite good looking in his younger days. His face, now lined, still reflected a strong jaw, full lips, high cheekbones and dark, intense eyes. His hair was mostly white, but still threaded through with black. He was tall and thin. His regal bearing made him appear even taller than he was.

Queen Edith was almost a comical opposite in looks. She was short, stout, with dingy gray hair and had the dullest eyes Catherine had ever seen. She could not even identify the eye color for the appearance was so washed out. The queen's lips were non-existent, although there was a thin red line where her mouth ought to be. She had a very high forehead, a long hooked nose, and not a single redeeming quality to her face.

"Oh dear God," thought Catherine, "let Ambrose look like his father!"

Catherine greeted the King and Queen, who then moved aside to introduce Prince Ambrose.

"Prince Ambrose, I am delighted." Catherine held out her hand. The Prince knelt before her, took her hand and kissed it.

"Queen Catherine, the delight is mine, I assure you." He looked up at her.

As she looked down at the prince, Catherine's smile was sincere and spontaneous, but no one was the wiser that it was from relief. The prince did not possess his father's coloring, but he had the king's looks. He was tall and lean. His face was more his father's, leaning toward handsome, but his coloring was definitely his mother's. His eyes were his best feature, a deep sea green that sparkled as he smiled.

After inquiring about the comfort of their quarters and rest, she turned to introduce Bella, who was standing nearby.

"May I present my lady in waiting, the Lady Isabella, originally of Acquapendente." Bella curtsied and raised her eyes to meet theirs. "It is my understanding that at one time it could well have been possible that Prince Ambrose was presented as a possible suitor to Lady Isabella. Is this true, Your Majesty?"

"It is indeed, Queen Catherine." The king's discomfort was evident, but did not appear extreme.

Catherine smiled. "Lady Isabella confided in me that she thought her father may have declined Prince Ambrose as a suitor." Catherine thought it best to present the refusal as something out of Bella's hands. "It would appear," Catherine continued, "that Lady Isabella's loss is a tremendous blessing for me and my kingdom." Catherine smiled winningly at Prince Ambrose who bowed and smiled.

"Thank you, Your Majesty."

Catherine noted the tenor of his voice, which was very pleasant. Prince Ambrose presented as charming and good looking, but Catherine detected something else…a reticence, a resignation perhaps. She made note of it.

She continued, wishing to put the last of the discomfort behind them, "I am sure you heard that Lady Isabella lost her husband and parents in an attack by a fanatical group claiming to be acting on behalf of the Pope."

The King, to his benefit, moved to Bella and took her hands, "Lady, we did hear of the attack and were very grieved. Your father was a respected Noble. Please accept our most sincere sympathy."

Bella smiled. "You are very kind, Your Majesty. My father spoke kindly of you, as well. I am glad to meet you at long last."

The discomfort was replaced by a comfortable cordiality. The group enjoyed a pleasant visit.

Prince Ambrose was actually a pleasant enough fellow. It was easy to imagine him as a lady's man. He was twenty four years of age, older than any of his siblings when they married, and Catherine sensed that his father was more relieved than happy about the marriage. Under any other circumstances Catherine would have found this prospect appalling. Given the true intention of this marriage, she was inclined toward relief, as well. The prince may be more amenable to the arrangement she intended than she had hoped.

Chapter Nineteen

The evening of the Banquet to honor the future King seemed like the perfect opportunity for Robert to address the matter with the bishop. Robert watched him closely as the evening was drawing to a close. Before Thomas Capshaw left the banquet, Robert was gone.

Robert waited inside Bishop Capshaw's private quarters. He did not have to wait long. He heard footsteps, but when he heard the bishop speaking with someone he quickly slipped behind the heavy draperies that hung along one full wall of the bishop's quarters. A split between two of the panels allowed him to see a good part of the room, but not all of it. At first he could not see them, until they made their way to the sitting area. Robert had a good view of them there, and he recognized the young boy with the bishop as the son of one of his soldiers.

"I am delighted, young man, that you are considering a religious life for yourself. There is no higher calling than one in which God, Himself, calls you."

"Yes, Your Grace," said the boy.

"Don't be shy. The room is grand, but don't let that frighten you. We are both the same in God's eyes."

The boy could not have been more than eleven or twelve years of age. He often served mass with the bishop.

The bishop led the boy over to a small sitting area, "There are some matters of importance we need to discuss in order for you to dedicate your life to God, my son."

"Yes, Your Grace."

The bishop poured two cups of wine and gave one to the boy. "You have made a manly decision. Let us toast your life of devotion."

The boy held his cup nervously in both hands. The bishop sat down next to the boy and lifted the boy's cup to his lips. "Priests need to become accustomed to the taste of wine; the sacrament of communion demands it. You may as well begin now."

The boy drank the sweet wine.

"Tell me," the bishop continued, "how long have you thought about the holy life of a priest?"

"Since I was very young, Your Grace. " The boy was obviously nervous.

"I must admit that I have noticed when you serve Mass with me. You seem very devoted to God and the church. "

"Thank you, your Grace," the wine seemed to be helping the boy relax just a bit. He did not sound quite as nervous.

"Drink up," the Bishop encouraged. "What do you know of how the church deals with heretics?"

"I know that they are to be imprisoned and may be put to death for crimes against the Church," said the boy.

Thomas Capshaw raised a single eyebrow at the boy. "Do you know of any heretics?"

"None, your Grace," answered the boy

"And if you did?"

"I would report them to you, your Grace."

"You are wise beyond your years," cooed the bishop. He poured the boy more wine and indicated that he should drink some more. "And do you realize that the same punishment applies to those who do not report heretics?"

"I did not know that, Your Grace. "

"You are quite certain that you know of no one who might question the tenets of our sacred religion?"

The boy thought for a moment and answered that he was aware of no one like that. He assured the bishop that if he did he would report the person.

"Very good answer. I'm glad you're on our side. We must stick together on matters of Church importance." He stood, walked to his bookshelf, then back, where he stood over the boy in an intimidating manner. He looked down and said, quite sternly, "We understand each other in this matter, then, do we not?"

"Y..yes, Your Grace," the boy was clearly frightened by this turn of events. Robert wondered where this was going. He did not have to wait long.

"Alright." He sat next to the boy and put his arm around him. "I am sorry to have had to scare you a little, but I find that it helps me to determine those who are truly devoted to our church. I can see that you are indeed a righteous boy. Let's turn to other matters, then. As your Bishop, and your teacher in matters of the spirit, I must ask you certain questions about yourself. The Pope insists these matters be addressed. Your answers and actions are important to your religious life."

"I will answer anything you ask, Your Grace."

"Have you ever been with a girl?" asked the Bishop.

"Well, I have girl cousins, your Grace. Our families do much together, so I am with them," the boy answered innocently.

The Bishop smiled. "The question is meant to ask if you have had sexual relations with girls."

The boy's puzzled look expressed his confusion.

"Young man, girls and women alike are temptresses. They possess an evil within them that causes even the holiest of men to become aroused. Do you know what I mean by aroused?"

"I am sorry, Your Grace."

"Do you trust me?" the bishop's voice took on a strained tone.

"Yes, Your Grace."

"I will need to show you what I mean so that you can avoid this temptation. God needs for you to understand this fully so that you will know how to deal with this matter as a priest. Please stand here in front of me."

Robert clenched his jaw. It took all of his will to stay put.

When the boy stood the bishop instructed him to remove his clothes. He didn't hesitate to do what he was asked. As the boy stood naked, Robert could see that the Bishop developed an erection. His robe tented in front of him. Robert seethed. He wanted nothing more than to leap from his spot and rescue the poor, unsuspecting boy, but he also recognized that the longer he waited to make his presence known, the more power he would hold over the Bishop. He waited.

"Turn around for me. I need to be sure that you do not have any markings of the devil."

The boy turned, but with a look of concern on his face. The bishop smiled again. He was toying with this boy, Robert thought, the way a cat toys with a mouse before destroying it.

"All right," said the Bishop kindly, "I am going to lift my robe up to show you what is meant by being aroused." The Bishop lifted his robe to reveal his enormous penis, fully engorged. The boy's eyes widened. "I do this to aid you in your spiritual journey only, my boy. Now, come here. You need to know what arousal feels like so that you can learn to control it and avoid it at all costs with regard to women. It is a sin, but you must know how to control your reactions to women in order to conquer sin. Do you understand?" The Bishop was nearly hoarse with desire.

"Yes, Your Grace."

At this the Bishop reached out for the boys limp penis and began to gently stroke it. It was not long before the boy hardened. The Bishop leaned forward and placed the boy's penis in his mouth. The boy let out a small gasp.

"You need to feel very familiar with all of this, now. Kneel and do the same to me." The bishop leaned back. The boy reached for the Bishop's cock and began to stroke it. "Put it in your mouth!" the Bishop cried hoarsely.

Robert could take no more. He leapt out from behind the curtain. "Do no such thing!"

The bishop was in the throes of such passion that it took him a moment to react. He blinked, and then he looked in horror at Robert.

"Boy, put on your clothes and never return here again," Robert said sternly. "Your Bishop is the devil in disguise. Never forget that."

The boy was so confused that he did not move. "Go!" ordered Robert.

The boy scooped up his clothes and ran for the door.

"How dare you!" the Bishop recovered his senses and stood, allowing his robes to drop back down around him.

"How dare I?" Robert leaped over a table and was in front of the Bishop in a few long strides. His movements were so quick and so powerful that the Bishop cringed and his arms flew up instinctively to protect himself.

"How dare I?" demanded Robert, his face nearly purple. "You have the audacity to use God and the church to satisfy your own sick lust, and you ask 'how dare I'? Sit down, Your Grace," Robert's disdain of the Bishop's title was clear. When the bishop remained standing and attempted a glare at Robert. The Captain repeated his order with more force. "Sit down. We have a few things to discuss."

The bishop sat. "First," said Robert through gritted teeth, "if I ever catch you with a young boy again, I will slice off your cock, shove it in your own mouth and then slit your throat." He paused, waiting for the image to register with the Bishop. The bishop paled. "Second, if *anyone, ever,* accuses the queen of heresy I will personally gather every boy in the kingdom with whom you have played your little games to accuse you of heresy and then I will slit your throat." Robert paused, leaned over the Bishop, who was forced to lean back in his seat. "Have I made myself perfectly clear?" spittle from Robert's mouth sprayed onto the Bishop's face as he asked this last question. He looked directly into the Bishop's eyes and did not alter his gaze until the Bishop finally spoke.

"Yes," was all the Bishop said. He tried to sound indifferent, but there was fear in his eyes.

"Good," said Robert. He turned and left the room.

The Bishop sat without moving for some time. Then he gulped down the remainder of the wine.

Chapter Twenty

Catherine and Ambrose had few encounters during the weeks since his family arrived. He was, quite clearly, not political nor did he seem very bright. He was not interested in the plight of the poor or in issues regarding the Inquisition. He was easy enough to look at, but beyond his looks, he seemed to have very few redeeming qualities. During the times they spent together, Catherine noted his eyes wandering, following many of the young women who roamed the castle.

During one of their afternoons together, she took Ambrose to see the paper mill. She often enjoyed stopping in to watch the process of paper making. It was a simple formula, but the end product was something that made her quite proud. Although making paper was relatively new to Montalcino, paper factories had been in existence throughout Italy for many centuries. It was only in the last ten years, after Catherine's father toured a paper-making factory in Fabriano that he decided to try the technique at home. Montalcino's paper was made of diluted cotton and linen fiber.

Catherine took Ambrose into the sorting room. Two women graded and sorted rags of cotton according to grade.

"You can see," Catherine showed him, "how the quality of this rag is much superior to the ones here." She held both the rags for him to feel the difference.

"Once the rags are sorted they are brought next door to be stamped." Catherine guided him toward a door. Before she opened it she said, "You can already hear it's quite noisy." She opened the door and led him through, shouting, "The rags are diluted in water then pounded to break down the fibers."

Several men were pounding the wet rags with sections of large logs suspended from beams. The noise was deafening. The rags were then placed in hot water mixed with lye to cook.

They moved to yet another small room. "Here you will see the vat men passing screens into the mixture. What they pull up is basically a mass of interwoven fibers." Ambrose watched as the screen emerged from the vat covered with pulped and twisted material. As they watched, the mesh screen was placed over a slanted table. "The excess water," Catherine explained, "is drained off and this wooden frame, the deckle, is fitted over the fibers and pressed." When the deckle was removed, the material was lifted and placed between two pieces of felt, where the excess water was pressed out.

"What you have left is a piece of paper that is then hung to dry."

Ambrose nodded. "I am impressed. I thought only the larger cities produced papers."

As they made their way back to the castle Catherine said, "For some time we were prohibited from such endeavors. Papermaking was prohibited by anyone within a fifty mile radius of Fabriano. There were even fines levied against anyone caught attempting the trade."

"You are very close to Fabriano," Ambrose noted.

"About fifty miles," she smiled. "But we are so small an enterprise that we are no threat. We mostly make paper for Montalcino merchants and residents."

"What is the most difficult aspect of the process?" he asked as they made their way through the doors of the castle.

Catherine laughed. "In the summer months it's bugs! I've lost count of the samples of paper that have come across my desk with mosquitoes imbedded in the paper."

She took Ambrose to her office where she took a small stack of some of the finest paper made in Montalcino out of a drawer. It was wrapped in a velvet ribbon. "For you."

He bowed and smiled. "Thank you. It is beautiful."

In some ways Catherine was dreading her wedding night, but she found herself curious about it, as well. She wondered if she would respond to her husband. It was hard to imagine what the wedding bed would be like. She felt no physical attraction with Ambrose. She thought about him rarely, if at all. The kind of desire and longing she felt with Bella did not exist. Still, she could not help but wonder if the sensations would be as pleasant. She hoped they would.

Regardless of her response to this man, she had been rehearsing what she intended to say to him about their future together as husband and wife. She had no desire to hurt him; he had done nothing to deserve being hurt. She was using him, but she suspected from comments made by both him and his parents, that he was using her as well. All the better, then, for both of them.

The wedding was scheduled. Preparations were made. The guests invited.

Catherine insisted the surrounding townspeople be allowed to celebrate the event. She wanted to give them reason to hope, even as she despaired over the fate of her country and her ability to prevent her church from persecutions. Parts of the castle and grounds were to be opened to them and Catherine instructed the staff to be sure that tables were set with refreshments following the wedding ceremony.

The morning of the wedding arrived. Bella woke to find Catherine lying next to her weeping silently. She lay on her back, the tears streaming from her eyes and filling her ears.

"Oh, my love," Bella exclaimed and reached over to pull her to her breast.

"I cannot believe this is going to happen, Bella." Catherine could not hide her anguish. She was certain her heart was breaking. "I wish so much for some other way."

"Be brave, my sweet queen. Our nights will be ours again soon enough. "

"I don't think that I can bear this burden."

"Catherine, you won't bear it alone. When your ability falters, remember I'm with you in this. Remember, always, that I am here, loving you, waiting for you, wanting you. Remember this." She kissed Catherine--a kiss filled with such love and tenderness, passion and promise, that Catherine allowed herself to be transported to a world where this wedding did not exist. Bella made love to Catherine on the morning of her wedding in a way that helped her to know that she could bear anything as long as Bella was with her.

When they finished their lovemaking, they lay entwined together, for some time. Finally, Bella spoke, "I will call for breakfast, and then we must prepare you for your day."

They ate in silence. When they were done, Bella had Marie fill the bath, and dismissed her. Bella bathed Catherine without words. As she dressed Catherine in her wedding attire, they didn't speak.

Catherine's dress was unusual. Although pure white silk, it was trimmed in gold, and more resembled the robes of a monk than the wedding dress of a queen. It draped in soft, flowing lines from her shoulders to the floor, the train flowing behind her for several yards. Instead of a veil, there was a wide hood that lifted and draped softly over her crowned head and could be pushed back. The dress, though not at all conventional, was elegant, simple and seemed a purer expression of the queen than the more traditional styles of lace and bustle that were being worn. Bella did Catherine's hair and applied her makeup.

Bella helped Catherine into her wedding dress and stood back to look at her. She was stunning. Bella's eyes filled with tears. She turned and went out onto the balcony. She would not leave her quarters this day. She would not be present at the wedding. She did not expect to see Catherine again for several days.

That her own lady in waiting did not attend her wedding would be overlooked because of Bella's condition. Neither Bella nor Catherine could bear the thought of having to endure the others' presence for the ceremony or the reception that followed.

Catherine watched Bella for a time, waiting to see if she would turn to say goodbye. But she never turned back. The hardest part of this day for Catherine culminated in her next move. What she wanted to do more than anything was to walk out onto the balcony with Bella and forget about this entire facade. If she were entirely honest with herself, what she really wanted was for this day to celebrate her love for Bella. That, she knew, could never be.

After what seemed an eternity, Catherine closed her eyes, bowed her head and turned. She left her quarters without looking back. That very act took more of her strength than any of her life.

Bella heard the doors close behind Catherine. She turned back toward the room. Her face drenched with her own tears. As with Catherine, it took every ounce of Bella's fortitude to keep from running after Catherine and begging her to call off the charade. Now that Catherine was gone, she went to the queen's bed...her bed...and wept while desperately trying to drown the sound of the clanging church bells.

The wedding itself was a beautiful Sunday affair.

Though custom was for the bride to be given away at the door of the church, and vows to be exchanged there, Robert insisted that the queen be married at the altar, where she was not vulnerable to attack from anyone with a view of the church.

Catherine placed her trembling hand on Robert's steady arm and they walked down the aisle of the church. Her free hand held a bouquet of white roses trimmed with knotted gold, silk ribbons. The pews, draped with a variety of flowers and ribbons, were filled to capacity. Every guest bowed or curtsied as the queen floated up the aisle.

Catherine set her eyes on the bishop waiting at the altar, thinking that if she could focus on her hatred of him, she might be able to disguise the dread she felt playing out this miserable game. Bella had hidden the pasty pallor of her face with fine rose colored powder. But Catherine was afraid that the sadness in her eyes was evident to all who had the courage to look her in the face.

The bishop looked resplendent in his formal robes. His miter sat regally on the top of his head and he appeared to tower over everyone and everything in his vicinity. As Robert and Catherine approached the altar, the bishop kept his eyes focused on Catherine, and she met his gaze with determination. If this was a battle, she was going to win. She was glad she decided to dispense with the formal procession of the bishop, cross bearer and witnesses to precede her up the aisle. And, although it had been a bone of contention, she had refused the traditional groomsmen and maids of honor. Ambrose's parents were unhappy that their other two sons would not be at the altar in their regal attire, but Ambrose was surprisingly supportive of Catherine's desire to limit the wedding party to just the two of them.

As she and Robert approached the altar, Robert leaned to kiss her cheek. He whispered softly in her ear, "Be brave, my dear cousin, it will be over soon...and I will check often on your true beloved."

Catherine's eyes filled with tears of gratitude and despair; despair for the fact that she was not marrying her true beloved; gratitude for Robert's understanding and his words; words that she knew helped her to appear as the happy bride shedding tears of joy.

She turned to accept the hand of Prince Ambrose who was dressed in full, formal, royal robes. His outer robe was crimson, trimmed in gold. On his head he wore the crown of the Prince of Perugia. Catherine wondered at the irony that there was probably not a woman or girl present who did not wish to be standing next to the dashing Prince, when she wished to be anywhere else.

The wedding ceremony was a Nuptial Mass, enhanced with special music. The bishop said an opening prayer, and followed the prayer with a psalm reading.

The homily, although blissfully shorter than the bishop's usual Sunday sermons, was a treatise on the importance of marriage as a holy sacrament.

Catherine felt her jaw clench as the bishop focused on the exclusivity of "a marriage in the eyes of God," and the importance of all persons respecting the holy sacrament between Catherine of Montalcino and Ambrose of Perugia."

Catherine was angry that she had not thought to have Robert warn the bishop to be brief and encouraging on this day. Now, as he began his not so subtle diatribe to unnerve her, she was furious at her lack of foresight.

"Any person," the bishop was droning louder and louder, "who tempts a married person to stray from the vows of holy matrimony is a sinner and will suffer the fires of earth along with the fires of hell! It is our responsibility as stewards of the faith to insure this does not happen! We must be vigilant for the couple married here today..."

Catherine heard a loud clearing of the throat meant to get someone's attention. She didn't turn, but recognized the interruption as Robert's throaty tenor. She looked at the bishop, who paused only briefly before continuing on a much lighter and more appropriate theme.

Following the sermon was the exchange of vows. Catherine dreaded this part of the ceremony. She hoped the sadness in her voice was noticed only by her, or that it was interpreted as something other than what it was. In her heart she was saying her vows to Bella, couched in a prayer that Bella might feel them and be comforted by her love.

Following the vows, the couple took their first Eucharist together as husband and wife. The bishop offered a nuptial blessing and led the congregation in the Lord's Prayer after which a final blessing was given.

It was over. She was married. And Catherine was certain she'd never been more miserable than at that very moment. As she walked back down the aisle on the arm of her husband she had a vision of herself ripping off her wedding gown and running up to her quarters...to Bella. But instead, she planted a smile on her face and went through the motions of the happy bride.

Following the ceremony, the bride and groom made a tour of the town in the royal coach. Crowds lined the streets of Montalcino and cheered as the couple rode by and waved. Periodically, Prince Ambrose tossed coins into the crowd, which generated even more cheering and excitement.

The reception took place in the Great Hall. Before dinner, Ambrose's oldest brother had the guests served sweet liquor and a variety of strong drinks. Once the guests found their way to their seats he stood, encouraging the guests to lift their cups in salute to the bride and groom. The hall erupted with a shout of "Per cent'anni!"

The food and wine flowed. Children ran around collecting the mesh bags filled with candy covered almonds. Musicians filled the hall with music throughout the night.

There was much drunkenness and dancing. Periodically, during a lull in the festivities one of the men would yell, "Evviva gli sposi! Hurray for the newlyweds!" And the guests responded with thundering applause. Even the bishop seemed to be having a good time. He sat at the head table with the bride and groom. Catherine noticed he had consumed enormous quantities of wine. At one point he leaned over to her and said, "It's too bad that your father isn't here. He would have enjoyed this immensely." Catherine thought he sounded melancholy, but she determined that he was just as drunk as everyone else and dismissed the sad tone and watery eyes as the effects of too much wine.

Nevertheless, at the mention of her father, she smiled sadly in return and responded, "He would have."

And while it was true that King Edward would probably have drunk himself into the night, and danced and celebrated with great exuberance, Catherine was glad that she did not have to hide her true feelings from him. She was certain she would have been incapable of deceiving her father. She was not even sure she could fool her husband.

The queen had no intention of sharing her private quarters with her husband. There was a room just down from her quarters sometimes used for special guests. She had that room turned into a marriage suite, where she intended to spend as few nights as possible. The king was given his own private quarters across from the marriage suite.

The marriage suite was decorated with a bed, draped with heavy curtains, a small dining area and a privy room. It was not lavish, but had a tapestry on one wall and a fireplace. The tapestry covered nearly the entire wall. It depicted a wedding scene of a bride and groom dancing amid a crowd of onlookers as servants poured wine from large jugs into smaller pitchers.

It was to the marriage suite that the bride and groom departed the reception, accompanied by the rowdier family and friends of Ambrose.

The newlyweds finally detached themselves from the revelry in the hall, which had not diminished, and walked into the wedding suite. When the doors to the suite closed Catherine perused the romantic setting before her, she could not help but think of Bella and it was all she could do to stifle a groan of pure sadness. The room was quiet, save for the crackling fire in the fireplace. After the noise of the hall, the quiet echoed in Catherine's ears.

Candles were lit, warming the room in a soft, yellow glow. Wine was poured into two goblets on the table. The bed was turned down and the linens were covered in rose petals. Ambrose removed his crown and robes, carefully placing them on the bench situated at the foot of the bed. He handed Catherine a goblet of wine and picked up the other. He lifted his goblet to her and said, "To us, my dear Catherine, and a long and happy marriage."

Catherine lifted her goblet in return and smiled. She had been dreading this night and now, here it was. Her stomach was in knots. After they both drank he took the goblets and set them down, too soon for Catherine. She had hoped that they might talk for a while, but he reached for her and pulled her to him. She was nervous. Bella told her what to expect, but the knowledge did not decrease her anxiety. Although she and Ambrose responded to the entreaties to kiss throughout the reception, she felt her stomach rise up into her throat as the time for kissing, as a prelude to the rest of the evening, was at hand. She attempted to say something, but he reached to hold her head in his hands and bent to kiss her. She felt his beard first and it quite startled her. Then she was aware of his lips and the sweet smell of the alcohol on his breath. His tongue began to probe her mouth.

He stopped and looked at her and smiled, "Let's move to the bed."

Standing at the side of the bed he began to undress her, and she allowed it without resistance. Her gown had no buttons or fastenings of any kind, so he bent to lift the hem of it up and over her head. Her undergarment was just as long, but tied in the front with an interlacing ribbon. He untied the ribbon and his fingers pulled the ribbon out from each eyelet in a slow, sensual motion. As the last of the ribbon came free, the garment fell from her shoulders and dropped to the floor. Her breasts were exposed. She felt awkward, vulnerable. His hands reached to cup them, and his mouth sought her nipples. After moving from her breasts, kissing his way back up to her neck, he knelt in front of her and started to roll her leggings down. As she stepped out of them Ambrose ran his hands up the inside of her thighs, then around to her buttocks. He pulled her hips toward him and buried his face in the mass of thick, black, curly fur. Catherine did not anticipate the quick inhalation that escaped her as the sensation from his beard startled her again. She did not like the scratching of his facial hair, but she forced a smile. Ambrose looked up at her and smiled in return. He stood and undressed himself.

Catherine watched. He didn't seem to feel any discomfort in his nakedness. In fact, he almost seemed to be showing off. What she had taken for a slender build under his garments was actually more muscular than she expected. And there was an abundance of hair on his chest, his arms and his legs. As he proceeded to remove his garments one at a time, she became more and more curious and even a little excited. She found herself anxious for him to reveal his manhood, wondering what it would look like, hoping that she would find qualities in his male member that attracted her to him in at least some small way.

His body was solid. She detected no softness, even his buttocks were firm. She saw that he was erect beneath the last of his undergarments. His member pushed at the fabric, looking as if it were demanding release. When, at last, he pushed his leggings down, his penis nearly sprung to attention, quivering up and out, pointing at her. Catherine could not help but stare, at first in amazement, then in horror as she remembered that she was about to host this part of him within her own body. She closed her eyes and swallowed.

"Don't be afraid," he said gently. "Touch it," he encouraged. She hesitated and he gently reached for her hand, pulling it slowly toward him. He guided her hand around the shaft and slowly moved it toward the base. It was hard and warm. When she had taken over the stroking for a bit he stopped her. "That's enough," he whispered.

He pulled her onto the bed. His hands roamed her body somewhat frantically, while his mouth found her nipples. Bella's hands were soft as silk on her body, his, though not rough, were firmer, stronger. They kneaded her, whereas Bella's lightness of touch caused the tiny hairs of her body to reach up as if to close the minute gap that existed between her skin and Bella's hand. She felt the hardness of Ambrose against her and his urgency increased. She wished he would slow down. Bella made every stroke, each kiss, every breath count as if it were the most important stroke, kiss, breath. It was all happening much too quickly for her to process her own emotional reaction to every touch. In spite of her desire for him slow down, she also just wanted to be done with it, to have the experience behind her.

He moved his fingers between her legs, sliding them up and into her, creating lubrication before he entered her. As he positioned himself over her she held her breath, she was afraid and suddenly did not feel ready. He separated her legs.

There was pain, but it was not as bad as she had expected. The entirety of the event could not have lasted more than fifteen minutes. While it was not unpleasant, she was disappointed that she didn't feel more aroused or satisfied. She did not realize until it was over, but she really was hoping for something more...for something to awaken in her that she knew other women felt... something satisfying and fulfilling. That she felt so indifferent to the experience saddened her in some strange way...especially since this relationship would exist in some capacity for as long as they both lived.

Ambrose was already asleep beside her. Catherine lay awake for some time. Her thoughts were of Bella. Though she did not want to compare the only two lovers in her life, she could not help but crave the slow and sensual way Bella drew her into lovemaking, the teasing, talking, and the gentle, light touching. With Bella, the anticipation of lovemaking was as sensual and fulfilling as the act of lovemaking itself. She cried a little, and fell asleep dreaming of covering Bella's lips, her mouth, her neck, and her breasts with slow, tender kisses.

When she woke the next morning it was not yet dawn, although there was a soft light starting to illuminate the eastern horizon. Catherine looked at her sleeping husband and wondered what their life would be like. She hoped her plan to conceive a child and keep her husband at arm's length would succeed without much difficulty. Time would tell. For now, her concern over Bella's pregnancy was at the forefront of her worries.

Catherine rolled onto her side and watched her husband sleep. As she did, her thoughts tumbled within her. There were times she still worried God was against her. Perhaps this marriage was her punishment. There were still times when she sought to feel God's presence as she had before Bella entered her life. Whether it was her own belief that God didn't accept their relationship or her fear that God did not approve, she ceased feeling God in her life as she once had. Her faith did not alter, nor did her prayer life. They were as much a part of her as her own breath. But once she acknowledged her love for Bella could not be denied, she accepted her life might be one of constant spiritual conflict. If God didn't want her to love Bella, then God would have to remove the temptation. She could no more stop loving Bella than she could stop being queen. God made her queen. Perhaps, she argued with herself, God brought Bella to her as well. Robert's words of so many months ago gave her more comfort than he would ever know. Robert. She smiled to herself. He always said the perfect thing when she needed a perfect saying.

"Love is a gift from God," he had said. And with those words she gave herself permission to let flow the feelings she had been denying for Bella. But in truth she still struggled with her decision, worrying that God had turned from her.

As she looked at Ambrose sleeping, she wondered, if Bella had never existed, would he have made a good husband? Then she sighed. She knew she would never feel for Ambrose even half of what she felt for Bella.

She rose, put on a robe and walked over to the window. The sun was coming up. She watched the sky turn blue, a few clouds reflecting the orange glow of the sun. Once she had given herself to Bella, she knew there was no turning back. Her love was an undeniable truth. It didn't change anything; it simply acknowledged another part of her she had not known existed. And yet, the acknowledgement seemed only that. It was as if she finally unlocked a door within her...a door she passed time and again without noticing. When Bella entered her life she finally looked at the door and wondered at its existence. When the knocking started gently on the other side of it she ignored it. But the knocking did not go away, it persisted. It demanded to be answered. What greeted her on the other side turned out to be nothing less than water for a soul dying of thirst. Refusing to drink meant certain death. Refusing to drink was not an option.

Ambrose woke when the sun was fully up. He saw Catherine standing near the window. "Buon giorno," he said.

"Good morning," Catherine smiled at him. "You slept well."

"You played a role in that," he smiled seductively. "I hope our activity last night enhanced your sleep, as well."

"I slept well," Catherine replied. She couldn't tell if he wanted to know about her sleep or his lovemaking. Either way he did seem eager to please her and that did endear him to her. She did not have the heart at this point to crush him with her plan to sleep with him only until she conceived.

"I ordered us breakfast," she said, indicating the table where breads, fruits, nuts, cheeses and warm ale waited. "I hope you're hungry."

"For my wife only," he smiled and strode toward her, pulling her to him.

Catherine could think of nothing she wanted less than her husband's amorous advances. But even as she struggled to think of excuses out of lovemaking, she thought perhaps it would increase her chances of becoming pregnant, so she gave in with as much enthusiasm as she could muster. She did not think it possible, but it was easier the second time. It wasn't better, or worse, just easier.

Chapter Twenty One

"Lady Isabella," Robert said as Bella entered the dining hall on the morning after the wedding. "I hoped to see you today. Will you do me the honor of accompanying me this afternoon for some fresh air? I'll order a carriage and we can ride down to the lake."

Bella smiled at Robert. "Your chivalry is noted...and accepted."

As Robert and Bella rode slowly out of the town limits and into the forest, Robert asked, "How are you, Lady?"

"You are kind to ask. I am managing. And you, Robert, how are your wife and that beautiful son of yours?"

Robert's face lit up at the mention of his son. "Ah, my little Gio. He makes me laugh. I didn't expect that. He is so comical and engaging. I truly did not anticipate such a small child could possess such a character!"

Bella laughed, too. "He sounds delightful. I look forward to getting to know him."

A shadow crossed Robert's face. "I will need to work hard to keep him so delightful....there is so much that can endanger him that I worry I may not always be there to protect him. May I confide in you?"

Bella was immediately concerned. "What is it?"

He told her of the episode in the bishop's quarters.

"I have tried to put it from my mind, though I can't help but wonder, what if that were Gio? What if my own son were to be lured into such an unholy trap by such a wicked man? Lady Isabella, I am not weak, but I have found myself near tears when I think of such a thing happening to my own son! I believe I would murder such a man on the spot."

"It sounds," said Bella, "as if you came close to doing so with the Bishop. Your restraint was admirable. And I don't believe your feelings in this matter make you weak. Rather, they reflect your resolve to protect those you love and keep them safe. That, my dear friend, is your strength."

They rode in silence before Bella spoke again. "Robert, how is it that you can be so outraged by the behavior of the bishop, and yet so accepting of my relationship with Catherine?"

They reached a small gurgling brook. Robert stopped the carriage and helped Bella down. Her movements were awkward due to her pregnancy, but she managed with his support. They walked to a spot near the brook, where he helped lower her to sit on a boulder. He looked up. A bit of sky that was visible through the trees. His eyes closed, he took a breath and exhaled it slowly.

"I never told anyone this story. Not Catherine. Not my parents. No one."

Robert sat near her on a fallen tree.

He looked at her. "Anna was my nursemaid. My first memory is of being held by that woman. I remember her smell…lavender. She was soft as down and when she held me I felt so loved and protected. She made me laugh. She loved me and I loved her. When I grew out of my need for a nursemaid I begged my mother to keep her on as my caretaker." Robert laughed at the memory, "I am certain I wore her down with my badgering. She finally relented and Anna continued to care for me.

"About the time I turned seven, Anna married one of the soldiers in the king's guard. She still continued in her role as my caretaker, but no longer lived in the room next to mine. It remained her room, so that she could be nearby when I was ill, but she spent nights with her new husband." Robert stopped speaking and for a moment the only sound was the wind blowing gently through the leaves of the trees.

"About a year after she married she began to waste away," Robert continued. "I could feel that her body was shrinking when I hugged her. Her laugh disappeared, as well. She was no longer the jovial, loving woman I had known.

"One day, some of us were playing a hiding game. I hid in the closet in the room that was Anna's. I left the door cracked so I could see if anyone entered. Anna came in and fell onto the bed. She was weeping. I had never heard anyone weep like that before. I wanted to climb up next to her and comfort her the way she used to comfort me, but I was afraid and stayed hidden."

Downstream from where they sat, a doe and her yearling appeared at the edge of the brook. The doe looked at them briefly and decided they were not a threat. The animals drank their fill, then crossed the brook with a splash and leapt away into the forest on the opposite side of the water.

"Go on, Robert," Bella encouraged.

"While I was trying to think about what to do there was a knock on the door. One of my mother's attendants, Portia, came in and asked Anna what was wrong. She reached out to comfort Anna and Anna cried out in pain. Portia removed Anna's doublet. She was covered in bruises and scars. Portia was furious and insisted that Anna tell my mother, but she became frightened and begged Portia to say nothing. She said her husband was one of the king's own and beyond reproach. Anna was afraid that if anyone found out about her beatings her husband would only beat her more. I could hear the hysteria in her voice."

Robert's own voice cracked a bit and he paused in his recounting. Bella waited without speaking. He picked up a twig and twirled it in his hands.

"Then one night Anna came into my room. I pretended to be asleep. She went into her room adjoining mine and closed the door. Shortly after, my door opened again and Portia passed through. I waited and when I thought it was safe I went over and peeked through the keyhole. I watched Portia tenderly undress Anna and cry over her bruises. I saw Anna's face transform as Portia kissed each bruise and each scar. My Anna returned…my happy, smiling Anna. I was so glad to see her smiling that I failed to realize that they had both taken off their clothing…." Robert stopped, suddenly embarrassed.

"I'm sorry, Lady Isabella. I did not intend to tell so much."

"I am glad you did. Please don't feel ashamed." Bella smiled. "What happened to Anna and Portia? Where are they now?"

Robert closed his eyes and fought back his tears, "Executed."

Bella gasped and her hand flew to her heart.

"Anna's husband found out about Portia. They spent several years in prison, convicted of crimes against the Church. They were burned alive." Robert cracked the twig he had been playing with and threw it on the ground.

Bella could not hold back her sob. She knelt in front of Robert and held his hands. "Please tell me you did not watch?"

"I did not know until after." He smiled and sadly shook his head. "I cannot say if I would have gone to watch. To this day I don't know if I would have had the courage. I imagine my Anna, though, and I take comfort from the knowledge that at least she died knowing Portia loved her."

Robert shook himself from his memories and said, somewhat brightly, "And so, my Lady, now you have heard two stories from me, one of lust and one of love."

"You have shared more than your stories with me, Robert. You have shared your soul and I am grateful. I understand more than you could imagine. And I believe your Anna knows how much you loved her."

happy for Robert. As she looked at Gio she could not help but hope that she might have her own little one to hold soon. But even so, she felt a pang of sorrow. This happy family, for whom her heart felt so much joy, would never exist for her in such a way.

The baby was as rotund and jovial as his grandfather. Robert doted on him, and Petra seemed happier than ever. She remembered when Robert first met Petra. He seemed unaware that all of his conversations revolved around this tiny woman with a smile that brightened everything around her. When Catherine finally mentioned this to Robert he was surprised and denied it. But soon there was no denying how he felt about Petra and it was clear she felt the same about him. They married six months after they met, much to the delight of all the parents, and with the queen's blessing.

Lord Giovanni was holding his namesake. He stood and gave the baby back to his mother. "Your Majesty, how are you?" Catherine heard a touch of concern in his voice and wondered how much he knew…or suspected.

"Lord Giovanni, I am well, thank you. And you, I see, are in your glory!" she indicated his grandson.

"I am blessed beyond my dreams to have lived long enough to know this moment," he said. He appeared overcome with happiness, which made Catherine glad. After his wife died he was lost for some time. It was good to see him happy again.

"Petra," Catherine addressed Robert's wife, "You have given two of my favorite men much joy."

"Majesty," smiled Petra, "It is I who hold the joy from the three men in my life." Petra went on, "I hope you will know this joy one day," she said sincerely.

"Thank you. Now, I wonder if I may steal your husband for a moment. I understand we have some business to discuss?"

Petra nodded and Catherine and Robert walked off to a quiet corner of the Great Hall.

"Are you well, Majesty?" asked Robert

"As well as I can be." They sat near the fireplace facing each other. Catherine looked out at the crowd that was milling in the Hall. The bishop sat alone and stared uncomfortably at her. She smiled in his direction and nodded a greeting to him. He nodded back, but did not smile.

Catherine turned her attention back to Robert, "Bella says that we have something to discuss."

"I am not sure that this is the place to discuss it, Majesty."

"I have been sequestered for three days with a husband who has little insight into the world around him." She bore her eyes into his. "I am hungry for anything that might stimulate my mind, please tell me."

Robert had to laugh, but cautioned her, "I will tell you, then, but you must refrain from revealing any expression that may indicate your revulsion. And do not, under any circumstances, look in your bishop's direction."

Catherine nodded and kept her head down as Robert moved close and told her the story of his encounter in the bishop's private quarters. She was furious, but didn't allow any emotion to give her away.

When, finally, Robert concluded his story he told her to smile as if he had just told her something amusing. She smiled.

"Do you think the Bishop is convinced by my marriage?" Catherine asked.

"At the very least you have confused him. He no longer has the support of the majority of the Privy Council regarding your *witch in waiting,* as he has begun to refer to Lady Isabella. My father-in-law indicated that the Nobles were afraid the Bishop was correct in saying Bella had power over you. Now they question him, saying your marriage clearly indicates otherwise. So, even he has been forced to restrain his relentless pursuit of heresy against you and Bella."

"What of the boy that was with the bishop that night. Have you seen him again?" asked Catherine. A server passed by with a tray of wine goblets, Catherine reached out to take one. When the servant was out of earshot, Robert answered.

"No, Majesty. But I have found several other boys who have had similar 'religious' encounters with him. If he knows what is good for him he would do well to begin to support you more than he has in the past," Robert smiled.

Finally, she looked up at him. "Robert, you are indeed my protector."

They stood and Robert returned to his family. Catherine resumed her place next to Ambrose.

Catherine dined with her husband that evening in the marriage suite. When they were done she told him she did not feel well and suggested a stroll in the gardens. The days were beginning to lengthen, so there was still a little light.

When they returned to their room Catherine claimed to feel no better. She suggested that Ambrose enjoy the comforts of his own private quarters. With her apologies she claimed need of privacy, stating she did not wish to trouble him with womanly issues.

"I understand," he said. "Is there anything I can do?"

"No, thank you," she said as she turned for the door. "Marie will tend to me. I'm certain I will feel better in the morning."

She bade him goodnight and left for her quarters.

Bella's kisses greeted her with happy intensity. They were starved for the touch, smell, and sight of one another. When they finished making love they lay entwined in each others' arms and talked well into the night. The absence of actual intelligent conversation in the past days was more of a hardship on Catherine than the expectations of the marriage bed. She hadn't realized how full of stimulating discussion, ideas and processes her life was. The realization made her appreciate her role as queen more fully. Her appreciation of Bella also increased.

The other thing that increased was the size of Bella's belly. It seemed that in the few days of absence Bella had grown much larger. Catherine loved to lie with her head on Bella's chest and feel the movements under her hand as the baby inside kicked and moved. Bella continued to fight with the whole idea of this child, but she enjoyed Catherine's excitement. The process that Bella was enduring was one that intrigued Catherine. When she thought about what was happening inside Bella's body, about the actual growth of a baby occurring within a woman, she found herself in awe. She looked forward to the baby coming and, in a realization that surprised her, she was excited about being present at the birth. It was all such a miracle.

In the morning they called for a light breakfast and continued talking. Catherine, it seemed, was starved for much more that Bella's body.

"I will be glad to resume my regular duties," Catherine admitted as she pulled a piece of bread from a small loaf.

"What do you have planned today?"

"It's been awhile since I looked at anything regarding paper production. Then, I will meet with the Council to see what they dealt with while I was indisposed.

"I don't envy your constant dealings with them," said Bella. "I wish they supported you more and you didn't have to be on your guard so relentlessly. I can't imagine having to weigh every word, and every silence," she emphasized this last, "so carefully."

"At first it was difficult. I had expected, simply by virtue of my title, the Council would defer to me as they had my father. I sat long meetings with them as my father prepared me for my future role. The meetings then were so full of discussion. Even though I knew that my father came to loathe what the bishop stood for, there was a respect for him as king that dominated the meetings. When my father had made up his mind about anything, a decree, or even a law with which the council was clearly at odds, they would defer to him...even our *dear* bishop," Catherine said as she shook her head and rolled her eyes.

"How did he handle the bishop's authority regarding the Inquisition?" asked Bella.

"That was difficult for him." Catherine paused. "He was very frustrated with his inability to exercise his power over the bishop in matters of sentencing. It was agony for him to know that he could not protect his subjects from the injustices meted out."

"Your father sounds like someone I would have liked immensely," Bella offered. "I wish I could have known him."

"I wish the same, my love," Catherine's sadness was apparent. "I believe he would have adored you."

"Do you think he would suspect...about us?"

Catherine poured some ale and leaned back in her chair pondering the question. "I don't know. Probably."

"How do you imagine he would respond?"

"I like to think that he'd be as accepting as Robert, but I don't know for certain. He would likely have insisted on a marriage, any marriage, for appearances sake. Then I believe he may have closed his eyes and cautioned us to be careful. It would have been very difficult for him, I fear."

"What about your mother?"

Catherine laughed. "That is something I don't even wish to imagine!"

Bella smiled and asked, "How did the bishop come to his role in your father's kingdom?"

"Now that is an interesting story." Catherine smiled as she thought back on her father's defense of Thomas Capshaw.

Although it was morning, Catherine called Marie to draw a bath. She could think of no lovelier way to spend her first morning back with Bella. When the bath was ready, Marie was dismissed.

As they slipped into the bath Catherine told of how Thomas Capshaw and her father grew up as childhood friends. Thomas was the son of one of her grandmother's ladies in waiting. As queen, her grandmother was adamant about setting up a school for the children of the castle.

"Thomas and my father were the same age and became very close, much like Robert and I, I suppose, but with a different outcome altogether," Catherine offered. "Thomas's father was a bit of a brute, as my father told it. And Thomas was more of a mama's boy."

"That could not have pleased his father," Bella suggested as she stepped into the tub with Catherine.

"No. And when Thomas expressed interest in pursuing the priesthood, well, you can imagine! His father was sorely disappointed, as he wanted his only son to follow in his footsteps as a land baron. His mother, of course, was delighted with his choice and encouraged him to pursue a monastery. When his father died there were no impediments to his quest for priesthood and he entered a Jesuit monastery."

Catherine soaped a sponge and ran it along Bella's legs as she told of how Thomas returned to the castle upon the death of her grandmother. Her father was happy that Thomas was able to fulfill his dreams of becoming a priest.

"As king, my father had the ability and the authority to appoint Thomas to the position of priest for the Royal Family."

"That must have been quite an accomplishment for a newly ordained priest," Bella interjected.

"Quite…and not lost on the bishop of the time!" Catherine took a drink from the cup of ale she had placed on a stool beside the tub. "At first, Thomas was instrumental in questioning the techniques and persecutions of the church, though it is hard for me to imagine that. His difficulty with that aspect of his role was clearly at odds with his calling. He and my father would spend longs nights in conversation about the Inquisition. It was actually Thomas Capshaw who helped form my father's resulting rebellion. So, as surprising as this may sound, Bishop Capshaw is responsible for my passion to right this terrible injustice. And, it is he who continues to fuel my passion by his reversal of ideals."

Bella reached for Catherine's hands and placed them on her belly. Catherine felt the baby kick within Bella. She smiled as the kicking pushed against her hands. Even though Bella still hated the thought of giving birth to this child, her enthusiasm about the pregnancy seemed to help Bella relax. Feeling the movement within Bella was one of the things that Catherine was convinced was pure miracle. She smiled at Bella.

"What happened?" asked Bella, acknowledging Catherine's smile with one of her own. "When and why did he change?"

"According to my father, Thomas was called to Rome. When he returned several months later, he had been made a Bishop. He became an official 'authority' on heresy and how to approach 'crimes against the church'. He returned from Rome an entirely different man than the one who had left. My father realized that something had changed, but Thomas would never allow him close after that. They were suddenly at odds about the Inquisition and the king realized the need to exercise caution as the result of Thomas' newly acquired power. While he never talked about it, I could tell that he grieved his friendship with Thomas. It was gone forever."

"Your father not only lost a friend, but a spiritual brother, as well," sympathized Bella.

"He lost more than that, I fear. My father was a deeply pious man. Even though he didn't agree with the Inquisition, he always believed it would pass, with the help of those good men in the church like Thomas Capshaw. He desperately wanted to see the end of the Inquisition in his lifetime. He believed that he and Thomas, together, could effect change from the inside, for his own subjects at the very least. Then after Thomas's return, that belief faded."

Catherine was quiet for a time, thinking back on painful memories. She swirled her hand absently in the water.

When she continued, she didn't attempt to hide the sorrow in her voice. "He lost his faith in so many ways. He always believed that God put him and Thomas together to fight for justice. When he lost Thomas, he lost part of himself, the part that needed to believe that good men remained good men in spite of temptations put before them. Thomas's change cut my father to his soul. It was after losing much of his support on the Council to the bishop that he lost his confidence in dealing with life itself. In many ways I believe that's when he started to die. He only lived for a year after Thomas returned from Rome. I watched as he deferred more and more to the Council, and the Council deferred more and more to the bishop."

"I am so sorry," Bella offered sadly.

They got out of the tub and dried. Catherine dressed for the day, but Bella slipped into a light gown. They sat at the table again.

Catherine continued. "When my father died and I assumed my role, I thought, foolishly, that the Council just needed a strong royal leader again. It didn't take me long to realize not only was it too late, but as a woman, the battle would be endless."

They opened the doors to the balcony and stepped out into the sunlight. Catherine's gaze drifted to a far off place. Bella placed her hand on Catherine's and they stood for a bit, letting the warmth of the sun filter into their bones. The sounds and smells of the surrounding forest, pines and chestnut trees, wafted up to them. Catherine inhaled deeply then took Bella's hand to draw her back inside where she kissed Bella.

With her hands on either side of Bella's face, she said, "I don't know how it is possible, but I love you more than I did a few short days ago." She left for the day, happier than she had been in some time.

Chapter Twenty Three

"Your Majesty," said Bishop Capshaw, "we did not expect you today." I understood from the king, that you were not well last evening and spent the night in your own quarters."

Catherine heard the insinuation and the slight emphasis on Ambrose's title. She attempted to diffuse both. "My husband spoke correctly, Your Grace. But I am much better after a *good* night's sleep. Shall we get down to business, my Lords?"

The Council shared a number of decrees they wished to establish regarding land and water rights. She agreed to all the decrees. Where possible she always tried to give in where she thought she could. In that way, when she did feel the need to stand her ground, she hoped they'd be more inclined to agree with her. At least that was her strategy.

Once the matter of new decrees was addressed, Lord Giovanni gave a report on several more attacks by the fanatical group. One of the attacks was in the southern part of the kingdom. Two were in the north. The attack in the south happened between the two northern attacks and was much too close in time to have been the same group. This information was alarming, as the attacks had been random and few enough that the assumption was that it was only one rogue group with whom they were dealing. Clearly, at least one other group had formed.

"Where is your delegate?" Catherine asked the bishop.

"The last word received is that he is on his way back from the eastern part of the kingdom, Highness."

"What was his communication to you?" asked Catherine.

"Fears are high, Your Majesty. As a result, it is difficult to get people to discuss what is happening. He has spoken to the servants of only one household that was attacked, and those servants were frightened to say anything for fear of reprisals."

"When your delegate arrives, I should like to meet with him, with your permission, of course."

"Of course, Majesty." He nodded curtly to her.

"I am planning to make another visit to Rome," Catherine informed them. "The new Pope, Marcellus II, seems to have a gentler and more humane approach to leading the Church and I will, again, attempt to convince the Holy See to assist us in deterring the fanatical groups that plague the countryside." Indeed, Catherine was relieved to hear of the election of the new Pope, but she also desired a reason to take Bella to Rome. Once the baby was born she wanted to give them time to travel and be alone together. And, it was true that Pope Marcellus was said to be quite fair and intelligent in his approach to issues of people. She had high hopes for a positive relationship with the new Pope.

The Bishop gave them a new list of interrogations scheduled for the upcoming weeks. While it was not necessary for him to do so, it was politically conducive to insuring his continued support on the Council. The Nobles expected to know if any of their own family had been named.

The meeting concluded and Catherine joined the Council for the midday meal. Her grandmother had begun the custom early in her reign as a gesture of respect for the Council members. Her father continued the ritual. Catherine gave thought to dispensing with the custom, but she found it interesting that often more in-depth discussion of the meeting topics took place over the meal. When that was not the case, the meal gave her opportunity to engage with the lords with whom she felt an affinity-- namely Lord Giovanni, Lord Romeo and Lord Como. The ability and ease with which she could interact with them was always a welcome treat for her.

Chapter Twenty Four

It was May. Bella was in the full bloom of her pregnancy, and bored with her inability to do much. She was uncomfortable, irritable and anxious over the coming birth. Catherine wanted to surprise her with an outing to the flower fields, which she expected to be in full spring glory. Thoughts of bringing Bella back to the place of their first kiss made Catherine smile.

She invited Robert and his family to join them. She hadn't had the opportunity to visit with Petra of late, and little Gio was growing up quickly. She wanted to be a part of her little cousin's life. Lord Giovanni was invited, as well.

And so a picnic party was arranged to the flower fields. As there was no way Bella could ride a horse in her condition, Catherine ordered a covered carriage for them. A separate, open carriage was arranged for Petra, little Gio and Lord Giovanni. Robert alone rode on horseback.

Catherine was as anxious for this outing as she had been for anything for some time. She quickly grew tired of the charade of her marriage. Although she spent several nights a week with her husband, the energy required to manage delight in the task was enormous. And there was the additional need to make certain that it was obvious to everyone the couple was, indeed, spending many nights alone together.

The morning of the planned outing Catherine left Ambrose sleeping in their bed and stole into her quarters to awaken Bella. Bella was unaccustomed to seeing her so early on mornings after she spent the night with her husband.

"I have a surprise for you, my love. Get up, let's have some breakfast. Then you must prepare for an outing."

Bella's moods had become as unpredictable as the end of the Inquisition itself.

"Sometimes," Catherine confided to Robert, "nearly as frightening. I never know if Bella will burst into tears or be outraged at an unexpected event."

Robert laughed at Catherine's frustration. "I find it enormously amusing that I have been warned about a woman's moods during pregnancy, while you are surprised by them!"

Much to Catherine's relief, Bella was delighted with the idea of a surprise outing.

Catherine closed the carriage curtains so she could offer Bella the full impact of the flower fields. As they rode along in the dim light of the carriage Catherine talked only of the picnic and her delight at spending the day in such wonderful company. She was as excited as a little girl giving her first gift.

A knock. "Majesty, we have arrived."

"Close your eyes, Bella," demanded Catherine. Her excitement was so contagious that Bella complied. "And do not open them until I tell you."

Catherine opened the door of the carriage. She and Robert assisted Bella out, her eyes still closed. She then took Bella's hand and walked her to the front of the carriage and stopped.

From directly behind Bella, hands on her shoulders, Catherine whispered into her ear, "Open your eyes, my love!"

Bella's quick intake of breath left no doubt that the scene before her was as wondrous a thing of beauty as she had ever known. One hand flew to her mouth, the other to Catherine's hand on her shoulder. She was speechless. The view spread out before them, acres upon acres of yellow and purple flowers in a sea of green grasses, a clear, blue, pristine lake in the distance, and the Apennines as a backdrop, still covered in snow. In Catherine's mind there was no higher praise for God's glorious work of art than a single, heartfelt gasp.

The group enjoyed a wonderful day sunning, chatting, reading and walking. Bella struggled awkwardly to pick blooms to carry home.

That night Catherine dined with Ambrose, who seemed genuinely dismayed about being excluded from the outing.

"Did you not even consider that I might like to join you?" he asked.

Catherine was taken aback. "I am truly sorry, Ambrose. It never occurred to me that you might enjoy something like that."

"Whether I might or might not have enjoyed the particular place is not what bothers me," he said. "I am your husband and I would have liked to have been included. At the very least I should have been asked, even if my answer was no," he pouted.

"Ambrose," Catherine got up and walked around behind him. She slipped her arms around his neck, "I didn't intend to hurt you. I do apologize. I didn't want to wake you, you were sleeping so peacefully."

"I suppose I forgive you, then," he turned and pulled her into his lap. She felt his erection and gave in to his amorous overtures. When he was finished he fell asleep. Catherine slipped out of the marriage suite and went back to her quarters.

When she arrived Bella was already in bed, genuinely exhausted from the day. Catherine found her sleeping among petals of yellow and purple. She smiled and slipped in next to Bella.

The next morning brought unbelievable news. Pope Marcellus was dead. Catherine's letter requesting an audience could not even have reached him. He was in office a mere twenty two days. It did not seem possible. Catherine sat at her desk and dropped her head into her hands. The reports she received stated that the Pope died of a weak constitution. The intense and rigorous schedule was too much for his frail disposition. "God only knows," she thought, "who will be elected now." She felt unsettled about this Pope's death. Something did not feel right about it.

Chapter Twenty Five

"Marie! Marie!" shouted the queen. "Fetch the midwife! Lady Isabella's time has arrived."

As they waited for Marie to return with the midwife, Catherine walked Bella to her old pallet and held her. Between her labor pains Bella could not contain her tears...or her fears.

"Catherine, please. I am afraid. Don't leave my side."

Catherine grasped her hands. "I am here. I won't leave you."

"What will become of this child? I can't love it!" Bella was nearly beside herself with her anxiety.

"Don't think about that now, my love. God will help us."

Catherine felt bile rise in her throat. If God didn't approve, then God would need to act. And therein lay her biggest fear...that God would act. Her heart was nearly always prepared to lose Bella. And now, today, as Bella's pains overtook her, and caused her to cry out, Catherine felt certain the loss was imminent.

Marie arrived with the midwife and they set to work for the birth. Bella was experiencing contractions about ten minutes apart.

"Majesty," the midwife directed Catherine, "you need not stay and bother yourself."

"Don't leave me!" Bella grabbed Catherine. Her face was full of fear.

"I intend to stay," Catherine informed the midwife. "Direct me as you will."

The midwife continued her evaluation of Bella. "I anticipate no problems. Lady Isabella seems ready for a normal enough birth. Marie and I can tend to the birthing; you may feel free to be a comfort to Lady Isabella."

Catherine positioned herself behind Bella in such a way as to support Bella's body and hold her hands. When the pains overtook Bella, she squeezed Catherine's hands tightly and cried out. Catherine offered her words of encouragement, wishing there were more that she could do.

Time seemed to stretch endlessly with no change. After nearly six hours, Bella was still not experiencing contractions closer than eight minutes apart.

"Lady Isabella, please try to relax and let the baby begin to move down." The midwife pressed on the top of Bella's swollen belly in an attempt to push the baby down.

"Bella, you must try to help the baby. Please do as the midwife says and relax," Catherine urged, choking her fear down.

The midwife instructed Marie to go to the kitchen and bring back some items. Marie returned a short time later. The midwife busied herself at the dining table then marched to the pallet.

"Here, drink this!" she commanded. She gave Bella a mixture of raw egg, sugar and ale.

Bella drank. "Oh, God, that's awful!" she gagged.

"Drink it anyway, you need something to help you relax and keep up your strength." The midwife said authoritatively.

Bella dozed on and off between contractions for several more hours

"What's happening?" Catherine asked the midwife. "Why is this taking so long?"

The midwife shook her head. "It's her first child, sometimes first babies take longer. It is not unusual for first labors to go on for twenty hours. But it would help if she wanted this baby. I have seen this kind of holding on before, when the woman does not wish to have the baby. The body simply fights against letting go."

Bella cried out as another contraction took hold of her. "I don't want the child, but I want this ordeal to be over. Do something!"

Catherine felt more helpless than ever in her life. All she could do was wait and watch as Bella went through this agony. She wished she could endure this for Bella.

Bella's head was cradled back against Catherine and Catherine's lips were next to her ear. "Bella," she whispered, "if it were within my power I would birth this baby for you. I cannot bear to see you suffer. Please, please, I beg you, do not give up. Do not leave me. I can bear anything but that." She continued to hold Bella, rocking her ever so gently.

After four more hours they were all exhausted. Bella continued to doze between contractions. Catherine remained alert and watchful, still holding and rocking.

After another two hours, the contractions had progressed only minimally. Catherine watched in horror as the midwife reached up and pulled a sharpened goose quill from her hair. As the midwife made to insert the quill between Bella's legs, Catherine stopped her. "What are you doing?" she demanded.

"Majesty, I need to break the woman's water to move things along. Neither Lady Isabella nor the baby can endure much more."

"Have you done this before?" Catherine was near panic.

"Yes, Majesty."

"Is it dangerous?"

"No more dangerous than letting the labor continue. Her contractions should be much closer together by now."

The midwife inserted the goose quill. They didn't have to wait long for the water to spill from Bella. The midwife reached her hand inside Bella and felt for the baby's head.

"The baby is positioned correctly. There should be no problem with the birth. Push now!"

Bella pushed, but she was weak and her attempt was feeble. The contractions progressed a bit more.

When the contractions were just over two minutes apart the midwife said, "Marie, push down on the lady's belly. Lady, push again! Hard!"

Catherine was still cradling Bella from behind. She had her arms wrapped around Bella, who held tightly to Catherine's arms. "Push, Bella, push!" Catherine pleaded.

Bella pushed with a howl that came from deep within her. The midwife reached for the baby's head as it emerged.

Catherine held Bella tight and watched the baby slither out of Bella.

At first there was no noise, just a bloody newborn being held by the midwife, who stuck her finger in the baby's mouth, then turned it upside down and slapped it. It gasped, and finally let out a cry, a pitiful cry, but a cry nonetheless.

Bella collapsed back onto Catherine in a faint as the baby delivered. The midwife looked at Catherine and said, "There is nothing left now but the afterbirth. It is a boy child. Marie, clean and swaddle the child to deliver him to his mother."

Catherine slipped herself out from behind Bella and helped to rearrange her pillows and covers after the midwife pulled the soiled linens away.

As the circumstances surrounding this pregnancy were so unusual, the usual joy and celebration was not expected. In fact, no one, the midwife included, quite knew how to respond to the birth of this child.

Marie cleaned and swaddled the baby. When she was done she brought him to Lady Isabella, who had regained consciousness as Catherine was wiping her forehead with a cool cloth. She turned her head to the window and refused to even look at him.

Catherine saw the pain and fear in Bella's face. She looked at Marie, smiled, and reached for the bundle.

If Catherine thought that denying her love for Bella was impossible, what happened to her next was nothing short of miraculous. She hadn't expected or prepared for anything but a resigned acceptance of the child. At first she was only aware of the weight and warmth of the child. The scent of him wafted up to her nostrils and she looked down. Her reaction was instantaneous and overwhelming. This was no child of the devil.

"Oh!" whispered Catherine as she looked at him, "hello." He looked back at her, blinking, and gurgled. Never had Catherine felt such a tug at her heart. She looked down at the face of an angel, and she fell instantly and completely in love. Catherine's awe and instincts surprised her. She knew, without doubt, that loving and protecting this defenseless little bundle gave new dimension...new meaning to her life.

"Bella, Bella," Catherine whispered, "he is beautiful."

Bella refused to look. "I don't want to look at him. Take him away, Marie."

Catherine handed the bundle back to Marie who put the baby in the cradle that had been brought to the quarters. She turned to Bella. "You're tired after your ordeal. Rest now. I'll be right here."

The midwife informed the queen that a wet nurse had been located. Marie and the midwife cleaned up and left the queen alone with Bella and the newborn.

Catherine picked up the baby, and sat cradling him in her arms. She and the baby both slept. A peaceful look graced her face. A short time later she woke up and looked again at the sleeping baby in her arms. When she looked up, Bella was watching her. She smiled, "How are you feeling, my love?"

"Lighter," Bella said with a snort.

Catherine looked down at the baby, then back at Bella. "Your son," she glowed, "is beautiful."

Catherine stood and took the baby over to Bella. She sat on the pallet beside her. "I know you never wanted this day to come, but it has arrived. You must accept the fact that you are the mother to this child...whether or not you wish it so."

Bella's face crumpled into a mask of pain and tears.

"I am not capable of mothering this child, Catherine," she whispered. "Don't ask me."

Catherine was afraid for Bella...and the baby. While she believed Bella would learn to love her child, there was a touch of uncertainty. Regardless, it was time for Bella to deal with things. "For all these months I have lived with your fear," she said, "I know that you believe that this child is of the devil. Listen to me...if this is the devil, then I will be content to live in hell for the rest of my days."

Bella's eyes filled with fear as Catherine leaned toward her. She shook her head. "No, no, Catherine, please. I'm not ready. I cannot do this."

Catherine ignored Bella placing the baby in her arms. Bella was forced to accept the bundle. She didn't take her eyes off of Catherine's, but when the weight of the baby settled in her arms he made a small noise. Reflexively, she looked down into his face.

Catherine could not see Bella's face as she first looked at him, but she saw Bella's body relax. The fear and anger that she knew Bella had braced for dissipated at first sight.

Bella looked up at Catherine, her eyes brimming with tears and surprise.

"How can this be?" she asked.

"Perhaps that is the definition of a miracle. It cannot be…but it is." Catherine settled next to Bella, the baby between them. The three of them slept peacefully.

The baby woke them up with a pitiful little cry. Bella picked him up.

"I think he's hungry," she said instinctively.

Catherine started up to fetch Marie to call the wet nurse, but Bella asked her to wait. She wanted to see if the baby would feed from her own breast. Catherine helped Bella to untie her dressing gown and lower it to reveal her breast. As Bella brought the baby up he instinctively began to root, looking for his source of nourishment. As he latched onto her nipple and began to suckle, Bella let out a little gasp, "Oh, my, you are a hungry little one!" She looked up at Catherine and smiled, "He is beautiful, I am blessed…for you both."

Catherine was filled with joy and relief.

"What will you name him?" Catherine asked.

Without hesitation Bella answered, "James. After my father."

"James," repeated Catherine. "It's a fine name."

It was out of the question to ask the bishop to baptize the baby. In an attempt to subtly cast doubts about her, the bishop had taken to ignoring Bella at the communion rail during Mass. Rumors started to spread that he refused her communion because she was a witch. Bella had not attended Mass for several weeks.

"If he thinks I am a witch," Bella said over breakfast, "he will certainly not look favorably on my son."

Catherine filled a plate with fresh melon for her.

Bella reached for the plate. "I want that hypocrite nowhere near my baby, especially not in light of what Robert saw!"

Both of them were determined to protect the child from the lecherous beast.

"We'll ask Father Tim to baptize him," Catherine said. "I'll ask him to perform the ceremony next week. It's perfect. He can openly arrive at the castle without arousing any suspicion. He will be here to administer sacraments to you and your child. Since the Bishop unreasonably excluded you from communion he cannot be offended if you must seek your spiritual needs elsewhere."

Since Bella hadn't returned to Church, she was in danger of furthering accusations of heresy against her. Now that she had James's soul to consider, it seemed an easy task to request that Father Tim arrange to come to the queen's private quarters to say mass.

"I look forward to meeting Father Tim. Perhaps when he is finished with his usual Sunday mass in the village he can say mass for us here in your quarters and then dine with us. That would give you time enough to discuss other matters with him."

"I'll send word to him," said Catherine.

Father Tim arrived the next Sunday just as Catherine was leaving the bishop's mass. She was unwilling to forego one mass for another. It seemed imperative to her that she know what the bishop was preaching. It gave her information about him and it kept him careful about what he might be insinuating behind her back.

As she made her way from the chapel to the castle, Catherine saw Father Tim sitting on a bench talking to some children. The children were laughing.

She approached. "Father Tim, you will spoil our children with too much fun," she laughed. The children scattered, still laughing as they ran.

He rose to greet her. "Your Majesty. It is good to see you."

She guided him toward the castle and together they walked.

"Thank you for agreeing to meet with us on Sundays," she said.

He looked at her. "It is my pleasure, Your Majesty. But, I have been giving considerable thought to your request. Do you believe it wise for me to come every week? This is the bishop's territory. In reality, I must defer to his authority. He will not be pleased. I am worried that we risk engendering his wrath further than we have already."

They'd reached the main entrance to the castle. A guard opened the doors for them and they stepped inside. It took a moment for their eyes to adjust to the darker atmosphere after being in the full sunlight.

"Of course," Catherine said. "I apologize. This is my battle. I did not intend to create difficulty for you," replied Catherine.

"I believe we can make an excuse for the Baptism today. His refusal to include Lady Isabella one sacrament is reason for you to believe he would refuse another. But, is he aware I am here today to baptize Lady Isabella's child?"

They were climbing the large, stone stairway that led to Catherine's quarters on third floor.

"Not as yet, but he will undoubtedly know by the end of the day. It's his doing that created the need. I will accept his wrath in the matter and present your visit as being at the command of your queen if I hear that he has been angered."

"How is your relationship with the bishop, Majesty? Is he still searching for ways to brand you a heretic?" asked Father Timothy.

"In his zeal to find yet another way to bring me closer to heretical accusations, I am afraid our dear bishop went too far when he refused Lady Isabella communion. We believe he is trying to portray her as a witch."

Father Tim stopped and looked at her. "That is a serious accusation. She must be very frightened."

"I believe our good Captain has addressed the issue with His Grace in such a way that we need not worry about his zeal for some time," Catherine smiled, then sobered. They continued walking. "Father, I wonder if you would sit with me before we proceed?"

They had reached the third floor and were near a bench in an alcove near the queen's quarters. She sat and indicated her desire for him to do the same.

"Of course, Your Majesty." He sat beside her and waited.

It was some minutes before Catherine spoke again. "In our past dealings regarding victims of this Inquisition, I have been--" she paused searching for words. When she continued, her voice was soft and low, "I have been less than compassionate for certain subjects...whose actions I have perceived as...against the teachings of Christ." Catherine struggled, not knowing how to express that she had opposed championing those who, like herself and Bella, had been persecuted. Father Tim, his head bowed, listened attentively.

Catherine continued, "You urged me to be compassionate to all of God's children. I ignored you. As a result, there were those of my subjects who were tortured and executed. I justified my actions, or inactions, because of what I believed." As she said this, her heart was breaking, thinking about the way she had simply turned her back on those whose relationships she had thought sinful in the sight of God.

"You have always acted according to your conscience and with the best of intentions, Majesty," said Father Tim.

"I was wrong, Father," Catherine was shaking. "I have come to believe that I allowed those persecutions because I could not accept my own inclinations. I…."

Father Timothy held up his hand to stop her, "My dear queen, you need say nothing more."

"But, I as much as condemned those innocents as if I were the bishop himself," she whispered as she looked down. She couldn't meet his eyes.

"Majesty, we are, each of us, on our own spiritual journey. With God's help, we see things when we are ready to open our eyes. Some are never ready, for to see requires action. Many depend upon their blindness in order to survive. You are not one of those. And your new understanding and remorse means that those souls did not die in vain."

"The knowledge I now have changes everything."

"It is not knowledge that changes us, Catherine," he waited until she looked up at him, then looked so deeply into her eyes that she was certain he saw into her soul, "it is how we choose to act on that knowledge."

"What must I do to be forgiven?" whispered the queen.

"Ask."

"Forgive me," said Catherine quietly.

He placed his hand on her head, "In the name of Christ, you are forgiven your sins. Go…and sin no more."

She wanted to continue to talk to Father Tim about this, but did not yet feel strong enough to speak of her own struggle. She still felt scared. She still missed feeling God's love and still feared He did not approve. In spite of Father Tim's absolution, she didn't feel absolved. Her heart remained weighed down by her burden.

Bella was waiting. She thanked Father Tim and together they went into her quarters.

Father Tim smiled as Bella walked toward him with her hands outstretched. Before Catherine could introduce them Bella said, "You must be Father Timothy. I have heard so much about you. I am Lady Isabella."

As Bella finished introducing herself she looked to Catherine. Father Tim blinked and smiled.

"Lady Isabella, it is a pleasure to meet you."

They sat and shared pleasantries. Then the priest said, "Lady Isabella, I understand that our Bishop has excluded you from taking the sacrament of Holy Communion."

Bella poured wine for all three of them and handed a cup to Father Tim. She nodded. "Although I understand his motive, I believe he feels he has hurt me by the act. If I thought he was truly a man of God I suppose I would be hurt. But I see his act more as a bad cook denying a meal to an already satisfied patron."

Father Tim laughed. "I believe our good Bishop would be appalled to hear you utter such blasphemy."

Bella immediately looked horrified. "I am sorry; I tend to speak too freely at times. It was not my intention to…"

The priest held up his hand, smiling, and reassuring her, "You may speak freely with me, Lady Isabella, I was making light of what is really a serious topic. Your queen and I have long dealt with the tyranny of the bishop. It is not often that I am afforded an opportunity to be in the company of those who share my feeling."

Bella smiled and visibly relaxed. "I am at your disposal in the fight against such despicable deeds as those of the bishop. How can I assist you?" She offered him some olives and bread.

"Bella," Catherine said, "Father Tim thinks his coming here will endanger his tenuous relationship with the bishop. We need to find another way to meet with him."

"Perhaps," Father Tim offered, "a Sunday afternoon outing to my village, where Lady Isabella can hear mass?"

"No matter what we do he will see through our guise, but I should be able to convince him that it is in his best interests to allow you to serve us Mass in your own village," Catherine offered as she sipped her wine. "That will make Robert's presence necessary, as well."

"I will be glad of less skulking about in the forest, Majesty. Although I know our meetings are held with the utmost of secrecy, I always worry that one of us will be followed."

The baby's cry caused all three to turn. James was awake and hungry. Bella excused herself from the sitting area and went into the queen's bedroom to feed the baby. She returned a short time later and introduced her child to Father Tim.

He took the baby gently. "He is beautiful," said the priest. "Shall we baptize him?"

When the ceremony was complete, Catherine called for a meal. James' soul was now safe, and he was officially named.

When they first began their outings to the village, the bishop objected. He made an appointment with Catherine and was in her office. "Your Majesty, it is not right for the queen to seek mass and confession from someone other than her own bishop in her own castle church," he protested.

"Your Grace, I accompany Lady Isabella, who has been refused Holy Communion by my bishop. She was so aggrieved by this action that we have been forced to seek her spiritual requirements elsewhere. Did you expect her to stop attending mass or confession?"

She had him. She was secretly delighted to have angered him and see him have to relent as he said, "You are quite correct, Majesty. Perhaps I was hasty to judge her."

"Perhaps," was all Catherine said.

In actuality, Catherine knew the bishop was more concerned with the fact that she was now regularly in the company of Father Timothy. She knew the Bishop Capshaw did not trust him, and had long suspected that he was sympathetic to the Reformation.

"Majesty, I would be happy to accept the Lady Isabella and her son at our own mass. I am willing to apologize to her."

Catherine watched him choke on his own words. "That is very gracious of you, but I believe Lady Isabella is quite content with both the Mass and spiritual counsel of Father Tim."

"Majesty," he said as his face turned a bright shade of red and the veins in his temples visibly pulsed, "I would prefer that you both resume taking your spiritual requirements here."

"I have not ceased attending mass here, Your Grace, and I will continue to do so. I also continue in my confessions with you, do I not?"

"You do, Majesty. Is there a reason you find it necessary to repeat both mass and confession with Father Timothy?" he asked.

"I am unaware that the Church limits our ability to partake in the sacraments."

"It does not, Majesty. But I have reason to believe that your priest may be involved in the Reformation activities that are spreading across Europe. I would not want you to become entangled in something that might put you at risk. Your Father Timothy may already be in a difficult position."

So, he was trying to scare her into cutting ties with Father Tim. Catherine directed an icy glare at the Bishop. She was done playing games.

"Lady Isabella and I enjoy our Sunday outings to the village. I don't anticipate any change in that routine. As to your suggestion that Father Timothy may be involved in heretical activities, I have no knowledge to that effect...nor do I have any reason to suspect that your information is anything but a desperate attempt to frighten me. I am well aware that your authority over village priests gives you the right to remove and control them." She stood and leaned over her desk. "If anything alters Father Tim's status in his village...if any accusations of heresy befall that good man, you will pay the price for your own hypocrisy," she waited while her words took effect.

The Bishop's face was livid with anger. "Majesty," he said curtly, through gritted teeth. He stood and turned to leave her office.

"Your Grace," she called to him. He turned slowly. "You may take your leave."

Chapter Twenty Six

Catherine and Bella had been visiting Father Tim for some months. Their Sunday afternoon ritual was something to which both women looked forward. It gave them an opportunity for a regular outing with James and time to enjoy the beauty of the kingdom between the castle and Castiglione d' Orcia, where Father Tim lived and worked. The residents of the village looked forward to their queen's arrival as well. Her visits brought extra income to the impoverished little village. Queen Catherine traveled with no less than four guards and a servant. After mass they all dined at one of the local taverns. Catherine was sensitive to alternating between the few that existed.

Before Father Tim said mass for the women, he always prepared for Confession. It was there that they made their secret plans to help the most recent victims of the interrogations. Father Tim sat in the confessional and opened the windows on both sides of his seat. There, Catherine was on one side and Bella on the other. In this way they were able to share the necessary information needed for the upcoming week.

Following the mass one Sunday, Catherine asked Bella if she would mind accompanying the entourage to dine. She wanted to visit with Father Tim alone.

Catherine and the priest sat near the front of the small church. The castle church was grand and quite well appointed, but Catherine found herself in love with this little chapel.

"I love this place," she said as she looked around.

"There is a sweetness here I don't find in other places where I have said Mass," Tim responded. "I am glad you like it, Majesty."

He waited, knowing she would begin when she was ready.

"I have been unsettled about something for some time," she started. "And I believe I can speak to you about this."

"You may speak to me about anything, Majesty. And even though this is not a confessional, please know that what you tell me is between you, me and God."

She smiled and knew she was safe.

"Am I doomed to hell?" she asked abruptly.

"For what, Majesty?" He was startled by her question.

"I believe you know that Lady Isabella is more...is not...that her title of Lady in Waiting is a guise only."

"Ah. I wondered if you struggled with yourself over this."

"I know we sin in God's eyes."

"Has God told you this?" Father Tim asked.

"The scriptures and the teachings of the church are very clear on this, are they not?"

Tim sat quietly for a moment. He took a large breath and exhaled slowly. "Majesty, Catherine," he started to reach for her hands, and then stopped, realizing his near breech of protocol. "It grieves me that you, of all people, think you are doomed to hell. And, no, I do not think the scriptures doom you."

"What is meant, then, by 'a man shall not lie with a man'?" she asked.

"Would you like my interpretation?" he smiled as he said this.

Catherine looked at him with mild puzzlement.

"You know the Bible was written many years after Christ died and rose again. The men who wrote the Gospels were far from the actual events they wrote about. They wrote from memory, they wrote from inspiration, yes, but they were men trying to remember for us, as best they could, what they learned from our Savior."

"But they were with Him, they knew him, He taught them."

"And they, like us, were tarnished by their own pasts, their own beliefs, their own prejudices and prides, their own jealousies. And, they were responding to their own times and situations, to specific problems that arose."

She struggled to connect what he was saying to her feelings of guilt and fear.

He stood, walked over to the altar, and then back to where she was sitting. "Do you believe in what the church is doing to heretics?"

"You know I don't," she said, frowning.

"This is no different. This Inquisition is based on the fears of our Church leaders...and their *interpretations* of Christ's teachings. Do you believe Christ wants His Church to execute people for questioning, for wondering, for healing, for interpreting?"

"No, of course that can't be what Christ intended."

"But the wise leaders of our Church have decided this is what's best for us. How is it that you don't believe in the Inquisition practices?"

"I understand your comparison," the queen stood and wandered over to one of the stained glass windows. She remained standing with her back to him.

"But something still troubles you," he said.

Catherine turned back and walked over to the altar. She looked up at the figure of Christ hanging from the cross. "I used to be able to feel the presence of God with me in such intimate ways. When I sat in church, or walked the flower fields or simply prayed in my quarters, I felt Divine energy fill and surround me. I have not felt God's presence since...for over a year."

"Since you interpreted your feelings to be something that God abhorred?" Tim asked.

"I have difficulty discerning how God sees me differently from our bishop," she said, her back still to him.

Father Tim walked over to her. "Look at me. I am telling you that love is God's greatest gift to us. Christ was love and He taught us that love is everything. There are many kinds of love, the love you have for your subjects, for your parents, for your family," he paused, "for Bella. Love is love, it is kind, and it is good. What the Bishop engages in is not love, but a lust that hurts and destroys others. What you have with Lady Isabella is a true love. Sometimes, God loves us through others, and God loves others through us. Who are we to say it should be this one or that one. It is who it is, and if Bella is who God sent, then to fight it is to refuse God's gift."

"Is that your 'interpretation'?" Catherine asked with a smile.

Father Tim laughed softly, "I suppose it is." He paused briefly. "But I would ask you to try something the next time you pray. You may find that you agree with my 'interpretation.' Instead of approaching God feeling like a sinner who is damned to hell, perhaps you might thank God for bringing Lady Isabella into your life. Love can be a calling as much as the monastery or the convent. If God has called you to love her, then your struggle is only within yourself. If you believe that you are sinning by loving Bella, then *you* block your own communication with the divine. Perhaps if you can accept that Bella is God's way of loving you, His presence will fill you once again."

Catherine smiled, feeling more grateful for his presence in her life than she could express. "Is there any way we can make you Pope?"

"That is not an office to which I aspire, Your Majesty."

"Before we join the others, will you pray with me?" she asked.

"Happily, Majesty."

Chapter Twenty Seven

On the morning that Mary DeMarco was slated to be burned at the stake, Catherine was irritable. She had been irritable for days. Sometimes, in spite of their best efforts to help innocent victims like Mary, it was impossible to save them. By the time they were brought before the Bishop for interrogation they were spent. The days, or weeks, they were forced to endure the cold, dark conditions of the castle keep were dismal. The cells were infested with lice and rats. Food was minimal. Prisoners were forced to defecate on the floors of their cells. Guards were often cruel and sadistic.

Physical torture to extract confessions from witches was supposed to have been banned years earlier. Prior to that, devices of torture kept the Inquisitors quite busy. The use of such implements as the rack caused accused witches to confess to almost anything. Under threat of torture by the iron maiden or the bastinado, a woman would not only confess to being a witch, but would denounce others as being witches as well. There were stories that told of women under torture who admitted that they and others turned themselves into horses and galloped through the skies. Some six hundred women in France admitted to copulating with demons.

Suspected witches were tortured in the cruelest of ways. Stripped naked, all their body hair shaved, they would be "pricked." The Malleus Maleficarum, a treatise written in 1486 by Heinrich Kramer and Jacob Sprenger, detailed how to deal with witches. The treatise advised that witches bore a "devil's mark," a numb spot on their bodies. Pricking with a sharp object would, apparently, divulge this numb spot. When the numb spot was not detected, some suffered red hot tongs on their nipples and genitalia. The torturers became aroused from their activities, and sometimes this alone was all the proof needed for identifying a witch. The women were forced to admit that they were causing the men to become aroused through their sinful powers. They said anything to stop the pain and torture.

It was considered progress that these types of torture were no longer accepted by the Church. But that was little comfort to Catherine on the day of Mary DeMarco's execution. Catherine suspected that Thomas Capshaw was using his position to show her he still held power over her.

Catherine went to her office early. Her thoughts swirled. Her heart was heavy. As she watched the smoke from Mary DeMarco's pyre begin to rise she realized how very much she hated Thomas Capshaw. She silently declared war on him.

Catherine stood at her office window and forced her thoughts to turn from the bishop to Mary DeMarco. She threw herself into prayer for the woman and her family. She watched as the smoke from the pyre thickened and blackened. She could not see the fire itself.

She never attended the executions, preferring to focus on praying for the victims. When Catherine was ten years old her father took her to an execution. It, too, was the burning of a woman convicted of being a witch. The King and Catherine sat in an enclosed carriage.

The charges against the woman were read aloud and she was tied to a stake. King Edward sat across from Catherine. He reached out, held her chin and looked into her eyes with such sadness that Catherine thought he might cry.

"Catherine, my child, you need to witness what is about to happen because one day you will be queen. What you are about to see is horrible. I want you to be horrified so that you will take up my mantle and continue to fight against this kind of persecution. These poor people are being crucified for greed and political reasons. No one, not the priests, or the Pope, or even a king or a queen, has the right to do what you are about to see." He paused and looked to see the torches being held to the dried kindling. "Watch, Catherine, and never forget what you see. Let the flames that burn this poor woman ignite a fire in your heart to carry you into battle against this travesty."

Catherine's heart raced as she watched the flames lick up around the feet of the sobbing woman. The woman started screaming for help. Her garment caught fire quickly, and the flames engulfed her, catching her hair on fire. The woman's head twisted back and forth as she howled in pain. Catherine forced herself to watch when everything in her screamed to turn away. As the smell of burning flesh and hair reached her nostrils she could take no more and buried her head in her father's neck. She begged him to take her away from here. "I promise I will never forget, Papa. Please take me home!"

When word reached Catherine that Mary DeMarco was dead, she nodded to the soldier who brought her the news. When the soldier left, Catherine dismissed her secretary and went to her quarters. Once there, she proceeded to vomit.

The queen was with child.

Chapter Twenty Eight

May 1555

Catherine's pregnancy brought much happiness and relief. Ambrose strutted as if he had proved his virility beyond a doubt. Catherine understood that this child would solidify the unity of their two kingdoms against any enemies, and wondered if his father would be proud of Ambrose at long last.

Bella chatted excitedly.

"Think what this means! James will have a playmate, a brother or a sister! And now you can stay here. I don't have to suffer the lack of you so often!"

Although Catherine knew that Bella had resigned herself to accepting their necessary separation for up to three nights per week, those nights were unbearable for them both.

"I ache for you more than know when you're with him." Bella said. "I didn't realize how jealous I was. Now I feel like I can tell you how awful it was."

Catherine was glad she would no longer have to endure Bella's moods when she returned from the marital suite. Sometimes Bella was distant for hours afterward. The effort it took to reconnect with Bella after her time with Ambrose seemed harder and harder. She understood and sympathized with Bella's feelings, but was glad all of that might soon be over.

She was relieved for other reasons, as well. At last, she felt she could put an end to the charade her life had become. Ambrose would still be her husband, but now she could dispense the marital bed. If all went well with the birth of this child, she hoped to never have to sleep with him again. There was still the matter of informing him of her intention, but now that she could, she was happier than she had been in some time.

While Bella was anxious for Catherine to return to her private quarters soon, and for good, she was prudent enough to realize that to wait until this baby was born would be the wisest course of action.

"At least," Catherine said, "I have reason enough to decline Ambrose's amorous advances for a time. And, I can claim need of my own quarters more often."

The truth of her own words fell hard on her as the pregnancy exhausted Catherine in ways that made her question how women desired to give birth more than once. Her discomfort as the baby grew made her irritable. She slept much, and once her sickness passed she was ravenous much of the time.

Ambrose was solicitous of her. His concern seemed heartfelt, but she had difficulty when he attempted to be close, and she bristled under his touch more and more.

Bella laughed at her. "You have a short memory, my love. It wasn't so long ago that you raved about how my pregnancy made me more beautiful! How beautiful do you feel?"

Catherine groaned and turned her back on Bella. Sleep and food were the only things she tolerated with any good humor.

Sofia Catherine was born on February 20, 1556. The birth was without complications, quick and easy. Bella was present, along with Marie and the midwife. Catherine's water broke shortly after the midday meal and Sofia slipped into the world before dark. It was as if the little princess fully intended to command her world. She arrived without difficulty and with a cry that demanded attention. The kingdom rejoiced at the arrival of an heir, celebrating the birth of the princess. If Ambrose was disappointed the child was not a son, he didn't show it. He actually seemed delighted at the birth of his daughter.

The presence of two babies now living in the queen's quarters increased the need for more servants to attend to the needs of all involved. Catherine and Bella needed to exercise more caution in their relationship. It had been a fairly simple task for Bella to appear to have spent the night on her pallet near the cradle with James. In reality, she only stayed until he fell asleep, then put him in his cradle and moved to the queen's bed. Bella was an early riser, so she was always up with James before Marie arrived to assist the queen. With the arrival of Princess Sofia, however, new arrangements needed to be made.

They discussed various scenarios. Bella suggested that perhaps the time had arrived for her to have her own quarters. Catherine thought about having the wall to the adjacent room torn down to create a nursery for the children with ample space for the nursemaid.

"Damn it, why are we required to do this?" said Catherine suddenly. "Let's cease with the facade and require my servants to attend to both of us without question."

"Don't even entertain the thought of telling them!" Bella was adamant. "Just because you are queen does not put you above the Church's laws, or," she emphasized, "your bishop's intent to burn you at the stake!"

Catherine could be quite headstrong, however, and it was never easy to change her mind once she determined to act. But Bella's fear and anger worked to her advantage. Catherine abandoned the idea.

And so a small room across the hall from the queen's chamber was made into a nursery for both the children. Mary, the oldest daughter of a soldier in the Queen's Guard, became the caretaker for Princess Sofia. It didn't take long to determine that Mary was quite capable and was given charge of James, as well. The arrangement shifted the focus from the queen's quarters, alleviating the need for the continual presence of servants to attend to the children.

Mary was a sweet girl of thirteen. She loved children and could not have been happier at her assignment of the Princess. The care of the babies was easy for her, given her own family. As the oldest of seven children, she was responsible for a great deal in her own family's household. Although she still possessed the face of a little girl, her abilities were commendable, and appreciated by all who saw her with the children.

Chapter Twenty Nine

Shortly after the birth of Sofia, Catherine and Robert were meeting in her office. The weather was unusually cold, even for early March. They sat near the blazing fire. Ambrose's sexual exploits were the focus of their attention.

"How often does he engage in this behavior?" Catherine stood and moved closer to the fire.

"Fairly regularly. At first he limited himself to the castle. That was at the beginning of your pregnancy. But I started a few rumors about how the queen would not tolerate disloyalty among her subjects and I believe Ambrose found his supply of castle women dwindling. That was when he began cavorting in town. There are several taverns he frequents."

"Does he have any idea that he is being watched? I cannot imagine he doesn't know."

Robert was unable to hide his smile. "Actually, I believe he thinks he has fooled us. On several occasions he attempted to disguise himself."

"No! As what?" Catherine laughed.

"Once as a soldier." Robert got up to add another log on the fire. "Another time he dressed in common clothes."

"Do the townspeople recognize him?"

"I believe some of them do," he said. "Most are oblivious."

The newly added log caught and flamed. Catherine sat again and watched the flames dance in the hearth. She was quiet for a bit, thinking.

"Thank you, Robert." She stood.

Robert started toward the door. "One more thing." he said as he turned back toward her. "Do you remember my telling you about the young soldier I suspected of releasing Lady Isabella's rapist?"

"Of course. He was given leave for his grandmother's funeral, but disappeared after that. He never returned to the castle."

"We finally found him...or rather, we discovered what happened to him. He was murdered...apparently on his way back here. Reports are that he was in a fight with patrons of a tavern."

Catherine's eyebrows knit together in concern. "Do you suspect foul play?"

"Well, it is a little too convenient. I am still looking into the matter. My understanding is that he was not the sort to go looking for trouble." Robert pressed his fist to his chest, bowed and left.

That evening Catherine left the nursery after saying goodnight to James and Sofia. Ambrose was heading in that direction.

"Before you go in, may I have a word?" Catherine asked.

Ambrose nodded and fell in step beside her as she walked down the hallway. "I see no further need to share the marriage bed," she said abruptly. She didn't intend for her voice to sound as cold as it did, but she heard the coolness echo in her ears.

Ambrose stopped walking and turned toward her with a puzzled expression. "I have no difficulty understanding the importance of you producing an heir," he retorted, "but I was under the impression the marriage bed was less a 'need' and more of an enjoyment."

"Ambrose, it has come to my attention that you enjoy your sexual exploits outside our marriage." Catherine resumed walking, avoiding looking directly at him. "I am inclined to allow you to continue your indulgences and only ask that you be discreet in your dalliances, at least more so than you have been thus far."

He did not resume walking with her, and when he spoke Catherine was forced to stop, turn and look at him. He stood still, with his hands on his hips. "Perhaps," he responded with as much haughtiness as he could muster, "I would be less inclined to dally if my wife were more inclined toward her wifely duties."

Catherine glared at him and smiled a cold smile, but she did not feel cold, she felt her face flush with anger that boiled close to the surface. "My dear husband," she began, "this was a marriage of convenience from the beginning. How could you not know that? We were not in love. I arranged this charade to form a political alliance and produce an heir." Catherine wanted to stop talking, but her words seemed to have formed a life of their own. The venom continued to pour out of her mouth without caution. "You have a title and a respectable position. You have gained as much, if not more, from this marriage than you could ever have hoped to attain. Be satisfied with that. Your freedom to indulge your sexual appetite is given you. All I require is your discretion."

"I suppose that you think you are being discreet with your *lady in waiting?*" he spat.

She felt exposed and scandalized by his remark, but she stared at him with narrowing eyes and without kindness, "You are fool, Ambrose. I would suggest that you be thankful for what you have been given in this arrangement. I know your father is much relieved to have you off of his hands." After a pause she continued. "And should you ever refer to Lady Isabella in such a manner again…or ever bring up my 'wifely duties' in the future, I guarantee you will regret having a tongue." She whirled away, glad her quarters were nearby.

Chapter Thirty

Catherine was pale and shaking when she closed the doors behind her.

"My God, what is it?" Bella rushed to her.

Catherine told her about the confrontation with Ambrose.

"Do you really think it was wise to anger him?" Bella asked fearfully.

"What does it matter?" Catherine tried to make light of the situation, although she felt sick to her stomach. She reached the chair near the fireplace and nearly fell into it. "I thought it better to deal with the matter forthrightly and be done with it," she said as she collapsed.

"Don't you think this will return to haunt you…us? What about the bishop?" Bella was pacing.

Catherine took a big breath and tried to sound unconcerned, although she was quite upset. "I am less concerned with the bishop these days. He seems to have toned down his rhetoric against us since my discussion with him. Would you like some wine?" She got up to pour herself a cup. Her hands trembled so much that she could not hold the cup still, but managed to pour some wine into her cup.

"You, of all people, need always to be wary of that man!" Bella said, her voice tight. "And even if it is true that he is less of a threat, you have a child to consider! And you cannot ignore the fact that Ambrose is Sofia's father as much as you are her mother. Catherine, I truly believe that you must make some effort to placate the man. You have enough enemies without making one of your husband."

Catherine took several large swallows of wine, hoping for the sweet liquid to calm her nerves. Suddenly terrified, she sat back down, dropped her head and sighed. "I know you're right. I have known it since the words left my mouth, but I didn't know how to make things right once they were said."

Bella stopped pacing and knelt down in front of Catherine. She took the cup from Catherine's still shaking hands and placed it on the table next to them.

"Alright, alright." She put her hands on Catherine's lap and was quiet for a moment, then asked, "What does Ambrose do now that he has the title of king? What is his role in the court?"

"Nothing really. There have been no expectations placed upon him. On occasion the Council has engaged in discussion as to how to best utilize his skills. Apparently," she said with considerable sarcasm, "they are having difficulty finding a suitable position for a royal stud."

"Catherine!" Bella exclaimed. But they both started laughing and could not stop.

"Antonio," Catherine said to her secretary before she entered her office, "please call for my husband."

"Yes, Majesty."

When Ambrose entered her office he gave Catherine a curt nod and said, "Majesty."

"Please come in and sit down, Ambrose." She gestured to a comfortable chair across from her desk. He sat. Then she rose and went around her desk to sit next to him.

"Ambrose, I wish to apologize for the other day. My words were spoken without thought for your feelings. It wasn't my intention to injure you in such a cruel and thoughtless way. Can you forgive me?"

"I am not certain that I care to forgive you," he said, almost petulantly. He would not meet her eyes.

"I understand. But I ask you to consider that we are both the parents of a beautiful child, who will depend on us to love her together, whether or not we share a bed. Perhaps, for her, we can find a way to be friends."

"I will consider it." His right knee bounced up and down as he picked at a cuticle on his finger.

Neither of them spoke for a bit.

Finally, Catherine broke the silence. She stood and walked back around to the other side of her desk. "You are aware that the Privy Council is considering how best to utilize your role as king?"

"I am aware, yes."

"I wonder if you have given thought to what you might like to do as king."

Ambrose looked at her with a quizzical expression. "I was under the impression that my opinion was not of any great importance in the matter," he said, unable to disguise his resentment.

"I would like your thoughts…it is your future, after all," Catherine said as softly and kindly as possible.

"Since I had thought I would not be consulted in the matter I gave no consideration to how I might be of service. I simply thought to await my instructions," he said without emotion, almost as if he were unconnected to his life.

In a flash of insight, Catherine realized that he had never really been part of any decision-making regarding his life. When she first wrote to King Christopher about the marriage possibility, his response was that the family would be greatly honored by the joining of their two kingdoms…and he accepted on behalf of Ambrose. Catherine met privately with King Christopher in the weeks leading to the marriage. Even then Ambrose was not included in most of the discussions regarding his own wedding. It was during those discussions that Catherine became aware of what an embarrassment Ambrose was to his family. They were anxious to be rid of him. That the queen had proposed this union was a windfall for King Christopher's family. Now, as she heard Ambrose respond to her questions with such detachment, she understood that he had given up on ever having a say on his own behalf.

"Ambrose," she offered quietly, "I have given thought to your role. Understand that this is not a directive, nor is it at the advice of the Privy Council, and I am truly inviting you to think about my proposal before you make any decision." She waited before continuing. "Once Sofia is a bit older and can travel, perhaps in about a years' time, I am compelled to travel the kingdom. My father did so periodically and always returned with a more realistic perspective of what was truly happening with his subjects. I wonder if you would be willing to sit on the Privy Council in my absence?"

"In what capacity?" he asked suspiciously.

"As a regular member of the Council you will participate in the general running of the kingdom. Perhaps you might like oversight of the paper production. I noticed that it was something you seemed interested in when we toured the mill." She paused to see if he might have any reaction. He remained quiet, but appeared thoughtful. She continued. "The Council, like most, has the ability to issue decrees and create laws. Ultimately, as queen, I have final say, but as much as possible, I allow the Council the freedom to manage the kingdom." Catherine knew that a position for Ambrose on the Council might prove dangerous for her, especially if she were unable to make any kind of amends with him, but she could think of no other way to determine his true abilities...and alliances, than to put him in a position where he would be required to participate, but not lead. A year should give her the time necessary to assess where his loyalties lie. By then she should be able to tell if it would be wise to give him authority to lead the Council in her absence.

"I don't think I am interested," was all Ambrose said.

"Ambrose," she said gently, "I really do not know all that much about you. I don't know where your skills or your interests lie. I want to know. Whether or not either of us is happy about how things have turned out, we are husband and wife for the rest of our lives." Catherine got up and walked back around to the other side of her desk, sitting next to him again as she talked. "Will you at least sit in on Council meetings for a while to see what goes on? You may find that you are interested in some aspect of what the Council does."

"I will consider it," was all Ambrose said.

Much could happen in a year.

Catherine was not inclined to take the evening meal in the great hall. Although customary for the court to dine together, since Bella's arrival Catherine preferred the evening meal in her quarters. At Bella's insistence, they began to join the castle residents. There, the king and queen sat at the head table, with Bella seated next to the queen on her left side. As Bella predicted, the simple change seemed to have the effect of softening Ambrose's anger at Catherine. One evening Ambrose addressed Catherine's proposal.

"I have been giving thought the Privy Council."

"Ah," said Catherine, actually delighted. "And what do you think?"

"I believe that I might enjoy such a position."

Catherine smile. "I am glad, Ambrose. I will notify the Privy Council that they need not trouble themselves with finding a role for you."

"Thank you."

"If it suits you," she added, "I should like to present this as your request, to which I give my wholehearted approval."

Even with his previous lack of involvement in any political arena, Catherine hoped that Ambrose recognized what she was offering. If the request came from him, as opposed to being at the direction of the queen, he would be seen as less a puppet and more master of his own life. He turned to her and gave her a grateful smile, as warm as she had seen in some time. "Thank you."

Bella slipped her hand under the tablecloth and gave Catherine's hand a squeeze.

Chapter Thirty One

The children were growing. James was almost three and Sofia was one. Ambrose had served on the Privy Council for almost a year, and Catherine noted that he seemed to come alive when dealing with issues of architecture; he also seemed to greatly enjoy his role overseeing the production of paper. He was a neutral addition to the Council, but it was difficult to ascertain whether this was genuine neutrality or if Ambrose just kept his true thoughts to himself.

Things in Rome had changed much in the past year since Pope Paul IV came to power following the quick and untimely death of Pope Marcellus II. Catherine's heart sank when she heard of the election of Marcellus's' successor. He was a man so vile that all thoughts of going back to Rome to plead for help vanished.

Prior to becoming Pope, Cardinal Giovanni Pietro Carafa played powerful roles in Rome and throughout Europe. At sixty eight years of age he became Cardinal and convinced Pope Paul III to stamp out heresy. He offered a "New Inquisition" that was designed to eliminate heretics not only in Spain and France, but throughout Italy and all of Rome.

Carafa, as Cardinal, assumed leadership of the Inquisition. He personally oversaw the building of prisons and torture chambers for heretics, ensuring that the cells and implements of torture met his standards for breaking those accused of heresy. At one time he proudly stated, "Even if my own father were a heretic, I would gather the wood to burn him."

As Pope Paul IV, Carafa was determined to show no leniency, no mercy to heretics. His primary targets were Protestant reformers, those guilty of sexual misconduct, and Jews. Although twenty three previous Popes had guaranteed the protection of Jews, Pope Paul IV abolished those protections and created ghettoes into which he banished them.

No one was safe from the threat of interrogation, imprisonment, torture, or death.

The worst of it for Catherine and the kingdom of Montalcino was that Pope Paul IV was cousin to her own detestable council member, Carfaggi.

Father Tim shared more and more stories of torture and execution. His brother, Thomas, travelled widely and kept Tim apprised of the Inquisition "progress" in other countries. Montalcino was not the only Kingdom under pressure to rid itself of heretics; many countries and kingdoms lived in terror under this Pope.

Catherine knew of a particular case in Venice. A young university student who accepted the teachings of Martin Luther was imprisoned for over a year. He didn't oppose the Catholic Church, only favored the teachings of Luther. For this, the young man sat in prison. Under a different pope, the young man might have eventually been freed. But upon becoming Pope, Carafa instituted a new form of execution, boiling alive in a vat of oil, tar and turpentine. The young student was made an example and became the first to experience this form of punishment.

Catherine was so enraged by the crimes of the Church that there were times she thought about pushing more openly against the Inquisition. At one point, when torturing women to get them to confess to being witches was banned, Catherine hoped that all torture might fall by the wayside. Now, with Carafa in power, torture was more common place, and it was encouraged in the most sadistic of ways.

During Sofia's first year, Sunday Mass with Father Tim in the village of Castiglione d' Orcia continued. Catherine, Robert, Bella and Father Tim continued to strategize ways to help the innocent victims. But, Catherine remained frustrated by her inability to accomplish more. Since Pope Paul, their ability to help the accused became less and less effective. Inquisitors became more ruthless in their attempts to convict heretics. In their fear, people were less able to defend themselves and the number of executions in Montalcino rose.

Under Carafa, the types of attacks that Bella's family had experienced were spreading like wildfire. Bishop Capshaw remained complacent and did nothing to discourage the illegal activity. Even if he wanted to investigate and stop the rogue attacks, he became far too overwhelmed with the increasing number of interrogations. Between the interrogations, his participation on the Privy Council, and his ecclesiastical duties, he could not be bothered with hunting the fanatics. And Carfaggi continued to breathe down his neck to interrogate more accused heretics.

"Majesty," he replied when she asked him about his delegate at a recent Privy Council meeting, "I have dismissed him. I have much more need of an assistant to aid me in the interrogation process than in trying to hunt this group that is so elusive."

Since Carafa's rise to Pope, the bishop was now interrogating nearly one person every day. His passion, if he ever really had any for this aspect of his role, began to diminish. His questions took on more of a rote, list-like, presentation. Although his questions were pointed and intimidating, he lacked interest in the outcome. Even if the evidence presented was questionable, he sentenced based on the evidence alone. He no longer cared about whether or not he felt any conviction about the crime or the person he sentenced, or whether he was sentencing to imprisonment or death. There were exceptions, however.

The bishop became particularly harsh with crimes of a sexual nature. He doubled his efforts and intensity with regard to sexual aberrations following a recent visit from a Vatican emissary. Catherine knew about the visit because the bishop was absent from a Council meeting. Lord Carfaggi was absent that day, as well. Robert discovered the visitor from Rome was under direct orders from Pope Paul, Carfaggi's cousin, to meet with Bishop Capshaw. Although details of the meeting were unknown, Catherine detected a change in the bishop after the emissary left Montalcino. She sensed fear, and that surprised her.

She was unaware of how much the change in Rome, from Pope Julius, then Pope Marcellus to Pope Paul IV, terrified Bishop Capshaw. His reasons, known only to him, and Carfaggi, in the Kingdom of Montalcino, were known by many in Rome.

When Thomas Capshaw had learned of Carafa's election, he became violently ill. He knew he needed to convince the watching eyes of the papacy that he was a changed man, no longer engaged in his sinful ways. Still, he worried that Carafa would come after him. Since becoming Pope Paul IV, Carafa was even imprisoning Cardinals.

Chapter Thirty Two

Ambrose's involvement on the Privy Council, failed to establish his loyalties. If he had any, they were not apparent to Catherine. He seemed, more often than she was comfortable, to side with the Bishop when the Council was divided on issues, but these seemed largely to be regarding matters of land disputes. At times, he opposed the Bishop, and his opposition appeared to center around using additional kingdom monies to fund Inquisition expenses. The Church, including the bishop and priests, were supported by the kingdom through taxes. Catherine was hopeful. Ambrose voted against an increase in taxes for the bishop to hire additional assistance for Inquisition interrogations. "Perhaps Ambrose might be his own man, after all," she thought.

Catherine wanted to give Ambrose a trial run at leading the Privy Council, so she arranged a pilgrimage to nearby Bolsena to visit the Grotto of Santa Cristina.

The descendants of Monaldeschi della Cervara still ruled Bolsena, and Catherine and Bella were guests of the family in the fortress that had been built in stages from the 11th through the 14th centuries.

Their rooms in the castle were comfortable and offered them spectacular views of the Lago di Bolsena, an enormous lake born of an ancient volcano.

"I am not certain why," she told Bella shortly after they arrived, "but the story of Cristina of Bolsena intrigues me."

"What do you know about her?" Bella asked as they wandered the castle.

"Only that she was a child martyr subjected to years of torture in the third century."

"Who tortured her, and why?" Bella was aghast.

"Her father did. He was a wealthy pagan magistrate, who was furious at her conversion to the Christian. She was submitted to many horrors. I remember they put her in a pit of snakes, and even threw her in a furnace once. After her father's death, his successors continued to torment Cristina, hoping to get her to give up her faith."

"Why, on earth, do you want to know more about such a cruel, horrible story?" Bella wanted to know.

Catherine smiled at Bella as she answered, "I suppose because the legend holds that Cristina came through all of her tortures unharmed. I am fascinated by the possibility that a child's faith could be that strong, that unwavering. I wonder what gives a saint that kind of faith."

"What you wonder," laughed Bella, "is how you can get some of that faith for yourself!" They walked to one of the walls near the top of the Borgo and stood looking out at the lake. Bella asked, "How did she eventually die?"

"By an arrow through her heart."

"Ah, so she met her end anyway? Too bad. I would have liked to have met her, although she would be quite old by now," Bella teased.

"I am ignoring you." Catherine said.

Catherine and Bella joined a few other pilgrims as the basilica bells chimed. An old priest, along with a nun, led the pilgrims to the altar in the center of the Grotto where the tomb of Saint Cristina was located. There, a basalt stone revealed impressions of two small feet said to be made by Cristina as she stood on the stone. A new, recently built, architectural Ciborium with great, pink, marble columns, housed the stone with the saint's footprints along with a Reliquary containing another stone. The additional stone was the result of yet another miracle that took place in the Grotto of Santa Cristina. In 1263, a Bohemian priest, plagued with doubts as to the real presence of Christ in the Eucharist, was on his way to Rome. He stopped in Bolsena and was saying Mass on the tomb of Cristina. At the moment of consecration blood began to drip from the host, staining the altar cloth and some of the stones in the floor. The corporal and stone, both blood-stained, were housed beneath the new Ciborium.

After Mass Catherine and Bella walked the well-worn stone path to the shore of Lake Bolsena. Catherine looked out at the Isola Bisentina. It was all that remained of the volcanic cone. The island, though small, had a long history and was home to many chapels and a prison known as the della Malta.

"Do you want to go to the island?" Bella asked as they wandered the empty shoreline.

"No." Catherine was firm. "Although I am certain it's beautiful, the history is not one that draws me."

"What do you know, my love?"

Catherine stopped and turned to look at the little island. Her face clouded as she recalled stories her father told her about the many people who had been imprisoned there.

"There is a prison on the island at the very bottom of a tower, many meters down. Many accused of heresy were lowered from the tower to the prison below and left to rot there, including an abbot and even a group of monks.

"The island was also home, for many summers, of Alessandro Farnese," Catherine said with some disgust.

"Pope Paul?"

"The third, yes."

Bella linked her arm through Catherine's and propelled her back up the hill to the bustling town of Bolsena. As they made their way back up the hill, Bella said, "It is amazing to me that such a sweet, beautiful place could be home to such a violent history."

"It does cause one to wonder," Catherine shook her head, "when a Pope like Paul the fourth actually creates an institution to revive the violent annihilation of those considered heretics. How can they justify such brutality? How do they reconcile it with the teachings of Christ? I am baffled."

Bella led Catherine back to the Rocca, to the glacis of the Fortress. There they sat, enjoying the afternoon sun as they sipped wine and nibbled on fresh bread drizzled with olive oil. As they looked out over the lake and the town of Bolsena, Catherine said, "I often wonder why Christ has not intervened to stop all of the ghastly things done in His name."

The remainder of their time in Bolsena was spent relaxing, walking along the lake, and making love without the worry of the kingdom intruding. It was the first time since inheriting the throne that Catherine fully allowed herself to shed her royal duties.

They returned to Montalcino after two weeks in Bolsena. According to Lord Giovanni, Ambrose did well managing the Privy Council. They met just once while Catherine was gone, but nothing notable arose in her absence.

Catherine made plans to begin to tour the kingdom. Her first visit was to be Pienza, which was little more than fifteen miles from Montalcino. Traveling with a large group, it might take two days, but a single rider on a fast horse could reach Catherine in a few hours. Lord Giovanni would be able to reach her if necessary.

Her entourage consisted of herself and Bella with the two children, Mary, the children's caretaker, Marie and two additional servants, two cooks, Robert, and a complement of ten soldiers.

As the soldiers and servants prepared for the trip, a general atmosphere of excitement filled the air. Most in the party had not accompanied the monarchy on such a venture. The cook's wagon was filled to the brim with food, flour, grains, cheeses and olives. Several barrels of wine were packed. A supply wagon carried everything they might need.

The morning of departure brought the castle residents to the courtyard to see them off. There was much hugging and kissing. They finally left in a cloud of dust at midmorning.

Nestled in the foothills of the Apennines, Montalcino was rough terrain. But the mountains were beautiful in spring, and spirits were high. It had been a long time since the Monarchy traveled the kingdom.

Even at their young ages, James and Sofia sensed that they were on an adventure.

Catherine hadn't been convinced they should take the children, but Bella had insisted.

"I have no intention of leaving James anywhere near that bishop of yours when I am not here. And you should be wary of him regarding your own daughter."

And so the children accompanied them.

Bella opted to ride a horse beside Catherine. Sometimes, James rode on the horse with his mother. Mostly, the children stayed in the carriage with Mary and Marie. But for the carriage and the wagons with their supplies, the journey would have been much quicker. No one minded. The pace was relaxed.

Camp life was surprisingly enjoyable. The first night, Bella and Catherine were set up in a fairly large tent with two down-filled pads for sleeping. The children and Mary had their own tent. The rest of the party shared tents as they wished, although the soldiers slept on the ground surrounding the party in a wide perimeter around the group. Robert slept in a small tent set directly near the Queen and Bella.

The campfire provided warmth and a good spot to sit and tell stories. Following the first evening meal, Catherine encouraged storytelling and enjoyed listening to the laughter and conversations that hummed around the campsite. Once conversations and stories began to fade, Bella brought out her harp to play. She had begun to make up melodies to the Psalms. Her music was a perfect end to a long day of traveling. James and Sofia fell asleep listening to her. The rest of the camp was close to follow their lead, save the soldiers on watch.

The night before they reached Pienza, the activity around the campfire was a bit more subdued. The second day of traveling was more difficult as one of the wagons broke a wheel and needed to be repaired before they moved on. Most everyone was tired by the time they made camp. As the meal drew to a close Remy, one of Robert's soldiers, asked, "Your Majesty, have you ever been to Pienza?"

"Once," she smiled. "I came with the King when I was twelve years old. Things were different then. It will be interesting to see if Pienza has changed much."

"What was it like, Majesty?" Mary was eager to know as much as she could about the world.

Catherine leaned back into her chair. Her head lolled back. Her eyes closed. When she opened them again she said, "I thought Pienza the most charming place I had ever seen. Perhaps that was because it was the very first time I had traveled outside of Montalcino, but I remember everything about that visit."

Everyone settled around the campfire as Catherine began her reminiscence of Pienza.

"My most vivid memory was of the flowers. The homes were nestled together much like the Borgo in Montalcino, but every single windowsill had a window box overflowing with colorful flowers. You could smell them as you passed by. And the streets were lined with vendors all selling different types of flowers. There was color everywhere I looked. I remember thinking that someone should paint a picture of all that beauty. And like an answer to a prayer, as we moved along the main street, there it was; an oil painting of Pienza, hanging in a shop. I made the king buy it for me. It hangs in the entrance to the Great Hall."

"That is Pienza?" Mary asked. "I love that painting. I always stop to admire it on my way to meals."

"That is Pienza as I remember her. One of the other things I remember is the people, full of joy and love. Of course people always greeted the King well, but there it felt as if they were really glad of his visit. Almost like children excited for the return of their father from a long journey. So much laughter. Such happiness…"

The queen's voice drifted off.

"Are you implying that we need to be more exuberant in our greetings to you, Majesty?" someone joked.

The queen laughed, too. "I would never compare the company here to anyplace else. But I do hope you get the opportunity to experience the Pienza of my memories. You won't forget it, I assure you!"

Pienza had a town hall, surrounded by a Borgo containing smaller homes and shops. Cobblestone streets wove out and around the town hall. There were slightly larger, individual houses on the outskirts of the moderately sized town. Like most of the towns and villages in the kingdom, farms spread out past those. Because of its location, still in the foothills, farms were sparse, as growing conditions were difficult. Most farms made their earnings from raising animals for food.

As they moved closer to the town the countryside rolled with green hills and wildflowers. Here and there they passed a farmhouse. Goats seemed the primary livestock.

Robert sent a small band of his soldiers ahead to prepare the inhabitants for the arrival of their queen, while the group set up camp on the outskirts of the town. Catherine did not wish to rely on the hospitality of the town's people. Her plan was to visit with the local officials, the town priest and as many villagers as possible. Beyond that, because she didn't know what to expect, she left her plan vague. She knew an Inquisitor had been here for months in the past year, but she had only information from the bishop about the results of that visit, and his reports were suspect. Information from other sources was limited during the winter months, so Catherine was glad she decided to find out for herself how the village fared.

Catherine, Robert, Bella and several soldiers rode into Pienza late morning. They were to meet with the local government officials and then enjoy a midday meal with them prior to meeting with the local priest. While she did not know what to expect, she wasn't prepared for what greeted her…or rather what did not greet her.

As they entered the main street of Pienza, the first thing Catherine noticed was the absence of people. There were few villagers lined up to greet her, and they were reserved in their greeting. They bowed and welcomed her, but with reserve and suspicion. The smiling, open, friendly people she remembered had been replaced by stiff, frightened citizens.

The second thing Catherine noticed was the total absence of flowers. It was spring, yet not a single flower adorned a windowsill. Pienza was grey and lifeless.

She almost cried.

The party continued through the main street on horseback.

"If Pienza could change this much in such a short time, I fear for what is happening in the rest of the kingdom," Catherine whispered to Robert.

"It does not bode well, Majesty," Robert said sadly.

"I would never believe this was the place you described so beautifully," Bella said with fear in her eyes. "I am afraid for what you will discover here."

Just outside the town center they came upon a gallows and a heavy charred beam jutting up from the ground. The company halted as the queen held up her hand. Catherine stared at the charred remains of the beam, and closed her eyes. At first, she was overcome by visions of the burning she had been forced to witness with her father. She banished the memory quickly replacing it with prayers for those who were executed there. "Heavenly Father," she prayed silently, "give peace to every man, woman and child murdered here in your name. Help me to fight this wickedness with the strength and spirit of these innocents. Lead the way, I beg You. I cannot do this alone."

The local government was comprised of the Chief Magistrate, the town sheriff, the town council and, directly related to the size of the town, any number of under sheriffs. In this case, the only people present were the Magistrate, sheriff and three men from the town council. The local priest was also invited to join the gathering. They met in a moderately sized room in the offices of the Chief Magistrate. The room was sparsely furnished with a wooden table and ten mismatched chairs. There was a table with a pitcher of water and several cups to one side.

Once everyone settled, Catherine addressed the group.

"Gentlemen, my father, King Edward, taught me the importance of visiting the villages of Montalcino. Pienza is the first of the kingdom I am visiting. I remember well my visit here with the king a few short years ago." She paused and looked around at the men seated around the table, then she walked to a window that overlooked the village square. "I am disheartened to see the changes that have taken place in Pienza since then. Please share with me your opinions and what you perceive as the reasons for such changes."

There followed an uncomfortable silence. None of the men present looked her in the eye. Finally, the Magistrate, because he was the leading member of the town, offered, "Majesty, you must forgive our poor reception. It is no reflection upon our affection for you, or our memory of your dear father. Pienza has fallen on hard times."

Catherine, knowing that the hard times did not relate to financial struggles, realized that they were concerned that she was disappointed in her reception.

"Please don't misunderstand. My concern is not due to lack of fanfare celebrating my arrival. Nothing could be further from the truth. I only want to know how the good people of Pienza fare, given the changes in Rome, and the recent visit of the Inquisition officials." Catherine waited patiently, knowing that it might take courage to speak up, if they did at all. She did not know these people and did not know who might be a spy for the Inquisition. She knew to be cautious in how she presented herself. The danger was in appearing to be opposed to the Inquisition.

"Majesty," the sheriff said, "you will be hard pressed to find anyone in Pienza who has not been directly affected by the interrogations, imprisonments or executions this past year. The Church has done its job well."

It was a safe enough statement to make without implicating himself, but Catherine heard the distress in his voice. She decided to change her tact.

"What is the current population of Pienza?" asked Catherine.

"Prior to the arrival of the Inquisitor, the population was approximately two thousand, Majesty," answered the Magistrate.

"And now, good Magistrate?" Catherine looked at him.

"Unclear, Majesty. Quite apart from the executions, many fled to hide in the mountains. Some hide within their own homes. Because it is the duty of the government to administer the punishments of the Inquisitor, our own people live in fear of us. We haven't been able to determine an accurate count of our citizens since the Inquisitor left us."

"How many citizens of Pienza were executed for heresy?" asked Catherine.

"Seventeen for heresy, fourteen for witchcraft and twelve for sexual aberrations, Majesty."

Bella attempted to stifle a small cry. She failed. Every eye in the room turned to her as she covered her mouth with a shaking hand. She blinked away her horror, took a deep breath and apologized for the interruption. Bella, closed her eyes and lowered her head.

The queen swallowed her concern for Bella and turned back to the Magistrate. "How long was the Inquisitor here?"

"Two and one half months, Your Majesty."

"How many imprisoned?" she asked.

"Thirty four, Majesty."

"How many interrogations?"

"Approximately two per day for the seventy eight days the Inquisitor was here. Some days more, some days less, Majesty."

The sadness in the Magistrate's voice seeped into Catherine's soul. She looked around the table at the men who sat there, and she could see that each of them had been broken. She knew she took a risk in asking her next question, but she needed to ask.

"Were any of you interrogated?"

All of the men at the table shifted uncomfortably in their seats. Almost in unison, they turned to look at one of the Council members. He was a short, unwell looking soul with a look of such sadness that Catherine was not surprised to hear it come through in his voice. He looked up at her.

"Majesty," he said, "I was interrogated by the Inquisitor. My wife and daughter were accused of witchcraft..." the man stopped speaking. Although Catherine was afraid to hear what happened to his wife and daughter, she asked, "And what became of the investigation?"

The councilman opened his mouth to answer, but no words came.

"Majesty," the sheriff offered, "Councilman Bruggia's wife and daughter were convicted of witchcraft and burned at the stake."

Catherine expected to be enraged by the things that she heard, but instead, she was overwhelmed with sorrow. She sat back in her seat and looked around her again at this broken town council.

"Father," she finally turned to the town priest, "were you present at the interrogations?"

"I was during some of the questioning, Majesty, but I was not active in the interrogation process," he answered.

"Did you know the Inquisitor prior to his arrival in Pienza?"

"No, Majesty. He was sent from Rome and not someone with whom I was acquainted."

"Were you asked for your opinion during the interrogations, or after?" asked the Queen.

"I tried, on several occasions, to offer my opinion of the accused, Majesty." Here the priest paused and looked around. I...when..." the priest seemed fearful of continuing.

"Father," said the queen, "I am not here to judge or condemn either the Inquisitor or the good leaders of Pienza. I am here to seek information about what is happening in my kingdom. While I understand your reluctance to speak, I beg you to be truthful. There will be no reprisal from me." She hoped that this would give him the courage to speak openly about what happened. If he believed her and was not afraid of her condemnation, then the only reason for him to hold back would be fear of one of the other members seated at the table. Since she would be meeting with him privately after the meal, his openness now would give her information regarding the rest of the Council. If he spoke openly in front of them, then she would know that she was in reasonably safe company.

"Majesty," the priest ventured, "I tried, initially, to defend many of the accused, offering my knowledge of them as good Catholics. The Inquisitor accused me of interfering with the interrogation process. It was made clear to me that my opinions were irrelevant." The priest looked down. Quietly, he said, "I was not brave enough to offer my opinion after that."

Catherine looked at the young priest, then around at the rest of the men at the table. "You are all brave in ways that have yet to be defined," she said, "and we have all become cowards in the face of this new Inquisition."

The meeting lasted a very short time. After that a meal, light refreshments only, was brought into the council room. Everyone picked at the foods. No one was hungry. Following the meal Catherine, Robert and Bella met privately with Father Guiseppi. They followed the priest to his small chapel. He was as broken as the rest of Pienza, yet responsible to continue to serve both the population and the church. It was clearly a role that demanded much from him. In his eyes, Catherine saw that he was haunted by all that happened.

"Father, tell me about Councilman Bruggia's ordeal," Catherine said as they sat in pews at the back of the chapel.

The priest shook his head, his eyes closed. He took a deep breath and looked up at her. "As a member of the Council, Bruggia has made enemies. Who does not in a position of authority?" He shrugged his shoulders. "He angered several local residents when he sided with a friend over land rights. My suspicion is that the angered residents found their revenge when the Inquisitor arrived, although the accusers were never identified."

As Father Guiseppi paused briefly, Bella wandered up to the altar out of hearing range.

"Lady Bruggia and her daughter were no more witches than you and I," he continued. "There was no defense because no one knew what the exact charges were, or who the accusers were. The women were tortured until they confessed that they were witches. They even claimed to drink the blood of animals in secret ceremonies. Their screams could be heard throughout the town." He began speaking softly so that only the queen might hear him. "Their torturers were not from here. They came with the Inquisitor. Councilman Bruggia was forced to watch."

Robert moved closer to where the priest and Catherine were sitting so he could hear what was being said.

"After the women confessed, they were burned. Poor Bruggia has not left his home since. Today is the first time anyone has seen him in public since the executions. He only came out of respect for you, Majesty. He will, in all likelihood, return to his home and die a slow death. He is, even now, only a shadow of his former self."

Catherine dropped her head and sighed deeply. "I am ashamed of what my Church has become," although shame is not the feeling that flooded her body. She was terrified by the story she had just heard. "I wish I could find some way to restore peace to the people of Pienza," Catherine sighed.

"Majesty, you may not feel like it is much, but I tell you that just being able to share their stories with you may give your people more comfort than you imagine. Just knowing how you feel has given me solace. It is important to know that we are not alone."

"I would be happy to meet with some of the families that have suffered. Please make the arrangements."

"I would be honored, Majesty. Although I cannot speak to who might be willing to share their story with you, I am glad to arrange the meetings."

Over the next four days Catherine met with many families. Only she and Robert ever returned to the village after the first day. When they returned to camp that first evening, Bella told Catherine that she would prefer to stay in camp with the children for the remainder of their time in Pienza.

"I don't think I will be much help as you meet with people. Perhaps it would be better for both of us if I stayed here." Catherine readily agreed, anxious to spare Bella the pain of reliving her own ordeal.

One story was much like the others. Grief and sorrow stacked upon more grief and more sorrow. Catherine returned each evening to the campsite wondering how the kingdom could survive.

As the villagers spoke to her, she felt, more than heard, the underlying anguish and fear that had replaced joy and life in the Pienzans. She noticed that those who were spared torture, imprisonment and execution did not appear any happier than those who endured, or watched their families suffer the torments. But what surprised Catherine most was that those who admitted to being the accusers, whether they accused of their own accord or out of fear that they would be the next victim, had the same vacant, lifeless expressions as those who suffered the unspeakable.

The Turano family, or what was left of them, had owned the now vacant shop where Catherine's father purchased the painting of Pienza for her.

Peter Turano arrived at the chapel with three of his five remaining children; a boy of thirteen and ten year old twin girls. The children stepped forward and bowed to the queen. Their father knelt, "Majesty." Catherine greeted them and invited everyone to sit. Father Guiseppi sat protectively near the children, who seemed comfortable in his presence.

Father Guiseppi had given Catherine some of the details of the family's ordeal before they arrived. She knew that there had been two older siblings, boys, who were executed by beheading. Their mother was burned at the stake.

"Signore Turano," Catherine began, "Father Guiseppi has told me some of what has befallen your family. I am interested to know a bit more, if you are willing to share with me."

"I will do my best, Majesty."

"Do you know how your family came to be accused of heresy? Do you know the exact charges?"

He leaned over, his shoulders drooping, and rested his elbows on his knees. "My two oldest sons often travelled the countryside in search of new artwork for our shop. Mostly, we carried unknown, local artisans, but the boys enjoyed venturing farther and farther from home. They both became enamored of the larger cities. Two years ago they pressed me to go to Venice. I saw no reason …."

As their father paused in his story, one of the twins went over to him and wrapped her arms around his neck. "Papa."

He looked at her with the most tender affection, placed his hand on her cheek and said, "I am fine, Cara Mia. You can go back and sit."

The child shook her head and stayed at her father's side.

He continued. "Venice captured the hearts of my sons. When they returned home they were excited about some books they found at a small shop on the outskirts of the city. One of the books was authored by Martin Luther."

"His books have been prohibited." Catherine shook her head sadly.

"It was as if the Inquisitor knew about the visit to Venice, and the purchase of the books. Our home was searched and the books found. My sons were arrested. We were all interrogated…even my little ones."

Catherine looked over at the two children still sitting with Father Guiseppi. She smiled and held her hands out for them to come to her. They hesitated and Father Guiseppi said, "It's fine, go ahead."

The children took her hands and sat next to the queen as their father looked on and smiled.

"The little ones, fortunately, had no knowledge of the meaning of the books. We, my wife and I, did not know what happened to the boys after they were interrogated. When we found out that the boys were to be executed, my wife insisted on speaking with the Inquisitor. I fear she defended them in a way that angered the Inquisitor. Though I cannot say for certain, I believe she was executed as an example." Signore Turano stopped and closed his eyes momentarily. "She was a devout Catholic, Majesty. There was not a soul who knew her who did not know that. She was no heretic, but she loved her sons. Her sin was that she tried to protect them." He swallowed hard, holding back his tears, though a few leaked from his eyes and splashed onto the floor.

"She was burned...and the books with her. Then my sons were executed."

"Were you forced to watch?" Catherine asked.

"I would have been there anyway. I could not protect them any longer, but I did not want their last moments of life spent only in the company of their tormentors. But the little ones were forced."

Catherine looked down at the two children sitting on either side of her. She pulled them close to her and kissed the tops of their heads.

"Is there anything I can do for you and your family, Signore Turano?"

"Thank you, Majesty. We are fine. We have one another."

Robert accompanied Catherine to Pienza for the visits, but he did not remain present with the families as they met with her. Sometimes, Father Guiseppi stayed, when the families requested his presence, at other times Catherine met alone with the families. Robert was always near, guarding the premises.

At first, Catherine shared some of what she heard during the day on the short trip back to the campsite. After two days, however, she offered nothing of her visits. They rode the two miles back to the camp in silence. Each evening she was more tired, more sad and withdrawn. She began collapsing in on herself.

The atmosphere in the camp took on a heavier mood. The lightness and excitement of the adventure was replaced by the solemn reality of the queen's burden. As Catherine entered the camp each evening it was as if a dark cloud of despair moved in with her. Even James and Sofia felt the oppressive weight.

Catherine forced smiles and greeted the servants and soldiers, but she could not disguise the heaviness enveloped her. She sat at the campfire as before, but her gaze disappeared into the fire. Nightly stories lost their animation and conversations were quieter. There was no laughter.

Catherine's comforts were the children and Bella's harp. She was able to unlock her gaze from the fire when Sofia and James climbed into her lap. Sofia nuzzled her face into Catherine's neck and played with her mother's hair. Sometimes she fell asleep with her little fist wrapped around a long lock of Catherine's hair. James laid on her other arm, curling up to listen to his mother play the harp. Somehow, the weight and warmth of the two children brought Catherine back from where she had gone. She felt grounded by the babies, and a little less adrift in her melancholy.

When they finally left Pienza it was with a different queen. Catherine spoke when spoken to, but otherwise disappeared beneath a mantle of pain. She began to look like the very people she had visited. Bella knew that look. Bella had lived within the walls of that same place and knew Catherine needed help to find a way out, or she might be lost forever.

When the group set up camp the first evening after leaving Pienza, Catherine wandered off to be alone. Bella followed a short time later. She found Robert some distance from Catherine. He was watching, but did not intrude on her. Catherine sat on a boulder near a stream and, as had become her habit these past days, stared at nothing in particular.

Bella stood next to Robert. "Have you ever seen her like this?"

"No, Lady. She has gone somewhere I do not know."

Bella heard the worry in his voice. "I know the place. And when she returns we will need to be ready."

Robert looked at her gratefully and whispered, "Please help her."

Bella went to Catherine. "Where have you gone, my love?"

"I am here," Catherine sighed but did not look up.

"In body perhaps, but you left the essence of your spirit with the people of Pienza."

Catherine didn't respond. Bella continued, "Catherine, tell me what you are thinking. Tell me what you are feeling!"

Catherine turned her gaze to Bella. "Nothing." The look in her eyes was dead.

Bella knelt in front of her. "Talk to me. Tell me what is going on, please. I cannot stand to have you so far away from me."

Without looking at her Catherine said, "There is nothing to tell. There is nothing to do."

"What do you mean?" Bella pressed. "You just spent four days listening to people pour out their sorrows to you. That is something!"

"No, it isn't," Catherine said almost absently. "I could do nothing but listen, helplessly."

Bella reached out and grasped Catherine's hands. "You gave them your heart, my love. Heart is what has been missing for them. Don't underestimate how much that must have meant to them."

"They have lost everything, and I don't have the ability or the power to replace what they lost."

Bella stood. "So, will you be lost with them? Do you need to join them in such a way as to lose yourself, as well? Catherine! Look at me. Come back to me!"

"I have nothing to say...nothing to give." And she lowered her gaze even further to the ground in front of her feet.

"You must...you will! I will not lose you. Have I not suffered enough? Have I not been where you are now?"

Catherine's gaze returned to the stream. Bella watched her retreat and her heart sank. They stayed like that for a time, Bella standing and Catherine sitting. Finally, Bella sat next to Catherine and said softly, "When I was lost in the place where you are now, it was you who found your way in and led me out. I have tried these past nights to give you time to feel the grief and heartache of your subjects. And I have tried to comfort you, bring you back to yourself, our children, me. But, you've locked yourself into that place and will let no one in. Is there nothing I can do or say to help?"

Catherine said nothing, but shook her head as she continued to stare into the stream.

"Very well." Bella stood to leave. "I shall leave you there if that is what you wish."

Bella waited to see if her words had any impact on Catherine, but she continued to stare into the water. Bella was scared, but decided to confront Catherine.

"But know this, my queen, it's a coward's place." Her voice was steady, tinged with anger as she dropped the challenge at Catherine's feet. "And you are a coward to stay there. I will not stand by and watch you cower behind the walls of despair you have built around yourself. I thought you were stronger than that. You, Queen Catherine, have abandoned us all. Perhaps your bishop is right, women do not have the strength to lead in times of crisis. It's too bad. I thought to be part of proving him wrong." Bella turned to leave, but Catherine leapt to her feet, grabbed her by the arm and spun her around.

Catherine's face was full of fury. Her nostrils flared. Her jaw clenched. The rage in her eyes startled Bella, but even in her brief response of fear, Bella was glad to see anything but the dead look she had become accustomed to these past days. Catherine's chest heaved, her breath burst in waves of anger. Bella waited, staring her down. Catherine's grip on her arm was painful, but not nearly as painful as the loss of her beloved this past week. She held Catherine's glare and finally said, "What will you do, continue to hide behind your hopelessness, or stand and fight for your people?"

Catherine released Bella with a cry of outrage. Her scream echoed throughout the valley as she fell to her knees. She picked up a small boulder with both hands and slammed it into the ground before her as she released another scream. As Bella and Robert both watched, Catherine lifted and pounded the boulder into the ground again and again. Her cries accompanied the pounding until she was spent and could lift the boulder no longer. Too exhausted to continue, Catherine collapsed onto the boulder and sobbed as though she might never stop. Bella knelt and pulled Catherine into her arms, letting her weep until she could cry no more. Robert stood watch, his own tears blurring his vision. His queen was back.

Chapter Thirty Three

The plan was to return home after Pienza, but the queen was in need of Father Tim. Robert sent soldiers back to the castle to inform both Ambrose and Lord Giovanni of the delay. He changed the route to bypass the more difficult terrain in order to reach Castiglione d' Orcia. They made good time. It took two and one-half days to reach the village.

Father Tim was surprised, but glad to see the queen. He invited Catherine, Bella and Robert to share his humble quarters during their stay, but they declined. They had everything they needed in camp, and did not want to be far from the children.

Their regular visits to Castiglione d' Orcia had given Catherine a false impression of how much the Inquisition impacted other towns. She was familiar with life in Castiglione d' Orcia, and the difference between it and Pienza was striking.

Father Timothy dined with them. Camp dinners were simple fare, but the supply wagons carried a table and chairs for the queen and a few guests. As dinner drew to a close, everyone wandered off to other campfires or prepared for sleep. Father Timothy was left with Catherine, Bella and Robert.

"Majesty," he addressed Catherine, "while I am delighted at your surprise visit, I can see in your eyes that you are deeply troubled. What has happened?"

The small secluded campfire around which they sat seemed to envelope them in a miniature world of their own. Flames flickered, casting shadows around and between them. The smoke of the fire rose straight up, but then briefly bent toward Catherine engulfing her. She closed her eyes and waited for the pillar of smoke to change direction again. When it did, she opened her eyes and looked into the flames trying to figure out how to start.

She wasn't sure where to begin. She still felt quite fragile and a little afraid the hopelessness might take her over again. She worked diligently to keep it at bay, but it was a stealthy enemy following her every movement and shadowing every thought, every breath. If she wasn't cautious, she might inhale the wispy, featherlike edge, then it would be too late and the cloud would consume her again.

Bella reached out and placed her hand on Catherine's arm.

Catherine began. "We have just come from Pienza. The things that greeted us there were so disturbing that I don't think I have the will, or the desire, to face them elsewhere. I was ignorant to the realities of the Inquisition. But I am ignorant no more." She paused, looked into the fire, the continued. "In Montalcino I created my own ignorance by blaming Bishop Capshaw for our suffering." She looked up from the flames with a sad smile. "I suppose it was easier to think that the kingdom was unaffected by the brutalities, much like your own Castiglione d' Orcia. I wasn't prepared for the total devastation of towns like Pienza. I don't know how to fight against such a foe as the one my own Church has created. The enormity of it is overwhelming."

She stopped. The cloud skirted around the edges of her being, still threatening. The smoke from the fire wafted toward her again, but then shifted in the opposite direction as if it had been warned of the danger in staying that course.

Father Tim sighed, "My Queen, this is a war. Sadly, it is a war about power and greed, land and money... but it is disguised as a spiritual war. It's difficult to know how to fight such an enemy. Those who try are paying for it with their lives and their land. You cannot fault yourself for floundering in this battle. If you did not falter you might speed full and foolish into the fight without proper weapons and protection."

At the mention of weapons Robert asked, "What kinds of weapons are there for such a battle? How do I protect my Queen from such invisible assaults?"

"You cannot, my dear friend," Tim shook his head sadly.

"Then how can she prepare herself?" asked Bella. "She cannot do this again."

Father Tim looked directly at Catherine. "You must arm yourself with the Spirit of God's Truth." He stopped and seemed to implore each of them, "You all must. Don't misunderstand, you must still be ready to protect yourselves with swords and armor, but you must also protect your spirits."

"How can we do such a thing?" Catherine asked. "And how do we know if we are acting within the Spirit of Truth? If I say that my truth is God's truth, and the bishop says his truth is God's truth, whose truth is true?"

The priest smiled, "The Spirit of truth is characterized by humility and with openness, a readiness to be surprised. If it is truly the Spirit of God guiding us, we will not be so convinced that we have it all figured out; we will always be peeking around the corners of our beliefs and habits to see how else God might be revealed."†

Father Tim saw Bella smiling at him. He smiled back and continued.

"Perhaps, more importantly, the Spirit of Truth is characterized by love. If what we think is the truth is not loving and kind, merciful and understanding, concerned about caring for the least among us, it is not the Spirit of God. Jesus said over and over again that *love* is the defining reality of God, and therefore the defining reality of our humanity."† Tim paused, "God is love, Majesty, therein lies the true truth."

No one spoke. The stars began to twinkle overhead. Night noises crept in around them. Smells from the burning cedar wrapped them peacefully.

"I need to make my way back to the village. You will stay for a few days, I hope, Your Majesty?"

"Yes."

Robert stood. "I will have two of my soldiers accompany you to the village."

"Thank you."

As he was leaving Catherine said, "I should like more conversations over the next few days."

"I am at your service, Majesty."

Later, alone in their tent, as Catherine and Bella lay close together, Bella asked, "What did you think of what Father Tim had to say?"

"I hear him and I think 'of course, that makes perfect sense…that is exactly what Christ meant'. He clarifies the teachings of Christ for me in a way no one has before. But I need more. How do I deal with the horrors, how do I listen to the sorrows, without falling into them? I need to know how to surround myself with that truth, the certainty of that truth, especially when I am in the midst of such hideous evil as being perpetrated by this Inquisition.

"You do need that, and if anyone can help you to find a way to prevent the loss of yourself in trying to help your subjects, it is Father Tim."

"Bella…"

"Yes, my love."

"Thank you."

Bella propped herself up on her elbow and reached to run her hand through Catherine's hair. She stroked Catherine's cheek and laid her head on Catherine's shoulder.

"I love you," Bella whispered. And they fell asleep wrapped around one another.

Over the next few days Catherine met often with Father Tim. Sometimes Bella or Robert joined them; other times Catherine met with him alone. The woods around Castiglione d' Orcia provided a peaceful setting in which to walk and talk. The canopy of leaves overhead was bursting bright green as the first buds began unfolding. One morning Catherine and Tim wound their way along a well-worn animal path. A mountain stream gurgled along with them.

"Majesty, your prayer life is critical during this time. You must be in communication with God to sustain yourself."

"You are right, of course. But I find it is difficult, with the change in routine, to be steadfast in prayer."

"You may find that your style of prayer can change with your change in routine. Prayer does not always require a certain ritual."

"What do you mean?"

"I believe that prayer has to do with searching not so much for God, who is always near, but for our own way of being with God, which can be somewhat obscured. Each of us must struggle to sift through practices and teachings, through our own resistance and bad habits, in order to find our own way to connect with God."†

He reached out his hand and helped her step over a fallen log. "Over time I have utilized various means to do this…walking in these woods is one way. Sometimes I find I am able to find God in music, or reading. Other times I find God in my relationships with others. There are times when the ongoing struggle with my own demons and limitations lead me to the Divine. But within each of these means there is a common thread – the search for the kinds of experience that God promises: peace, truth, confidence, creativity, vitality and love for others. This is always the same…how I might get there is different." †

Catherine thought about this for a while as they walked. Slowing only slightly she said, "I told you once that I had lost my ability to feel God's presence."

"I remember. You were convinced that God had abandoned you because of your love for Lady Isabella."

She sighed as she resumed walking at her normal pace again, "I still have yet to feel God's presence the way I did before. But, as I listen to you, I am aware that the feelings I experience when I hold Sofia, or sit quietly with Bella, are similar."

"Ah, Majesty, there it is. Searching for God is like a fish searching for water. We live in God; the divine is the air in which we live and move and have our being. We are all part of God's body. The whole of creation is God's body; rich and poor; plants and animals; mountains, sky, rivers; all races and tribes." †

The path opened onto a sunlit meadow. Catherine smiled and stepped into the sun, turning her face up to its warmth. Tim followed.

"How does God abide what the Church is doing now? How does He tolerate this violence being done in His name? And, please don't begin by telling me about free will," she begged.

Father Tim couldn't help but chuckle. "Majesty, it amazes me how much of my own questioning comes through in your questions. The answer is that I don't know how God tolerates what is happening. I imagine Him to be greatly sorrowed, as we are." Tim folded his hands and brought them up to his lips, then dropped them again. "I can give you my thoughts, but know that they are mine. When I consider all we know about God, I am reminded that we are made in God's image. If that is so, then perhaps God, also, struggles with the dark side of His own nature. If we are created in His image, then we must assume that evil, or at least the potential for evil, is part of God."

Catherine stopped and looked at Father Tim with something akin to horror, "Surely that must be blasphemy! Are you not afraid to even think such thoughts?"

"At first I was, yes. But the more I considered this possibility, the more I studied the scriptures, the more I meditated on this thought, I could not deny that the possibility was there. Have you read the Old Testament?"

"Of course."

"The God of the Old Testament was a bit frightening to me. Do you find Him so?"

"Yes, actually, even somewhat vengeful and unpredictable. The stories of slaughter and slavery always disturbed me," Catherine responded. She remained standing still as he went on. She felt that she needed to understand what he was getting at before she could continue along this path with him.

He remained standing with her. "And the story of Noah, tell me what speaks to you in that lesson."

"That God abhorred what man had become," she said. She looked at Tim and a smile slowly spread across her face. "I think I see where you are headed." She began to make her way to the center of the meadow.

"God is ever changing...as we are. If we are all part of God, if God is in us and we are in God, as Christ has taught, and if we are made in God's own image, then why can't God use us to refine His own being?" Father Tim was becoming rather animated as he spoke. "God's own free will and His own realization of how humanity acted on the darker side of that free will may have been just what determined God to send us Jesus Christ."

"As a way to help us choose a more loving path for the whole of humanity?"

"Why not?" asked Father Tim.

"You have managed to bring us around to 'free will', Father. "Don't think I haven't noticed," the queen laughed.

"It was unavoidable, Majesty," he chuckled again. "I apologize. But, think on this; the Divine love of Christ is the inner force that insistently brings life out of death; that keeps searching for ways to recreate harmony and justice when parts of our body rebel against our innate divine nature and hurt other parts of the body." † He stopped again and looked at her. "This Inquisition is like a sore festering in the body of God. Part of the Body is sick, but we cannot abandon it, we must nurture it back to health. We must bring truth and love to the parts in need."

"And how do we deal with the parts that are creating the sickness, the parts that attack the other parts?" They strolled to the far edge of the meadow.

"With God's grace, we bring truth and love to all parts. We must try. That is our task."

"I don't believe it is in me to love someone like the bishop." Even thinking about Bishop Capshaw drove her anger to the surface. "And when I see the evil that has befallen the children in my kingdom, I feel only my desire to rid us of this scourge."

"It is not easy to love someone who behaves in such hateful ways, especially those with the power to convince many that they are speaking for God, or acting on God's behalf. We must be vigilant in reminding ourselves that God loves even the most hateful of us. You, as Queen, are in a difficult position." He indicated that it was time to turn back. "You must mete out punishment to criminals, and be fair and compassionate in your dealings with your subjects. I do not envy you, Your Majesty. Yours is a complex and heavy duty. You have the power and the authority to execute, imprison, banish or forgive." Tim stopped and looked Catherine directly in the eyes. "You, more than most, must rely on the grace of God to fulfill your duties in the spirit of love and truth."

As they stepped out of the meadow and back into the forest, Tim held a branch out of the way so that Catherine need only bend a bit to get back onto the path.

"I will tell you the truth, Father, there are times when I wish I were a simple peasant."

Father Tim laughed. "I know the feeling well, Majesty! But I will share this with you; I am thankful to God every day for you as my monarch. No matter the struggle that you endure, I know that God is with you because you invite Him into your heart and soul. I believe that you rule from a place of truth and love. Know that my prayers are with you always. And know that God is with you…whether you feel his presence or not."

Chapter Thirty Four

Catherine and her entourage returned to the castle for a respite before resuming her tour of the kingdom. She was anxious to see how Ambrose was faring in his role as king. It would also be nice to bathe and sleep in her own bed.

The forward guard rode ahead to announce the return of the queen. The courtyard was full of families to greet the returning travelers. The soldiers who had come straight from Pienza to inform the king and Lord Giovanni about the unscheduled stop in Castiglione d' Orcia had reported that life in Pienza was dismal, so many of the castle residents were present to find out what had happened. Even King Ambrose waited in the courtyard, most urgent to greet Sofia.

"My daughter has grown in her short absence from me!" Ambrose exclaimed as he lifted Sofia into his arms. He buried his face in Sofia's neck and proceeded to make her shriek with joy. The king's delight in his daughter was apparent. Catherine could not deny that he loved her, and Sofia was equally enamored of her father. Ambrose might lack in many areas, but his love for Sofia was not one of them.

At dinner in the Great Hall that evening, Catherine refrained from inquiring about the Privy Council. She had already arranged to meet with Ambrose tomorrow for details. He asked about the journey to Pienza and the subsequent change in plan to visit Castiglione d' Orcia.

"Word reached us that things in Pienza were quite difficult," Ambrose said.

"You cannot imagine," Catherine answered. A server filled her goblet with wine and stood back.

"Were you in any danger?"

"Never." She looked at him and detected his concern. "I would not have taken Sofia if I thought there might be any risk involved." She was offended at the hint of concern over their daughter's safety. But then she realized that Sofia was his precious child as much as hers and she added, "But I doubt I will take her on any more of these journeys. She will be better off here with you."

He visibly relaxed. "What happened there? Can you tell me?"

"An entire town died," she said sadly. "There are still people walking around, breathing, and eating. But they no longer really live. The heart and soul are gone from Pienza. I don't know if it can ever return to what it once was...I doubt it."

He reached out and patted her hand. "Let's hope that Pienza is an exception." His concern surprised Catherine.

"I will tell you more about it tomorrow. For now let us enjoy our meal. I am glad to be back."

As Catherine pondered how much to share with Ambrose, her eye caught the blush of a young woman at a table off to the right. The woman had been obviously sharing a look with Ambrose. Ambrose tried to hide his smile at the woman, but his demeanor radiated as he looked at her. She wondered who the young woman was, for she did not recognize her.

Chapter Thirty Five

Ambrose did well on the Privy Council during Catherine's short absence. When they met in her office the day after her return from Castiglione d' Orcia he was direct and comprehensive in reporting the few things the Council addressed while she was gone.

They returned to their previous nights' discussion of Pienza. Catherine didn't try to hide her sadness from him.

"Can you imagine," she asked him, "returning to Perugia and finding the life gone from everything?"

"It is a shame," he offered, "that the Church must resort to such extremes to save souls from hell."

"Ambrose, do you really believe that such extremes are necessary?" She had been standing looking out the window behind her desk, but when he said this she turned to look at him.

"I am a Catholic," he said a little defensively. "I have never been drawn to, or called, to any kind of religious life. I don't pretend to know or understand the things our religious leaders claim to know and understand. I have never questioned the demands or requests of my Church." He rose to pour himself a cup of water.

Catherine waited for him to finish filling his cup, then looked at him and said, "We have never discussed anything of any importance, Ambrose. I don't really know you, and I suspect you don't really know yourself."

Ambrose put his cup down and glared at her, "You don't know what you are talking about!" he began.

Catherine shook her head and put her hands up to stop him, "Ambrose, all I meant was that I believe you have never been given a chance to know yourself! I saw how it was with you and your father," she said trying to assuage his hurt feelings and convince him that she was not attacking him. "I am only saying I believe you may not have given yourself leave to think about certain things because your thoughts never mattered. Please don't be angry. I meant no harm."

Ambrose sat down again. He took a large breath and slumped somewhat in his chair. "You are right, of course. As the third son of a king with two strapping, strong sons already, I was a clear disappointment to my father. I didn't enjoy the martial arts, or any of the things that brought my father joy when he compared me to my brothers. The things that interested me became a wedge between us and I eventually gave them up at my mother's urging."

"What kinds of things?"

He got up again and strolled over to an oil painting of the flower fields. "Painting mostly. My father did not approve."

"I am sorry, Ambrose. I didn't know."

He shrugged. "It's of no consequence now. The king is happy...I am no longer the constant reminder of his failure in his own home. I have, by marrying you, made my father happy. You were right when you once said that I was an embarrassment to him."

Catherine winced. "I do wish I had never uttered those words."

He shrugged again. "If you had been wrong in what you said, I would have been less injured, I suppose. It does not matter any longer. The truth is that I am happier away from the Kingdom of Perugia as well. It was never easy to be the younger, gossiped-about prince." He smiled at her.

Catherine turned back to gaze out the window and said, "Have you really never given thought to how the Church purges itself of heretics."

Ambrose stood and went to join her at the window. He didn't answer for some time and when he did he spoke quietly. "The torture and executions disturb me." His voice was a whisper, as if he were afraid that someone would hear him. "I do hope we live to see the end of them."

"Do you ever wonder how Christ would respond to the executions?" she asked softly.

Ambrose said nothing but shook his head sadly. Together they stood looking out over the castle courtyard. Finally, he turned to leave.

As he made his way toward the door Catherine said, "My secretary, Antonio, enjoys painting. I will ask him where he obtains his supplies if you like."

Ambrose stopped dead with his hand on the doorknob. After a moment he said, "Don't trouble yourself. I have not held a brush in so long I have likely forgotten."

211

At the next day's meeting of the Privy Council Catherine dispassionately told the Council of her visit to Pienza, telling only the numbers and facts of what she found there. She knew to be cautious of how she presented the information and opted to keep her feelings about the abuses out of her report.

Lord Giovanni had already heard the details from Robert. When Catherine was finished with her report, he urged the queen to make Ribolla her next visit. He was anxious to return home to see for himself that all was well, or not. He desperately wanted to accompany the queen, but Catherine was not willing to leave Ambrose in charge of the Privy Council for such an extended period of time without her strongest ally.

"I have already decided to visit Ribolla next, Lord Giovanni. But I must insist that as I visit each of your homes," she looked around at all of her council, "that you remain here to attend to the running of the kingdom."

Later, she confided in Lord Giovanni that she was not yet ready to leave Ambrose in charge without her most trusted advisor at hand. He understood, but begged the queen to return to Montalcino with all due haste. He would not rest until he was reassured that his home, his extended family and his village were spared the fate of Pienza. He hadn't been able to make his usual fall trip home to Ribolla since last spring. He had been ill with a severe case of gout during the summer and fall and was unable to travel. Once winter set in, there was no way to make it out of Montalcino through the snow covered passes.

The queen's trip to Ribolla would take considerably longer than the one to Pienza. Ribolla was on the far western border of Montalcino. The trip alone would to take four days.

Against Catherine's insistence, Bella refused to leave James behind and Catherine finally gave in. Sofia was to remain behind with her father.

The day before the queen departed for Ribolla, the Privy Council met. Catherine opened the meeting with a report from Captain Moretti, who sent news from Perugia. King Christopher's border regiment found and executed a rogue band of murderers masquerading as "Inquisition" enforcers on the eastern border of Montalcino.

"Apparently, the group went into Perugia thinking they could evade our troops. Captain Moretti had already advised Perugia's border patrol to be alert. Our Captain knew he was close to capturing the leader of the group and feared the brigand might try to seek refuge across the border."

"My father," added Ambrose, "has offered to extend one hundred of his troops to guard the border and southeastern part of Montalcino."

Catherine smiled at Ambrose. "And we have accepted his generous offer."

She thought to herself, "You are coming into your own…and liking it, I see." Then aloud she said, "King Ambrose will have the details of the movements and reports from the troops by next Council meeting."

"When do you leave for Ribolla, Majesty?" the Bishop asked.

Bishop Capshaw already knew she was leaving the next day, but Catherine heard in his query his desire to confirm that she would be gone soon.

Catherine shuffled through some papers and answered the bishop without looking up. "Nothing has changed, Your Grace. We depart tomorrow."

"I am wondering, Bishop Capshaw," Lord Giovanni said, "about your thoughts on the queen's report from Pienza. Have you given any consideration to the drastic number of executions there? "

"I have not, Lord Giovanni. It is not my place to question my Pope or my Church. The Pope himself sent the Inquisitor to Pienza. He must have had reason to do so and I do not question my Pope," answered Bishop Capshaw firmly.

"Forgive me, Bishop, I believe you may have misunderstood. I was not maligning the Pope or his Inquisitor. My concern was for the number of Pienzans who were found guilty of heresy and other crimes. The question was related more as to whether or not you thought the numbers unusually high for such a small community?" Lord Giovanni replied cautiously.

Catherine knew that every word relating to the Inquisition was carefully couched in the knowledge that Lord Carfaggi was related to the Pope. And Lord Carfaggi never let an opportunity pass to remind anyone that he was the Pope's cousin.

"As the followers of Martin Luther spread their disease among us," the Bishop retorted, "there will continue to be increases in the numbers of interrogations and executions. I have no doubt that the Pope is aware of how the disease is spreading and how to stop it. As you well know, Lord Giovanni, even in our own little Montalcino, I am besieged with new accusations daily." At this he picked up a stack of papers and held them up. "These are new reports of heresy just this week, and just locally. All reports must be investigated. If the numbers are reflective of anything, let them reflect the quick cleansing of heresy." He dropped the pile of papers back onto the table with a smack. "The sooner we stop the spread of the disease, the more souls we save for Christ." The Bishop nodded curtly to Lord Giovanni, as if that should end the discussion.

"Perhaps," suggested Lord Carfaggi as he directed an unsympathetic glare toward Lord Giovanni, "Lord Giovanni is concerned because the queen is now traveling to his own home."

Catherine felt her heart quicken as Carfaggi attacked her favorite. Carfaggi knew that Giovanni was sympathetic to the queen. He, like his cousin the Pope, did not care for anyone who did not, wholeheartedly, support and encourage the elimination of heresy. She also knew that in spite of his kind hearted nature, Lord Giovanni could take care of himself. Catherine was glad to see that he was not about to cower in the face of Carfaggi's threats. Giovanni leaned forward in his seat, directing an equally chilly glare at Carfaggi.

"Any man would be a fool to be unconcerned, Lord Carfaggi." Lord Giovanni stared his opponent down. "Do you suggest that it is unreasonable for me to worry about my hometown; to be disturbed by the possibility that my family, my friends, my neighbors might succumb to the influence of heretical ideas and be executed?"

Lord Como stood abruptly. His chair scraped against the stone floor and caught, falling with a loud crash. "I am appalled at what is happening not only in Montalcino, but everywhere! We are all frightened for our loved ones, Lord Carfaggi. How can we look around us and not be afraid? Let's not pretend that we have not, all of us," at this he looked directly at Carfaggi, "at one time or another, been grateful for our ability to learn the names of the accused before their arrest. The information the Queen brought back from Pienza *is* alarming, no matter who should have reported it."

"Perhaps," Lord Romeo interrupted, "my Lords, it would do us well if the Bishop were to lead us in prayer for Montalcino…and our queen, before she leaves for Ribolla" His aversion to discord generally resulted in a direct attempt to calm things. It was difficult to say no to a prayer.

Following a brief prayer, the council moved on to other business and adjourned prior to the midday meal. Ambrose left hurriedly.

The queen's party prepared for their departure early the next morning. Catherine was anxious about leaving Sofia, but as Ambrose held out his arms for their daughter after Catherine kissed her goodbye he said, "You have made a good decision to leave her. She will be fine."

In another cloud of dust the group departed. Ambrose held Sofia, who waved and shouted "Bye…bye!" until she could see her mother no longer. Mary reached for Sofia, but the king said, "I will bring her to you in a bit, Mary, I should like some time with her this morning." They made for the courtyard to wander and spend some time outdoors.

After spending the morning playing with Sofia, Ambrose arrived in his quarters to find gifts of an easel, several canvasses, a palette, brushes and powders for mixing paints. A note accompanied the gifts: "Ambrose, use them well and often. Perhaps someday you will paint a portrait of our daughter."

He stared at the easel for some time before reaching out to run his hand along the canvass. It was a while before he realized that he hadn't moved and his eyes were filled with tears. It was the most thoughtful gift he had ever received.

Robert and Catherine rode side by side on the first day to Ribolla.

"You should know, Majesty," he said softly so that no one else might hear, "the King appears to have fallen in love."

Catherine stopped her horse and looked at Robert with surprise, but said nothing. He held up his horse to stop with her and waited until she urged her horse on again.

"Tell me," she said with a smile.

"His nightly exploits started to decrease significantly when you were in Pienza," Robert said. "Apparently, at that time he also started to see a young woman who is a new resident of the castle."

"Who is she?"

Robert described the woman Catherine noticed looking at Ambrose in the Great Hall. She was young, but had a sweet look about her. Catherine remembered that Ambrose could barely contain his glow when their eyes met.

"She is the niece of Lord Como. She was here visiting with her family."

"Is her family still with us?"

Robert cleared his throat, "No. She is now staying to *assist* her uncle."

"Does Como know?" she asked as she turned to see if the rest of the party were catching up to them.

"I don't think so, not yet, anyway. Ambrose is actually making an effort to be discreet."

"Do you think she has anything untoward in mind? Does she want something from him, or me?"

"I actually believe she is in love with him, as well."

"In that case, allow them whatever you can. Ambrose deserves some happiness, do you agree?"

"I do. As long as his relationship poses no threat to you or the kingdom, I will let it be, then."

Catherine thought of Ambrose as she continued along on her ride. She was glad he found someone to love, and who loved him.

The journey to Ribolla was uneventful. The soldiers hunted for game along the way and there was plenty to eat. It took four days to get to Ribolla.

The outriders alerted the officials in Ribolla that the queen's arrival was imminent. As in the case of Pienza, word had been sent ahead, but journeys being what they were, unexpected hardships along the way could lengthen or shorten the arrival time.

The streets were lined with people, all of whom cheered for the Queen. Many subjects approached her to offer gifts. The reception was so different from the one in Pienza that the queen was hopeful the devastation would be limited. Her hope was short-lived.

The meeting with city officials was much the same as in Pienza. While none of the officials had suffered the same fate as Lord Bruggia, the numbers were just as startling. Because the population was greater, the interrogations, tortures and executions were proportionately higher. The local priest, Father Mario, was willing to arrange for meetings with villagers, but made it clear that he did not wish to be present.

Father Mario had the appearance of someone who should be dead, but continued to live. He was old and thin, his pallor had a yellow tinge. He had an odor about him that was sharp and unpleasant. Perhaps once, Father Mario had a full head of hair, but now his head sprouted sparse clumps of long, dingy grey string. For all intents and purposes, he had the look of someone who had given up...on people, on faith, on God and on life. He looked like he hated to be there, or anywhere, but lacked the motivation to do anything about it. Queen Catherine was just as glad he would not participate in her meetings. His very presence filled the room with a ghastly air.

Meetings with the townspeople were much the same as the meetings in Pienza. Although, here in Ribolla, there seemed a bit more hope. Catherine was concerned that the hope seemed to stem from her presence. She had no hope to offer. She had no help to give.

"Tell me what happened when your wife and daughter were first accused of witchcraft?" Catherine sat before yet a third devastated man, and it was only her second day in Ribolla.

"The men who came to arrest them gave us little information, except that, Majesty. We did not know where the accusations came from, or what to expect." This husband and father of two more of the

Church's victims fell apart before her very eyes. His face showed his attempt to maintain a stoic mask, but the harder he tried the more the mask dissolved and his pain crept through until, finally, he broke, burying his face in his hands, weeping uncontrollably.

Catherine reached out, placed her hands on either side of his head and simply held them there. After a while he was able to regain control of his emotions. "I apologize, Majesty. They were all I had. I am so lost without them."

Her words of comfort seemed so meaningless that she stopped dispensing them. What could she say to people who had lost everything? All she could do was listen.

She returned to camp exhausted.

"Love," Bella said when Catherine lay back on her down pad in the tent, "We must find a way to help you in your task. You can't do this day after day...it will destroy you! Have you armed yourself as Father Tim suggested?"

"I suppose not. But I do not even have the strength to try right now. Please just let me nap a bit before supper."

"For a short while only then. I have something I think might help." Bella left Catherine already dozing and went to pack a light supper for two.

"Time to wake up, my queen," whispered Bella in Catherine's ear as she kissed it gently. "I have a surprise for you. Come." Bella took Catherine by the hand and led her out of the camp. A horse carried a small basket hanging from one side of the saddle. Robert followed at a distance.

After they walked a short distance through the mountainous terrain, Catherine heard the sound of rushing water.

Bella tied the horse to a branch. "Do you remember when I was still carrying James and you surprised me at the flower fields?"

Catherine nodded and smiled.

"Now I must ask you to trust me. Close your eyes and let me lead you. Don't open them until I tell you."

Catherine closed her eyes. They walked, Bella leading, for about twenty yards.

"Open your eyes, my love."

The sight that greeted Catherine was magnificent. They were next to a wide river, rocky, coursing over boulders. Pine trees and aspen surrounded them, all whispering as a gentle breeze whistled through branches and needles. Catherine inhaled deeply of the pine scent, and looked up through the branches to a sky so blue she could not describe it. But what filled Catherine with awe was the waterfall spilling from high above.

"Wait here," Bella ordered. When she returned she had the basket. Robert stayed with the horses and she pulled Catherine toward the waterfall. "Come, come, I have to show you."

As they climbed the rocks surrounding the river and moved ever closer to the waterfall, rocks jutted up to create private, secluded spots, each one of which would nurture the weary soul. Bella refused to stop at any of them pulling Catherine farther on.

"You will not be disappointed. You must trust me!" Bella urged.

Water cascaded over the huge rock overhang. They slipped behind the waterfall to the most private, special spot God ever created. Catherine marveled at the sheer beauty and simplicity of the place. Rock and water. Marvelous. As she moved closer to the water and felt the spray mist her face she couldn't help but smile. Life sprinkled onto her, into her. When she finally turned around there was a blanket spread with cheese, wine, olives, bread and grapes and Bella. Bella was propped against a rock. She held out her arms and Catherine slid into her, resting against her. They sat in silence listening to the sounds of the water. They ate some, and listened some. Finally, Catherine sighed and sat up. She turned to Bella.

"It's as if the water washed away the sorrow I carried with me from Ribolla. I am renewed. How did you find this place?"

"Lord Giovanni told me about it. He told Robert exactly how to find it and with the help of one of Robert's soldiers, I sought it out today with James. He loved it. It will be a wonderful place for him in the day, and for you every evening, I think."

"Bella, it is perfect. I haven't felt this relaxed and peaceful since Bolsena."

"I think, my dear, that this is exactly what Father Tim was talking about when he said that communion with God did not need to be limited to a certain kind of prayer."

"I believe you're right. As usual."

Catherine resumed her position lying against Bella for a while longer. Bella stroked her hair. After a bit Catherine reached up and pulled Bella into a kiss. They made love behind the waterfall, the cold, gentle mist creating a shivering sensation that enhanced the pleasure they found in one another. The setting sun filtered through the falling water. Catherine found it magical to look on Bella's body and see how the moisture formed tiny beads on the light hairs. The tiny droplets sparkled like crystals.

As the sun drew nearer the horizon they made their way back to camp.

Although Catherine did not realize it at the time, the beauty of that place would carry her through some of the most difficult days she would ever know. That secluded waterfall alcove became her chapel and her saving grace while she was in Ribolla.

In the days that followed, Catherine met with several of Lord Giovanni's family. She was grateful to have them to rely on, since Father Mario was no help. But the person with whom she felt the most affinity was Lord Giovanni's youngest son, Benito, who had his father's warm personality and gregarious laugh. He also looked most like Lord Giovanni and that made Catherine always glad to see him.

When they first talked, they agreed to meet every evening at a large tavern on the outskirts of the city. As they sat, sipped ale and picked at bread and cheese, they talked.

"Benito, what do you know of the people who have been executed in Ribolla?"

"I don't claim to know many of them, Majesty, but the ones I did know were good people, as were most I am afraid." His voice took on a melancholy tone that Catherine knew all too well.

"Please tell me what you know," she said. "And I warn you not to hold back in an attempt to protect me from the ugliness."

"Very well, Majesty. But please stop me if you …"

She held out her hand. "Benito, the people of Ribolla have suffered in ways that stagger me. If they can endure the torture, perhaps it is a small tribute to them to have their queen care enough to listen."

He smiled and took a long drink of ale. As with so many others, Benito took his time before beginning. It was as if the tellers of the stories needed to brace themselves for returning to the memories that were too painful to be kept close to the surface. Finally, he began.

"I have a friend, a good friend. We grew up together. His name is Pietro. Pietro had…has an older sister, Rosa. She was a beauty. At one time I was much taken with her, but she had eyes for only one man. That man was her downfall, I am afraid."

"He was married?" Catherine asked.

"He was the priest."

"Father Mario?" Catherine asked, aghast.

"Good God, no!" laughed Benito. "That shriveled up old patron would not know love if it spit at him in the eye!"

Catherine could not help but laugh, too. "I am sorry, Benito, please continue."

A server came by to check on them and they did not speak again until he was far from the table.

"No, Rosa's love was for Father Paolo. He was a young, handsome priest with an eye for many of the women of Ribolla. For him, Rosa was just another plaything. Pietro and I knew what was going on with Father Paolo and Rosa because we followed her. She did not know, of course, until we confronted her. We were waiting one day when she came out from the church after meeting secretly with the priest.

"Pietro accused her of sinning, in the eyes of God and the church, and threatened to tell their parents. She didn't care. She was in love. She thought the fact of his being a holy man of God absolved her from any sin." Benito turned his cup in his hands. "She thought Father Paolo loved her, as well. Pietro tried to tell her she wasn't the priest's only lover, but she refused to believe him. "

"Did Pietro tell his parents? "Catherine asked.

"He was going to, but then he decided it would serve no purpose except to upset them. She, Rosa, was not going to stop loving her priest at any cost. In the end, it cost both of them."

Catherine waited silently for him to continue.

"When the Grand Inquisitor arrived he met with Father Mario. Father Mario knew about the exploits of Father Paolo and so the accusations began. Rosa was interrogated. She lied about the relationship with Father Paolo, of course, until the imprisonment and torture began. She found herself in a cell with several of Father Paolo's lovers. Most were tortured and already confessed to the Inquisitor. Eventually, so did Rosa. She has languished in prison ever since. She will be there for some time."

"What happened to Father Paolo?"

"He was executed."

"How?"

"Drawn and quartered."

"My God!" Catherine exclaimed. She dropped her head and briefly buried her face in her hands.

Her stomach heaved into her throat as she remembered that a series of other tortures generally preceded the actual drawing and quartering. Sometimes a hand or a limb would be cut off and burned in sulpher; other times limbs or breasts were lacerated with red-hot pincers and hot oil or molten lead poured into the wounds. Catherine did not want to know if any of these were suffered by Father Paolo. It was enough to know that his four limbs were tied to the harnesses of large plow horses, driven in different directions, to be dislocated and eventually ripped from his body. She knew that this torture could last for hours and that sometimes the severed limbs would be placed next to the torso of the victim…which might still be alive. All parts were then usually burned. She held her nausea at bay.

Eventually she looked up at Benito. "How is your friend Pietro?" she asked.

"Consumed with guilt. He wonders if he had told his parents if they might have been able to do something. He wishes he could go back and force Rosa to stop the affair with the priest. He tortures himself for what happened."

"And you?"

"I am fine, Majesty." He gave her a winsome smile. "How can I not be fine in the presence of one so extraordinary!" he exclaimed. "My father was right, you are beautiful and kind. I am so glad to have an opportunity to spend time with you."

Catherine recognized his need to move on to other topics. It was one of the ways that many tried to keep their own demons from taking over and consuming them. She joined him. "You are so like your father, Benito. He is a blessing to me. I am grateful for him every day."

They talked for another hour, moving in and out of general discussion of family, Benito's life, his father, and tragedies of others in Ribolla. Benito told her everything he knew about various executions and tortures. Catherine left with the impression that he did, in fact, feel better after sharing the stories with her. Perhaps listening offered more than she imagined.

Each evening Catherine and Bella retreated to the waterfall as soon as Catherine returned from Ribolla. Some days they just sat and enjoyed the sound of the water as they ate. Some days Catherine talked about the day and the people she met. On occasion Catherine shared some of their stories, but only if Bella asked.

Sometimes Bella found that hearing the stories of others helped in a strange way to link her to the people Catherine met. She felt less isolated in her own waning grief. It was as if each story she heard joined with her own, creating a tapestry of kinship and sorrow. She was not alone and somehow that comforted her.

Chapter Thirty Six

On the last day that Catherine spent in Ribolla the sheriff reluctantly agreed to accompany the queen to the prison to meet with two of the convicted heretics. Catherine hadn't met with any of the prisoners in Pienza. After learning about Benito's friend, Rosa, she wanted to meet her. She wasn't sure what she might say, but prayed for guidance as the sheriff led the way to the cell. Robert accompanied them.

She and Robert followed the sheriff, who carried a torch as their only light. As they walked down the stone steps deep under the interrogation rooms, the air became cooler, the light waned sending shadows along the walls from the torch. Smells drifted up the dark, dank stairwell. The lower they went the more intense the smells. Catherine recognized the stench of human waste. She covered her nose and mouth with a handkerchief. Her breaths became shallow.

"It is a prison, Your Majesty. As such the conditions are filthy. Are you certain you wish to continue?" asked the sheriff.

"I am fine, Sheriff." But she was not fine, she was terrified. She wanted to turn and run back up the steps and out the door. Run and run all the way back to her waterfall. She imagined standing in the flow of the falls, cleansing the smells and filth away. Her heartbeat slowed, her breathing returned to normal.

But when they finally reached the bottom of the stairwell Catherine thought she would retch from the stink. "How could anyone survive here?" she thought.

Soon enough her nostrils became somewhat accustomed to the smell. Some of it was mold and mildew. The rock walls were wet in places and slippery from the constant ooze of water seeping through the pours.

They stopped at a cell door. The sheriff held his torch up to light one on the wall outside the cell.

"This is the cell of Rosa Pucci and Bettina Torino, Majesty." The sheriff unlocked the heavily padlocked door and placed a chair inside for the queen. The women were told that the queen wanted to meet with them and warned to behave themselves. After lighting a small torch high on the inside wall, he stepped outside. Robert checked inside the cell, nodded to Catherine, and stood guard in the hall. The sheriff disappeared.

The cell was small; about eight feet by eight feet. There were no windows. A hole in the floor on the opposite side of the two women served as the privy. The torchlight cast an eerie glow. Whatever clothes the women originally wore were now nothing but thin rags, barely enough to cover them, let alone keep the damp, cold air at bay. As the light flickered on the women she saw they were struggling to get up to greet her.

"Please, please, don't get up!" She insisted.

They looked frightened and Catherine quickly tried to reassure them that she was not there to punish them further or pass judgment.

"I came to find out for myself the conditions and circumstances surrounding your imprisonment," she started. "Which of you is Rosa?"

"I am, Majesty," said the smaller of the two women.

Catherine could tell that at one time she was probably extraordinarily beautiful. Although her hair was matted and dull now, she imagined how it might once have flowed long, silken and raven black across her shoulders. Her eyes, so sad and lifeless, were the blue of the Aegean Sea. They surely sparkled with life not so long ago…they would never sparkle again.

"Rosa, I learned your story from my friend, Benito."

At hearing this Rosa hung her head.

"You need not feel ashamed, Rosa. You are not the first to be a fool for love, nor will you be the last. How long are you to be imprisoned?"

"Two years, Majesty."

"And you, Bettina?"

"The same, Majesty. I was the same fool for the same lover."

"Were either of you tortured for your confession?" asked the queen.

Rosa looked at Bettina, who answered, "I was, Majesty."

"How were you tortured, child?"

Bettina did not answer. She looked to Rosa, but the other woman kept her head bowed and would not meet her gaze. Bettina lifted what was left of her dress to reveal what was left of her feet.

"My God, child, what did they do to you?" Catherine gasped, her hand flew to her mouth. Her gut heaved and she fought against being sick. They were not even feet any more, but scarred masses, barely recognizable. There were nothing but hideous, deformed and blackened nubs where the girl's feet should be. Catherine wondered how she had even tried to stand when she entered their cell.

Bettina was silent.

Rosa told of Bettina's torture. "They tied her feet together in a leather sack and dragged her to a fire. Boiling water was poured over the leather sack. It ate away at her skin and some of the bones, as well."

The queen could only shake her head in disbelief. Slowly, she felt her horror being replaced by anger.

"Were you tortured, as well, Rosa?"

"Yes, Majesty." Rose lowered her head and seemed reluctant to tell of her torture.

"Rosa..." Catherine could no longer remain sitting. Her sorrow propelled Catherine off her chair onto her knees in front of the women. "Tell me what they did to you."

Rosa nodded, her eyes closed, her head dropped. Sounds, sharp exhalations, short bursts, emanated from her. "Do you know what 'the pear' is?"

Catherine could barely hear Rosa, her voice was only a whisper. "No."

"It is a metal instrument shaped like a pear." She stopped.

Catherine waited.

"I...I was stripped naked and tied to a table. The pear...the pear opens up from the handle." Rosa began to shake, violently, and could not continue.

Catherine reached out and pulled Rosa to her breast. "Stop, child. You needn't continue. Hush." The smells that originally assaulted the queen disappeared as she comforted Rosa, stroking her head, hoping to calm the girl. "These women," Catherine thought, "and so many like them are the true warriors in this battle. They are sacrificing themselves in droves in places like this all over Europe. How have we let this happen?"

"Majesty," Rosa said tentatively as she began to calm and regain her ability to speak.

"Yes, child."

"Will you see Benito again?"

"Yes."

"Will you tell him that I am sorry."

"I will."

"And, Majesty, would you ask him to tell my family that I am sorry, and to tell them that I love them and miss them?"

"I will. Benito told me that your brother misses you terribly. It sounds like he still loves you very much. I will be sure that your family gets the message."

It was time to leave. Catherine spontaneously grasped each of their hands and pulled them to her, enfolding them in an embrace. "I am so sorry for what has happened to you. I wish that I could release you from this hell and give you back your lives this very day. Know that I will never forget you, either of you. You will be in my thoughts and prayers. I vow that as long as there is breath in me I will fight to end this...this savage brutality. I am so sorry. I am so sorry," she whispered. She held the two women close and cried with them. "God give you peace, and the strength to endure until you are released."

Catherine rose on shaky legs. Before she left the cell, she removed her cloak and wrapped it around the women.

The sheriff locked the cell door again and turned to lead the queen up the stairs. Her heart ached within her breast and she fought the desire to stifle a sob. She stopped at the foot of the steps and reached to lean on the wall to hold herself up. As she worked to regain control of her emotions she felt her strength returning. The sheriff stopped partway up the stairs and turned to wait. But she did not follow.

Her spine began to straighten and her shoulders slowly squared. As her body transformed, so did her demeanor. "Take me to see the torture chamber," she demanded.

The sheriff looked at Robert, then back in horror at the queen. "Majesty, no, please, why?"

"Now," she ordered.

"Yes, Majesty."

Robert followed, a small smile on his face. He remained silent.

She could not see all of the room for the darkness. They remained beneath ground level so there were no windows. The single torch carried by the sheriff did not illuminate the entire room. From what she could see there were several chairs and a desk. A fireplace was on one wall. A large black cauldron hung from a swinging arm inside the hearth. There were benches and tables scattered throughout the room.

"Light all the torches," Catherine commanded, swallowing her fear.

"Yes, Majesty."

As the sheriff lit each torch, the intent of the room could not be mistaken. Even though she did not understand the uses for all her eyes beheld, there was no question but that this room was used to inflict the most unimaginable pain. She forced herself to look, to take it all in, steeling herself against the dread and loathing.

Along one whole wall chains hung from hooks buried in the stone. The ends of the chains bore metals cuffs. The height of the hooks and length of the chains were too high to allow the prisoner to stand on the ground.

Whips and branding irons lay on one of the tables. Their uses were evident.

"What is this?" the queen asked as she stood before an odd metal A-frame rack.

"It is a cicogna, in some places known as a 'scavenger's daughter', Majesty." The sheriff was reluctant to go on.

"Sheriff, I am determined to know the use of every item here, so don't waste my time by making me ask for details."

"Yes, Majesty. The cicogna is used to compress the body. The head is strapped to the top point, here." He pointed to the rounded top of the A. It was easy to see that a head would nestle inside of the circle and could be fixed, unmovable. "The arms are tied here in the middle and the legs to these bottom portions. Once the prisoner is tied the head is swung down and the legs forced up. The knees are bent and the body is pressed together until blood is squeezed from the nose and ears."

With grim resolve Catherine moved to the next item, what appeared to be a giant iron shoe. She said nothing, but looked expectantly at the sheriff..

"An iron boot, Majesty. The feet are placed inside and the boot locked. Wedges of wood are then forced between the knees until the pressure breaks the leg bones."

Some items the queen encountered needed no explanation. An iron maiden was in one corner. It was a large sarcophagus shaped iron body the inside of which contained hundreds of spikes. Catherine reached to touch one of the points. It was covered in dried blood. "What kind of mind thinks to create such things?" she thought to herself.

She spotted what could only have been 'the pear'. "Tell me about this device," she ordered.

Even in the dim light, the sheriff turned crimson. She saw his jaw clench.

"It is called the La Pera." He picked it up and turned the handle which acted as a crank to open the metal sections of the pear shape. "It is inserted into the victim and opened."

"How," Catherine insisted, "where is it inserted?"

He looked at her with eyes that did not hide his fury at being forced to tell her. "In the mouth, the anus, and for women, between their legs." His tone had become almost defiant.

Catherine expected to be enveloped within her dark cloud of despair upon entering this room of evil. But as the sheriff explained each item, as she absorbed the intent of each torture, as she imagined how the pear would tear and rupture the tender insides of its victim, she felt a fire start to burn within her.

Robert had not left the open doorway. He watched and waited as Catherine explored the room and the devices. His eyes never left his queen. He saw the tears in her eyes when she left the women's cell. Now, as he watched, her face transformed. Her eyes narrowed and enlarged. Her jaw clenched, her nostrils flared, her lips pressed together and disappeared. He saw the veins on her forehead become pronounced. Her shoulders drew back and her back straightened. She was furious.

He felt, more than saw, that this room, this day, this knowledge would redefine the course of her life…and so his, as well.

When they left the torture chamber Catherine and Robert made their way to the tavern where they were to meet Benito for one last time. They didn't speak as they rode the short distance to the tavern.

Benito rose and greeted the queen. After they ordered refreshments, she told him of her meeting with Rosa and the messages that she sent. She did not share the torture. The smells clung to her nostrils and made it difficult for her to eat, so she satisfied herself with some wine. Benito, tears in his eyes, thanked her and promised to deliver Rosa's message of love to her family.

They did not stay long in the tavern. Catherine and Robert were anxious to begin the journey back to Montalcino.

Benito walked them outside. One of Benito's servants was waiting with a horse.

"Majesty, I have been greatly honored to have spent time with you. You are truly everything my father said. Please accept this horse and these gifts from the sons of Lord Giovanni. We are your faithful servants."

Equally balanced in large baskets on either side of the horse were many jugs of wine made from Lord Giovanni's own vineyards and fine wool from the sheep raised by the Lord's family. But the gift that touched Catherine most was the blanket woven for her by Lord Giovanni's family. It held the queen's crest intertwined by a grapevine to the coat of arms of Lord Giovanni's family. The workmanship was incredible and the wool softer than any Catherine had ever felt.

"Thank you, Benito. And thank your family for me. I am honored and will tell your father that you serve him well and proudly." She kissed him affectionately on both cheeks.

On their return to camp, Robert rode quietly next to his queen. She was weighing all that her time in Pienza had revealed to her.

Periodically, she snorted, or spat out a curse as they rode. Finally, he spoke.

"You are planning something." He smiled. "I hear it in your curses and see it in your face."

She said nothing and Robert looked up into the sky. Clouds had begun to form overhead.

"I am afraid, my dear cousin," she finally said, "that it will no longer be so easy for me to fight this Inquisition quietly. The Church has created and unleashed a hideous monster on my people. It has served the church to conveniently turn that monster over to secular authorities. Does it not strike you as cowardly for people like our bishop to be able to shield their eyes from the brutalities they order inflicted upon their victims?" she asked.

"What do you intend?"

"It is all well and good for the church to pretend that it remains holy and removed from the tortures. Perhaps a visit to the torture chambers is in order for our dear bishop and our council members."

He drew up on the reins of his horse, stopped and turned toward her. "Are you certain that is wise?"

She stopped, as well. "Would you send your men into battle without knowing the first thing about fighting? Would you give a man the authority to command soldiers without first insuring that he knew how to fight and lead…how to teach…what to expect in battle?"

"What is it you expect to accomplish by forcing the bishop to the chambers? Don't you think this will just make him hate you more?"

An ominous, low roll of thunder reached their ears. They urged their horses to move on.

"Perhaps, but I care nothing for his hatred anymore. I will not be able to live with myself if I don't stand up to this injustice. The people of Montalcino deserve a monarch willing to do more than sneak around the back of the Church offering meaningless support. If I can't show that I'm willing to fight openly for my people, I don't deserve to be their queen."

"A martyr is of little help."

She laughed, "I wonder what Christ would have to say about that?"

Again Robert smiled. They rode silently for a while. The wind was starting to pick up and the sounds of thunder were advancing.

"Cousin," Catherine offered softly, "this is my battle. I choose it. I do not expect you to join if you do not feel so inclined."

Robert laughed out loud, "You know well I am yours to the end of my days. I have no choice in the matter."

"I know that you have always felt so. But you have a family now...a son to consider."

"And you a daughter. What of it?"

"I know what I am asking," she stopped again, pulled up the reins of her horse and looked straight at him. "Be certain. The risk is great that we may pay for this with our lives."

"My life would be worth nothing to my family if I couldn't do what I was born to do. I am with you, my Queen. Your battle is my battle...and I could not be prouder to serve you than at this moment."

Rain began to fall and they slapped the reins onto their horse's backsides to race the downpour back to camp.

The moment Catherine and Robert entered the camp Bella sensed the change. She saw it in Catherine's face, in the way she rode her horse into camp. Even though she didn't know what that change was, she recognized the look of absolute resolve in Catherine's eyes. Whatever it was, she instinctively knew that life would be different from that moment forward.

The rain stopped and the sun broke through the clouds again. As Robert and the men broke camp, Catherine and Bella made for the waterfall one last time.

"Bella," Catherine said as she continued to tell the story of her day as they walked the muddy path, "if you had been in that cell and met those women, heard their stories, you would understand why I can no longer be so complacent about the plight of my people."

Bella moved to avoid a puddle. "I do understand, Catherine. You forget that their story is mine, as well. You forget that I could just as easily be in a prison cell of my own, or dead."

"I am sorry, love. I haven't forgotten. Painfully, I remember how we found you and the agony of your recovery. And I am aware that you still have your night terrors. You are part of why this must stop. I can't continue to do so little when I hear stories like yours and Rosa's and so many in the kingdom who have fallen victim to the Church. If I don't stand and fight for them, then what right do I have to expect them to fight for Montalcino...for me?"

"And what good will that do when you're dead?" Bella stopped and looked at Catherine, her eyes beseeching.

"Bella, I must do something!"

"But you *are* doing something! The work we do with Father Tim is something! Why must the something you do be something that could end your life?"

They were walking again and were almost to the little alcove behind the falls. Catherine waited until they had slipped behind it and turned to Bella.

"It's not enough, not for me, not anymore. If I allow Montalcino to collapse under the crushing weight of a Church that has thrown away its compass, then I have no right to be queen. You ask 'what good will it do when I am dead?' and I am forced to ask 'what good is it that I am alive and do so little to help?' I am sorry, Bella. I know that my stance frightens you, but I need you to believe that there is no other way for me. I need to know that you believe I am fighting for a just cause...and with just reasons. Please tell me you are with me."

Bella turned from Catherine and walked to the far side of the alcove. The sound of the rushing water was the only sound for some time. Catherine knew she was asking much. She knew that Bella was as frightened as ever, but she also knew that she had no choice. She loved Bella with her whole being...and she hoped that Bella loved her because of who she was...because she would not turn her back on her people. Catherine leaned against the back of the cove and waited. Finally, Bella turned and walked back across the alcove.

"I am with you," Bella said as she slipped her arms around Catherine's waist and whispered in her ear. I will fight with you, by your side. Together we will find a way to give the people of Montalcino the hope they deserve."

Catherine pulled Bella into a great kiss, and behind the roar of the waterfall, they made love one more time.

Chapter Thirty Seven

Their return to the castle was uneventful, but nothing prepared Catherine for Sofia's refusal to greet her. Ambrose tried to coax the child into her mother's arms, but Sofia clung to him refusing her mother's entreaties. That evening, Bella tried to assuage Catherine's feelings.

"She is still a baby! All she knows is that her mother disappeared."

"Did you see her face? It was as if she didn't know who I was!"

"Give her time." Bella went to Catherine and slipped her arms around her waist from behind. "She needs to get to know you again," Bella whispered into her ear.

"She didn't need to get to know her father again when I took her to Pienza!" Catherine wriggled out from Bella's arms.

"We were gone considerably longer this time. To her it must have seemed like an eternity. She will come around, but you need to be gentle with her and give her that time."

Catherine sat in her favorite chair near the fireplace. Though the fire was not lit, she was warm. The summer was hot and muggy. Her cloths stuck to her and made her uncomfortable. When she finally stood she made her way to the doors.

"Oh, you're probably right. I'll go to say goodnight to her."

"Spend some time with her, Catherine. Here, bring her the gift you brought back from Ribolla."

Catherine held out her hands for the cloth doll she found at a shop in the square at Ribolla. The doll itself was cotton material stuffed with wool, but it was the clothes and the hair that Catherine could not resist. The doll's dress was made in layers of fine blue satin trimmed in even finer white lace. The hair was long, black yarn pulled back and tied with a matching blue satin ribbon. Finally, the eyes were painted on. They were blue to match the satin and were so close to the color of Sofia's own eyes that Catherine could not resist purchasing it. Although Sofia's hair was not yet very long, it, too, promised to be dark and long, like the doll's.

Catherine looked at the doll and smiled, then turned and crossed the hall to the nursery.

Mary was readying the child for sleep when the queen entered. "Majesty," she bowed.

"Give me a few moments with Sofia, Mary."

"Of course, Majesty."

Mary left the room. Sofia refused to look at her mother. She picked up a wooden figure that lay in her crib and began to play with it.

Catherine made her way slowly to the crib. "You can be mad at me if you want, my sweet one. But I brought you something." Catherine saw she had piqued Sofia's interest. Sofia's head briefly and almost imperceptibly turned, but then she returned her attention to the wooden toy. Catherine placed the doll in the crib on the opposite side of where Sofia busied herself. Sofia looked up and could not contain a little cry of delight when she saw the doll. The wooden toy was immediately abandoned as Sofia reached for the gift and pressed it to her heart.

It filled Catherine's heart to see Sofia's face transform from recalcitrance to pure joy. She reached out to stroke Sofia's head, then bent down and kissed the top of it. "Goodnight my little love. Sweet dreams."

Catherine's first order of business on the day after her return, was to meet with Lord Giovanni. She knew he would be anxious to hear about her visit to Ribolla. She invited him to join her for a private midday meal in her office.

"Lord Giovanni," she rose to greet him as he was announced. She extended her hands and he knelt to kiss them.

"Majesty. It is good to have you home."

"Come, sit." She led him to a table that was prepared with a small meal. A servant was waiting to serve them. Catherine dismissed the servant so that she could speak without caution to Lord Giovanni.

As she doled out a mixture of black and green olives in a marinade of olive oil, vinegar and herbs, Lord Giovanni poured his own Ribolla wine into two goblets and lifted his to her. "To long life, Queen Catherine."

She raised her cup. "And peace."

Over the meal Catherine told him about her visit to Ribolla. She began by singing the praises of his family, especially Benito. She did not hide her great affection for his youngest son. Once she had reassured him that all was well with his family, she picked up her wine goblet, stood and walked away from the table.

Lord Giovanni almost stood, as well, but she indicated for him to remain sitting. She walked over to the window and stood looking out quietly for some time. When she finally spoke it was to tell him about her visit to the prison and the story of Rosa and Bettina. She told the story without ever looking back into the room, without moving from the window. When she finished she finally turned to find Lord Giovanni wiping tears from his face.

"I know Rosa. I have known her since she was born. Her father and I have done much business together. He must be shattered."

Catherine moved back and sat at the table again. "There is more."

He looked up at her and waited.

"After I met with the women I went to see the torture chamber."

His eyes opened wide, "My God, whatever for?"

"It seems to be the fate of my kingdom that torture is more commonplace than we ever imagined. Does it seem fair to you that my subjects, our people, our family and friends, are subjected to things that we will not even allow ourselves to know?"

Lord Giovanni lowered his head and covered his eyes. "No," he whispered.

"I want you to know that I plan for Robert to take me to see our own chamber later today. You are welcome to join us." She paused before continuing. "And because I love and respect you, I want you to be prepared." Again, she paused, stood and walked over to the window. "At tomorrow's Privy Council meeting I intend the council to join me in a visit to our chamber. I will not accept any refusal. I will make it clear that to refuse means abdicating position on the council."

She waited to see how he would respond. When he did not she turned. He was sitting, hands folded against his forehead, eyes closed, leaning heavily on the table. She waited.

"You are my Queen," he said softly as he raised his head, opened his eyes and looked at her. "There is no question but that I will do whatever you request of me." He stood and walked over to her. "Are you certain this is how you wish to proceed? You understand what this means? You are declaring war on your own Council."

She remained facing the window. She closed her eyes. Her face was creased with pain. She lowered her head, "I know."

He reached out and pulled her into a great, ferocious hug.

The next morning, when the Privy Council gathered, Catherine was called. She entered the room with steely resolve. Even her gown, though simple, was a grey, cold color. The council stood and bowed. She let them remain standing longer than usual before she finally said, "You may be seated."

She, alone, remained standing. The room was eerily quiet and the atmosphere charged with tension. Even the colors in the room hesitated to reveal themselves, as if they were waiting to determine whether it was safe to cast a beam.

Catherine did not need to draw herself up, for she walked into the room at full height and regal stature. She stood at the head of the table and waited until all eyes were upon her. In what could only be regarded as an open act of defiance, Carfaggi waited until it was obvious that he could delay no longer. He finally raised his eyes to her. She was waiting for him; her look was frigid. She raised one eyebrow and nodded, leaving no question that she was not amused by his attitude.

She began. "My Lords, Your Grace, I have learned much from the people of Pienza and Ribolla. And what I have learned is this; we are cowards. We have closed our eyes to the suffering we have allowed in the Kingdom of Montalcino. I don't doubt that Inquisition tortures will continue. I am not so naïve as to think that the Church will abolish the Inquisition any time soon. But before any of us condone another torture on behalf of our Church, you will know what happens to the human body before you close your eyes and your ears to the evils of the torture chamber." She paused to let her words sink in. She let the echo of what she said ring in their ears. And she waited.

The tension turned to general discomfort. Some squirmed in their seats, others shuffled papers. Finally, Carfaggi broke the silence.

"Majesty, are you suggesting that the Church should abolish the Inquisition?"

"The Church will proceed as the Church sees fit," she said curtly. "I do not seek to interfere in the teachings of the Catholic Church. But," she bent forward and thumped her fisted hand on the table, "I will be damned if I will continue to allow my Church to force *my* government and *my* soldiers to torture *my* subjects so that Church leaders may live with a clear conscience!"

Carfaggi's nostrils flared. She saw him shoot a look at the Bishop that said, "You had better control your queen."

"Majesty," the Bishop sputtered and protested. "You cannot be serious about this. Surely you realize that this action pits you against the Church."

"The Church declared this war hundreds of years ago, Your Grace. And we have all allowed the war to continue....why? Because we believe this is what Christ wanted?" She thought that when this time came she would be frightened. She felt stronger than she had in some time. She was angry, and she made no attempt to hide her anger. "You, more than anyone in this room, should know that Christ's message was one of love. This is not love! Come with me, gentlemen. I have arranged a little tour for you." She turned and started for the door.

"I will not accompany you in this folly, Majesty!" Lord Carfaggi stood, a look of defiance and horror on his hateful face.

She stopped and turned around very slowly to look at him. "I am not surprised, Lord Carfaggi. It is all well and good to give the dirty, bloody, work to others, is it? I didn't think you had the stomach to come with me." She looked around at her Privy Council. "Gentlemen, this is not a request. I intend my Council to know what tortures are being inflicted on the people of Montalcino. I do not make this command lightly. What you will see is not for the faint of heart. It will change you. We have lived our aristocratic lives above the sounds and sights of the torture chamber." She walked back toward them. "Oh, we know some of what happens there. We have been present during some of the executions. But we have lived our privileged lives pretending that the tortures and executions have nothing to do with us. Well, they have everything to do with us and I will no longer sit idly by while the people of Montalcino suffer. Nor will my Privy Council!"

No one moved. She waited for the impact of what she said to register. On the slim chance that they did not fully understand what she said, she decided to make perfectly clear her intentions.

"Captain Robert will take us to the chamber. I expect the whole of my Council to accompany me. You may refuse, if you like, Lord Carfaggi, but from this moment forward, the council is comprised *only* of those who accompany me now." Catherine turned and did not look back. She didn't know if Carfaggi followed, or, for that matter, if any of them followed her. Robert strode slightly behind her and on her right side. Together they led the way to the torture chamber. She knew what to expect as she and Robert both toured the chamber the previous day. While the variety and numbers of instruments were less than the larger chamber at Ribolla, she hoped the effect would be the same.

As they walked the long narrow hallway past the Great Hall through the courtyard and into the west wing of the castle, she wondered who was following. Her pace was quick, her back erect and she didn't give any indication that she was in the least bit afraid. Though her heart was racing and her hands were trembling, she wanted to give the message that she didn't care whether they followed her or not.

She was fairly certain that Carfaggi would come. He would not willingly give up his position of power over her threat. She was less certain about Navona and Romeo, as she perceived them as too tender to tolerate such cruelties. So it was with great surprise that she turned at the entrance to the chamber to see all of the Council present except Lord Bagglioni. She had not bargained on losing him.

Captain Lorenzo met them at the entrance to the chamber. Robert had arranged for him to conduct the tour.

Catherine took a deep breath.

"Captain Lorenzo will describe everything you see," Robert said. "I caution you, he will spare no details about how the human body responds to each device."

The Captain opened the door to the chamber. All the torches were lit. The Council filed into the room silently.

Catherine watched the faces of the Council as each device was described. She watched as both Giovanni and Romeo paled. Lord Como, usually so outspoken, was silent. She saw he had broken into a sweat and looked for something solid to lean against. She hated to do this to them, but she could think of no other way to shock them out of their complacency. This was necessary, of that she was absolutely convinced. She knew that both the Bishop and Carfaggi would seek to find their revenge. But she refused to turn back. Her course was set.

Chapter Thirty Eight

Lord Carfaggi fumed at the Bishop. "How dare she! Who does she think she is to force us to that stinking hell hole?" They were in the Bishop's quarters. The Bishop had called for a bottle of wine and dismissed the servant as soon as it was poured.

He didn't answer Carfaggi's question, but thought to himself, "She thinks she is the queen, you pompous ass."

Thomas Capshaw was no more pleased about the turn of events than Carfaggi. This whole change put him more directly in the middle of the war between the Pope and the queen. Carfaggi, as the Pope's own emissary, was certain to put him under even more pressure to rid them of this heretical queen. But the queen had his hands tied because of Robert's discovery of him with the boy. He would have to figure out a way to satisfy both of them to save himself. His mind raced.

Carfaggi was still raging, "Your future is at stake here, Capshaw. The Pope will know about your queen's little episode before too long. What she has said is nothing short of blasphemy! She will burn for this!"

"Lord Carfaggi, no one wants to see that woman burn more than I. But we must plan our strategy carefully." He stopped and smiled, an evil smile. "I believe that I can give you...us...what we both want, to rid ourselves of this queen. I have a plan."

"Tell me." Carfaggi's eyes narrowed suspiciously.

"What would be better than one of us accusing our queen of heresy?"

"I do not care to play guessing games! Tell me what you have in mind." Carfaggi was pacing.

"You are aware that I have been looking for ways to create suspicion and accusation against our queen for some time. It is not easy. She is well protected." He stood to pour himself a second cup of wine. "Even if I had succeeded in having her accused and convicted we might not have been any better off because there was no heir. Who knows into what hands this monarchy will fall."

The bishop took the bottle of wine over to Carfaggi, who waved him away.

"Now there is an heir," the bishop went on, "and one whom we can mold."

Carfaggi was not impressed, "The child is young. I am ready to be rid of this queen now."

"As am I, Lord Carfaggi, but do you not see the beauty of waiting a bit?"

"I don't see the beauty in anything that delays ousting that bitch!" Carfaggi drew himself up and folded his arms over his chest. He looked down his pointed nose at the Bishop.

"Not even," the Bishop lowered his voice and raised his eyebrows, "if it is her own daughter who accuses her of heresy and brings about the queen's death?"

"How long?" Carfaggi asked after a thoughtful pause.

"As soon as the child is old enough to appreciate having attention lavished upon her. I will make her dependent upon me and the doctrines of the Church. I will subtly implicate her mother, and that companion of hers, so that she will begin to draw her own conclusions about her mother's heresy. Do you not see how perfect a plan this is? Then we will help her to rule the kingdom of Montalcino with the iron fist of the papacy."

"What of her father, the King?" Carfaggi remained unconvinced.

"He adores the child. I don't think he will be a problem as long as he believes that I have the child's best interests at heart."

"I am leaving for Rome in a few months, Capshaw. I will share your plan with the Pope. If he approves, then so be it. If he doesn't...well, we will have to see. I am more inclined to move quickly. Her persistence in traveling around the kingdom makes me uncomfortable. She continues to endear herself to her subjects. And our ability to monitor her activities weakens when she is gone from the castle."

Weeks passed without further incidence on the Council. Catherine was still pondering whether or not to replace Lord Bagglioni. She spoke with him after his refusal to accompany the group to the torture

242

chamber. All he said was, "I am old and tired, Your Majesty. I have seen enough pain in my life. I do not wish to see more."

The Council, of course, wanted a replacement. She knew the Bishop and Carfaggi had someone in mind, but even they must know she would resist whomever they recommended. Then, one evening at dinner in the Great Hall Ambrose brought up the topic of the empty Privy Council seat.

"Do you have it in mind to replace Lord Bagglione?"

"I haven't yet decided. I rather like the fact that we are down again to seven members. An uneven number prevents me from having to break ties when votes are taken."

"I see your point." Ambrose cut into a juicy piece of roasted quail. "You do know that the Bishop and Lord Carfaggi have someone in mind."

"That's no surprise. Are they pressuring you to convince me on anyone in particular?"

"That should also come as no surprise. Yes, they are, but I think they are more interested in whom you might want."

"I suspect I already know the men they would like. It will never happen. I would rather keep things as they are," Catherine said as she sipped her wine.

When she finished eating he said, "Sofia is two now. I don't think it too early to bring her to Mass."

Catherine looked at him quizzically. "She is young yet. I believe we can wait a while longer." In spite of her calm demeanor, she was disturbed by his suggestion.

"Bishop Capshaw has raised the issue with me. He believes it is important for the child to become comfortable in the church," said Ambrose.

"She is two. She is comfortable anywhere she is." Catherine did not want to create acrimony between Ambrose and the Bishop, but it frightened her that the Bishop was pressing so soon.

"I tend to agree, but the Bishop is rather insistent on the matter," Ambrose seemed uncomfortable. He cleared his throat and avoided eye contact with her.

Catherine sighed. "Let me have tonight to think about it, then. Come to my office in the morning and let's discuss it further." She wanted to talk with Bella before making a decision.

"Fine," he said with relief evident on his face.

The next morning when Ambrose arrived at her office he was carrying a wrapped package, tied with a ribbon. He had a nervous smile on his face as he approached her desk. She came around and indicated the chair next to her.

As he sat he said, almost shyly, "I...have something for you." He held out the package.

Catherine was quite taken aback. "A gift? What is the occasion?"

"No occasion. I just want you to have it."

She reached out to accept the package. The ribbon alone was beautiful; soft yellow, and wide. The gift took up all of her lap and was wrapped in a piece of muslin cloth. As she uncovered the cloth she exclaimed, "Oh, Ambrose!"

Catherine held the oil painting up to admire. It was a remarkable likeness of Sofia. She was not only touched, but very impressed.

"You," she turned to look Ambrose squarely in the eyes, "are a gifted artist. I am so glad you have started painting again. You captured her innocence and her obstinacy, both!"

His head lowered as he blushed. Then he looked up at her with a shy grin. "I never thanked you for the gifts. I am glad you like it."

"I love it. Thank you." She bent to kiss his cheek. "Sofia is fortunate to have you for a father."

She set the painting on her desk, determined to find a good place to hang it, and turned back to him.

"About the Bishop...and Sofia attending Mass. You seemed uncomfortable when you raised the subject last night. What is it that bothers you?"

"I wish I could say." Ambrose turned in the chair and crossed his legs. "There was something that didn't feel quite right. Perhaps I am reading too much into his request, but I did sense that he had another reason. I just can't tell if the reason is related to you, or Sofia."

"Knowing the Bishop," Catherine offered carefully, "it may be both." She strode over to a shelf that contained many books and maps and ran her hand across some of the books as she thought. "Your instincts are probably correct, so perhaps we might err on caution's side. Do you see any harm letting her attend the Mass?"

He reached up and scratched at his beard. "Not really, and she would be with both of us, me when you are gone."

"It's enough His Grace detests me. He came to you for a reason. I see no reason to refuse his request if you don't."

Ambrose sighed deeply and his whole body relaxed.

Catherine smiled at his obvious relief. "When I am in residence, then, we can bring her to mass if he feels that strongly about it. We don't want to anger the Bishop over such a trivial issue." Catherine did not like that the Bishop seemed to be setting his sights on her daughter so soon. She had expected that he would attempt to sway the Princess at some point, but was distressed that he would attempt such a pointless position this early.

On Sunday, Catherine, Ambrose and Sofia attended Mass.

Chapter Thirty Nine

"Your Highness," the bishop said as Ambrose entered the Privy Council meeting, "I was happy to see you were able to convince Her Majesty to bring the child to Mass on Sunday."

Ambrose sat at the head of the table. Catherine was not feeling well and asked Ambrose to preside over the meeting.

"I would guess the queen was quite resistive to bringing the child," sniffed Lord Carfaggi.

"It wasn't a problem," Ambrose said.

"Well," Carfaggi continued with an irritated look, "have you found with whom she intends to replace Bagglione?"

"She has not yet decided."

"Well, has she given any indication she is even thinking on the matter?" Carfaggi pressed.

"I am afraid I have no information for you, Lord Carfaggi. The answer, again, is no."

"Perhaps," Bishop Capshaw interjected, "the king is not yet comfortable sharing information with the council." He paused, waiting for Ambrose to look at him. "Or, perhaps the queen doesn't trust him enough to tell him anything."

Carfaggi picked up where the Bishop left off. "I should hope, Your Grace, that the king has enough wisdom to know when to share things with the Privy Council. After all, it is Montalcino that must be served by this group, and not Her Highness."

Ambrose got up and went to pour himself some water, trying to hide his discomfort at the attack. His brain worked to think of something to say that would not seem defensive or foolish. When he returned to the table, Lord Giovanni requested the council turn to more pressing topics.

Summer was over before most in the kingdom were ready to let go of the long, warm days. Autumn charged in with full glory. October was near. It was time to prepare for the Chestnut Festival. The castle was surrounded by chestnut trees. For more winters than Catherine cared to remember, the meaty nuts provided the only protein for the residents of Montalcino. Without the chestnut, many would have starved when the snows piled so high that there was no way to hunt and the food reserves depleted.

It always amazed her how many different ways they could find to use chestnuts. Quite apart from roasting them, many creative recipes were invented—from soup to stuffing. Catherine was especially fond of breads and muffins made from ground chestnut flour.

The annual Chestnut Festival symbolized the strength and character of her people in a way that made Catherine especially proud. The festival incorporated music, dancing, food, wine, contests and games. In particular, she enjoyed watching the children scatter among the giant trees as they vied to see who could catch the most falling chestnuts. The child to catch the most won a prize, but it was their laughter and pure enjoyment of running and trying to avoid being hit by dropping nuts that offered the most amusement to the onlookers.

Catherine also loved Castiglione d' Orcia in the fall. The ride through the foothills was easy and she loved skirting around the shadow of the Apennines during the change of season.

When they arrived at the little church in Castiglione d' Orcia, Father Tim was talking to someone near the altar. Robert had entered first, to make sure it was safe for Catherine. He stopped when he saw the stranger.

"Robert!" Father Tim greeted him. "It is safe, please come in. Come in. This is my brother, my sibling actually, not another priest." Father Tim walked over to Robert, Isabella and Catherine.

"Majesty, my I present my brother, Thomas."

Thomas knelt before the queen, "Majesty."

"Please rise, Thomas. It is a pleasure to meet you."

"The pleasure is mine, Majesty. My brother has told me so much about you."

"And this is the Lady Isabella," continued Timothy.

"Lady Isabella, I am delighted." Thomas bowed. "And the concerned looking fellow with the sword must be Robert, Captain of the Queen's Guard?"

"I am." Robert nodded.

"I assure you, Captain, I have nothing but the utmost respect and admiration for your queen. And I am unarmed." Thomas smiled engagingly.

"Thomas just returned from Spain," Father Tim said. "His travels took him through parts of France and the Kingdom of Sardinia,"

Catherine wondered if Thomas shared his brother's views on the Inquisition. Until she had some indication, she listened.

"I've met with many who are disillusioned with the Church. Majesty, know that you are not alone in your fight against injustice. I have seen, and heard, things that chill my blood. I don't know how my brother continues to wear the robes of a priest in the Catholic Church. When I think of the…"

"Thomas," Father Tim interrupted him, "perhaps we can discuss that later. For now, Queen Catherine and Lady Isabella have come to hear Mass."

"My apologies, Majesty. As my brother can tell you, my zeal tends to overtake me at times."

"Thomas, will you stay for Mass? I am very interested in hearing what you have learned in your travels."

"No thank you, Majesty. I don't share my brother's spiritual leanings. I will be at the tavern. No offence intended."

"None taken, Thomas," the queen laughed. "Your honesty is refreshing. We will join you after Mass."

"I look forward to it, Queen Catherine." Thomas bowed and retreated.

Thomas was ordering his second ale as the queen's party joined him. They sat at a secluded table in the far back of the tavern.

"Majesty, I know you want to hear about Thomas' travels," Father Tim began, "but you need to know that his stories make your experiences in Pienza and Ribolla seem like child's play."

Catherine looked at Bella. "I intend to listen, but don't expect you to stay."

"I am staying." Bella stated firmly.

Robert arrived with several bottles of wine. The innkeeper brought a platter of cheeses, breads, oil, olives, fruits and nuts. Goblets were placed around the table and the wine was poured.

When the servers finished pouring the wine and left, Thomas began. "The majority of my time was spent in Spain, but I met with people from all over Europe. Primarily, it is the Protestants who are the targets of persecution. I'm sure you've heard that the King of France has publically declared he intends to exterminate all Protestants from France."

"With a cry of 'turn Papist, or die!'" Catherine shook her head as she put her goblet back on the table.

"It's true, Majesty. Those who refuse are put to death. Those not put to death suffer imprisonment, their houses are burned and property stolen. Their wives and daughters, after being ravished, are sent to convents. If they try to escape, they're pursued through the woods, hunted and shot like wild beasts."

He stopped, "Perhaps I am forging ahead too quickly. I apologize, Majesty. It isn't my intention to startle or offend you."

"It's fine, Thomas. Please continue at your own pace. I will stop you if I need to."

Thomas nodded and took a breath. "In all the provinces of France, it is the bishops, priests, friars and the clergy who work to keep up the cruel spirit of the military. An order was published for demolishing all protestant churches.

"Ferdinand and Isabella laid the groundwork for their unspeakable cruelty well. Since their deaths, their successors have taken their Spanish Inquisition to new levels. Expeditions in new parts of the world are still being funded, so it isn't just their own people they murder. I have heard Bartolome de Las Casas speak on the horrors he witnessed in Haiti, Cuba and the New World. Natives of those lands are being decimated in droves…as if they were nothing more than soulless beasts."

"Who is this de Las Casas?" asked Isabella

"A Spanish colonist, Lady, and a priest. One of the good ones, although he did not begin as such." Thomas smiled at his brother as he said this. "Originally he was a supporter and puppet of Ferdinand and Isabella. He traveled with Columbus to some of the lands I mentioned, and was present during the attacks on the native population of Cuba. It was there that he found his conscience rebelling against the slavery and slaughter of the natives. That's when he became a Dominican priest. He travels back and forth across the Atlantic debating openly for the freedoms of the Indians of those lands. Many of them have been forced into slave labor."

"Where is he now?" asked Catherine as she accepted cheese and olives Bella placed on her plate.

"For the last many years he has been writing and speaking. He has made several court appearances in defense of the Indians."

"I am glad to know that someone is out there making a public stand, but I wonder why he is allowed to get away with his public position?" Catherine was intrigued.

"De Las Casas himself has wondered, Majesty." Thomas smiled. "If you want my opinion, I think it's because these new worlds are far enough away to be considered nothing by way of threat. The great Ferdinand and Isabella didn't consider the natives of other lands to be people. But that is just my opinion."

"One that seems based in careful consideration and knowledge." Isabella offered.

Thomas nodded to her. "Thank you, Lady Isabella, but I don't deserve your praise. I may be privy to much information, but it is people like de Las Casas who are fighting for the rights of others who deserve your respect. I am simply a carrier of information. I don't have the courage to do anything with the information except pass it along to those who might be able to do something."

"Nevertheless, Thomas," Catherine leaned across the table and placed her hand on his forearm, "you must not underestimate the power and importance of the information you provide. And the mere fact that you are willing to travel, supplying this kind of information puts you at risk. It takes a great deal of courage to do what you are doing."

"Thank you, Queen Catherine. I am only glad there are people, like you, willing to listen." Thomas paused to take a long drink of his ale. Then he continued. "And I wish that there were more people like you. I wonder if you know that you are the reason I am here."

Father Tim playfully feigned astonishment. "Brother, you mean I am not the sole reason for your visit? I am hurt."

Thomas laughed and turned back to the queen. "My brother knows well why I have come, Majesty. You should know that word of your sympathy is spreading beyond your little kingdom. When I heard about you I determined that I must meet you. You can imagine my delight when Tim told me that he was working with you to fight for freedom."

"I am afraid that's an exaggeration," Catherine said. "There are times that I wish we might openly fight, but that has not been the case. Your brother wisely points out that the earth is filling with the bodies of martyrs right now. His is the voice of reason and caution as we search for new ways to help."

"There are times when I wonder if anything will ever help. Especially when I learn of how difficult things are in other places." Thomas's face darkened and he lowered his head to hide his tears.

Timothy placed his hand on his brother's shoulder. "Majesty," Tim gave a worried look across the table. "I hesitate for you to hear some of what Thomas has related to me." Tim paused and didn't seem willing to proceed. Catherine waited. The determined look in her eyes was one that said to the priest, "You know you will tell me…and do not make me ask." It was a look that all present, with the exception of Thomas, had come to know over the years.

Tim closed his eyes and dropped his head in surrender. "Bohemia. Things are very bad in Bohemia and Portugal. The Portuguese government ordered all non-Catholic children under the age of fourteen be taken from their parents and retained in the country as fit subjects for Catholic education. You can imagine the distress of the parents. Many of them murdered their own children to defeat the ordinance; many killed themselves as well."

No one spoke. What was there to say? The sounds of the tavern continued around them oblivious to the sadness that consumed the table of the queen and her guests.

Finally, Thomas continued. "No one, however, has suffered more than the Protestants of Bohemia. Racked, burnt, sawn asunder, thrown from rocks, torn by wild horses, cut to pieces, skinned alive, hanged, drowned, stabbed; some were boiled in oil or had boiling lead poured down their throats. Many were crucified with their heads hanging downwards."

More silence.

Then, finally, Catherine asked, "How many?"

"Some I have spoken to have told me that the country may be nearing a new population count of one million...maybe lower."

"That is impossible!" Catherine cried. "Bohemia has three million people!"

"No longer, Majesty." Thomas dropped his head into his hands, then picked up his ale tankard and drained it. "In many places they locked up people in churches and forced them to kneel before the Host. If they didn't kneel willingly their legs were beat with clubs until they fell down; others were gagged, and when they had propped their mouths wide open, the host was thrust down their throats. Many were detained in prisons until they died, and one was kept in a loathsome dungeon so long that his feet rotted off."

Thomas looked up to see that Bella had visibly paled. "I am sorry, Lady Isabella. Perhaps I need not be so graphic."

Bella took a deep breath and shook her head. "No, Thomas. If this is what is happening, then I must hear it. Everyone should know this, and be sickened by it. Please, don't try to shield me."

Thomas ordered another ale and looked to Catherine, who nodded for him to continue.

"If anyone tried to avoid the tyranny, to flee to the woods or other private places for shelter, edicts were published forbidding everyone from entertaining them, upon pain of forfeiting great sums of money for every night's entertainment. Country people were fetched out of their houses, out of their very beds, by hoards of soldiers, who drove them like beasts in the worst of bitter weather. They filled the prisons, towers, cellars, stables...even hog-sties, where they died with hunger, cold, and thirst. Marriage, burial and baptism are forbidden to the Protestants, and if they perform the rituals privately they are imprisoned, or else put to great fines. In some places they are shut up in privies, in the hope that they might be poisoned with the stench."

Thomas stopped. Again, the only sounds were those of the tavern, silver on plates, the steady hum of voices around them, laughter.

"It is incomprehensible to me," Catherine broke the silence, "that the horrors we have witnessed in our little kingdom can be considered tame by comparison."

She ached. Her heart faltered within her.

"You have presented us with staggering numbers of deaths." Robert said. "If Bohemia alone has murdered two million, how many more have been eliminated in other areas?"

"I don't think we will ever know." Thomas poured himself another mug of ale.

"I cannot," Bella started, shaking her head "comprehend how we have allowed this to happen! "Why are not more people standing up to this abuse?"

"Some are, Lady," Thomas said "just not enough of us."

When they parted, the queen thanked Thomas, bid him farewell and safe travels. He was leaving in the morning to try to make Venice by weeks' end.

Chapter Forty

The evening ride back to the castle was full of emotion…but devoid of words. Bella sniffed and cried her way back. Robert occasionally filled his lungs, blowing the air out between gritted teeth as his head shook back and forth.

Catherine was mobilized by her anger, she felt her fire fueled and fanned. Her mind raced with thoughts, both murderous and frightening. She did not understand how God allowed these things to happen. How did these atrocities go on and on? Where the hell was God? Why didn't He do something? And that was when it struck her like a blow to the chest. God had nothing to do with this. God wasn't even present. This was not God's doing. It was a mistake to think that God was going to answer her prayers, or anyone's. If He hadn't heard them by now He was deaf. They were on their own to fight or die, or give in to the evils perpetrated by men who called themselves God's representatives. God had abandoned them.

That night in her quarters, Catherine was restless. She paced back and forth near the doors leading to the balcony. Bella tried to help her calm, but she would have none of it. The meal sat, mostly untouched, except for the ale which Catherine sipped.

"Catherine, let me draw you a bath." Bella offered as she reached her hand out to lay it on Catherine's arm.

Catherine shook her off. "I don't want a bath."

"Please, then, sit with me. Let me hold you. I can see today upset you."

"I don't want to be held." Catherine continued pacing and did not look at Bella.

"But I do. Catherine, please. Today upset me, too. And now you are worrying me. You think I don't see that look in your eyes? That I don't feel the shift in you?"

She stopped her pacing and glared at Bella. "I am angry…angrier than I have ever been in my life."

"So talk to me," Bella pleaded. "Let's be angry together! Sometimes you act as if you are the only one who is allowed to respond to the things going on around us!"

"I am not ready to share what I'm thinking. Just let me be, can you?"

Catherine threw open the double doors to the balcony and went outside. Then she spun around, went to the table and grabbed the rest of her ale and returned to the balcony. Even there she paced. When she stopped pacing she stood looking up at the stars. Her teeth ground against one another as she went over and over the things that Thomas told them. "If God cannot be counted upon," she reasoned with herself, "then we have to take care of this on our own." She was unsure how, exactly, to fight, but the fight built within her as she resumed her pacing. She stopped and pushed against the half wall of the balcony with all of her might, stifling a scream.

Bella went to the doors. "Catherine, please come inside. It is cold with the doors open."

"Then close them and leave me alone," she barked.

Bella closed the doors and went to prepare herself for bed.

A while later Catherine entered the bedroom. "Bella, I am sorry. I know you have feelings about what we heard today. What you seem to forget is that, as queen, I have a responsibility to try to do something about it!"

Bella was sitting in bed working some needlepoint. She looked up and delivered an icy stare at Catherine.

Catherine felt the sting of the look. "Please, don't be like that. I said I was sorry."

Bella's face did not soften. "What you seem to forget is that I am affected by your responsibilities no less than you. When you decide you must act I am forced to act with you, or at least support your action, no matter how I might feel about it. And much of what you do *as queen* takes little of me into account."

Catherine felt her defenses rise up. "Don't be ridiculous. You are always part of what I think and plan and do. You are included in everything."

Bella nearly flew off the bed. "I am not talking of being included, I am talking about being considered!" she shouted with her hands on her hips and her eyes blazing.

"You are not making any sense." Catherine dismissed her, "You are behaving like a typical...like a...."

"Like a woman?" Bella finished. "Oh, well here is some news for you, Queen Catherine, I am a woman...and one who supports you in spite of my feelings. Do you think I enjoy following you all over the kingdom and watching you take on the woes of all of Europe? Do you not, for one selfish moment, imagine that I might enjoy a quiet life of reading, riding and watching our children grow without having to worry that your position...your fight...your damned royal title might doom us at any moment?"

Catherine's defenses shattered instantly. Her heart crumbled as she understood what Bella was saying. "Bella...I had no..." Catherine started apologetically.

"I am not finished!" Bella interrupted as she strode around the bed to stand face to face with Catherine. "I am a typical woman because I continue to support you and all that you believe in and strive for regardless of my own fears. I do this because I love you...and I love you because I have no choice. If that makes me ridiculous then..."

Bella was unable to complete her thought. Catherine could take no more. Remorse flooded her and threatened to drown her. She had to stop Bella; had to stop the words, the anguish of what Bella said. Catherine was crying, pulling Bella close, and kissing her hard. There was everything in her kisses... desperation, fear, anger, outrage. "Stop, Bella, please. Forgive me. Forgive me!" Catherine begged as she covered Bella with kisses. They were kisses that screamed the need for survival, held the last vestiges of hope, and pleaded for life in a world gone mad with murder.

Catherine pushed Bella against the bed with the intensity of her kisses. Bella found herself responding in spite of and because of her own anger. She turned and pushed Catherine down on the bed tearing at her doublet. Catherine lifted her head but Bella reached up, slid her fingers through Catherine's hair and pushed it back down onto the bed, all the while her lips, tongue, teeth probing, searching, desperate. Then

Bella's hands were on Catherine's breasts, her knee pressing hard between Catherine's legs.

Catherine was moaning, arching, needing, but she rolled on top of Bella and her hands were everywhere at once stroking, squeezing, satisfying. Catherine became Bella's desire. As Bella neared her climax her fingers clawed at Catherine's back, but Catherine, suspended in some otherworldly realm, did not notice. She was Bella's hunger and her nourishment, her faith and her despair, her life and her death. When Bella finally cried out Catherine heard all of life in her cry, but she did not cease her raw, intense lovemaking. Catherine's hands, fingers, lips, teeth, tongue, hair…every inch of her continued to ravish Bella, until Bella cried out again and again…and again.

When the morning sun filled the bedroom, Bella rolled over to reach for Catherine, but she was not there.

"Catherine?" she called, the fear evident in her voice.

"I'm here." Catherine came through the doors from the sitting room. She sat on the side of the bed and reached her hand out to stroke Bella's face gently. She smiled. "I thought to let you sleep."

Bella kissed Catherine's palm. "What have you been doing?"

"Just thinking."

"Do I want to know?"

Catherine closed her eyes and took a deep breath, then opened them and looked at Bella. She spent the last hour feeling the intense guilt of her unintentional disregard for Bella's feelings. "My love, I am so sorry. You have given so much of yourself. I have not considered your feelings. You are right that I always expect you to simply go along with whatever I feel I need to do because of my title. It isn't fair to you…and yet, you never complain." Catherine's shame overwhelmed her and her eyes reddened and misted. "I never meant to hurt you. I would do anything to make it up to you."

"Catherine, I was angry last night," Bella said as she reached to take Catherine's hand in her own. "My succor has not changed. I will continue to support you, and the kingdom, in any way I can."

"But you have needs, too," Catherine said through her tears, "and you were right to point out that I have ignored them. That was never my intention. I do promise to be more considerate. Please forgive me?"

Bella opened her arms and Catherine climbed onto the bed and curled into them.

"After last night I think you may have accumulated quite a huge surplus of forgiveness," she smiled.

Gratefully, Catherine wrapped her arms tightly around Bella. "I don't ever want to lose you," she whispered.

Chapter Forty One

January 1561

Just before Sofia's fifth birthday the Bishop asked Ambrose to bring Sofia to the church.

"King Ambrose," the bishop said, smiling happily, "how nice to see you and the Princess."

"You did request us, Your Grace" Ambrose replied.

"I did, indeed, Majesty." He led them to the front near the altar. I believe Princess Sofia is old enough now to appreciate some of the more intricate aspects of our faith, I believe. She is nearly five years old now, is she not?" the bishop asked although he knew, to the hour, Sofia's age.

"What is it that you have in mind, Your Grace?" Ambrose asked.

"To begin Princess Sofia's religious training, King Ambrose," he replied. "It is time."

The bishop decided to address Sofia directly. He had no real experience in dealing with children, but had led Lord Carfaggi to believe that he had been setting the stage to endear himself to Sofia for some time.

"Princess Sofia, do you like coming to Mass?"

Even at her tender young age Sofia knew that there could only be one answer to this question. "Yes, Your Grace."

"What is your favorite part of the Mass?" he asked.

Sofia scrunched up her face and thought for a moment. "Sometimes I like the music best, when it is not so sad. Sometimes I like Communion."

The Bishop was surprised that Sofia liked that particular Sacrament. "What is it about Communion that you like, Princess?"

Sofia looked up at her father, as if she were unsure that she should give her answer honestly.

The bishop saw the look and moved quickly to reassure her, "Princess, come here," he sat down on one of the pews and forced himself to hold out his arms. She went to him and climbed onto his lap. "I want you to feel comfortable here in the church, and with me.

Whatever your reason for liking communion, you may tell me. I am your bishop and we are going to be great friends, you and I. Now, tell me, what do you like about communion?"

With the honesty that only a child could give, Sofia looked the bishop square in the eye and said, "I am always hungry at Mass."

The Bishop's limited experience with smaller children did not prepare him for her answer. He smiled and told her he understood completely. "I am often hungry during Mass myself, Princess. But let us keep that as a secret between us."

The bishop looked up and smiled at the King, then turned back to Sofia. "Would you like to see where we keep the Communion wafers between Masses?" he asked.

Sofia's eyes grew wide as she nodded enthusiastically.

So began the subtle and manipulative road down which the bishop hoped to ally himself with the future queen.

He knew he would have to involve King Ambrose as much as possible, but over the years he was unable to determine whether King Ambrose was sympathetic to the church or to the queen. He remained frustrated in his attempts to identify the king's loyalties. He thought, at first, that Ambrose would be a malleable subject. When Catherine first announced that Ambrose was to join the Privy Council he was surprised, but considered it a boon for himself. He had no doubts, initially, that he would be able to control the new King, thereby gathering all the evidence he might need to have Ambrose accuse the queen of heresy. Ambrose, to his surprise, remained aloof and unreadable. Bishop Capshaw had never read a man as wrong as he had read Ambrose. If he did not succeed with regard to his plan with Princess Sofia he was doomed.

To Carfaggi's disappointment, the Pope had liked Capshaw's idea and encouraged Carfaggi to be patient. The Pope wanted this queen under his control, and he was willing to wait. But the bishop knew once the Pope had *Queen* Sofia, he would have no more need for Bishop Capshaw.

Following the visit with Sofia, King Ambrose sent the bishop a note stating that he and Queen Catherine wished to wait until the princess was older to begin formal religious training.

Chapter Forty Two

Spring 1561

Mary sat in one of the gardens working on a needlepoint as Princess Sofia and James played nearby. On warm spring mornings she always brought them outdoors for some fresh air before the midday meal. She established a routine with them early on, and found they both responded better to a structured day than to one allowing them too much time without guided activity. Mornings outdoors allowed them a bit of both.

The morning was soft, warm, and held an abundance of clouds. Sofia and James were digging in a pile of dirt left by the gardener, who'd left gone to retrieve some new vine cuttings.

At six James was all boy, digging contentedly and making a huge mess. He did not care that he was becoming covered in mud.

"James, stop!" Sofia ordered. "You are getting dirt in my moat!"

"Sorry, Sofi. I'll help you rebuild it." James adored Sofia. "We need water, too."

A shadow passed over the children. Mary looked up.

"Your Grace!" Mary jumped up and put down her needlework and knelt before the bishop. He held out his ring for her to kiss.

"How are the children doing, Mary?"

While it was unusual for the Bishop to know the names of any servants but his own, he made it a point to learn the name of the primary caretaker for the princess.

Mary stood. "They are good children, Your Grace. It is a joy to care for them."

The bishop looked over to where the children continued digging, then back at Mary. "It is time to begin formal religious training for the princess. Because of your role, it makes most sense that you and I arrange a time for you to bring her to me for her lessons."

"Of course, Your Grace."

"I should like you to bring her to the Church every Wednesday following Mass. It will just be for a short period every week."

"I understand." Mary nodded.

"And, Mary, the king and queen have left this arrangement in my hands," the Bishop lied. "Please don't bother them with the details, or for that matter, even our conversation regarding the princess. They have made it clear that all of this is up to me. I don't want to burden them more than they are already with running the kingdom."

"I understand, Your Grace."

"Good. Then I shall see you tomorrow after Mass."

Mary curtsied. "Tomorrow, then, Your Grace."

After that, Mary dutifully brought Sofia to the church once weekly after Mass.

Each week as she was leaving, the Bishop reminded Sofia about their secret. "Now don't forget, my little princess, our meetings are just a secret between you, me…"

"And God!" Sofia beamed. "I won't forget, Your Grace."

To further insure that Sofia remembered to keep her secret, and to help her look forward to coming, he always ended the short times by giving Sofia a special treat. Usually, it was some confection, but on occasion he gave her a little toy.

Chapter Forty Three

October 1563

In the fall of Sofia's seventh year a tutor was hired to begin in earnest on her studies. The tutor, a scholar from Venice, was a homely man in his thirties. Mario Barone was short, stocky and hairy. At first glance one would not take him for a scholar, rather, he had more the look of a blacksmith gone soft. His pudgy face was smooth and his nose bent a little awkwardly at an angle, as if it had been broken one too many times. He had overly large ears, but kept them covered with a full, thick, long head of brown hair. His eyes, dark and bright, were his best feature. They were intense and shining, open and intelligent. Although not much to look at, he possessed a fine mind and his ability to train his young charge was admirable.

"Your Grace!" Sofia exclaimed delightedly when the Bishop entered the room where she and her tutor spent a good part of the day working. Sofia ran from her table and threw her arms around him.

"Ah, my sweet little princess, how are you today?" He picked her up and hugged her. "Oh, but, Sofia, you are forgetting your manners. Please introduce me to your teacher," he said more playfully than sternly.

As the bishop put her down, she dutifully introduced Mario Barone, who knelt and kissed the Bishop's ring.

Bishop Capshaw said, "I don't mean to interfere with Sofia's lessons, Master Barone. But I wanted to meet the great teacher she has told me so much about."

"Your Grace, it is an honor to meet you. It is evident that you two have a special relationship."

Thomas Capshaw looked down at Sofia and winked. "We do, indeed." He looked down at the open book from which Sofia had been reading. "And what are we learning today?"

"Numbers," Sofia said brightly.

The Bishop squatted down in front of her and whispered loud enough for Mario to hear, "Numbers are important. Unless you know your numbers and counting how will you be able to figure your purchases of candy?" As he said this he slipped a small confection into her hand.

The bishop stood and turned back to her teacher. "I would like to visit with you regarding certain aspects of the Princess' education, Master Barone. I wonder if I might impose upon you to dine with me this evening in my private residence."

"You are too kind, Your Grace. It would be an honor."

"Seven o'clock, then," he turned to Sofia and smiled, "and you, my dear, back to work!"

Master Barone arrived at the Bishop's private residence at precisely seven o'clock. In anticipation of his arrival, Thomas placed a book with detailed drawings of Michelangelo's works on the table near where they would sit before and after dinner. He had stolen the book from the library at the Villa Guilia when he was in Rome. He left it open to a sketch of the statue of David. The nude statue created quite a stir when it was unveiled.

One servant was on hand to serve dinner and wine. The bishop handed the tutor a glass of wine and invited him to sit.

"Master Barone, how do you find life here in our quaint little Montalcino?"

"Please, Your Grace, call me Mario."

"Mario, then."

"I like it well enough. It is quiet and seems friendly," he replied as he sipped at his wine. "This wine is quite delightful, Your Grace."

"I am glad you like it. The grapes are grown locally, and the vintner is a friend. I save his finer wines for special occasions."

Mario blushed, unable to conceal his delight at being 'special'. "I am honored, Bishop."

"Not at all, it is we who are honored to have a scholar, at long last, in our midst. I love our little kingdom, but must confess to feeling quite alone in my search for more sophisticated companionship." The Bishop stood and strolled over to his bookshelf. "I spent an extended period in Rome several years ago, and have greatly missed the discussions among scholars and great leaders." He smiled at Mario.

"Rome is quite the place, is it not, Your Grace?"

"It is a delight for all of the senses."

"Have you ever been to Venice, Your Grace?"

The Bishop sat down again, this time a bit closer to the teacher. "I have not had the opportunity. My duties here in Montalcino take up too much of my time."

"Ah, Your Grace, that is a shame. I believe you would find Venice even more enchanting than Rome."

Bishop Capshaw started to ask about Venice when his servant indicated that dinner was ready to be served. The men made their way to the dining room.

"Tell me about Venice." Thomas said as he indicated for Mario to sit.

"Some of the most learned men and most gifted artisans spend time in Venice. It is a seat of great learning. I guarantee you would never tire of finding good conversation. And Venice is a vision of grandeur and beauty. The architecture and the waterways are an unimaginable feast for the eyes."

"I will have to make it a point to travel there someday then." The bishop lifted his wine glass. "To Venice then, and to Montalcino's good fortune at having secured such a remarkable tutor for our princess."

They dined on roasted pork in a honey glaze. Pork was an especially telling entrée to serve as it allowed the host to determine whether or not the guests might be averse to eating pig. Avoiding pork gave rise to the suspicion that the aversion may be religiously motivated.

Mario had no problem with the meal, eating everything with gusto.

When the meal was complete, the Bishop asked about the princess and her studies.

"She is really quite a remarkable student, Your Grace. Her ability to grasp more complex ideas with regard to mathematics and languages is really surprising for her age."

Thomas led them over to the more comfortable couches where the art book was open. The couches were arranged to allow for ease and comfort of conversation no matter where one sat. The Bishop sat directly across from Mario, so that the tutor could not avoid the drawing of David.

"I have found the princess to be very astute. I am glad you find her so, as well. I have spent several years working on her religious training."

"That explains the closeness of your relationship."

"Yes. And I have no desire to distract her from her studies with you, Mario, but it is important that her religious studies continue with me."

"Of course, Your Grace. How may I be of assistance?"

Bishop Capshaw rose and poured them each a glass of hazelnut liquor. "The King and Queen have placed Sofia's religious training in my hands. Since she will someday inherit the throne, her knowledge of the Catholic Church and the tenets of our religion are of utmost importance. Do you agree?" The Bishop raised an eyebrow in question.

"Without a doubt, Your Grace."

The Bishop remained standing after giving Mario the liquor. "I should like a bit of time with her, say, two times weekly, for her religious instruction."

"I do not foresee that as a difficulty."

"Good." The Bishop moved over to the couch where Mario sat. He sat down close beside him. "Two mornings a week, then, after Mass. I shall come directly to your classroom and spend time with her there."

"Whenever you like, Your Grace. I am at your service."

"Thank you, Mario. Now, let us turn to more interesting subjects. Have you seen this statue of David in person?"

Mario turned his focus to the drawing in the book that Bishop Capshaw was pulling over toward him. The tutor flushed ever so slightly.

"I have not, Your Grace, but I hear it is magnificent."

"Truly," the Bishop answered. "I had the opportunity to be staying at the Villa Guilia in Rome when Michelangelo was staying there."

"What was he like? Did you actually meet him?"

"He was so unlike his creations...slovenly, uncouth. An interesting man, but very unsociable, lacking in good manners. I had difficulty marrying the man to his work. His paintings and his sculptures are so magnificent that one expects him to have an air, a presence, himself. But he does not. I was disappointed to be honest."

The Bishop leaned over the drawing, and as he did so he allowed his hand to rest on Mario's knee in a preoccupied sort of way. "His attention to detail is amazing. Look, here," he pointed to the musculature in David's torso, "you would be astonished to look upon exquisite attention to detail. It makes you want to reach up and touch the marble, certain it might come alive under your touch." Here Thomas allowed his finger to casually drift over David's penis. "And. if you haven't seen the ceiling of the Chapel in Rome, you must do so before you die."

Mario swallowed the remainder of his liquor in one gulp. Thomas got up to pour him another glass.

"Oh, no, Your Grace. Thank you. I really must be going." The tutor stood and made for the door. "It has been a delightful evening, but I must prepare for tomorrow's lessons. Forgive me for rushing off."

The bulge beneath the tutor's robe was all Thomas needed to know that he had succeeded in his goal for the evening. After Mario left, he sat back and poured himself another glass of the sweet liquor. He smiled to himself as he paged through the drawings of Michelangelo.

"Now, my sweet Sofia, we will be meeting in your classroom two days a week. How will you like that?" Bishop Capshaw asked the princess on the first day of his arrival in her classroom.

"I like that just fine, Your Grace," Sofia answered happily. "And James will like it, too. He is to join me for lessons starting today!" she announced with obvious great delight.

This fact caught Thomas off guard, but he recovered quickly. "I am certain that I would enjoy meeting with James, too, but don't forget that our little meetings are for us alone. You are the Princess, after all, and require special lessons that are only designed for Royalty, my dear."

"Oh," Sofia looked sad.

"But if you like I will talk to your parents about including James. Would you like me to do that?"

"Oh, yes, thank you, thank you!" Sofia lit up at the suggestion.

"But," the Bishop continued, "you must let me talk to them. You must not utter a word."

"I understand. It will be another secret," the child whispered conspiratorially.

The Bishop smiled and wrapped Sofia in his arms in a great hug, disappearing before James arrived.

A few days later Master Barone was in the middle of the children's Latin lesson when the caretaker, Mary, entered the classroom. James ran up to her and threw his arms around her. Sofia waited, smiling, until James had finished his greeting.

"Princess Sofia," Mary smiled as Sofia allowed herself to be wrapped in a warm hug. "You are to come with me for a bit."

Sofia looked to Master Barone. "It is fine," he said, "you will be back soon."

Mary took Sofia down through a small door at the back of the library, through a secret passageway that led to the chapel where Bishop Capshaw waited.

"But what about James?" Sofia asked him after she arrived.

"I am afraid it is not to be." The Bishop shook his head sadly apologetically.

"But why...why can't he come, too? Doesn't he need to learn about God?"

The Bishop dropped his head as he answered, "Princess, I tried to obtain permission for James, but your mother would not allow it. I am sorry," he lied.

"But how will James learn about God?" Sofia was concerned.

Bishop Capshaw got up from where he sat next to Sofia and walked toward the altar.

"Come here, Sofia."

Sofia went to him and knelt next to him in front of the altar.

"We must pray for your mother so that she might come to understand that James needs this instruction, as well. I fear that she and Lady Isabella believe they are fulfilling James' religious instruction by taking him to Mass with Father Timothy in Castiglione d' Orcia." Thomas Capshaw bowed his head and folded his hands in reverence and prayed. Sofia emulated him as the bishop began to pray. "Heavenly Father, please help the queen to see that her sins harm those she loves...and those of us who love her so dearly." He opened his hands and turned them toward the crucifix in supplication. With a look of utter pain, and tears in his eyes he continued, "Lord, show us the way to help Sofia's mother. She does not understand the harm that she does to the children."

Sofia's tears dripped down her face and fell onto the stone floor of the altar as she listened to the bishop. He was quiet for a time, then whispered just loud enough for Sofia to hear, "Yes, Lord. I understand."

Thomas Capshaw turned his body to sit upon the stone step to the altar. He opened his arms to Sofia and she climbed into his lap. "It will be fine, little one. But God needs us to be in constant prayer. We must pray in earnest that your mother will, in time, come to understand what you already seem to know."

"What is it, Your Grace? What do I know?" Sofia looked up at him.

"You know that God is here...in this Chapel. You know that God loves her...and that I love her. But she does not know that. The Queen imagines that I despise her."

"She does?" Sofia's eyes opened wide. "Why?"

"Satan and Father Timothy have poisoned her mind. Not all in the Church are of God. We must pray that she finds her way back to the truth."

Fear flowed from the child's face. Sofia wriggled off the Bishop's lap and knelt at the altar. Her tears flowed as she prayed. "Please, God, help my mother."

"Sofia," Bishop Capshaw said softly as he walked her to the door. "We must not speak of this struggle to anyone. God wants your mother to come back to Him on her own. You must not let her know that we pray for her soul and her return to grace." He knelt in front of her and his eyes filled with tears. "I will continue to try to arrange for James to be allowed to come here with you, but only if you promise to say nothing about our visits, or how concerned we are for her soul."

Sofia threw her arms around the Bishop's neck and sobbed into his shoulder. "I promise. I promise." When she finally finished crying he released her and placed his hands on her face.

"It will be fine, my little Princess. Have faith. God is on our side." He smiled at her as she sniffed.

He opened the doors to the Chapel where Mary waited to return her to class.

That evening at dinner in the Great Hall Catherine noticed that Sofia ate little.

"What is it, Sofia? Are you feeling ill?" she asked.

"I'm not very hungry," the child responded.

"Come here, love." Catherine opened her arms and pulled Sofia into her lap. Sofia allowed her mother's arms to enfold her. She sank against her mother's breast and released a sigh so large that Bella reached out to feel the child's face.

"What is it, Sofia?" Bella asked. "You seem so forlorn...like you have lost your best friend."

"Nothing." But as she buried her face against her mother again, she began to weep. Catherine excused herself from the dining table and carried Sofia up to her quarters where she sat with her in the rocking chair that still remained from when Sofia and James were babies.

As Catherine rocked her daughter, she stroked her hair and whispered, "Whatever it is, my darling, all will be well. Just cry if you need to. Sometimes we all need to cry."

Sofia fell asleep in her mother's arms.

"Ah, Master Barone," Bishop Capshaw said. Both men were leaving the dining hall at the same time. "I have been craving some intellectual company this evening. Will you do me the honor of joining me for a drink in my quarters?"

"Oh, Your Grace," he stammered. Mario blushed and could not meet the bishop's eyes.

"I will take any refusal as a personal insult, I must warn you!" the bishop said playfully.

"Well, then, Your Grace, it appears I have no choice. I would not want to insult you." Mario Barone smiled.

The Bishop poured them each a glass of wine and brought one over to where Mario sat.

"To stimulating conversation," the Bishop raised his glass.

"To stimulating conversation, then, Your Grace." Mario Barone lifted his glass and touched it to the Bishop's

"Have you read Homer?" Bishop Capshaw began.

The tutor looked with some surprise at the Bishop. "It is impossible to avoid Homer when studying the classics. Have you read Homer, then?"

"It was impossible to avoid many things when I was in Rome. Homer, Dante. I must admit that I was surprised to find so many in the Church well versed in the classics."

"What of the ban on such materials, Your Grace?" Master Barone's expression was one of concern. "Have not such materials been banned by the Church?"

"They have indeed." Thomas Capshaw rose from his seat and walked over to his extensive bookshelf. "And not only have such books been banned, but you are probably aware that Pope Paul was instrumental in having the genitalia of the works of Michelangelo, as well as others, covered. He felt they were obscene and had no place in the Church."

"I had heard that, yes." Mario stood and walked over to join the Bishop at the bookshelf. He began to look through the titles that lined the shelves. "And how do you feel about the bans, Your Grace?"

"May I confide in you, Master Barone?" the bishop lowered his voice to a whisper.

"Of course."

"It saddens me that such great works of art, poetry, philosophy and science are forbidden. I believe that such works are important to the improvement of civilization. How can we progress, as a people, if we deny the exploration and discussion inherent in the creation and expression of thought?" The bishop turned away from the tutor, hiding his face. He shook his head and walked back over to the couch where they had been sitting.

"You are an unusual man, Your Grace." Mario continued to peruse the bookshelf. "One full of surprises."

"Not unpleasant surprises, I hope?"

Mario Barone smiled as he made his way to sit next to the Bishop. "Not unpleasant, no. One, in fact, whose sentiments reflect my own."

"Perhaps, then, I might confide in you about something."

"Of course, what is it?" the tutor said with worry.

"I am concerned about Princess Sofia's safety." Again, the bishop stood. He placed the fingertips of his hands together, tapping them ever so slightly as he paced in front of Mario. "I am more relieved than you know that she has you to teach her." He sat back down, closer to Mario, as he continued. "I am in a difficult position as her confessor and her bishop. It is my duty to protect her from heretical thoughts and ideas…to teach her the difference." The Bishop looked directly into Master Barone's eyes, searching them.

Mario Barone's face registered a mild look of fear. "Your Grace, I would never teach the Princess anything against the Church!"

The Bishop placed his hand on Mario's shoulder. "I believe you. And I trust that you have Princess Sofia's best interests at heart. But I wonder if I might ask you a favor."

"Anything, Your Grace."

Bishop Capshaw brought his hands together, interlacing his fingers, and rested his chin on them momentarily. "I have reason to believe that the Princess may be in danger."

"How so?" Mario's look was one of both fear and shock.

"I am not at liberty to discuss the matter, and I am still investigating, but the important thing is that the time the Princess spends with me be absolutely confidential. I will continue to have Mary pick her up and deliver her to me at the church, but do not want James to know that she is with me." The Bishop paused here and seemed hesitant to continue. Finally, he said, "This is the difficult part, Mario," and here he rested his left hand on Mario's thigh, "I believe it vital to Sofia's safety that absolutely no one knows about her studies with me.

Although her parents have assigned her religious studies to me, I don't want to worry them with my fears about Sofia's safety."

"Do you not think it wise for the king and queen to be apprised of the danger?" Mario asked.

The Bishop drew his right hand across the tutor's shoulders as he leaned against him. His left hand still rested on Mario's thigh and slid slightly upward toward his groin as the Bishop leaned in to whisper. "Mario," the Bishop drew himself close to the tutor and whispered in his ear, "it is from the queen I believe she is in danger. I can say no more."

The teacher said nothing, but adjusted his posture to try to hide his erection.

"Now," said the Bishop as he leaned back in his seat, "about Homer. What is your opinion of how he portrays Ganymede's abduction by Zeus?"

Chapter Forty Four

Summer 1566

In spite of Lord Carfaggi's objection, Catherine announced plans to visit Radicondoli. She had made it a point to visit the hometowns of every other Privy Council member and had still not been to Carfaggi's home. It was time.

"Your Majesty," Lord Carfaggi pleaded, "I have been in continual contact with my family, my friends and my business associates. I assure you they have things well under control. You needn't bother yourself with a trip there."

"It's no bother at all, Lord Carfaggi. I don't wish to slight the good people of Radicondoli. They are as much a part of the kingdom of Montalcino as all my other subjects. And, I look forward to meeting with your family".

The threat Carfaggi posed during the years of his cousin's reign as Pope diminished slightly after Carafa's death, but Lord Carfaggi continued the harsh criticism of heresy; and he still had friends in high places in Rome and throughout the kingdom of Montalcino. The new Pope, Pius IV, was slightly more moderate in his views, but there were few changes with regard to the Inquisition.

As Catherine thought about leaving for Radicondoli, she was aware that Sofia was more subdued than usual. One evening at dinner, Catherine watched as Sofia kept her head bowed and hands in prayer. She stayed in prayer long past the grace given by Bishop Capshaw.

"Bella," she nodded in the direction of Sofia. Her look conveyed her concern.

Bella shook her head. "Something is troubling her. I have tried to get her to talk to me, but she just seems to disappear within herself."

"She has always been serious, but lately she seems perfectly unhappy. I think I will speak with Master Barone, perhaps her studies are weighing on her. She puts so much pressure on herself to excel at everything."

As the women spoke in low whispers at the main table, Mario Barone watched. He saw the Queen indicate her daughter to the Lady Isabella. He looked to the Bishop, who had also noted the focus of their concern. Bishop Capshaw looked at the tutor and sadly shook his head.

"Your Majesty," the Queen's secretary announced, "Master Barone, the tutor, is here."

"Thank you, Antonio. Show him in."

"Your Majesty." Mario Barone bowed.

"Please sit, Master Barone. Would you like some wine?" she offered as she poured herself a cup.

"No, thank you, Highness."

She sat in the seat next to him. "I will get right to the reason I called you. I have noticed disturbing changes in my daughter recently. I am concerned. How are her studies proceeding?"

Mario raised his eyebrows, his shoulders shrugged slightly. "Her studies reflect no problems, Majesty. She is very bright, very attentive. Her ability to grasp more complex concepts is advanced for her age. I do not observe any difficulty with her learning."

"Would you say that she is eager regarding her studies?"

"Quite eager, Highness. She and the boy, James, both seem to enjoy their lessons immensely."

Catherine got up from her chair and moved to the other side of her desk. She sat. Her brow knit together as she pondered her daughter's recent behavior.

"Majesty, if I may speak?" Master Barone intruded on her thoughts.

"Please do."

"I would not be overly concerned. Princess Sofia is an excellent student. She is absorbing a lot of new information. It has been my experience that children often become more serious as they begin to understand more of what they are learning."

"You believe it will pass, then?" the queen asked.

"There are no assurances, Majesty, but if the issue is simply a matter of adjusting to new information, then yes, I believe it will."

The Queen stood and walked over to the other side of her desk. "Thank you for your time, and your insights, Master Barone. Please let me know if you have any further thoughts."

Mario Barone bowed and left.

When Mary arrived at the Church with Princess Sofia the Bishop was in prayer at the altar. His eyes were closed. It seemed he did not hear them enter, although the doors were quite noisy as they opened and closed.

Mary coughed discreetly.

The Bishop started and turned. "Ah, Mary, I did not hear you enter."

Mary curtsied, left her charge and waited outside.

"Sofia, come here."

Sofia rose and went to the altar to join the Bishop.

"I was deep in prayer for your mother…and for you. Please kneel and join me in prayer."

Sofia dutifully knelt, bowed her head and closed her eyes tightly as the Bishop prayed.

"Heavenly Father we beseech you to hear our humble prayers. The Princess and I love You. We know that You wish us to obey all of the rules of the Holy Roman Catholic Church. We know this is the one, true way to You and to heaven. We ask you to help the Queen, Sofia's dear mother, to understand that You love her and we are desperate to save her from the fires of hell…and from the fires of earth."

He paused in his recitation and looked down at Sofia who was intently praying and listening to his every word. He continued, "Lord, we know from Your teachings that Father Timothy does not follow the law of the one, true Church. The Queen is fooled by his teachings and allows herself to be led by this false priest. Please help her to see that if she continues her visits there she will be endangering herself and her family. You know, Lord, as do I, that it is at the urging of the Lady Isabella that the Queen has fallen into the trap laid by Father Timothy. Help her. You have made clear your desire for us to identify heretics, but we love Queen Catherine. Help us to know what to do. We are your humble servants. Please guide us and direct us as You will. And, Lord, help the queen to understand that her relationship with the Lady Isabella is sinful. Amen."

"Amen," whimpered Sofia through her tears.

The journey to Radicondoli was shorter than many of the others they had made over the years. Barring difficulty, Radicondoli was only a few days from Montalcino Castle. However, Robert increased the number of soldiers travelling with the Queen. Since Carafa's death, and the installation of Pope Julius, the number of fanatical attacks had risen. Robert wasn't taking any chances.

Bella no longer attended any of the town functions, preferring to stay in camp to work with James on his lessons.

"Why can't Sofi come on the trips?" James whined on the first day they were camped just outside of Radicondoli.

"We have discussed this many times," Bella answered patiently. "At first her father missed her too much and wanted her to stay with him. Now, she must attend to her studies."

James picked up a handful of rocks and tossed them, one by one, into the nearby stream where he and his mother strolled. "It's not fair. Why can't she just learn with me? You're a good tutor when we travel."

"Sofia must learn so much more than I can teach her, darling. She will be queen someday. She is required to learn things that you would hate learning." She reached and tussled his hair. "Besides, this will be a short trip and you will be back with Sofia soon."

"It's lonesome without her." He bent down to pick up an unusually shaped rock and turned it in his hands.

"And your mother is not so entertaining, is she?" Bella asked with a smile.

"Oh, you are entertaining enough," he teased, "especially when you try to beat me at chess."

He laughed and ran back to camp ahead of her.

Radicondoli was unlike any of the other towns and villages that Catherine had toured. It was a bustling hive of activity and culture. It did not seem possible that Radicondoli could even be part of the same kingdom as Ribolla and Pienza...at least not the kingdom of Montalcino that had evolved over the past decade. At first glance, one could even imagine the Inquisition did not even exist. The atmosphere was such that Radicondoli seemed untouched, unchanged by the horrors facing the rest of Italy or Europe.

As had become her custom, Catherine first met with the town officials and priests. The leaders of Radicondoli were cordial, but cool. A welcome meal was served in her honor, after which the parties were to meet and discuss the state of affairs in Radicondoli.

Radicondoli was about the same size as Ribolla. For this reason Catherine expected to find similar situations and similar numbers with regard to interrogations, imprisonments and executions. So it was with more than a little surprise that Catherine listened to the numbers presented by Radicondoli's mayor.

"Those are the total numbers," Catherine said, "reflecting the Inquisitorial investigations and consequences for the entire past year?"

"Is there a problem, Your Highness?" Mayor Como asked.

"You are telling me that there have only been twenty two interrogations...total...in one year?" Compared to Ribolla, this was miniscule. Ribolla had close to two hundred sixty interrogations in the same year.

"Yes, Your Majesty."

"How many executions?" Catherine asked.

"Five executions and twelve imprisonments, Highness." The Mayor stated again with some exasperation.

Again, startlingly low numbers compared to Ribolla. Catherine looked around the table at the men seated. Of the seven there, one was the mayor. There was the sheriff, along with one undersheriff, three city council members and the local priest. With the exception of the young undersheriff, all of the men looked her directly in the eyes without flinching. She felt their hostility and suspected she knew the reasons behind it.

Catherine stood. She saw no reason to prolong this meeting. It was painfully clear she would get no real information from this group. "I want all paperwork on the interrogations...names, investigators, accusers if available. As well, please provide me with the names and dates of all executions."

"Excuse me, Your Majesty," said the priest, Father Emilio, "but that information belongs to the Church. As such, the Church holds authority over the documents and only the Holy See can give permission to release them." The haughtiness of his response caused the Mayor to smile, although he tried to hide it.

"Father Emilio," Catherine responded with equal haughtiness, "I fully understand the authority of the Church in these matters. And the Church's authority ends when it turns its back on the actual horror it inflicts. That horror is then carried out by secular authorities. That would be everyone else at this table except you. Everyone else here is under *my* authority and answers to me." She looked around again. The smile was gone from the Mayor's face. No one ventured a glance at her…except the Undersheriff. That face told her everything she needed to know.

"Undersheriff Russo," she said, "You will bring all the documentation I have requested to my campsite this evening. I will leave several of my guards here to assist and escort you."

"Yes, Your Majesty."

"The Undersheriff will require the cooperation of everyone at this table to meet my demand." Catherine was still standing. She bent over the table as she spoke her final words. "If I do not have the paperwork I have requested by this evening, rest assured, gentlemen, I have the authority to replace every single one of you…and I will not hesitate to do so." She turned and left the room, allowing the door to slam behind her.

Robert was waiting outside the door. "I heard raised voices."

"Only mine, dear cousin." Catherine's pace did not slow and Robert fell into step next to her.

"What happened?" he asked.

Catherine stopped when she was far enough from the building. "I suspect that our Lord Carfaggi has enjoyed playing God in Radicondoli. His rule is near its end. I want you to leave three of your guards here. Send them into the room I just left. Tell them not to let the Undersheriff out of their sight. Given his ability to look me in the eye when the others lost control of the meeting, I suspect he may be the only one from whom we will get any real cooperation." She turned and started walking toward their horses. "I sensed the Undersheriff was relieved when I confronted the others. He is our man here. I want him protected. He knows what I want. Tell your men to guard him closely and bring him to us this evening."

Robert nodded and turned to call three of the five soldiers who had accompanied them to town. He gave them their instructions. Catherine, Robert and the remaining two soldiers made their way back to the campsite to wait.

Just as the cooks were serving the evening meal, Robert's soldiers and Undersheriff Russo arrived at the camp. As they dismounted Robert approached the Undersheriff.

"Do you have all the documents?" he asked.

"Yes, Captain."

"Come." Robert said as he directed the young man toward the dining table where the queen waited for them.

"Majesty," he knelt before Catherine. "I brought everything I could get my hands on."

"Rise, Undersheriff Russo. Please join us for a meal."

"Thank you, Your Majesty. And, please, call me Cologero."

"Very well, then, Cologero," she said. One of the cooks handed him a plate of roasted game, fresh bread drizzled with olive oil and a small mound of olives and cheese.

Catherine introduced Cologero to Bella. Robert joined them after he checked in with the soldiers who returned with Cologero.

Once Robert joined them with his own plate of food, Catherine raised her cup of wine and offered a toast. "To truth...and justice."

"Truth and justice," echoed Robert, Bella and Cologero.

After a few pleasantries, Catherine said, "Cologero, I sensed some discomfort from you at the meeting today. Your uneasiness did not appear to match the hostility of the rest of the party present. Please correct me if I have misread you." Catherine said as she tore a piece of bread and dabbed it in oil.

"You did not misread me, Majesty. I…it is…forgive me. I do not know how to begin."

"If I did not misread you, then know you are among friends. You may speak freely, without fear of judgment, or accusations of heresy." Catherine smiled at him.

Cologero took a deep breath. "Majesty, I have heard of your sympathy for victims of the Inquisition. Your reputation is one of fairness and justice. I all but lost hope that you would ever visit Radicondoli."

"Why? Did you think that I would avoid coming?" Catherine asked.

"Forgive me, Majesty. I had begun to believe the lies," Cologero paused and looked down.

"What lies?" Catherine asked, leaning forward.

"We have been told that Lord Carfaggi was in control of all of Montalcino. And given what's been happening here, it was very easy to believe."

Catherine held his gaze. "Lord Carfaggi may have control over Radicondoli. If he has abused his authority in any way he will answer to me." She took a deep breath and exhaled slowly. "I need to know as much as you can tell me. Clearly, your town has not suffered the same fate as the rest of Montalcino. I have my suspicions regarding this. But I cannot act on suspicions. I need proof."

"I am at your service, Majesty."

"Good." She refilled his wine cup and hers, as well. "First, why so few interrogations? While I am glad to see smaller numbers, I am stunned by the figure."

"Do you know Lord Carfaggi's brother, Domenico, Majesty?" Cologero asked.

"I have not had the pleasure, no."

"I would hesitate to call knowing that man a pleasure, Highness. He is a despicable creature. It is he who makes the majority of decisions for the Mayor, the Council and the local priests."

"How?" asked Robert. "Does he pay them to do his bidding?"

"That, Captain, would be more acceptable, and certainly much kinder." Cologero took a sip of his wine. "No, he rules through intimidation. He has all of Radicondoli convinced that through his brother, and therefore through the Pope himself, that he can save or accuse anyone via the Inquisitorial process."

"No!" Bella exclaimed. "And people believe him?

"They are afraid not to, Lady Isabella. The first few citizens who defied his position or his business requests found themselves facing the Inquisitor. I believe you will find their execution papers in the documents."

"I suppose," Catherine said as she shook her head, "that Radicondoli thrives because the Carfaggis thrive. I imagine that the kind of power that the Carfaggis wield lends itself to vast profits for their family and businesses."

Cologero nodded sadly. "There, too, Majesty, you will find that several former business associates of the Carfaggis have been in prison for some time. Their families are ruined."

"Who is it that oversees the interrogations and the Inquisition process for Radicondoli?" Catherine questioned. "I am unaware that Radicondoli has been visited by a Grand Inquisitor?"

"It has not, Majesty," the undersheriff answered. "Father Emilio has victims brought before him by order of Carfaggi. Then he and the Sheriff carry out the interrogations and hand down the rulings."

"Have any of the victims been unknown to the Carfaggis?"

"I believe two of them were not associated directly with Carfaggis. However, I have information that indicates that payments were made to the Carfaggi family for accusations made on behalf of a close associate of theirs."

Bella left and returned with a bowl of fruit and some sweet wine. As she set them down she asked, "Is every record you brought, in some way connected to the Carfaggis?"

"I am afraid so."

"That explains their attempt at keeping the records from you," Robert said to Catherine. "You were wise to have our guards present with Cologero as he pulled them."

Catherine nodded, then looked at Cologero. "How is it that you came to work for the Sheriff's office?"

"My father died saving the Sheriff's life when he was ambushed by the crazed son of one of the men being interrogated on behalf of Carfaggi. The Sheriff had just left the church when the son jumped him and attacked him with a knife. My father happened to be passing by and went to the aid of the Sheriff. As he pulled the madman off, he wheeled on my father and stabbed him to death, then ran."

"I am so sorry, Cologero," Bella reached out and placed her hand on the young man's arm.

"Thank you, Lady Isabella." Cologero sighed. "With his dying breath my father begged the Sheriff to watch over his family. As the oldest of four, it seemed my place to accept the job when it was offered."

"How long ago was that?" Robert asked.

"About a year."

"How is it for you?" Catherine wanted to know.

"It is not so bad, I suppose. I actually like the work, when it is honest. I think I would be quite good at it, given a chance. But having to deal with the greed and abuse of power is hard. For now, it is an income and supports my mother and my siblings. I cannot ask for more than that. I am grateful for the work."

Catherine stood. "It's getting late. We need to review the records immediately. I will have questions as I go through them. Cologero, are you up to the task of remaining here to answer questions?"

"Yes, Majesty."

"Good." She turned to Robert. "Set up torches in the large tent, along with a table and four chairs. Bella?"

"Of course, I will help."

The task of pouring over all of the documents was tedious, but necessary. Cologero's presence was essential. He was able to answer questions about connections to the Carfaggi family in almost every case. Hours later Catherine threw the last of the files on the heap. She stood and stretched her arms up, arching her back, and walked toward the tent opening.

"It is late, perhaps eleven?" she asked.

"About that," Robert guessed.

"We must act quickly. The element of surprise will give us an advantage. It is time to bring the Carfaggi family to justice."

"Tell me what you want." Robert stood, ready to spring into action.

Catherine turned to Cologero, "In spite of the hour, I wish to visit with the families of the executed victims. Can you lead me to them now, tonight?"

"I am at your service, Your Highness. I can take you to all five families."

"Here is my plan. Tonight we get the information we need from the families of those murdered. Once those connections to the Carfaggi's are made we will proceed to the prison. I assume," she turned again to Cologero, "that you have access to the prison cells."

"I do," he nodded.

"How well is it guarded at night?"

"Two guards only, Majesty. One in the upper office of the tower keep, one in the hall at the end of the cell block."

"When does the guard change?" she asked.

"Not until dawn."

"Good. We will be finished by then."

Bella, who was quiet throughout Catherine's questions asked, "What, exactly are you planning?"

"Just this; first we gather proof that the Carfaggis have abused the Inquisitorial system to benefit themselves. We will have all we need by dawn. We have fifty soldiers with us this trip. Five of those soldiers will be waiting at the Carfaggi home at dawn to arrest all family members. They will remain sequestered there until we determine which of them were involved." Catherine moved back over to the table but did not sit.

"The two guards at the prison will need to be kept with us to prevent them from alerting the rest of the Council and other town leaders, including the priest. We will have the Undersheriff with us, and you, Robert. How many others do we need to secure the prison and the two guards safely?"

"How many entrances to the prison keep, Cologero?" Robert asked.

"Just the one, sir."

"Will the guards submit to your demands?"

"They should, unless they fear that they will be punished for acting against the Carfaggi family."

Catherine looked at Robert, then back at Cologero. "I want as many of our soldiers free to arrest the entire Council, the Sheriff, the Mayor and the priest in as short a time frame as possible." Catherine paused and paced a bit.

"If our soldiers," she said, "simultaneously arrest the town leaders, we can put them in individual cells. That should be no problem since we will be emptying cells before they arrive." She smiled.

"Robert, I want you and Cologero to determine the number of soldiers needed to make each of the arrests. I don't want our men in any more jeopardy than necessary. But I want this done swiftly."

Yes, Majesty." Both Robert and Cologero said in unison.

"Cologero, you have just been promoted." She smiled at him. "With a considerable increase in salary, Sheriff."

He smiled at Catherine and bowed. "I am grateful...and proud to serve you, Highness."

Again she turned to Robert. "One more thing before you assign your company. Send two of them back to Montalcino Castle immediately." She wrote orders and sealed them with wax. As she pressed the wax with her seal, she said, "I want our own Lord Carfaggi behind bars before word of any of this reaches him." She handed him the orders. He thumped his chest and bowed.

Robert and Cologero left the tent to make the necessary assignments. When they were gone Catherine walked over to where Bella sat. She walked around behind Bella, bent and slipped her arms around her love and whispered in her ear, "Do not worry. I will be back tomorrow."

Bella smiled and turned her head to Catherine's while reaching her own arms up to encircle her neck. "I always worry," she said. "Tomorrows don't always hold what we expect them to."

If the five families of the executed were filled with fear at being awakened in the middle of the night by the Queen's Guard, they were even more surprised to find the Queen, herself, at their doors.

It was not difficult, or time consuming to gather the evidence needed to arrest those involved in the executions. The family members had already lost so much to the Carfaggi "empire" that signing affidavits quickly handwritten by their own queen was an easy task.

One of the families, the Guilias, had been so broken by the events leading to the execution of their father, that their mother committed suicide.

The Guilias were now a family of five children. The oldest was a girl of fifteen…with the eyes of a sixty year old.

"Rosaria," the Queen said when they arrived, "my only intention is to bring the people who did this to your family to justice…and quickly."

Rosaria looked at her siblings, each with the sad, vacant expression in their eyes that never failed to pierce Catherine's heart, and nodded.

"We need to know everything you can tell us about how your father knew the Carfaggis and about the events that led to his arrest and execution. Can you help us?"

What Catherine saw happen to that fifteen year old girl in a matter of seconds startled her. Rosaria bowed her head after looking at her brothers and sisters. Catherine thought she was about to break down weeping. She witnessed the breakdowns often enough to prepare herself for them…wait them out…know that those who sat crying before her would eventually pull themselves together and tell their story.

Rosaria Guilia did not cry, and when she did raise her head she looked the Queen directly in the eyes with a fire that matched Catherine's own fury.

"Bastards…all of them!" she spat through gritted teeth. "My father was a good man. He ran an honest business. He thought those men were his friends. He treated them with respect they did not deserve…always helped them, even when it was a sacrifice to himself. But when Carfaggi pressed him to make false accusations of heresy against another business associate my father refused." Rosaria stopped and shook her head.

"That," Catherine finished for her, "is when your father found himself on the receiving end of those same accusations of heresy?"

"Yes. There was nothing we could do. All of them were in on it. Too late my father realized how greedy and cruel his *friends* were."

"How have you survived since then?"

"Even though my brothers and I are able to raise the crops and tend the farm, we couldn't find anyone to buy our produce. So we grow enough for ourselves. We are self sufficient with the farm, but that is all. Everyone shuns us."

"Out of fear?" Catherine asked.

"Cowardice would be my answer, Your Majesty."

"Rosaria," Catherine looked at her younger siblings as she spoke. "The wrongs done to you and your family can never be fully righted. I can't bring your parents back from the dead. But justice will be done in your father's and mother's name…and on behalf of you and all who have been so damaged by the cruelty of these men."

Rosaria looked at the Queen with a puzzled expression. Catherine was busy writing down the names of those responsible for the family's tragedy. She laid the paper in front of Rosaria and asked if there was anything or anyone missing.

"No, Majesty." Rosaria signed the paper where Catherine indicated. "But what is it that you intend to do?"

"You will know by day's end," Catherine said as she rose and made her way toward the door. "All of Radicondoli will know. Don't leave your farm today. Wait here. My soldiers will be back to let you know when it is safe to leave."

"Yes, Majesty." Rosaria answered.

Catherine looked warmly at Rosaria's younger siblings. "Do you all understand what I am asking?"

The younger girls nodded, wide eyed, while the older boys both replied, "Yes, Your Majesty."

It was the same at each home they visited. They completed rounds of the five homes by four in the morning. The soldiers had their instructions, and directions, to the homes of each of the town leaders and the priest. They split up to make the surprise arrests. Catherine, Robert and Cologero went directly to the prison.

The two guards were startled out of sleep when they arrived. Both of them were directed to the prisoner cell blocks where they stayed with Robert without question. They were used to following orders.

Cologero unlocked the cells of those who were casualties of the Carfaggi government.

"Bring them upstairs and get them food and wine," Catherine ordered. Cologero took one of the night guards up to the kitchen quarters. The prisoners were escorted upstairs to the guard's upper room, where they were invited to sit. Catherine sat busily writing and the only desk in the room and did not speak to them at first. Cologero and the guard returned with bread, cheese and wine. The prisoners looked baffled and worried. Catherine had not yet told them who she was.

Finally, when they each had a plate of food and a cup of wine, she accepted a cup of wine from Cologero. She lifted the wine toward the shattered men and said, "Gentlemen, my apologies for the delay in your rescue. As your queen, I promise you retribution this day. To justice!"

Of the twelve originally imprisoned, only nine were left. Three died during their confinement. The men were confused. They stared at their queen. Slowly, the reality of what was happening began to dawn on them. Understanding seeped through the numbness. Slowly, one by one, they began to weep. Catherine turned to the window to give their emotions some privacy. As she did, she saw the first of the troops returning with their prisoners.

She turned back to the men, who were mostly dabbing their eyes. "Gentlemen, you are about to witness the beginning of your justice."

The door opened and three soldiers hauled in the Mayor, still in his night clothes and chains. He attempted a look of disdain as he said, "You will pay for this!" But there was only fear in his eyes.

"Take him to the cells," ordered the queen. "Lock him up. Put each of them in a separate cell and post enough guards to prevent them speaking to one another."

"Yes, Majesty." They disappeared down the stairway leading to the prison cells.

Before long the others arrived. The former prisoners watched, as those responsible for their unjust incarceration and ruin, paraded before them to the cells. They sat in silence, still disbelieving their own eyes.

All of the men responsible, with the exception of Domenico Carfaggi, were locked up.

Catherine turned to Robert. "Send as many as you can to reinforce the others surrounding the Carfaggi home. I'll return to camp before I begin his interrogation."

"Five of my men will escort you back to camp and stay to guard you, Majesty." Robert turned and signaled his five.

Catherine turned one last time to the men in the room. "You have all been through much. My soldiers will escort you home. Sheriff Russo will contact you regarding restitution arrangements. Go with God." She and Robert went outside.

"We'll need to leave a good contingent of men here to insure a smooth transition to a new government," she said to Robert as they walked toward the horses.

"I already have several in mind. They come from political families and understand the political process." Robert said.

"Good. You and Cologero begin organizing a list of men who might be decent candidates for the positions vacated." She mounted her horse. "I'll interview them before I leave." She turned to her horse.

"What of Carfaggi?" Robert called after her.

"Let him wait!" she called over her shoulder. "I will attend to him when I am good and ready!"

The sun was up. Bella and James were playing a game of chess when Catherine returned to camp. When she heard the horses, Bella looked up. A look of relief washed over her face. She looked at James.

"You haven't really had your mind on this game, Mother." James smiled at her. "Go ahead."

Bella went around the table and kissed the top of his head. Catherine was already walking toward them.

"Who is winning?" she smiled at them.

"Well, it hasn't been much of a contest," James rolled his eyes playfully as he nodded toward his mother. "Her mind has definitely been elsewhere. She was going to be mated in three moves."

"I was letting him win," Bella laughed. "He was so worried about you he couldn't concentrate."

Catherine went over and kissed the top of James' head as well. "Well, thank you both for your concern. Everything is fine." She started toward her tent. "But I am exhausted and need to sleep for a bit."

"You must be hungry, too," Bella said. "Can I bring you something to eat before you rest?"

"Thank you, just a light plate. I don't think I can stay awake long enough to eat more than a few bites."

Catherine was slipping out of the last of her outer garments when Bella entered the tent with a slice of bread and a few berries. "How did everything go?"

"It could not have gone better." Catherine plopped herself onto her down mattress and took the plate from Bella. "Thank you, love. The entire Council, Sheriff and priest are in custody. Domenico Carfaggi is surrounded by armed guards. He will be held until I am ready to interrogate him." She ate a few bites of bread and two of the strawberries. "As if the real Inquisition isn't bad enough, we have people like the Carfaggi brothers to contend with. Carfaggis and those like them are no different from the rogue groups murdering in Christ's name." She stopped, then said, "I take that back. These men are worse. The rogue groups at least believe they are working in the name of Christ, these men know they are motivated by their own greed and power. That is the bigger sin."

Bella took Catherine's plate and lay down beside her. She held her arms open and Catherine curled within them. "Rest, my love. I'll stay with you."

When Catherine woke, Bella was awake still holding her, stroking her head gently.

"What time is it?" Catherine asked.

"I don't know, but I heard the rest of the camp preparing the midday meal some time ago."

I could stay here forever," Catherine said as she buried her face in Bella's neck.

"And who would run the kingdom then?" Bella teased.

"Oh, let it run itself. I deserve a little time off."

"That's something I would like to see…you taking time off!" Bella laughed.

"Is that a challenge?" Catherine propped herself up on one elbow.

Bella laughed. "That, my love, is an impossibility!"

Later that day, the Queen's guards delivered her sealed orders to Lord Giovanni. When the Privy Council reconvened after the midday meal, Lord Giovanni was absent. King Ambrose expressed a desire to wait for him before beginning.

"I disagree, King Ambrose," Lord Carfaggi said. "I see no reason to hold up the entire Council for one man."

"Very well, gentlemen, Your Grace," King Ambrose started. "Have you all had the opportunity to read through the new taxation proposal from Lord Como?"

Before anyone had an opportunity to answer, the doors to the Council chamber opened. Lord Giovanni stepped through them, but did not close them.

His face held an unreadable expression as he remained near the doors.

"Do you plan to keep us waiting forever, Lord Giovanni?" Carfaggi said haughtily.

Lord Giovanni looked at Carfaggi without hatred, without malice, without annoyance.

"Gentlemen," he bowed ever so slightly, "I have received a communication from the Queen." He held up an official document clearly marked with the Queen's Seal. He looked at the document and paused before he continued. Then he read, "Lord Carfaggi, you are hereby placed under arrest by order of Queen Catherine for conspiracy to commit crimes of bribery, extortion, false imprisonment, kidnapping and murder of innocent citizens of Radicondoli. You are to await…"

Carfaggi leapt to his feet and screamed, "This is an outrage. How dare that woman try to arrest me!"

"...you are to await trial in prison until such time...." Again Lord Giovanni was interrupted by the fuming Carfaggi.

"I will await nothing!" he said as he made for the open doors, his eyes bulging from their sockets.

As he neared the doors, six of the Queen's guards stepped into the doorway, blocking his egress.

"Get out of my way!' he shouted as he attempted to push his way out of the room.

"Take him to the lowest portion of the cells," Lord Giovanni shouted to the guards who were restraining the screaming Carfaggi. "Keep him chained until the Queen returns and decides how to deal with him!"

Lord Carfaggi's screams could be heard fading as he was dragged to the tower keep. When his voice could no longer be heard, Lord Giovanni turned back to the Council, every one of them pale, stunned and speechless.

"Gentlemen, may I suggest we adjourn for the day?" he said softly.

The next morning, Robert and Catherine talked over a light breakfast.

"Things are under control at the prison. Cologero Russo will make a good Sheriff. You read him well," Robert said.

"Were you able to construct a list of possible candidates to replace our illustrious council?"

"Several men were discussed. Cologero will speak with them later today. I asked him to meet us here first thing this morning to join us for the trip to the Carfaggi home."

Bella stepped out of the tent and came over to join them. "How are you, Captain?"

"Never better, Lady Isabella. And you?"

"Fine, as well, thank you." She reached for a berry.

Catherine looked at Bella. "Robert, Cologero and I plan to interrogate Carfaggi. After that I will need to spend some time in town."

"How long will you be?"

"I'll try to be back by mid afternoon. It's important for people to see that their Queen has taken back control of Radicondoli. They'll need to know things will be different, and that we will be keeping a close eye on things for some time to come."

"How long do you think we'll be here?" Bella asked.

"A few days for us, I should think. A contingent of the guard will stay to insure all goes smoothly until Cologero has a solid base of support to handle things. That could be awhile."

As they talked, Cologero arrived. He joined them at the table.

"Did you get some rest?" Robert asked him.

"Enough," he answered as he held up his hand to refuse an offering of fruit. "Majesty, what is your plan?"

"After a good night of rest we will head to the home of Domenico Carfaggi and present him with a list of the charges against him. He will be arrested and you will take him back. Lock him up with the others." At this she called Marie to bring her paper, pen, ink and royal seal. "How did your prisoners spend their night?" she asked.

"Mostly whining that it was all Carfaggi, of course." He shook his head. "The Mayor cried openly and offered up both Carfaggi brothers in exchange for his release. He claims that the Carfaggis threatened him and his family if he did not go along with them."

"Do you believe him?" asked Bella

"To some extent I suppose I do, Lady. And if we were merely talking about some dishonest business dealings I would be inclined to feel sorry for them." Cologero shook his head again and his face did not mask his emotion as he said, "But they murdered innocent people for the Carfaggis. I don't understand how they could live with what they have done." He fought allowing his tears to fall. "Forgive me, you must think me weak."

Robert came to his rescue. "You do not know them well enough, Cologero," he laughed, "but you are in the company of two of the strongest women in all of Europe and I can tell you from experience that they find the tears of men like you and me to be a sign of strength."

"And honesty!" added Bella.

"We don't have time for too much of a show of strength," Catherine smiled. "Tell me about the men you are considering for the new government. I want to meet with them tomorrow."

When Catherine, Robert and Cologero arrived at the home of Domenico Carfaggi they were apprised of the situation. Carfaggi was so belligerent and combative when the Queen's guard arrived that they finally tied him to a chair and gagged him. Most of the servants continued to perform their duties. Several tried to leave but were prevented from doing so. Carfaggi's wife and daughters, he had no sons, had been in a near constant state of weeping and wailing in their rooms since the soldiers arrived.

Catherine thanked the guard and asked to be led to Carfaggi. He was still tied to a chair in his study. When the Queen entered he looked at her with a fury that made her glad he was bound and gagged.

"Bring his family!" she demanded of the guard.

Catherine walked around the room, observing the details, the luxury, the opulence with which Carfaggi had surrounded himself. She spotted a locked box on his desk. It was rather large.

"Sheriff," she called Cologero over to her. "Open this box."

He looked in the desk for a key, but found none. He walked over to Carfaggi and searched him. He found a key tied on a thin rope around the man's neck. It fit. He opened the box.

Catherine stared at the contents. "There must be enough gold in here to purchase a small country!" she exclaimed.

At that time the crying Carfaggi women were brought into the room.

"Silence!" the Queen demanded.

They stopped crying, although their sniveling continued.

Catherine held out her hand as she stood before Carfaggi, staring him down. Robert placed the role of charges against him into her outstretched hand. She continued looking into Carfaggi's eyes with a cold and a fire that, for a time, he matched. She did not look away. Eventually, he did.

"Domenico Carfaggi," she announced as she unrolled the document in her hands, "You are charged with assault, bribery, extortion, kidnapping, torture, false imprisonment and murder." She read the long list of the victim's names. "You will be escorted to the prison and held there until such time as a new government is in place in Radicondoli. You will be tried and most likely executed for these atrocities."

"No, Your Majesty," Lady Carfaggi threw herself at the queen's feet and started weeping even louder than before.

Catherine ignored her. Robert pulled the woman up and returned her to her seat where her daughters put their arms around her and they all started weeping again.

"Your brother is already under arrest at Montalcino Castle," Catherine continued. "He will be brought back to Radicondoli to face trial once all is in order."

She walked over to the large box of gold on the desk. "Your assets will be used to recompense the victims of your crimes," she added without emotion. "Meanwhile, this gold will go a long way to helping them get back on their feet." She looked at the Sheriff. "Please take this box of gold back to your office, Sheriff. We will call upon the families of the victims and begin dispensing it today."

"With pleasure, Majesty."

She turned back to Carfaggi, whose eyes held even more hatred than when she first arrived. "I intended to interrogate you, allow you to answer these charges. But in the short time I have been in Radicondoli I've heard and seen enough to convince me that you would stop at nothing to benefit, or save, yourself." She handed the list of charges back to Robert. "Then we would have to add perjury to your list."

She turned to look at the women. "You will be interrogated by the Sheriff, as will your servants. Captain," she said to Robert, "have your guards take him," she indicated Carfaggi, "and lock him up. I do not wish to see him again."

Catherine spent the better part of the next two days in the office of the non-existent mayor. Word spread quickly about the arrests and changes in Radicondoli. She found herself overwhelmed by citizens wishing to offer support and thanks. It was necessary to institute a system allowing only certain people access to the queen. The citizens of Radicondoli converged on the Mayor's office in droves, many desperate to tell their own horror stories of the Carfaggis. Hundreds wished to participate in the trial of the former leaders. All of them reacted to the events of the past two days with formidable emotion.

It was clear that Catherine would not be able to leave Radicondoli as quickly as she had hoped. She didn't want to leave Cologero with an impossible task. She interviewed many of the candidates for the vacant positions. Some form of government, no matter how inexperienced, needed to in place before she left. Also, she needed to return to the families of the executed and the former prisoners. They could not wait for justice, in the form of a trial, to be granted restitution for all they had lost. Many would not survive until then. She was determined to distribute as much of Carfaggi's gold to them as necessary.

"Bella, my love," Catherine said as she flopped down in exhaustion at the end of her day.

Bella helped her out of her outer garments, then lay next to Catherine and gently massaged her temples. "You are spent."

"I am, yes." Catherine responded with a sigh. "And, it won't be possible to leave as quickly as I had hoped. I am sorry."

"Your initial time estimate seemed ambitious. I'm not surprised."

Catherine looked into Bella's eyes. She reached up to place her fingertips on Bella's lips. Bella smiled and kissed each fingertip, the palm and the back of Catherine's hand.

"Would you consider coming to town to aid us tomorrow?" Catherine asked. "The guard is overwhelmed dealing with sorting through everyone who wants to have their voice heard. You could be helpful there. I value your keen political sense. If you might be present during the interviews for the new councilors and sheriff, as well as the Mayor, you can help me sort the wheat from the chaff."

Bella adjusted her body, slipping it partially under Catherine to hold her in her arms. "I could do that," she said as she reached to run her fingers through Catherine's hair.

Catherine pulled Bella into her arms and they lay together for a bit. "How is our James?"

"Bored. He misses Sofia," Bella said. "So do I."

"It's hard to be away from her, Catherine said sadly, "especially now when she seems to be changing so much."

"Perhaps," Bella said, "she will be back to her old self when we return."

Catherine did not respond. She had fallen asleep and was already breathing slowly.

The next several days in Radicondoli were full, dealing with people and situations of all sorts. Catherine would be keeping a close eye on the new government for some time. She very much liked two men for the mayoral position. Bella gave her approval to the choices. Catherine thought they might work well together and made one the Mayor and one a vice-Mayor. Councilors were chosen. Whereas there had been three council members before, she opted to create a larger Council, hoping to avoid the kind of triumvirate that existed with Carfaggis. More men meant more of a chance that at least some might remain honest and less tempted by bribery or power.

Her last day in Radicondoli was spent revisiting with families most grievously injured by the cruelty of the Carfaggis.

Catherine, Robert, Bella began their tour early in the morning. It was late afternoon when they arrived at the home of the Guilia children. The children heard much of what had happened from neighbors and were expecting them. They made a beautiful basket of fruit and vegetables for the queen as thanks for all she had done.

When the queen dismounted in the courtyard of their home, the younger children ran up to her. Before anyone could keep the children from the lack of etiquette, she knelt before them and opened her arms to embrace them. Only Rosaria stood back watching, knowing that it was an exceptional moment.

Finally, Catherine stood. She went to Rosaria, whose eyes had lost some of their fury. They were softer.

Rosaria knelt before Catherine and took her hands, kissing them. "Thank you, Your Majesty. Thank you."

"Stand, child," Catherine softly ordered. She linked her arm through Rosaria's and turned to her siblings saying, "I need to speak with your sister. I will bring her back shortly." Together Catherine and

Rosaria walked off toward the fallow fields. Bella, Robert and Cologero stayed with the children.

"Rosaria," Catherine said as they walked arm in arm, "you are a remarkable young woman. You kept your family together in spite of a most difficult situation." Catherine led them to a bench in the midst of a desolate, barren flower garden. There they sat.

"You have touched my heart," Catherine continued. "You may call on me for any reason. Obviously, you are capable of running this farm and keeping your brothers and sisters happy, but I sense the loss in you."

Rosaria looked at Catherine with a mildly puzzled expression.

"Don't let your anger, or your sadness, consume you, Rosaria. Don't lose yourself to those emotions."

Catherine reached up and placed her hand on Rosaria's cheek. The kindness in her touch opened wounds Rosaria was forced to ignore when she lost both of her parents. Tears spilled from her eyes and down her cheeks. Catherine wrapped the girl in her arms and held her as she cried a little.

When Catherine and Rosaria returned to the group the boys were laughing and playing happily in the courtyard with Robert. Bella was chatting with the two younger girls, as they showed her their treasures of special rocks and beads.

Catherine nodded to Robert. He brought the box with the remainder of Carfaggi gold coins. Much of it had been distributed throughout the day, but Catherine made sure that the lion's share was saved for the Guilia children. She took the box from Robert and handed it to Rosaria.

"Rosaria Guilia," she said with some seriousness, "this is the first of what I hope to be more to come. This was taken from the home of Domenico Carfaggi to help you and your brothers and sisters recover from what the Carfaggis did to your family." She handed Rosaria the box.

The children all gathered around Rosaria eager to see what was in the box.

Catherine continued, "What is in this box will never bring your parents back, but, hopefully, it will help you heal, forgive, grow stronger as a family...and help you begin to build a new life for yourselves."

Catherine mounted her horse and removed the key to the box from around her neck. She gave it to Rosaria and turned to ride off with her party.

Rosaria and the children waved and shouted goodbye.

The little ones gathered around Rosaria. "Open it, open it, Rosaria!" they shouted.

Rosaria slipped the key into the lock and turned it. They held their breath as she lifted the cover. A single, simultaneous gasp escaped them all. The box was one third full of solid gold coins...nearly one hundred of them. Rosaria looked up to see the queen riding away. The dam holding back the flood of her emotions finally burst.

Chapter Forty Five

Princess Sofia seemed more settled, less sad, when the Queen and her entourage returned from Radicondoli. She solemnly greeted her mother. It was James upon whom she focused her attention. She walked over to him as soon as he dismounted.

"Princess," he bowed to her once his feet were on the ground. "How are you?"

Equally formally, Sofia nodded her head and responded, "I am quite well, thank you."

"How have your studies fared in my absence?" he asked, still somewhat stiffly.

Sofia stared at him as if she were waiting for something, a sign perhaps. "My studies proceeded well," she responded.

"Hmmph," he ventured. "I thought you would be bored to tears without me to help you understand everything!" He could no longer hide his smile, or his delight at seeing her.

As soon as she saw his face break into his familiar grin, Sofia threw her arms around him and said, "It was awful. I missed you so!"

"And I was the one bored to tears without you!" he said as he hugged her back.

As a stable boy reached for the reins of his horse, James grabbed something tied to his saddle and said, "Come. I've brought you something."

They disappeared into one of the castle gardens.

On the Queen's first Sunday back from Radicondoli the bishop's sermon was more subdued than normal. His homily, unlike his usual, so filled with messages of fear and threat, lacked its familiar intensity regarding heresy.

Following Mass on Sundays, it was customary for castle residents to enjoy breakfast in the Great Hall. After the meal, Catherine and Bella made for their quarters to prepare for the ride to Castiglione d' Orcia, the first since their return from Radicondoli.

"Marie," Catherine said to the servant as she was assisting the queen into her riding cape, "please make certain Sofia is ready. Ask her to join us as quickly as possible."

Marie left the quarters with a curtsey, but returned a few moments later.

"Your Majesty," she said, "the Princess is not feeling well and has requested to stay behind."

Catherine looked at Bella. "She seemed fine this morning."

Bella shrugged her shoulders, "Perhaps it was something she ate."

"I'll go see her and be down to join you in a bit," Catherine said.

"Sofia?" the Queen called as she entered her daughter's room.

Sofia emerged from behind her privy screen holding her stomach. "Forgive me," she beseeched her mother, "I must have eaten something that doesn't sit well. May I be excused from going to Castiglione d' Orcia today?"

"Of course, darling," Catherine said as she reached to put her arms around Sofia. "I'll have Marie stay with you. We'll be back soon."

"Please, mother," Sofia pleaded with Catherine, "will you stay with me?"

"What is it? Shall I call the physician?" Catherine reached to feel her daughter's face. "You aren't warm," she said. She placed her arm around Sofia and led her to her bed.

As they sat on the edge of the bed Sofia wrapped her arms around her mother and began to cry, "Don't go. Please stay with me."

Catherine lifted Sofia's chin and looked into her tear-filled eyes. "Of course I'll stay with you," she answered as she held Sofia to her breast.

At Catherine's request, Robert accompanied Bella on the road. He assigned two soldiers to protect the queen. Then he, Bella and James went alone to Castiglione d' Orcia.

In spite of Lord Carfaggi's arrest Bishop Capshaw did not cease, or even slow, his relentless pursuit of control over Princess Sofia. If anything, he intensified his manipulation of her. Now that Carfaggi was eliminated as his overseer, the Bishop was free to imagine himself as the sole puppeteer controlling a new queen.

One week later, at Mass, the congregation readied for the bishop's sermon.

"Today's gospel," Bishop Capshaw intoned from his pulpit high above his castle congregation, "speaks to us about weeds among the wheat."

Princess Sofia sat between her parents in the front row of the chapel. Her attention fixed on the Bishop.

"In Montalcino our farmers know about weeds. Our mountainous terrain does not lend itself to easy farming." The Bishop tended to begin his sermons softly. "We are required to deal not only with weeds, but with rocks and boulders and even whole sections of land that are nothing but solid rock.

"But Jesus is not speaking to us of real weeds or real wheat. This parable, like all of Christ's parables, speaks of people. It is people, us, you and me, about whom the Lord speaks. And, He is telling us about the end of days, when the weeds...the wicked among us will be pulled up in the final harvest and burned.

"Who are the weeds, the evil about whom Jesus spoke? We know because our God has told us. The weeds are those among us who do not follow the word of the Lord as it is meant to be followed. The weeds are heretics!"

Sofia listened with all of her being. She not only heard the Bishop's speaking directly to her, she felt as if God, Himself, stood before her.

"Who are the heretics? Are they here? Do they sit among us in our very chapel? Do we live next to them, or with them? Are they the very people with whom we work and play and whose company we may enjoy?" His voice was beginning to rise. "Can heretics be the very people we love the most?" he asked in mock horror.

As he asked the last question, Bishop Capshaw's gaze settled on Sofia.

"Yes!" he boomed. Then more softly, "Yes. They can be those we love and those with whom we work and play and with whom we conduct business," he continued as he moved his eyes over the rest of the congregation. "They can even be those we love the most."

"Jesus was telling us just that. The weeds grow among us. They thrive along with the wheat. The danger is that the weeds may consume the good wheat before the harvest. Once the harvest time is come, then God's angels will pluck the weeds from among the good wheat and thrust them into the fires of hell!" The Bishop's arms raised and his hands clutched into fists. "But what are we to do meanwhile? Are we to allow the weeds to grow unhindered? Is that what Jesus was saying? Are we to allow known heretics the freedom to contaminate the rest of the crop? Do we allow the weeds to drop their seeds of sin and take up the good nutrients from the soil…away from the wheat?"

Catherine felt, more than saw, how Sofia absorbed every word of the sermon, and wanted to desperately cover her daughter's ears to save her from this hate filled diatribe. She could feel Sofia responding to the Bishop. More and more she noticed that words and sentiments expressed by the Bishop on Sunday mornings crept into her daughter's language. All she could do was hope that the message of love that Father Timothy delivered on Sunday afternoons might offer a counterbalance to the hate.

"No!" the Bishop yelled as he slammed his fist onto the pulpit. "No, we do not. But neither do we pull up the weeds." His tone was again softening as he looked directly at Sofia. "We do not pull up the weeds." He smiled at the Princess. "That is not our task. Our job, as good Christian wheat is to identify the weeds so that God and his angels can easily separate the faithful from the wicked."

Sofia was nodding.

The Bishop continued. "We cannot turn weeds into wheat. But as wheat, we must be stronger than the weeds. We must be more vigilant than the weeds. We must not allow ourselves to be strangled by the weeds lest we shrivel and die before the harvest. The leaves of us must point to the weeds and say, 'Here, Lord! Here…and there…there is a weed!' We must identify the weeds so that God and the Church can deal with them."

The sermon might have ended there, but the Bishop felt it his duty to hold his audience for as long as possible. He droned, yelled and bullied for another half hour.

For the second week in a row Sofia claimed illness and begged Catherine to stay with her instead of going to Castiglione d' Orcia.

"Sofia," Catherine said as she felt herself responding to her daughter's tears, "I will be back shortly." She reached out to hold Sofia, but the child turned away.

"I want you to stay with me," Sofia nearly demanded. "I'm sick!"

"I am going to Castiglione d' Orcia today. I wish you would come," Catherine implored. "If you are not well, we can arrange for a carriage. That way you can rest on the way there and on the way back."

"Please don't go." Sofia was in tears.

It took all of Catherine's strength to refuse her daughter. But Father Tim had planned for her to meet several men who were sent via his brother Thomas today.

"I must go. Your father will stay with you." She bent to kiss Sofia's head, but the girl pulled away and would not allow it.

Catherine and Bella immensely enjoyed when Father Tim hosted underground meetings. Whether the visitors from underground movements were followers of de Las Casa, or simply travelers Thomas had met in other parts of Italy and sent to meet with his brother, it meant that Father Tim would actually preach a sermon. On Sunday afternoons when only Catherine, Bella, James and Robert were present the priest refrained from delivering homilies, and just spoke to them about the message for the day, encouraging them to ask questions. Catherine still acted according to her own set of beliefs that she must protect her people as if God did not intervene or assist, but she still enjoyed his sermons.

Father Tim recognized the shift in the queen the first time he spoke with her after Ribolla. He didn't challenge or chide her. He simply accepted that her relationship with God was undergoing transformation. He had faith that Catherine would find her way back to God, and that she would be stronger for the journey.

"Welcome to all visiting our humble Castiglione d' Orcia today. I'm delighted to see new faces and meet new friends," Father Timothy said as he walked around to the front of the altar where he preferred nothing between himself and the congregation.

"Today's gospel consists of two parts. First is the original parable of Jesus, handed down from disciple to disciple for several decades. The second half is an interpretation of the parable, probably written some forty years after Jesus' death and resurrection, †" he began gently.

"The interpretation has Jesus telling us that his parable about allowing weeds and wheat to grow together is really about the end of the age, when angels will come and reap the final harvest, burning up all the wicked people, and rewarding the righteous in heaven." †

Catherine could not help but smile as she waited to hear how Father Tim's sermon would compare to the bishop's. She found herself wishing Sofia could hear it, too.

"This part was written during an extremely polarized and dangerous time. By 70 or 80 AD, the Romans had destroyed Jerusalem and scattered both Jews and Christians around the Mediterranean and Middle East. It was also during the beginning of violent persecutions against Christians. †

"It was, for the audience of Matthew's gospel, the end of the world. They expected Jesus to come back in their lifetime and deal with this horrifying violence, to get rid of those evil people who wiped Israel off the map and those who were destroying their Christian communities.

"They also expected Jesus to protect and lift up the persecuted faithful who were only trying to follow the gospel, and make them shine like the sun in heaven. It is an understandable hope." †

Bella reached out both of her hands, one to either side of her, to hold James's and Catherine's hands. Catherine recognized this small act as Bella's way of saying, "Listen, my two loves, this is important." Catherine squeezed Bella's hand.

Father Timothy walked slowly back and forth as he continued. "But what did Jesus mean when he originally told this parable? Taken by itself, it doesn't necessarily point to an end time when God would separate people into evil and good, burning the former and rewarding the latter.

"The parable is a simple farming metaphor. Jesus tells us to allow weeds to grow alongside wheat. The workers are instructed to avoid trampling through the tender shoots, ripping out what they thought were weeds, destroying the good grain in their zeal. No, let the weeds and wheat grow together until harvest time, when you can really tell the difference between them.†

"Told at a time before all the violence against Christians and Jews, this story seems to be about our tendency to judge one another, and to judge parts of ourselves we don't like. It is about the difficulty of sorting out good from bad, and how if we try to do this too vigorously, we'll destroy whatever good is there, too. Instead, we are to accept both the shadow and light within ourselves, and refrain from judging others as well, letting God sort these things out. †

"In our lifetime there are those of us who want to trample through the fields, furiously ripping out the weeds among the wheat."† Tim paused and looked around. He smiled as he made eye contact with each person present before he continued.

"But who is weed…and who is wheat? We all have the tendency to see ourselves as the wheat. How wonderful life would be if we could only get rid of those nasty weeds? Are those who cry the loudest, who run around arresting 'witches' and 'heretics' the weeds? Is their fear of evil any different than ours?

"The fact is that what we think is evil may reside within ourselves. The danger is in thinking that if I can eliminate the evil in the world around me, perhaps I will not be tormented by it within me anymore. Ah, but it is not so simple."

Tim watched as some of his visitors shifted uncomfortably in their seats. Their faces reflected disappointment and even anger as he spoke. He knew that these were good men, devoted to fighting the wrongs of the Church, but he also knew that in spite of this, and because of it, it was important to push them to examine their thoughts and actions in the matter.

"As we live alongside others who are very different from us we come up against our own fears, our own prejudices. We make judgments about others by the way they dress, by the language they use about religion or politics or heresy, and we shift them from the category of 'wheat' to 'weeds'. †

"But if we are willing to look closely at ourselves, we shed light on our shadow parts...those 'weeds' within each of us. We must offer God an opportunity to heal us. The way this healing happens, however, is not by ripping out our nasty weeds, but by transforming them into something healthy and good." †

Tim was winding down.

"Perhaps you are ashamed of something you desire. Perhaps the anger you try to hold at bay is a thirst for things to be set right. Perhaps your perceived lack of faith is a call to leave behind simplistic answers and travel bravely into the mysteries and paradoxes of the spiritual life." †

Catherine looked up. Her head had bowed as she listened to Tim. But as he spoke this last sentence, she felt certain he was looking and speaking directly to her. He was on the other side of the aisle, however, and looking out at some of the other visitors.

"Jesus advises us to let our weeds and wheat grow up together, until it becomes obvious what they are, when the Spirit will work with us, to transform us. Our inner weeds may turn out to be wheat, after all, and what we thought was good grain God may eventually reveal to be nothing but thorny weeds. †

"That, I believe, is what Christ wanted for the church. In the end, the vision of heaven is not a population that has been cleansed of all evildoers, and our own redemption is not us with big parts missing. Instead, heaven is a community whose members have finally found their true purpose, with all of their traits made useful, and each one of us happy that everyone there has a part to play in God's kingdom. † Amen."

The discomfort caused by Tim's sermon was reflected in the gathering following Mass. At first the tone was subdued, each member afraid to condemn the likes of Inquisitors or the failings of the Church.

As they gathered around the table in Father Tim's home, Catherine sensed the distress and moved to acknowledge it. "I didn't like to hear,

Father, that my own sense of righteousness might actually be fear of my own evil!" she laughed. "You are either very brave, or have shifted your alliance to stand with the Pope and the Grand Inquisitor," she announced when the entire group settled.

Tim laughed. "Not at all, Your Majesty. I only speak to what I have had to examine in myself. My own righteousness regarding the papacy and the persecutors of the innocent is both my shadow and light." He prayed over the food and wine, and indicated for all to help themselves.

"You mean," Bella chimed, "that unless we are willing to see all sides of ourselves, both good and bad, we are in danger of becoming more like those we see as all evil?"

"Precisely, Lady Isabella," Tim agreed. "It is in our nature to create our monsters outside of us. In that way we can feel good about slaying wickedness and evil without implicating ourselves."

One of the visitors, a man named Vincenzo, said, "But it sounded like you were defending the persecutors of the innocent."

"No, Vincenzo," Tim replied. "I would never defend the actions my Church has taken against its body. I only believe that we must be aware of the good and bad in ourselves. Without acknowledging that the persecutors of the Church may have some good in them that can be redeemed, we condemn our own wickedness without first acknowledging that we, too, are sinners.

"The kind of spiritual battle in which we find ourselves is a wrestling match. We need to examine the ways in which we enter these battles. What kind of victory do we hope for?" †

Vincenzo looked at Father Tim, his confusion evident on his face. "We hope to stop the atrocities of the Inquisition. Is that not the aim?"

"That *is* the ultimate goal, yes," Father Tim acknowledged. "But how do we accomplish this task? While I do *not* agree with those who persecute and condemn and torture others for their perceived heretical beliefs, I don't want to demonize and dominate the persecutors, to cast them out. I want to be in relationship with them, and hope that through this relationship we can find ways to be together, find ways to see the light in one another – and accept the darkness that lives in each of us, as well." †

"Why," asked Stephan, who had been quiet until then, "would I want to accept someone else's darkness? If I am a true follower of Christ, is He not all light? Do I not walk in His light? Is He not the light itself? There is no darkness in Christ."

"Really?" Father Tim responded, his eyebrows arched in question. Then he smiled and continued. "As I read the gospels and spend time reflecting on the life of Christ, what speaks to me the most is his own struggle with the light and dark within him. Yes, the light of Christ is what we know wins the spiritual battle, but it seems that he had his share of darkness with which to contend...as do we all." †

"How do you deal with your own dark thoughts, then?" Vincenzo asked.

Father Tim had just taken a bite of bread. He chewed slowly and took a sip of wine before he answered. "Years ago, I realized that every time I thought I had put my anger, my fear and resentments to rest, they found new ways to plague me. They found new ways to reveal their faces again and again. Eventually, I shifted my spirituality from trying to walk only as a child of light, with no darkness at all, to a spirituality of light and dark. Sitting in silence, as my inner demons revealed themselves, I let them be, feeling them, seeing them as they were, without any attempt to judge or rid myself of them." †

Bella was pouring wine from a carafe into Stephan's cup. She stopped and looked at Father Tim and interrupted him. "That must have taken an enormous amount of courage."

Father Tim smiled at her and nodded. "At first, yes, it did. But I soon found that as I befriended these thoughts, as they came out into the open, they lost some of their power. The problem with splitting off things we don't like about ourselves is that they only grow more powerful when they are forced into hiding. Out in the open they can be put in perspective, and we can even find a gift in each one of them, something that, I hope, contributes to our becoming whole." †

"Father," Vincenzo stopped him, "forgive my interruption, but I am still unclear on some of what you are saying. I think I understand what you mean by demonizing others. That clearly goes against what Christ taught us about loving our enemies. But, I don't quite grasp the part about accepting anyone's darkness…my own included. I am in this underground movement to fight for justice, not accept others' evils."

"Vincenzo," Father Tim looked at him and nodded, "you should stand firm in your convictions and fight for what you believe is right. But remember, we are, all of us, members of God's family. God will ultimately be victorious. Good will win in the end. Our security does not have to fearfully depend on us, or upon how much fragile progress we can make in our Church, our kingdoms…our souls. Our security is rooted in the eternal goodness of God, who loves us completely – our darkness and our light – and loves our enemies in their darkness and light, as well. So, even as we contend with the evils of the Inquisition, or the evils within our own souls, we have a safe place in which these struggles occur. We live in God." †

Father Tim looked around and realized that his sermon had continued. All eyes were riveted on him. "I feel as if I am still preaching. That was not my intent," he said sheepishly.

Stephan laughed and said, "I don't think that is a bad thing. You are making me think about things I have never before thought about. But, I still don't understand about giving my darkness a place to exist."

"Let me tell you a story that may help." Father Tim sat back and reflected for a moment before continuing. "Years ago, when I was a very young priest, I served in a small town where a very pious and devout family lived. The father was a pillar of the community, very religious. He had several children, but only one daughter, who was quite beautiful. The father became very involved with a local group who had taken up the cause of fighting heresy. In particular, the focus of the group was to target women whom they believed to be witches." Father Tim got up from his seat and walked around the table toward a window. He looked out for a bit before he continued.

"As you have already learned in your endeavors to right the terrible wrongs of the Inquisition, the women were not witches. Many of the men were unable to reconcile their carnal lusts to their wayward beliefs that such reactions to women were sinful. So they made witches of the women, blaming them for what they, themselves did not wish to see."

Tim turned toward the group and walked to the table where everyone sat. "You all know what happened then. They tortured women to get them to admit that they were responsible for inciting their sexual responses. They tried to rid themselves of what they perceived as evil, by blaming it all as something outside of themselves. They thought that if they could just rid themselves of the cause of the 'evil' being done to them, all would be well. And they did so by justifying their actions as God's will."

"I have seen more of that than I care to remember," said Antony, who had been quiet until that moment. He spoke so softly that it was difficult to hear him. His head hung down and shook slowly back and forth.

Stephan reached over and patted Antony on the shoulder.

Father Tim sat back down at the table.

"What happened?" asked Vincenzo.

"Eventually, his daughter became the group's focus. Because she was beautiful, it was inevitable. She was as sweet as any girl I have known, but her beauty made her vulnerable to the uncontrolled lusts of the men. In spite of her father's protests, the group tortured her until she admitted that she used spells to arouse them."

"Did they murder her?" Bella asked.

"No." Father Tim said quietly. "But they disfigured her horribly. Her father could not live with the knowledge that he had participated in the very same activities with other women. He knew his daughter was good, and pure, and *not* a witch. His shame was more than he could bear. He tried, unsuccessfully, to make the group understand that perhaps they were misguided. They turned on him and burned him for heresy.

"It is imperative that we examine our motives and actions within ourselves. If we don't, we risk the danger of becoming like those whose very actions we despise. We must fight the battles within ourselves before we fight the battles outside of us."

He stood again, "We live in God," he repeated. "That is our safe place to do battle. That is the only thing upon which we can truly depend – not a new pope, or new government leaders, not a perfected self or an enlightened Church. Our only place of ultimate safety is in God. Know that the outcome of the war has already been won, and it takes place in heaven itself. Take your battles seriously, but not too seriously. For we live in God, and all shall be well." †

On the ride home James was the first to speak. "I felt as if Father Tim were speaking directly to me--not about the witch stuff, but everything else. He really makes me think about my anger toward people I don't like."

Robert laughed, "I don't see how that's possible, since it was obviously me to whom he referred."

"Father Tim," Bella announced, "has the uncanny ability to speak to a multitude of listeners and cause each one to believe that they are the only one to whom he speaks."

Catherine remained quiet the entire ride home.

Chapter Forty Six

June 1568

"Why?" Sofia asked James as they wandered through the outer courtyard. "Why must you go to Castiglione d' Orcia?"

"I suppose I don't have to go," James shrugged. "But I enjoy going. I like the change of scenery. I like spending time with your cousin, Robert. He is teaching me the art of swordsmanship. Did I tell you?"

"Only a thousand times!" she laughed. "What about Father Tim?"

"What about him? I like him." James bent over to pick up a long stick on the ground. "This will make a great walking stick. I think I'll carve some designs in it for my mother!"

Sofia was not about to be distracted. "What is it about him that you like?"

James was already creating designs for the stick in his head. "About whom?" he asked.

"About Father Tim!" Sofia sometimes found it exasperating to carry on a conversation with James. His thirteen year old mind wandered so quickly from one thing to another that she often found herself having to work to keep him on a topic.

"Oh." James shrugged again. "I don't know. He is so kind. I like his face, too."

"Apart from his face," Sofia pressed, "what do you think about his philosophy?"

"What do you mean?" James held up the piece of wood in the air in front of him and it became a sword.

"His beliefs are not shared by the Church. You do realize," she stopped and turned to him so that he was forced to lower his 'sword' and face her, "that he openly defies everything that the Church is working to establish?"

"What are you talking about?" he said.

Sofia knew he really didn't understand what she was talking about. She had to take a breath. Her studies with the bishop really helped her to understand these matters. Sometimes she was still infuriated with her parents for not allowing James to study with her and the bishop. "Father Tim is a heretic." She finally stated. "The only reason that he hasn't been arrested and tried is that my mother protects him."

James stopped and looked at her aghast. "From what?" James expressed his concern.

"From the Church. From the Bishop." She offered impatiently.

James looked at her. "How do you know this?"

"I know." She looked at James and there were tears in her eyes. "James, please don't go there anymore. Please."

"Sofi," he dropped the stick, "what is it?"

"Do you promise not to tell?" she asked.

"Come here," he pulled her over to a secluded bench partially hidden under a trumpet vine. They sat and he reached for her hands. "Tell me."

"You must promise to say nothing!"

"I promise," he said softly.

"I'm worried you are in danger of going to hell. I know that the things that Father Tim talks about are against the Holy Church. He is a heretic and he is turning all of you into heretics, as well! I am afraid for you. Please promise me that you will stop going to Castiglione d' Orcia," she pleaded as she threw her arms around him and buried her head in his neck.

James wrapped his arms around her and just held her while she cried. He said nothing. Finally, when she had cried herself out, she lifted her head and looked at him questioningly.

He smiled at her, "Don't worry, Sofi. Everything will be okay."

He picked up the stick and walked her back inside.

The next Sunday after Mass and breakfast Sofia informed her mother that she would no longer accompany her to Castiglione d' Orcia.

"I don't like going. I will stay behind," she announced.

"What don't you like about it?" Catherine asked.

"I don't like riding all that way. It's too far. I would rather stay behind and study my lessons," she said.

Catherine sensed that there was more to Sofia's refusal. Part of her wanted to insist that Sofia come, but part of her knew that whatever her real reason, Sofia was growing up and she needed to let go.

"Very well." Catherine stood to go. "I will miss you, but I understand if you feel that your studies must come first." Catherine bent and kissed the top of Sofia's head. As she did she felt the sadness that all mothers feel when they realize that giving birth to the adult will be longer and more painful than giving birth to the baby.

"I don't feel well," James told his mother. "I think I'll stay behind today. Is that alright?"

Bella felt his face. He wasn't warm, but did appear to be a bit pale.

"Are you certain you will be okay? Would you like me to ask Mary to sit with you?" Bella offered.

"I'm sure it's nothing serious. I'll just rest and maybe read while you're gone," he said.

And so, for the first time since they were born, neither James nor Sofia accompanied their mothers to Castiglione d' Orcia.

Chapter Forty Seven

"Master Barone," the note from Bishop Capshaw read. "Please meet me in the Chapel this afternoon after the midday meal. I have something I need to discuss with you."

Sunday Mass had just ended. Mario Barone was having breakfast in the Great Hall. As he folded the note and placed it inside his robe his faced flushed. But no one noticed.

Mario Barone entered the deserted Chapel. "Your Grace?" he called out. There was no answer. He wandered around the Chapel exploring, wondering. His heart raced with anticipation of being with the bishop. He'd been secretly in love with him for months, but knew better than to admit his feelings. When he heard the doors to the Chapel open he turned to see the Bishop locking them.

"Your Grace," he said, working to contain his excitement..

"Mario," the Bishop approached him. "Thank you for coming."

"Not at all," the tutor responded. Then, almost shyly, "It is *my* pleasure." Quickly, he looked down.

Bishop Capshaw smiled. "Please, come and sit with me."

The Bishop led the tutor to the front of the Chapel, where he indicated a pew near the altar.

"Your correspondence sounded urgent," Mario suggested.

"I suppose that's because it is." Thomas Capshaw leaned in toward the tutor and lowered his voice. Although they were clearly alone in the Chapel, he nearly whispered, "I need your assistance with regard to the Princess."

"Anything, Your Grace."

Thomas Capshaw placed his hand on Mario's arm. He allowed it to rest there and paused before proceeding.

"As you know, I believe the Princess to be in danger," he started. "I believe that danger to be escalating." He closed his eyes, bowed his head and raised both his hands to his lips. After a moment he took a deep breath and dropped his hands. He strategically lowered his left hand so that it rested on Mario's thigh.

"I believe that I am in danger, as well," he proceeded. "I know too much."

Mario looked at him, horrified. "What can I do to help? I will do anything."

Thomas Capshaw searched the tutor's eyes as he filled his own with tears. "You must encourage the Princess to trust me above everyone else. Her life and mine depend upon it. And I must ask that you never reveal, to anyone, my work with the princess."

They held each others' gaze for some time. "Promise me," the Bishop pleaded.

"I" sputtered Mario, "I promise". His breath quickened. "I... of course. You have my word."

"Stay with me awhile," Thomas whispered. He slid his hand up to Mario's thigh as he looked soulfully into the tutor's face. "Don't go," he whispered hoarsely, as his hand continued up Mario's leg until it could go no farther.

The Bishop reached for Mario's hand and pulled it to his own erection. The mutual masturbation continued only briefly until the Bishop stopped and pulled the teacher up, propelling him toward the altar. There he lifted Mario's robe and shoved his undergarments out of the way. He turned Mario away from him and bent him over the altar. The Bishop spit into his hand to lubricate himself, then separated Mario's buttocks and entered him. The thrusting was hard, angry, and almost vicious. Mario grasped the opposite side of the altar and held on. After Thomas climaxed inside Mario he moved to the altar where he lifted his own robes and separated himself for the man to slip inside. When both men had satisfied themselves, they sat on the floor in front of the altar.

"I have wanted that for so long," Mario said. "I did not even hope that you might feel the same."

"I needed to be certain you were someone I could trust," the Bishop said. "As I began to know you, my feelings for you grew. I knew I was safe with you."

Mario was delirious with joy and leaned to kiss Thomas.

Thomas stood, quickly, avoiding the tutor's lips. "We should leave. We don't want to arouse any suspicion. Someone may have seen us come into the Chapel."

"Of course," Mario uttered. His face reflected his disappointment.

"If anyone should ask, you requested that I hear your Confession." The Bishop moved toward the doors and unlocked them. Mario left, but not without a backward glance filled with love. Thomas nodded. and closed the Chapel doors, shaking his head as he exited through the back. He smiled as he locked the door behind him.

Chapter Forty Eight

"James," his mother called softly as she entered his quarters upon her return from Castiglione d' Orcia.

"I'm here." He was sitting in a chair turned toward the window. He stood as his mother approached him. His face was a mass of confusion and hurt. Bella could tell he had been crying.

"What is it, tell me."

James sniffed and invited his mother to sit in the chair. He sat on the floor next to her and rested his head on her knee. Bella rested her hand on his head, gently stroking his golden waves. He favored her looks. She was so grateful for that. His body was growing tall and lean. His hair, wavy in golden locks, hung to his shoulders. He even had her blue eyes.

"Is Queen Catherine a heretic?" he asked without looking up.

Bella's free hand flew to her breast, her eyes closed as she paled. She didn't breathe for a moment, then asked, "What would make you think such a thing?"

He hesitated. "I've heard things about Father Timothy. It makes me worry."

"Do you fear that Father Timothy is a heretic, as well?" she asked.

"Is he?"

"What do you think?"

"I don't know what to think. I like Father Tim," he looked up at her. "And I love Queen Catherine."

"James, my love," she placed her hand on his cheek, "do you understand the meaning of heresy? Do you know what it means to be a heretic?"

"A heretic is someone who doesn't follow or believe everything the Church teaches," he answered simply enough.

"I believe you are old enough to know certain things," Bella said as she slipped off the chair and onto the floor next to him. Her heart ached with the knowledge that he was so distraught. She knew she must tread carefully, but wanted to help him. She decided to tell him the truth.

319

"Let me ask you something." She paused as she thought for a minute. "Am I a witch?"

He looked at her with horror. "What?"

She smiled. "Am I a witch?"

"No, of course not!"

She laughed at his response. "You needn't worry. You are correct. I'm not. But," she went on, "before you were born, while I was still carrying you, our bishop tried to portray me as one. He refused me Holy Communion to emphasize his point, intent to turn people against me."

"Why?" James asked.

"He perceived me as a threat when Queen Catherine and I became close. He didn't like the thought of anyone having influence over the Queen."

"That's absurd."

"Of course it is. But in his desire to get rid of me, he spread rumors that I was a witch. Fortunately, Robert took care of that. That is why we go to Castiglione d' Orcia to Mass."

James got up and walked over to his window. "Do you trust Father Tim, then?"

"With my very life. Father Tim is a good and gentle soul. He has a pure heart and works to help others who have been falsely accused of heresy." Bella stood and went over to the window to join him. "James, Queen Catherine, Father Tim and I try to make certain that people like the Bishop cannot make up lies about people and use those lies to hurt others. Do you think that makes us heretics?"

"No."

"According to the bishop, it does. I don't know how you came to your information, nor does it matter. What does matter," Bella said with conviction, "is that you always try to discern the truth. That is what you just did with me. I hope you always do so."

"I will," he said.

"I know you will. Trust your heart and it will always lead you." She reached out again and gently touched his face. "Your heart is much like Father Tim's. You always see the good in others."

"Was my father like that, too?" he asked.

Though not with as much frequency, James still asked about his father. Bella decided long ago that he would never know he was born of her rape. That one lie was one she justified as being in her son's best interest. She didn't want him to harbor any fear or judgment about himself regarding his origins. As far as James knew, and would ever know, his father was her husband, murdered by a fanatical believer's group.

"Yes," she said. "And he would be so proud of you."

In the childlike way that he used to, he threw his arms around her neck, hugging her and whispered, "I love you."

She kissed his cheek. "I love you, too."

Chapter Forty Nine

January 1569

Robert went to Catherine's quarters. She had sent him word that she was not feeling well and wanted his weekly report there. Bella let him in, and went in search of Marie to bring Catherine some hot broth and tea.

"You look a little pale, cousin," he said. "Are you certain you are up to this?"

She looked up at him through puffy, watery eyes after she sneezed into her handkerchief. She was miserable, but she said, "As long as I can sit next to my warm fire, curled under my blanket I'm fine." She managed a smile. "Please sit."

"I thought you should know I received word from Cologero that Domenico Carfaggi was executed yesterday."

"It is about time, I suppose. It's been more than a year, hasn't it?"

"A little more than two, actually."

She sneezed. "He was the last to be dealt with, then?" Catherine asked as she dabbed her sore nose with a handkerchief.

"He was the last in Radicondoli after the Mayor and the Sheriff were executed. The rest of that brood will remain in prison for another year."

Robert reached for the poker and stoked the fire.

"It sounded," Catherine said, "from my last communication from Cologero, as if the new government is functioning well. How many men do we still have there?"

"Only two. The transition has been complete for some time, but you were wise to leave them to support Cologero."

"Perhaps it's time to bring them home."

Marie entered with broth and tea. She drizzled honey in the tea for Catherine, and offered Robert a cup.

"No, thank you, Marie. I am nearly done and will allow the Queen to resume her rest."

When Marie left, he turned back to Catherine. "I think it time to send our own Lord Carfaggi back to Radicondoli for his trial."

"I suppose it is. Does he know about his brother's execution?"

"Not yet," Robert answered. He lifted the bowl of broth and handed it to Catherine as he took the cup of tea from her. "I will tell him as soon as you order it."

"Make arrangements to transport him to Radicondoli at your convenience. Tell him or not. He will know soon enough. I leave it to you."

Robert stood to take his leave. "Feel better, cousin. You look like hell."

She sneezed in response and closed her eyes with a groan.

April 1569

Catherine was in her office examining the quality of the latest batch of papers from the mill. Ambrose made improvements to decrease the amount of impurities able to enter during the pressing process. She was thinking of Ambrose, and of how much he enjoyed his role in the paper production. He did quite well, and, he'd become quite the artist. His oil portraits developed beautifully as his confidence increased. She had just stopped to admire his very first portrait of Sofia when her secretary knocked and entered.

"Majesty?" he said quietly.

"What is it, Antonio?" she asked without looking up.

"The Captain of the Guard would like a word with you."

"Thank you. Send him in." Catherine rubbed her eyes and looked up to see Robert enter the room. They had not met for several days, at his request.

"Majesty," he said formally as he bowed slightly at the waist.

Catherine stood. "Come in, Robert. Sit." She moved around her desk to join him in the small sitting area by the fireplace.

"Something has been taking up your time," she smiled. "Am I finally to learn what it is?"

His look was solemn. "You will not be pleased," he said.

"Go on." She leaned forward to give him her full attention.

"Two days ago, sometime shortly after Mass, I happened to be crossing the small servant hallway behind the kitchens, the one that connects to the secret passageway from the library. As I entered, I saw Sofia and Mary making their way down the passage."

"Why would Sofia be there at that time? She is with her tutor immediately after Mass."

"That, of course, was my question, as well," Robert said. "So, I followed them." He paused. "They went directly to the Chapel. They both went in, but Mary came out again shortly thereafter." Catherine felt her jaw clench and her face flush almost instantly. "What is that bastard doing with my daughter?" she demanded as she sat up, fear and anger both filling her.

"Don't panic. He has no interest in women in that way. As far as I can determine he has never touched her."

Catherine relaxed a bit, but still found the information unsettling. "Go on," she said as her eyes narrowed.

Robert shifted in his seat, crossed his legs. "I went around to the back entrance of the chapel. I couldn't hear what they were saying, but they talked only. Once I determined Sofia was not being molested by him, I went in search of Mary and interrogated her." He hesitated before continuing. "She has been delivering Sofia to the Bishop for 'religious training'.

Catherine leapt to her feet, the veins in her forehead stood out. "On whose authority?" she demanded.

"On yours apparently," Robert said solemnly. "At least that is what she has been led to believe."

"By Thomas Capshaw, no doubt." Catherine was livid.

"No doubt. Obviously, however, there is also someone else participating in this charade," he continued. "I went to see Master Barone, who claims he saw no reason to deny the Bishop access to the Princess. And since the Princess had obviously formed a close attachment with the bishop long before he arrived, he saw no reason to be concerned."

Catherine collapsed back into her chair. "How long?"

"Some years, apparently."

"Under our very noses!" Catherine was appalled. "Do you believe Mary?"

"I believe Mary was duped. I am not convinced about Barone. He seems to be covering up something, but I'm not sure what. He was very nervous under questioning and seems to be protecting the bishop. He won't implicate Capshaw, not even to save himself."

"Where is he now?"

"With Sofia and James, but I have a guard posted outside the door so that he cannot warn the bishop. As of today Mary will cease delivering Sofia to the Chapel. He is waiting for her now."

"I think we should pay our Bishop a visit." Catherine stood.

"I thought you might like to surprise him." Robert followed her out the door and to the Chapel.

The Bishop was kneeling in prayer at the altar when Catherine and Robert entered the Chapel. He didn't indicate that he knew, or cared, that anyone had entered.

Robert and Catherine moved to the front of the Chapel and sat, waiting to see how long he might keep them waiting, thinking it was Sofia. After many minutes the Bishop finally stood, crossed himself and turned around.

When he saw the Queen and Captain sitting in the front pew he blanched.

"Why, Your Grace," Catherine smiled, "that may be the first honest reaction I have ever observed from you. Is all well?"

In spite of the absence of color in his face the Bishop responded, "Why, of course, Majesty." But his eyes darted nervously at the doors of the Chapel.

"Are you expecting someone, your Grace?" Catherine asked.

"As a matter of fact, yes, Your Majesty," he replied somewhat shakily. "If you need to speak with me I would be happy to come by your office later."

"Who is it you are expecting?" Catherine stood and took a few steps toward the Bishop. Robert stood, as well, but stayed where he was.

Bishop Capshaw saw the look in her eyes and did not answer.

Catherine stepped closer to him and said coldly, "My daughter will not be coming for her 'religious studies' this morning, or any other morning," she spat.

"And why is that, Your Majesty?" the Bishop seemed to be recovering from his initial shock. "Do you not believe that she requires a solid religious education?"

"I will not play games with you, you hypocrite! My daughter is off limits to you. Is that understood?"

"I understand perfectly well, Your Highness," he replied coolly. "But I wonder how the Princess will feel about that?"

"Your arrogance is matched only by your hate." Catherine shook her head. "Someday soon you will have to answer to God for your pitiful excuse of a life," she said as she turned to leave. But before she left she turned back to him. "I watched you kill my father with your hate. I will be damned if you will do the same to my daughter!"

Thomas Capshaw was sitting in his quarters drinking later that evening. The queen's words upset him more than he thought possible. Was it possible his change after Rome was a factor in Edward's death? The mere hint tore at him with the claw of possibility. It was bad enough that he still grieved over Edward in the silence of his own soul. The suggestion that he might be responsible for contributing to Edward's decline and death had never crossed his mind.

He was well in to his third cup of wine when Master Barone arrived unannounced. A servant asked if he should be allowed entrance.

He nodded and sent the servant away for the evening. He remained sitting when Mario entered the room.

"I have been dismissed!" cried Mario as he threw himself upon the bishop.

It was obvious that he had been crying for some time. The bishop wriggled from his grasp and went to pour him a cup of wine.

"Here," Thomas said, "You need to pull yourself together."

"What am I to do?" Master Barone lamented, ignoring the wine that had been offered. "Where am I to go?"

Coolly, as he set the untouched cup down on a nearby table, the Bishop said, "There are other positions. You will find something. Return to Venice," he said casually with a wave of his hand.

The Bishop moved to the chair furthest from the tutor and sat, crossing his legs in a casually disinterested manner.

"I don't want to return to Venice. How can you even suggest such a thing?" Mario's blubbering started anew, making his homely face look even more uncomely.

"There are other places where the skills of an academic are needed." The Bishop held up his goblet admiring the craftsmanship allowing the beauty of it to totally engross his thoughts, as if it were the most beautiful item he had ever encountered.

Mario Barone knelt before Thomas. His eyes beseeched the bishop for comfort, for some tenderness. "I don't want to leave here, leave you," he sobbed. "I cannot bear the thought of it. I love you!"

Thomas stood, extracting himself yet again from the cloying embrace of the tutor. This slobbering display disgusted him. He wanted the tutor gone. "It appears you have no choice."

Thomas Capshaw might just as well have slapped Mario Barone across the face. The tutor fell against the chair, staring, slack-jawed. He watched the man he loved turn away. "Do you feel nothing for me then?"

"I am sorry for you," the Bishop said, never turning to look at him. "It is unfortunate that Mary was observed escorting the Princess to the Chapel. But there is nothing to be done about it now. I will be left to protect the Princess on my own. That, I fear, needs to be my priority."

"I see." Mario Barone pushed himself to a standing position, wiping his face on his sleeve. "I shall say goodbye then." He turned to go and took a few steps toward the door, but stopped. He looked back, his face filled with devastation. He waited for Thomas Capshaw to turn, but the Bishop neither turned nor said another word. He offered nothing by way of farewell or affection. Mario Barone closed the door to the Bishop's quarters behind him.

In the morning Master Mario Barone was gone.

Chapter Fifty

February 1570

The snow lay deep around the castle. It was the middle of another February. A new tutor had been in place for nearly a year. Although it was Sunday there was no outing to Castiglione d' Orcia, as the pass to the little village was piled high with snow. It would be some time before Father Tim would see the Queen again.

Bella saw the restlessness of the castle residents in the way they sniped at one another. Tensions were high.

"Catherine," she said at the meal following the Mass. "The staff and servants need some distraction from this confinement."

"What do you mean?"

"Open your eyes, my love. Don't you see how people snap at one another?" Bella indicated a minor disagreement on the far side of the hall. "Tempers are short."

Catherine followed Bella's eyes to see two servants glaring at one another. The anger was evident, although they restrained themselves from much more than a few harsh words and scowls.

"What do you suggest?" Catherine inquired with a smile. "I know you well enough to know that you already have something in mind."

"King Ambrose," Bella leaned across Catherine, inviting him into the conversation. "Don't you think that a celebration might benefit the mood of the castle? There's been nothing since the Chestnut Festival in October."

"What a splendid idea, Lady Isabella. I wish I had thought of it!"

Catherine looked back and forth between the two of them. "If I didn't know better, I might think you two were conspiring behind my back!"

Bella and the King looked at each other and had difficulty concealing their smiles.

"Very well, then." Catherine stood. Ambrose called for silence in the hall.

The residents and servants turned toward the Queen. Her face appeared a mask of displeasure. When the hall was finally silent she spoke.

"It has been brought to my attention," she said with a mock frown, "that perhaps the time might be right for a celebration to help us out of the atmosphere of gloom generated by this extended period of storm." She watched as the faces of everyone in the room changed, brightened, alerted. She smiled as she announced, "One week from today, in the Great Hall, I declare that we shall have a festival!"

The hall erupted in cheers and shouts. "And," she continued, "the festivities shall embrace the snow as well as proclaim the hope of spring!" She felt the excitement and happiness blossom in the hall, it inspired her on the spot. "I want to see sculptures made of snow in the courtyards. A contest! The most creative sculpture will win a prize!"

Catherine looked down her table to see James, Gio and even Sofia light up. "I expect all children of the castle to participate in creating a garden of delight from the snow that has buried us for so long!"

"In this hall," she continued, "with whatever materials we can muster, let's honor our flower field. Fill the hall with our faith that spring is coming, and our confinement limited!" She lifted her cup and shouted, "To the creation of our happiness!"

"To Queen Catherine," someone in the hall shouted.

"To Queen Catherine," echoed the simultaneous response from the entire hall. The noise that followed was filled with happy laughter and excited planning.

Catherine sat back down, pleased with herself and the response from the hall. But then she turned to look back and forth between Bella and Ambrose. She shook her head, and, grinning, said, "You two are dangerous together. I must keep a watchful eye, I see!"

No one was more excited than Sofia and James about the upcoming festival. They had spent a good part of their time lately bickering and avoiding one another. After James had resumed his weekly trips to Castiglione d' Orcia, their relationship changed. And since the winter confinement, whenever they were together, topics of heresy, Castiglione d' Orcia and Church doctrine dominated Sofia's conversation. She relentlessly hounded James at every opportunity.

James found himself spending more and more time with Robert and Gio. Robert made himself available to James, including him when they hunted or practiced swords or horsemanship. James and Gio got along well. They had their spats, but got over their anger quickly and moved on without difficulty.

The announcement of the festival was a welcome intrusion on the ever-present anger and frustration that had become a large part of interactions with Sofia. Her fears and worries about her mother's salvation, and James' seeming betrayal, had turned to reticence and anger.

But all that darkness was instantly banished with the announcement of a celebration.

"I haven't seen Sofia smile for so long I thought she had forgotten how," Catherine said wistfully to Bella as they made their way back to their quarters.

"She's changing," Bella offered.

"I miss her," Catherine lamented. "She's been so angry and distant since I denied her visits with the bishop. She took it harder than I expected. It troubles me."

Catherine sat near the fire. Bella went to stand behind her. She slid her arms around Catherine's neck and hugged her. "I know what you mean. But it's not only you she has distanced herself from. She barely talks to me anymore. Even she and James are distant lately."

"I've noticed. I'm also disturbed by how hostile she is with you. I tried to talk to her about it but..." Her voice trailed off. "Has James said anything?" Catherine asked.

"Not recently. Not since he expressed being worried about us visiting with Father Tim." She walked around to sit facing Catherine. "Are you certain Sofia isn't still meeting with the bishop? After all, if they managed to hide their liaisons for so many years, perhaps they have found a way to continue to meet."

"Hmmm," Catherine nodded. "I have thought of that already. Robert has the bishop closely watched during the day. There is no way that he is seeing her." Catherine got up and sat down on the floor at Bella's feet. She rested her head on Bella's lap. "I do not know how to break through all the lies and damage that bastard has done. How do I get my daughter back?"

She sighed deeply as Bella stroked her hair. "It breaks my heart that she is so resistive to you and Tim...and Castiglione d' Orcia...and..." her voice drifted off as she stared into the fire.

"And you?" Bella asked as she slid down and knelt in front of Catherine.

"And me." Catherine gazed into Bella's open, loving face. "I did so want to be close with her. I fought my own mother in so many ways, and miss her so much now, when it's too late to ask her forgiveness, too late to wrap my arms around her to tell her how much I love her." Catherine was silent, drifting in and out of her own memories. Bella rested her head on Catherine's lap, each lost in memories of long lost mothers.

"I guess," Catherine said, "I thought that I could do things differently with Sofia. I wanted her to feel the freedom to be strong, and independent, not stifled by harsh rules and formalities of regal life. I so wished for her to desire my encouragement and support as she grew into her role of monarch."

"Don't give up, my love. Give her time." Bella offered.

"I feel her resentment every time she looks at me," Catherine mourned. "Perhaps that is the way of mothers and their daughters. Or maybe this is my punishment for my own resistance to mine," she thought aloud.

"Perhaps," offered Bella, "this festival will heal whatever it is, and you shall have your daughter back."

Catherine leaned against the chair and cuddled with Bella. They kissed ever so softly and lingeringly. They sat, warmed by the fire, holding each other quietly.

The week of the Festival was filled with exuberance. The castle was abuzz with preparations. Minstrels practiced new songs. Flowers were crafted of various materials and strung together to be hung in the Great Hall. Summer foods were prepared, and if summer foods weren't available, the cooks worked to make winter foods, roots and other items from the fall harvest cellars, look like summer foods. All the activities delighted the castle residents, but the snow sculptures, by far, brought the most joy.

Sofia, James and Gio combined their ideas into one sculpture. It took work to merge their ideas, but eventually they managed to come up with something important to all of them. They took their plan to Ambrose to help sketch them out. He was happy to help them design their creation.

The day of the Festival arrived. Was it Catherine's imagination or was the bishop's sermon actually shorter and less hostile?

When the Mass ended, the residents made their way to the Great Hall. The doors were closed. The cooks, the bakers, the decorators all waited inside to open the doors onto their creation. A single guard stood outside the huge doors to the Great Hall. The Queen waited for all the residents to assemble. When steady hum of voices stilled, the guard knocked three times.

Slowly, majestically, the doors swung open. Those in front near the Queen exclaimed in wonder. Catherine walked in slowly, taking in all before her. It was a glorious sight.

From every candled chandelier streamed fabric flowers of every shape and color. The servants and cooks were stationed around the room at intervals, all dressed in summer attire. Huge fires burned in both of the fireplaces to warm the room comfortably, but the fires were hidden behind large screens of summer scenery.

Each table was adorned with a different color of tablecloth, picking up the colors of the flowers flowing from above. One large table held roasts of every kind, whole pigs and turkeys, lamb and beef roasts. Each sitting table was piled with vegetable dishes, pitchers of summer wines from the cellars, and summer ales. But one side of the hall was the table that made everyone exclaim.

Flower streams flowed down from a single point on a large chandelier to the each end of the massive table. There sat a sweet table beyond every child's imagination. Every confection was created to reflect an object of spring or summer. The outer perimeter of the table was covered with small, individual cakes all decorated as a different flower. There were as many different flowers and colors as could be imagined. Within the flowered cake border were candies and candied fruits. Catherine was delighted to see her favorite confection, Nipples of Venus. They were roasted chestnuts coated in brandied sugar and topped with a small toasted almond.

Light, lacey baked sugar fantasies drizzled with honey took the forms of birds, flowers, boats, suns and flowers. But the centerpiece of the table is what demanded the attention of the crowd. A huge cake, nearly the width of the table and a quarter of the length, was decorated to look like the flower fields surrounding the lake. Mountains of meringue created the look of the Apennines behind a blue frosting lake. The yellow and purple flowers surrounding the lake were a masterpiece of creation. The effect was dazzling.

Catherine made her way to the head table. She waited for everyone to find their seats, which took longer than usual, for the children had difficulty tearing themselves away from the sweet table. Once everyone was situated, she turned to the makers of this part of the celebration, the cooks and bakers and decorators, and simply clapped. The entire hall erupted into applause turning toward the proud group lined along the wall. They bowed and curtsied, unable hide their pleasure.

When the applause died down Catherine addressed the crowd. "Winter is transformed!" she began. She lifted her cup, already filled with wine, to the crowd. "To the joy you have brought to this day, and to the promise of spring!"

"To spring!" the hall resounded.

At once the minstrels broke into song and the feasting began. Laughter filled the hall. The heaviness of mood that had enveloped the castle just a few short days ago was gone, replaced by giddy chatter and celebration.

During the meal Bella leaned over to whisper to Catherine. "Look," she indicated the table where James, Sofia and Gio were seated.

Catherine smiled. The three of them were excitedly discussing something of great importance to them. It didn't matter what it was, only that they were animated, engaged in a way that had been missing for some time.

"Thank you, love," Catherine whispered in Bella's ear.

"For what?"

"For everything," Catherine said softly, "but, especially, for this. I confess I don't always notice the little things."

"You just needed a little nudge," Bella said, and under the table she gave Catherine's knee a squeeze.

When it seemed that no one could eat another morsel King Ambrose called the hall to silence.

"The outer courtyard," he announced, "has been a hive of activity this week. If you haven't had the opportunity to see the spectacular artwork being created there, you are in for a treat. Twenty snow sculptures have been erected by our children and await appreciation."

The children hurriedly donned their outer garments. Catherine and Bella had never seen so many children move so swiftly. The adults followed slowly, but no less excitedly, to the courtyard.

A light snow was falling. It softened all of the footprints and ruts from the week, creating the illusion that the sculptures created themselves, appearing to have sprouted out of the snow.

Catherine, Ambrose and Bella walked silently within the rows of sculptures as the castle residents gathered around the outer ring of them. Catherine stopped at each sculpture, asking the artists to step forward to tell about their creation.

One of the first at which Catherine stopped was a lighthouse. It was the tallest of all, towering some two feet over the heads of the Queen and King. A young man, about Sofia's age, stepped forward when Catherine asked for the artist.

"Here, Your Majesty." He seemed nervous, but very proud of his work.

"Why a lighthouse?" the Queen asked. "Have you ever seen one?"

"No, Majesty," the boy answered. "But my mother talks of the lighthouse on the shores of the village where she grew up."

"It's a fine rendering for someone who has never seen one. I can almost hear the waves of the sea crashing against the rocks."

The young man beamed.

At each sculpture Catherine chatted with the artist. Some of the work was magnificent in detail. Some, those done by the younger children, were smaller, but clearly gave much joy to those who participated.

There were several animals: a ferocious looking bear, the front end of a rearing horse, a lioness with nursing cubs.

Several of the children had attempted a rendering of the Queen. Catherine found it difficult to hide her smile as she spoke with the artists about her own likeness. They were all so earnest in their descriptions.

Sofia, James and Gio stood proudly next to their creation. It did nearly take Catherine's breath away. Set into a mountain of snow was a near perfect rendering of Montalcino Castle, its proportions almost faultless. The detail, down to each window was remarkable. The central tower easily supported the two adjoining wings. The main doors almost had the look of the carved wood. Each of the two surrounding walls appeared to be made of the original rocks set in place so many years ago. There was even a guard standing next to the guard house at the outer wall.

"I am most impressed." Catherine walked around the castle taking in every detail. "Most impressed." Then to herself she thought, "Sofia, you have your father's gift of artistry." She smiled as she congratulated the three children closest to her in the world.

The final work was clearly done by a smaller child. It, too, was a rendering of Montalcino Castle. Compared to the one done by her family it was pitifully small and inaccurate. As Catherine looked at it, part of the center tower collapsed.

The Queen noticed a boy of about eight standing nearby and saw him wince as his tower gave way. Out of the corner of her eye she watched him as she walked around the snow carving. He waited anxiously to be called. She made a show of taking her time to study his work, nodding and whispering to Ambrose and Bella.

Finally, she said, "Who is responsible for this castle?"

The young boy stepped forward, "I am, Your Majesty."

"I see." She looked down at him. "And did you have help?"

"I didn't need any. I wanted to do it myself," he announced proudly.

"Tell me about your castle," she commanded as she looked up to see the boy's mother standing nearby. She gave a smile and a nearly imperceptible nod to the boy's mother as she continued her interrogation of the boy.

"This," he announced as he pointed to the crumbling central part of the castle, "is the main tower, and this is the wing where my mother and I live, and this is where the Great Hall is..." The boy rushed through descriptions of his barely recognizable castle.

Catherine listened intently as he showed her everything. Robert had already informed her about this boy and his attempt to recreate the castle. The boy's father was one of his guard; he died in the spring of the previous year, succumbing to pneumonia. His wife and child stayed on in the castle. The boy's mother assisted in the kitchen.

"And this," the boy slowed in his presentation, "is the guard house where my father used to stand guard."

Catherine looked down at the boy. "What is your name?"

"Marco," he said seriously, then added quickly, "Your Majesty."

"After your father." Catherine bent and placed her hand on the boy's shoulder. "I remember your father, young Marco. He would be proud of you. Tell me," she asked, "what made you decide on Montalcino Castle?"

"Because it is my home, Majesty."

She smiled at him. "Mine, as well, Marco. I am proud to share it with the likes of you."

Catherine, Ambrose and Bella stepped aside and talked in hushed tones. As they did so they made a show of looking and pointing to all of the imaginative models surrounding them. Finally, King Ambrose said, "We have declared a winner to the competition.

"Marco Carrerro, please come forward!" Ambrose boomed.

Catherine took the golden medal on a strip of blue silk and placed it around Marcus' neck. She kissed him formally on each cheek and congratulated him on winning the snow sculpture competition. The crowd erupted in cheers and applause for the boy, who beamed so brightly that his smile threatened to melt all of the snow. After congratulating each of the participants on their creativity and abilities to work with such a difficult medium as snow, Catherine encouraged everyone back inside to continue the celebration with music, dancing, games and entertainment.

The mood in the ensuing weeks was much lighter, much friendlier following the festival. The flowered ropes stayed up in the Great Hall and the snow sculptures stayed intact, gracing the courtyard.

As the sun made its lazy way back toward spring, the decorations were finally removed. The grand snow creations were only melted mounds shrinking in the sun.

Spring arrived and fresh berries were again on the table. Catherine, Bella and James were just finishing a private morning meal in the queen's quarters when Sofia entered and walked over to peruse the table for food. At fourteen she was nearly as tall as her mother and had been developing in both body and attitude.

"Sofia, where have you been?" asked Catherine.

"Don't bother looking for your favorite berries," said James. "I ate them all when it seemed you weren't coming."

Sofia turned up her nose at James, then, without looking at her mother said, "I was in Church, if you must know."

"This long?" Catherine asked. "Mass ended two hours ago."

"I was with the Bishop." Sofia did not meet her mother's eyes. With the defiance that colored most of her conversations of late she said, "I've been seeing him regularly. I am learning all of the Doctrines of the Church, and he is helping me to understand the finer, more subtle points of the gospels."

Catherine's look of fear was mirrored in Bella's eyes. But neither James nor Sofia noticed.

"Whose idea was that?" asked Catherine with as much nonchalance as possible.

Sofia looked at her mother with disdain. "Why should it matter?"

"Because you will be Queen someday. You must begin to examine everything with a more critical eye." Catherine responded as she stood to walk over to where Sofia was. "We have discussed this before."

"Yes, yes." Sofia rolled her eyes as she sat at the table where her mother had been sitting. "I have heard over and over the importance of suspecting everyone!"

Catherine worked hard to keep the angry edge out of her voice. "It is not that you need to suspect everyone, Sofia, it is wise for someone in power to examine the reasons behind certain requests." Catherine fought the urge to forbid her daughter to see the Bishop. She was nearly immobilized by fear that Sofia was so beguiled such a misguided man. She flashed on how her father despaired when he realized that Thomas Capshaw was not the man he thought him to be. The thought of the same thing happening to Sofia terrified her. She knew she must be cautious, or she would lose her daughter, too.

"Mother, please. The bishop has only my best interests at heart. You may not trust him, but I do."

"Sofia," Bella offered her a dish of strawberries, "have you given any thought to allowing Father Tim to aid in your religious training?"

More and more of late, Sofia ignored Bella. She took the bowl of strawberries, but did not answer the question.

"Rudeness is not a quality that will endear you to anyone, Sofia. You have been asked a question." Catherine found it hard not to be exasperated with Sofia.

Sofia looked at Bella with indifference, "I honestly don't know what you see in that priest of yours. And why would I want to travel all the way to Castiglione d' Orcia when I have the kingdom's highest ranking priest right here in my own castle?"

"Sofi," James offered, "want to go riding with me this morning?"

"When?"

"Now might be good," he grinned his winning smile.

Sofia could not get out of the room quickly enough. "Let's go."

"James," his mother called out as they were leaving, "be sure you take at least one armed guard with you!"

Sofia was gone, but just before the doors closed James stuck his head back in and winked at his mother, "Don't worry, I will."

James saddled their horses while Robert assigned them a soldier. Once outside the castle walls they made for the forest. Up until then they hadn't spoken. When the muddy path in the forest widened large enough for the horses to walk side by side, James slowed to allow Sofia to move next to him.

"What has you in such a foul mood this morning?" he asked.

"Do you have any idea what a heretic my mother is?" she asked.

"Not again." James was tired of hearing Sofia berate her mother. "Your mother is no heretic! Is your bishop still feeding you that load of shit?"

"It isn't shit, James. It is the truth."

James reined up his horse to allow the guard to get a bit further ahead. "What are you talking about?"

Sofia stopped and turned her horse toward him. James' face held a look of innocence and concern. "Never mind," she said. "You wouldn't understand." She turned her horse back to follow the guard.

"Don't!" James demanded. "I hate when you do that to me. You engage me with a comment like that, and then you dismiss me like a pesky servant."

"Well, you can't be my friend while defending my mother!" Sofia was already shouting over her shoulder as she spurred her horse toward the flower fields. She passed the guard and hit the rise at the end of the forest line before either of them reached her. By the time James caught up with her she had left her horse to graze amid the few clumps of snow and sparse grass and was walking toward the lake.

James found her sitting on an old stump at the edge of the water. "Sofi," he said softly. "Tell me what's wrong."

She was quiet for some time. Her expression seemed to vacillate between anger and sadness. When she finally spoke, the combination revealed more anger than anything.

"I know things about my mother that no one else knows," she said.

James watched as her jaw clenched and unclenched. He waited for her to continue.

"Whether you believe it or not, she is a heretic. She fights her own bishop and her own Church!"

"So you believe that her stand against torture and persecution make her a heretic?" James asked.

"It is more than that. She openly rebels against the Church. She is at war with the Holy See. She defies the Bishop and all he stands for, all the Church is trying to accomplish! There is more, but..."

James waited for her to continue. "But what?" James asked.

"Her entire life is built on a lie." Sofia seemed to be winding down.

These tirades of Sofia's seemed to occur more and more of late. James usually let her rant until she was done.

He tried many times to convince Sofia that her mother was a good Queen, a good person. Sofia knew he really didn't understand the animosity between them, and long ago he stopped defending Catherine to Sofia. Every time he tried she became so angry they ended up not speaking for several days. Lately, however, she found that he seemed content to just listen while she ranted on about her mother. She hoped he was beginning to see her side of things. She was still worried about his soul, his salvation. She so wanted him to be on the right side of the war between God and the heretics, but she always stopped short of telling him what she knew about her mother's relationship with his own mother. James adored his mother. She knew the information would drive a wedge between them that could never be repaired. She always stopped just short of telling him.

Sofia finally came to the end of her diatribe.

When she finished James said, "Then you must think me a heretic, as well."

"I don't think any such thing!" She looked at him as if he were a child. "You are an innocent. You can't help but to do what your mother tells you to."

"You're wrong, Sofe." James stood and looked at her with tears in his eyes. "I choose to go with your mother and mine to Castiglione d' Orcia because I believe the Church has made a grave mistake. I believe in what Father Timothy stands for and I want to help those who are unjustly accused of heresy and witchcraft. I wish you could understand...I wish you would join us." He paused and waited for her to say something, but she would not look at him. He turned to head back to his horse. "I'm going back," he said. "I am suddenly very cold."

James mounted his horse and waited for her, but she didn't make a move to join him. He told the guard to wait with Sofia and returned to the castle alone.

Chapter Fifty One

Bella's birthday fell in the full of summer. Catherine planned a birthday picnic in the flower fields to celebrate the occasion. Robert and his family joined them, as did Ambrose and Lord Como's niece, Mirabella, who obviously cherished Ambrose. No one ever spoke of the relationship between the King and Mirabella, but Catherine made every effort to include them both in the goings on of family gatherings.

When the group settled and spread out the foods and drinks, the children, who were no longer children, but blossoming adults, took off for the lake, while their parents stayed back to lounge in the summer sun and talk.

Gio beat James and Sofia into the water and came up sputtering.

"How cold is it?" asked Sofia.

"Warm as bath water!" he laughed.

James jumped in, believing him, and came up with a start. "Don't believe him, Sofi! It's freezing!"

"You believe him every time!" Sofia laughed and sat on a rock on the side of the lake, dangling her feet and legs into the cold mountain water, glad for the rare opportunity to play. This was their sanctuary, their retreat from the real world. In past years they would steal away to the lake to enjoy each other. The water cleansed them of the winter's arguments and discord. Sofia watched the boys swim and float on their backs. She loved to watch them dive from the overhang into the deep water just over the rocks from where she sat.

Gio called them the "triumvirate." "Someday, the three of us will take all of Italy by storm," he called from the water.

"And just where will we take it?" teased Sofia.

"Oh, I don't know," he smiled as he shook water out of his hair spraying her. "But with you as Queen, me as your Captain and James, here, as your advisor I think we could rule all of Italy, maybe even the whole of the continent!" He dove, laughing.

James pulled himself out of the water. He and Sofia were grinning at him when he came up. "You are crazy, you know?" James said.

"Oh, I know." He came out of the water and sat on the rock next to them. "But what shall we do when our time comes?" he asked seriously.

Many of their summers were spent solving the problems of Montalcino and the world. They talked of exploring new lands, becoming wealthy, and they shared the deepest, most intimate desires of their hearts. They loved one another fiercely and passionately as only young people can. As only children, they were both siblings and friends to one another as they grew their own history around and within them, weaving their history like a tapestry. Somehow, no matter how tense things might be between them, when summer came and the lake called, all tension disappeared and they found their rhythm again.

The summer afternoon was warm when Sofia entered the Chapel where she knew Bishop Capshaw was waiting for her. She saw him sitting in the front pew talking with someone. When he heard the great doors close he stopped talking and rose to greet her.

"Ah, Princess Sofia, my lamb, how are you?"

"I am well, Your Grace, thank you. And you?" she asked.

"Quite well, quite well."

As he spoke this last, the other man stood and turned to her. He was of medium height, and dressed in drab, brown robes. There was a large, wooden crucifix around his neck. His face was severe, drawn, and dark. Sofia looked at him and then back to the bishop, who was smiling broadly.

"Princess Sofia," he soothed, "may I present my very good friend and colleague, Captain Dominic Bello. Captain Bello, this is Princess Sofia, about whom I have been raving for the past hour."

He smiled. It did little to soften his hard features. He looked at Sofia with unwavering intensity before moving toward her. He bowed quite formally and greeted her.

"Princess, an honor to meet you. Bishop Capshaw has, indeed, been glowing about you for some time."

"Thank you, Captain." Sofia's face relaxed into a smile.

"Sofia," the Bishop said, "I have asked Captain Bello to meet us because I believe he is someone you should know. He does important work for the Church. He has quite a formidable reputation," the Bishop smiled as he placed his arm around Sofia and led her to the second pew. Once they were seated, Captain Bello sat in the front pew and turned to face them.

"Captain Bello recently moved to Montalcino. He will be a great help to those of us who work so diligently to serve Christ and the Church."

"Your bishop is too kind, Princess. I am only a servant of God, here to help where and when I can. It is your bishop who deserves the credit for steadfastness in the eyes of our Lord." Again, he smiled.

The bishop smiled and bowed his head, seemingly embarrassed by the praise. "In any event, Princess," the Bishop continued, "I wanted you to meet Captain Bello." He paused and his face took on a concerned look. "You and I have become quite close over the years."

Sofia smiled broadly at the bishop. "And I am glad of it, Your Grace."

He smiled back at her and reached for her hand. "That is why, my dear, I believe it important for you to have someone else in whom you may place your trust when it comes to matters of the Church."

"I don't understand," Sofia looked at him quizzically. "Are you going somewhere?"

"I don't intend to, no," he said. "But because we are close, and the Queen seems intent on punishing me for our relationship, you and I must be more cautious."

"You mean because my mother does not approve of you teaching me about the Church?" It was a statement rather than a question. "You know I don't care what she thinks, Your Grace."

He patted her hand and looked at the captain. "You see what I mean about her courage now, don't you?"

Bello nodded, but did not even attempt a smile.

"Sofia." Thomas Capshaw grew intensely serious. "If you should ever have questions or concerns about anyone, whether they are questions of heresy, or witchcraft, or even worry about your own personal safety, I want you to promise me that you will seek out Captain Bello."

Sofia looked lovingly at Bishop Capshaw. "I will."

"He has many contacts and can address your concerns without hesitation."

"I am here to serve you, Princess. You and the Church," Captain Bello added.

"Thank you, Captain," Sofia said.

Chapter Fifty Two

May 1573

At seventeen James could not remember a time when the flower fields were not a significant part of his life. He never missed spring or summer playing among the blossoms. When they were small he and Sofia often sneaked away from their mothers to lie down in the midst of the flowers so that no one could find them. They stared up through the petals and watched the clouds roll by for hours. As they grew, some days found them in the lake, swimming until they were so exhausted they fell asleep in their mothers' arms on the way back to the castle.

Some of their outings included others, but mostly it was just James, Sofia and their mothers. Those were the outings James remembered most fondly, the times when he and Sofia would just disappear for hours and play. When they returned to the blanket near the rocks where Catherine and Bella would invariably be waiting, his mother would sometimes play her harp. He loved her voice. It was sweet and soft and it comforted him to listen to her. He felt very blessed to have a mother whom he loved so much. He wished Sofia and Catherine had a better relationship. It hurt him to see Sofia at such odds with the queen.

Sofia confided often in James, and even shared that both she and the bishop thought her mother could easily be accused of heresy against the church. James knew there was animosity between the queen and the bishop. When he asked his mother about it, she had smiled sadly and shook her head. That was when she told him that the bishop had always disliked having a woman for queen and tried for years to convince others that Catherine was a heretic. That was when he learned that the Bishop tried to brand his own mother a witch. It was also when he felt his feelings for Sofia change. Nearly all their lives he was in love with Sofia. He always imagined them marrying, but the more she tried to convince him to turn against her mother…to believe in her bishop and his hatefulness, the more he felt himself drifting away from her.

When he began to defend Queen Catherine, Sofia stopped talking about her mother. He was relieved as the whole subject had become quite uncomfortable for him. He genuinely loved Catherine and he knew Sofia would have to work things out on her own. "At least," he mused, "she has her father."

Sometimes James thought about his own father. He knew his father was killed along with his mother's parents. She told him stories about his father and their life together. He often imagined what his relationship with his father would be like if he were still alive. He liked to think that it would be as good as Gio's was with Robert. James loved Robert, who was the closest thing he would ever know to having a father.

These were the things that James was thinking about as he wandered the field looking for the most perfect flowers for Teresa. He'd only met Teresa a few short months ago, but he was smitten. He found himself nearly always distracted when he thought of her, which, lately, was constantly.

Teresa was the sister of one of his best friends in the regiment. He first spotted her in the Great Hall during one of the meals. He'd asked around and when he found she was sister to his friend, Enzo, he pressed Enzo to introduce them. Since then they had taken several walks in the courtyards and he often saw her watching him at drills.

His thoughts turned on Teresa as he wandered. They held hands on a few occasions and he loved the feel of her hand in his, it was so small, so delicate, he was afraid he might crush it with his enthusiasm. He thought of her face, sweeter than any face he knew. Her eyes were sable brown and a perfect match to her long hair. Her lips made him smile. He loved to watch her mouth as she talked. Her bottom lip was slightly larger than the top one, and they turned down ever so slightly into a small pout. When she smiled she lit up everything around her. He wanted desperately to kiss her. He planned to tonight when he brought her the flowers.

The basket was nearly full. He looked up to see how far he'd wandered from his horse. That was when he saw the man approaching his horse, moving quickly from the tree line. He called a greeting, but the man did not answer, and started running for the horse. He was dirty. His hair was long and matted, his clothing worn, hanging like rags from his short, stocky body. He had a long, dirty beard.

James called out again, but the man had reached his horse and was untying the steed from a branch where James had left him.

James dropped the flower basket as he started running for his horse.

"Stop!" James yelled. "Stop!"

He was only about a hundred yards away and he was a fast runner. The man was short, so it was a slight struggle for him to mount, nevertheless, he managed to get onto the saddle and was turning to make his way for the open field.

James was upon him before he could make any headway. He grabbed the reins of the horse and reached for the thief's leg. The man pounded James about his head and hands, trying to dislodge his grip. The fists landed with loud thuds on James's head but he did not release his hold. The horse snorted and reared and the man, unable to hold on, was thrown off backwards. James leaped on him in an instant.

The struggle was short. James had the clear advantage. He was young and strong. The man continued to struggle, grunting as he tried to maneuver out from under the boy, but James held him down easily. As James fought to turn the man over onto his belly he heard a loud crack. The sound was similar to the ice on the lake cracking as it contracted after a change in temperature. But it was summer, and the lake was not frozen.

James stopped. He wasn't sure what happened. He was confused. The man stopped struggling and looked up at James with an evil grin. It was then that James smelled the sulfur from the burning gun powder. Pain shot through him. His face contorted in agony as he reached down and felt the heat of his own blood pouring out of his chest.

"No," James whispered hoarsely just before he collapsed on top of his killer.

With a grunt the man pushed James's body off of him. His gun was still smoking. The thief had difficulty standing because he had fallen hard on his backside when he was thrown from the horse. His breath came in short, raspy bursts. He looked down at the boy who lay dead. With a snort he knelt to feel around the boy for anything of value. As he rifled through his clothing, he failed to notice two soldiers arrive at the top of the rise. They were on him before he had time to reload his pistol. He dropped it and drew a dagger.

"Drop your weapon and put your hands behind your back," ordered one of the soldiers. They already had their swords drawn. The man glared at them for a few seconds, then dropped the dagger and put his hands behind him, where they were bound.

"I am a friend of the bishop!" the murderer said quickly. "I demand to speak with Capshaw!"

"Shut up!" said the soldier whose sword still lay on the murderer's neck.

The other soldier, who happened to be Enzo, ran to James' body.

"James. James." Enzo knelt beside the boys' body and shook it. There was so much blood. It didn't take long to determine that James was dead. He got up and ran back toward the prisoner with his sword drawn.

"I am known to your bishop! Don't kill me!" the man pleaded. "I must speak to the Bishop Capshaw!"

Enzo stopped just short of running the prisoner through with his sword. His compatriot held him back. Enzo's whole body quivered with rage. This beast had just killed James, but at the mention of the bishop he knew he had best wait and let his captain handle things.

Enzo lowered his sword and returned to James' s body.

"James," he wept as he gently draped James' body across his horse. The prisoner was tied to the pommel of the saddle with a short rope. They made their way back to the castle.

Robert was admitted to the queen's office by her secretary.

"Robert, what a lovely surprise!" But she instantly knew something was wrong.

"What is it?" she went to him.

"Catherine…" he rarely used her name, still generally preferring her title as a form of respect. "Please sit. I have…I must tell you something. Please sit."

She sat in the nearest chair. Robert knelt in front of her and took her hands in his.

"I am so sorry," he began. His face was filled with anguish. His voice broke as he said, "It...it's James."

"What is James?" she demanded. She felt her body responding in panic to what she had not yet heard. It started as a roar in her ears and quickly flooded her entire body, culminating in an implosion in her gut. "What is James," she whispered through gritted teeth as her body started to tremble.

"James is dead, Catherine." He looked up at her. He did not want to have to say it again.

"What are you talking about?" she asked, still whispering in an attempt to control the blast threatening to tear her apart. "I just had breakfast with him. He is fine!" She pulled her hands out of his and stood up.

Robert stood with her and waited.

She wheeled on him. "Tell me it is not true! Tell me you have made a grave mistake!"

His eyes filled with tears. He shook his head slowly, sadly. "I am so sorry, Catherine. I am so sorry!"

Catherine stared at him, her insides ricocheted with horror, disbelief, fear and sorrow. Nonetheless, she knew she must forge on. Her glare subsided and was replaced by a look of resignation mixed with fear.

"Tell me everything," she said quietly as she collapsed back into the chair and slumped back.

Robert told her, about the flowers, and the horse thief, the pistol shot and the soldiers who heard the shot and found the murderer searching James' body.

She didn't move. When he finished she said, "Take me to him."

He did not question her, only nodded. Together they went to the infirmary where James's body lay.

As Catherine looked upon the body of her son, for he was her son, too, she could not help but feel that she had failed him. She had been protecting him since before he was born. And once he pushed into the world, she embraced his tiny being and loved him with all of her might. He was so precious, so good and kind. How could the boy who helped everyone feel better be gone? How could she have failed to protect him when he needed it most? And how, dear God, how would she tell Bella?

She reached out to caress James's face, the face she fell in love with seventeen years ago when she first laid eyes upon it. Of all of the deaths she had been forced to accept, she knew this one would stay rejected in her for the rest of her days. She felt her insides tearing apart, organ by organ. She felt pieces of her soul drifting away from her. She knew they would never return, but she let them go just the same. Part of her, the part that held joy and hope, simply transferred itself to the lifeless form before her. And she made no attempt to retrieve them before she left.

As Robert walked her back toward her private quarters she asked, "Do you have the murderer in custody?"

"Yes."

"Hang him."

"He claims to be a friend of the bishop's."

"I don't care if he is the pope, himself." Her tone was cold, detached. "Hang him."

"I will take care of it." Robert's highest need, however, was to protect Catherine. "But you must trust me to deal with it. I want to know what his relationship to the bishop is."

"See to it as you will." Haltingly, he brought his fist to his chest and bowed. She did not see him do so as she slowly, hesitatingly, opened her door.

When Catherine entered her quarters she asked Marie to leave. Bella was on the balcony strumming her harp. When she turned and saw Catherine was back early, she put down her harp and went to the sitting room.

Catherine turned to Bella after Marie closed the door. Bella saw Catherine's face and moved quickly to her and pulled her into a loving embrace. "What is it, my love? I have never seen you so stricken. Come, sit, before you collapse."

They sat on the couch. Catherine took Bella's hands in hers and held them between her own. Her head hung down, she could not look at Bella.

"My love," she started. Tears fell from her eyes. They splashed onto the hands in her lap. "I would rather face a thousand enemies with swords, than do what I must do now."

"Catherine, stop it. You're frightening me."

Catherine finally looked up, directly into Bella's eyes. She attempted to take a breath, but a strangulated sob escaped instead. "James," she said so softly that Bella did not hear her.

"What?" Bella asked.

"James is dead," she whispered. As the words left her mouth she waited for them to register with Bella. She was prepared for any number of responses, any of which would have been understandable. Tears, screaming, tearing of her clothes; Catherine was even prepared for Bella to strike her. She could have dealt with Bella's anger, her outrage, or her tears. But she was totally unprepared for Bella's calm.

Bella stiffened. Her eyes glazed over. Her breathing slowed. It was as if her body slowly absorbed the news. Gradually, her body softened and as it did it diminished, lessened as she sat, almost stoically, without moving.

There is a grief so profound that no words can describe it; no pouring of tears will cleanse it from the soul; no heartrending sob can shake it loose from life's endless breath; no anger filled scream will silence the deafening beast.

James was dead.

If Catherine's heart was broken by James' death, Bella's was shattered. Catherine made sure that James was cleaned and the bloodstained clothes removed before she took Bella to the infirmary.

She held Bella close as they as they walked toward the bed where James's body lay covered to his chin, Catherine was prepared to catch Bella should she collapse. She did not. She walked steadily, slowly toward her son's body. When she arrived at the bedside she stood, eyes unblinking. She stared down at him for the longest time. Catherine continued to hold her at the waist, waiting for her to say something, do something. But she stood staring, almost impassively.

Finally Catherine whispered, "Bella." Then again, closer into her ear, "Bella."

Bella blinked and moved forward. She placed her hand on James's cheek, then bent over touching her forehead to his. Before she stood again she kissed his forehead.

"Bring me a chair," Bella demanded. Catherine brought a straight-backed, cushioned chair from the corner of the room.

"Leave me," she said as she sat by her son's dead body.

The room was cool, silent. Catherine found a coverlet and placed it around Bella's shoulders and bent to kiss the top of her head. She left.

When Catherine returned, Bella was still sitting. She hadn't moved. Her eyes were dry. She still sat immobile, staring.

"Bella, come. You cannot stay here forever. We must leave. We must talk about what you want to do."

"I am not ready to leave."

"I know, my love, but we must. His body needs to be prepared for burial. Arrangements need to be made. I have already sent word to Father Tim."

"I am not ready."

"Very well, then. I will stay with you."

Catherine pulled up another chair and sat next to Bella. She wept softly. Bella stared.

Finally, Bella rose. She wrapped her arms around James and lifted his torso pulling it to her closely. To be taken in such a senseless act, and when he had so much for which to live, was the cruelest blow God could force a mother to endure. She broke and Catherine heard her shatter. Bella released a cry that sounded more like a howl. As she released James's body her knees gave out and she started to slide down the side of the bed. Catherine caught her and they slid to the floor where they sat until Catherine finally pulled Bella to her feet and guided her back to their quarters.

Bella refused to eat. She sat on her old pallet by the window for the remainder of the day. She did not cry again once they left the infirmary.

She was incapable of thought or speech or even breathing. Periodically, as if her body's need for air was suddenly recognized by some remote mechanism, Bella would inhale fully and her exhale would be an unending sigh. Catherine did not leave her, but kept watch.

James' body was prepared for burial. Catherine ordered a coffin specially built of rosewood and lined with silk. When all was prepared she brought Bella to the church where his coffin sat open in front of the altar. It was the evening of the day after James was killed.

Castle residents came to pray and offer their condolences. Catherine greeted them all and thanked them for coming. Bella greeted no one. She sat, a statue, unmoving in the front pew nearest the coffin.

Father Tim arrived. He prayed at length, silently. He and Catherine talked in low whispers.

"She has not moved," Catherine said in hushed tones. "She has only stared, sighing occasionally. She has been like this since I told her."

Father Tim placed his hand reassuringly on Catherine's shoulder. "We have both," he whispered, "seen enough to know that we need to watch closely, and give her time. All we can do now is be with her. And pray."

He approached Bella, who hadn't moved or indicated she even knew he was there. He sat beside her in silence for a very long time. Finally, he reached for her hand. She did not resist.

With his own tears falling Father Tim said, simply, "James was a gift and I will miss him."

Bella gave no indication she heard him, but then, slowly, she turned her head to look at him. Her eyes were cold, dead. Catherine saw them and shuddered.

The three of them stayed with James' body until dawn. Bella sat. Catherine worried about Bella. Only Father Tim prayed.

When sunlight streamed through the stained glass window, bathing Bella in a rainbow, she seemed not to notice, but finally said, "I want to find my parents' graves. They should be somewhere on my husband's land. Someone must know where they rest. I want James buried beside them."

Catherine did not try to convince Bella to change her mind, although she was sorely disappointed that Bella would want James so far from them. She would have preferred to bury James here, in the palace cemetery, where she might feel the essence of his spirit close by.

"I'll have Robert prepare for the journey, my love. We'll leave as soon as possible."

But she turned so Bella could not see the hurt in her eyes.

"Princess Sofia to see you, Your Grace," announced the servant.

The bishop got up from his reading chair and went to the entry himself. "Princess," he held his arms out and she fell into them crying.

"I am sorry to hear about James," he said. "I know how much you cared for him."

The bishop patted her head. "There, there," he said. "Come in and sit."

He led her to his sitting area and poured her a cup of wine. She took it gratefully and sipped at it.

"It is a shame about the boy," the Bishop continued.

"Will he go to hell?" Sofia asked abruptly. She always counted on being able to turn him away from his heretical viewpoints. Now, all she wanted was reassurance that he wasn't damned.

"Sofia," he shook his head and answered gravely, "only God can make that determination."

"But you are God's emissary here. You know the scriptures and the laws of the Church," she cried. "Please, I must know he will not burn in hell."

He took his time to answer her. When he finally did, he said, "Sofia, I was not privy to the boy's spiritual well being. You know his mother never allowed him to attend Mass here." He leaned forward in his chair. "And we both know how your mother has always felt about me. I tried, on several occasions, to convince both your mother and the Lady Isabella to bring James to Mass here in the Chapel."

He watched her face and knew that Sofia believed his every word. "What did they say when you asked?"

"They both refused, they preferred the boy to join them in Castiglione d' Orcia with that priest they were both so enamored of.

They did not even let me Baptize James. They sneaked their priest in to have him Baptized in *their* quarters."

"I am so sorry, Your Grace."

"It is of no matter now. I was quite hurt at the time, but in actuality, I have always been more concerned about their souls than my own feelings."

"Tell me if you think there is a chance that James is in heaven," Sofia begged.

"I would if I could, Sofia. I don't know. If he has believed the lies of the Castiglione d' Orcia priest, I am afraid for him. But I will pray for James' soul in earnest."

Sofia got up from her chair and wandered over to a sideboard along one wall. She had stopped crying, but her anger at her mother for years of refusing to see reason when it came to the bishop and the Church came crashing down on her. She felt it fill her soul and spread its venom into her bones. All these years she tried to help her mother and James through her prayers and supplications. If it weren't for his mother, and her own, James would be in heaven. Now she couldn't help him. Her fury built with surprising force within her. It was her mother's fault that James might go to hell. She struggled under the weight of having the responsibility for the souls of everyone on her shoulders. She slumped, briefly, then, all of the anger she felt about James's spiritual well being and now his death, in fact, all of the anger she felt, created a horrible rage that unleashed itself within her.

Her mother must pay.

Thomas Capshaw watched Sofia closely. He saw her face transform slowly, from one of grief, to one of anger. He felt his heart quicken. He saw his years of hard work begin the task of completing itself. He did not have to say another word. Her face, so grief stricken, the eyelids puffy, her nose reddened and dripping, lips swollen…all of her features underwent metamorphosis before his very eyes. Her shoulders drew back first, followed by the straightening of her spine, an unfolding from the base all the way up until her head lifted, straight and erect from her neck. Her eyes narrowed, the lids squeezed the last tears out then hardened, displacing the puffiness that had just been there. She held a handkerchief in her hand, but she ignored it, wiping her nose on her sleeve in a gesture so harsh it almost seemed violent. When her sleeve pulled away from her face the nostrils flared. A snort emanated from her nose. The soft, full, sad lips that first greeted him thinned into a single, angry line as he observed the alchemic miracle that filled him with hope. Her jaw clenched. He could see her teeth, and the muscles of her face just in front of her ears, grinding, creating a bubbling, roiling movement that told him he had finally succeeded. She turned to him, and she was not the same weeping, simpering child who entered his quarters a few moments before.

"It is finished," he thought jubilantly.

Sofia looked at him. "I have a confession to make," she said with steely resolve. "I fear that my feelings for James may have clouded my thoughts with regard to my duty." She began to pace before him.

"Whatever do you mean, Princess?"

Sofia's looked directly into his eyes, the blue of hers intense and determined. "I mean that I have known about the heretical activities of my mother and Lady Isabella, along with James and the Castiglione d' Orcia priest. I have been hesitant to report anything because I kept hoping that James might see reason and join me here with you." For the briefest of moments her anguish about James whisked across her face. She banished it and quickly grabbed hold of her anger again.

"I see," the Bishop got up and turned from her. "I wish you had shared this with me sooner, Sofia. Perhaps I could have helped in some way. Now it is too late for James."

"Your Grace," Sofia said. He turned and saw her grim determination. "They cannot be allowed to get away with this. It stops now. In the name of Christ, it stops now."

"What do you suggest, Princess?"

"I think it is time to call on Captain Bello."

He raised his eyebrows, attempting to create a look of fear to mask his joy. "Are you certain?"

With the authority of someone born to royalty she glared at him and ordered, "Call for him. I will be in my quarters. Send word to me when he arrives. I will tell him everything he needs to know."

Sofia left the bishop's quarters knowing beyond doubt that what she felt was the strength of her faith filling her. God was with her. God's presence filled her and she knew that the power coursing within her could only be the power of the Almighty. She never felt so strong, so sure, so certain of anything in her life. The words of Christ rose up in her breast, "If any want to become my followers, let them deny themselves and take up their cross daily and follow me. For those who want to save their life will lose it."

She knew that to be true to herself, she needed to be true to her faith. She knew that to follow Christ, she must give up her worldly concerns. She knew that her delay in acting before this moment was cowardice. And now James, the one person she hoped would come to see the light, would burn in hell for all eternity. She would be silent no longer. Her faith demanded that she act now, and without fear. The banner of Christ was before her, and she marched, determined, into the battleground. She was right and she knew, without a doubt, that she made the only decision there was to make.

Chapter Fifty Two

Catherine, Bella, Robert and the body of James left the castle early. The morning was foggy. A contingent of servants and a small group of soldiers accompanied them. Bella wanted a small private ceremony and didn't want a large party to announce any part of her private grief.

Sofia refused to go, claiming she would rather stay and pray for James's soul in the sanctuary of her own church.

Robert was uneasy about the journey to bury James. He couldn't explain it, but this trip caused him more anxiety than he had felt for some time. Because of it, he commanded additional men to ride ahead and report back at regular intervals. Whether it was the place to which they journeyed, the vulnerability of the women he swore to protect, or his own grief about James, he would not rest easy until his queen was back in her castle. When they returned, he intended to deal with the murderer, who thus far refused to speak with anyone but the bishop. The bishop denied any knowledge of the man and ignored all requests to see him. Robert felt the bishop was hiding something and wanted to investigate the connection fully.

A wagon carried the coffin. Inside, James's body was wrapped in muslin cloth. The coffin was draped with the royal colors. A complement of eight soldiers, plus the two forward guards and Robert made the journey. Two servants, one cook and a supply wagon followed.

It was a solemn procession. The soldiers all knew James. Not only was he well liked, but he was respected. He loved to joke with the others, and laughed just as easily when the jokes were about him. His recent state of mind over Teresa made him an easy target for kidding. But he was so much in love that he really didn't mind the teasing of his compatriots.

James would be missed. Of that there was no doubt.

By late morning they were approaching the granite cliff where, so long ago, Robert and Catherine rescued Isabella. Catherine wondered if Bella had any sense of the place as they drew near.

Catherine thought back on that day as they passed into the shadow of the wall. She watched Bella closely to see if any of the surroundings sparked a memory. But Bella just rode in silence, her head bobbing gently as her horse made its way along the path.

Catherine remembered finding Bella. Sometimes her heart caught as she thought about how different her life would be if they hadn't happened to hear her that day…if Bella hadn't been found. Sometimes Catherine was more convinced that it was she who was found and rescued that day. Where the path widened Catherine spurred her horse up to ride alongside of Bella. She reached out to take Bella's hand. "How are you holding up, love? Do you need to stop and rest?" she asked.

Bella simply shook her head.

The journey to Bella's former home would take a full day, but Catherine had no idea what to expect when they arrived. It had been years since she stopped asking for information about the estate of Bella's former husband. All this time and the information revealed nothing about who had been behind the attack on her family.

The forward soldiers were reporting back to the Captain at regular intervals. Once they moved well outside of the villages surrounding the castle there were very few farms or people encountered on the road. They'd seen no one for some time.

Robert was getting restless. It was past the time for the forward guard to report back. He didn't like that they were bordered to the right and front by dense forest. The granite cliff was well behind them and he didn't care to have them so vulnerable. There would be no cover for some time. He held up his horse to converse with the Queen.

"I don't like riding so close to the tree line of the forest, Your Majesty. There would be little time to react should we be attacked from the forest. The foliage is so dense that it is an easy place to hide in waiting. Although it's off the path, I am moving us to the center of the open meadow."

Catherine looked around as if seeing where they were for the first time. She'd been so absorbed in her grief that hadn't even realized where they were for some time. Finally, she said, "I agree. Let's move to the middle of the meadow." She had her sword, which she always wore when she travelled, but she never gave a thought to her chain mail, and left without it. If Robert noticed, he didn't say anything.

Robert ordered the soldiers to bear left into the openness of the plain and returned to the front of the line. They moved through the grasses at a slow pace. He scanned continually for any sign of the forward guard. They were now long past due. As he squinted at the horizon where the meadow and the forest merged in the distance he spotted a horse.

"Hold up!" he ordered. He watched and waited. His whole body was on alert.

Catherine trotted her horse up alongside his and looked ahead to where he was searching. She saw the horse. It appeared rider-less.

"There is an outcropping of rocks," Catherine pointed to them in the distance. "We can take cover there."

"Agreed." Robert turned to his company.

"Corporal, leave the wagon. Take the party to those rocks. Be alert for any danger," Robert ordered as he spurred his horse forward to head for the horse in the distance.

The company of soldiers acted quickly. Two of them raced for the rocks to determine the safest place among them. The other soldiers surrounded the queen, Isabella and the few servants, and moved them speedily toward the safety of the rocks.

Robert returned a short time later and instantly commanded two of the soldiers to climb atop the rocks to stand watch. The horse he found belonged to the forward guard. He brought it back with him. The guard was nowhere to be found and there was blood on the saddle. The other guard and horse were missing.

For now, they were safest in the rocks, but if night fell, they would be no safer there than in the open or in the forest. They couldn't wait long before making a decision to move ahead, or return.

Sofia left the Chapel with swollen eyes and a heart heavier than she had ever known. James was her whole history, her world, and she had failed to save his soul before he died. Knowing he would burn forever broke her heart. She spent the morning in the chapel praying for his soul, begging God to blame her for his misguided belief. Her rosary never stopped turning in her hands as she begged for his soul to move from purgatory to heaven, instead of hell. "If only I had been more insistent about him stopping the visits to Castiglione d' Orcia," she thought. Then, more sadly, "If only I had told him how I felt."

Even when he ignored her requests to cease going to Castiglione d' Orcia, she tried so hard to dislike him, but it was impossible. She could never be angry with him for very long. His charm, his disarming spirit, was impossible to ignore. That he would never torment her again with his teasing was not possible. The boy who held such a special spot in her own mother's heart would now leave a gaping hole in hers. Regardless of where his soul might rest for eternity, James was dead and she would miss him terribly.

As she left the Chapel, her vision still blurred by her tears, she bumped into Lord Giovanni.

"Your Highness, please forgive me. I didn't see you," he apologized.

"You are forgiven," she managed, "the fault was mine."

"Princess, you are crying," he spoke with the tenderness and concern of a father. As he always had with Catherine, he spontaneously wrapped his arms around Sofia. She could not help herself and fell to weeping in the comfort of his arms.

Lord Giovanni led her to a nearby bench and held her as she wept. When she was able to speak again she said, "I don't know how I can live without him."

"You and he shared something very special, Princess." He reached and wiped a tear from her cheek. "I have watched you grow up together, he was more than a friend, he was your brother. We will all miss James, but I know that for you and your mother his loss will be especially painful."

At the mention of her mother Sofia bristled. Lord Giovanni felt her stiffen and saw the anger flash briefly in her eyes. He knew Catherine and Sofia might comfort each other in the coming months as they struggled with their grief, but only if they could get past their anger.

"Sofia, your mother loves you so much. What causes you to distrust her so much?" he asked.

"My mother loves much, but she only pretends to love me. She loves James, loved," she added sadly.

Lord Giovanni took her hands in his, "Princess, you see her love for James because it's easy to see. He loved her back. It isn't hard to see love that flows openly between two beings," he offered. He hesitated before continuing, then smiled and said, "When you were small I had the opportunity to spend a great deal of time with you and your mother. She loved you with an intensity I never observed in her prior to your birth. It was a pure mother love I thought never to see in my queen. It delighted me to see how much she loved you." He paused. "You delighted in that love, as well, child. You used to adore her, you know."

Sofia looked at Lord Giovanni as if he were talking of another child and another mother. She didn't remember ever feeling that way about her mother, and she couldn't tap memories of her mother ever feeling that way for her.

"Princess," he continued, "it has been painful for those of us who adore both of you to watch you pull away from her."

"She brought it on herself," Sofia said defensively. "How could I continue to love someone who so opposed the teachings of the Church. My faith is the most important thing to me!"

"How is it that you came to believe that your mother opposed the Church?" Lord Giovanni asked gently.

"She can't tolerate her own bishop. She works against him even though she knows he is the true authority of the Church. He is a representative of God. She cannot tolerate anyone having any kind of authority over her, even God." Sofia stopped. She had made her point. Even Lord Giovanni would have to agree that her mother detested the bishop. She looked at him with all surety and confidence in her belief.

"Princess Sofia," he whispered sadly, "there is no more God-fearing or spiritual being than your own mother." He paused before he continued. "And your information comes, I believe, from the bishop, who has long hated your mother. Listen to me. I have watched that man try to undermine your mother for as long as she has been queen. It is he who has despised her and spread vicious rumors about her in an effort to accuse her of heresy against the church."

"She is a heretic. You think I do not know about her relationship with her 'lady in waiting'?"

"Your bishop has told you that?" Lord Giovanni asked.

"He did not have to tell me, I have eyes. But, yes, we have discussed the matter."

"Your bishop is a hypocrite, Sofia." Lord Giovanni's jaw tensed and his nostrils flared. "Let me tell you something about your religious leader. He is as vile a man as ever lived. He lures young boys to his quarters and uses his 'faith' and his God to defile them in ways that you cannot even imagine. Ask your cousin, Robert, if you want the truth."

Sofia didn't say anything. She did not like what she was hearing and couldn't trust herself to respond. Her body trembled with the effort of trying dismiss what Lord Giovanni said. Her mind reeled and she became dizzy. She closed her eyes and leaned back taking deep breaths. It could not be true. It was not true. She refused to believe it. She shivered.

Lord Giovanni watched her face and continued. "Do you know the story of how your mother met Lady Isabella?"

Princess Sofia shook her head.

"Robert and your mother were returning from Rome. They had gone to beseech the Pope for help with rogue groups who were terrorizing Montalcino. On their way back they found Lady Isabella. She was tied to stakes, naked, and was being brutalized by one of the men who participated in the torture and execution of her husband and parents. He dragged her off as her family was being burned alive on false charges of heresy."

Lord Giovanni paused and closed his eyes. He rubbed them and looked back up at Sofia. "Your mother brought Lady Isabella home and tended to her wounds personally. She was not expected to live. When she was conscious she was so frightened that she only allowed your mother near her. It was a miracle that she lived at all."

Sofia did not know the story. She listened intently as Lord Giovanni continued. "When Lady Isabella recovered, it was discovered that she was pregnant. Your mother could have discarded her. Quite honestly, most people would have."

Lord Giovanni went on to tell Sofia about the rapist, his branding and escape. "Your mother and my son-in-law have been plagued by regret that they could not bring Lady Isabella's torturer to justice….or find out what he knew about the men who killed her family."

Sofia got up on shaky legs and wandered a short distance away. As Lord Giovanni's words tumbled within her, she fought against allowing them to settle anywhere. This information did not fit with the portrait Bishop Capshaw painted of her mother and Lady Isabella. Her heart started racing and she thought she might jump out of her skin. She did not want to hear more. None of this could be true. She needed to make him stop talking. She needed to find a way to justify her action of last night. She returned to sit next to Lord Giovanni. "That does not make their relationship right. They live in sin," she said absolutely.

"Do they? Who determines sin, Sofia? Is it you, or me? Is it your bishop? Let us hope not!" he said somewhat emphatically. "It is God only who has the right to judge what is sin and what is not. Our job is only to love one another. Whatever your bishop told you, the love the queen and Lady Isabella share is profoundly sacred, of that I have no doubt…in spite of what your bishop may say about it."

Lord Giovanni rose and paced a bit in front of the bench where Sofia sat again. "Your mother," he continued, "is one of the most courageous and uncommon women I have ever known. I have more respect and admiration for her than for most men with whom I am forced to deal. It made my heart glad when my queen found love, for it brought forth her strength in ways that made her an even more passionate and compassionate ruler. Do you know why?" he asked.

Sofia shook her head. She didn't want to know, but she needed to know. She was confused. The things he said panicked her, made her feel desperate, anxious, and yet, they were filled with such love and acceptance that she found herself craving more and more. None of this information fit her image of anyone, yet the message was so tender and pure that it made her heart afraid.

"Because," he said, "love helps us to reveal the best parts of ourselves. Love uncovers the flame, the vehemence, in us that stays secreted away until it knows it is safe to lay itself bare. Love is that safe harbor."

Sofia desperately tried to hold back her tears. She clenched her jaw and closed her eyes, trying to sift through everything he said.

Finally, he stood. "Walk with me." As they began to walk across the courtyard he continued. "The bishop has duped you, Princess, and trust me, it's not because he cares about you. What has he taught you about love? Your Bishop detests all women, and he will turn against you when you are queen." He stopped and turned to face her. "He has tried to brand your mother as a heretic since before you were born. Are you aware," he asked, "that at one time he tried to portray Lady Isabella as a witch?"

Lord Giovanni turned and resumed walking. He waited to see if Sofia might respond. When she didn't he went on. "Your bishop has used you to his own end. He has turned you against your own mother. She does not deserve your hatred or your anger. She has only loved you from the day you were born."

Finally, Sofia asked, "If the Bishop is truly as bad as you say, why would my mother not warn me?"

"Would you have believed her?"

Sofia closed her eyes and bowed her head. She shook her head in answer.

"Princess," he stopped and lifted her chin with his finger, "she saw the hold he had on you, as did we all. She loved you too much to compromise your faith. She could see that your faith in God was twisted with your belief in the bishop. She didn't want to compromise your faith. When those of us who love your mother saw what was happening, we desperately wanted to intervene, especially your cousin, Robert. Your mother forbade us to say anything, insisting you would come to your own realizations in your own time. She wanted you to come to her on your own terms."

Sofia looked up at Lord Giovanni. "And why do you tell me this now?" she asked.

He smiled at her. "I am a foolish old man, Princess, but one who believes that God put us here to watch over one another. I have watched long enough."

Lord Giovanni turned to leave. "One more thing, Princess; as long as there is breath in me, I am here for you as I have been here for your mother. I am at your service, always." He bowed and took his leave.

He left Sofia standing in the courtyard.

Some betrayals are accidental; the unhappy result of a shift in feelings or circumstances that leave both the betrayer and the betrayed feeling like hapless victims; each submerged in their innocence, believing the other is to blame, when in reality no one is to blame. Life simply unfolded in such a way as to propel each into, or out of, the place of the lesson.

And then there are betrayals of purpose, those planned and selfishly contrived to the benefit of the perpetrator, designed to manipulate, seduce and mislead the innocent.

As the words of Lord Giovanni settled on her and seeped into her very being, Sofia saw her past from a different perspective. The insight hit her with the force of a blow that slammed into her, grabbing, clawing at her insides and hauling them out into the light of truth. The realization of the events she set into motion ripped her gut with a force that doubled her in two. She held back the scream building in her and looked desperately in the direction that Lord Giovanni had left moments before. She ran after him.

"Lord Giovanni...Lord Giovanni!" she called from the depths of her fear, her anger...and her sorrow.

Though far from her, Lord Giovanni heard and turned in her direction. She was running after him. When she caught up with him she grabbed his robe and cried out, "You must help me!"

"What is it?" he said, "Sofia, calm down and tell me."

"Oh, God," she cried as she sunk to her knees, still clinging to him. "He is going after them!"

"Who is? Sofia!" he grabbed her by the arms, pulled her up and demanded that she answer him. "Is the queen in danger?"

Sofia was nearly incoherent. Every time she tried to speak, her words were garbled by the sobs that wedged themselves between each word. Lord Giovanni grabbed Sofia by the shoulders, "Sofia, you must tell me what has happened. *Now!*" he ordered.

She took a breath and said. "Captain Bello, the Inquisition Enforcer. I told him the route they were taking. Please help me," she pleaded. "He is going to arrest my mother and Lady Isabella for heresy. He plans to put them in prison! We must save them!"

Lord Giovanni ran. He found Robert's second in command and told him of the situation. He mobilized a force.

Sofia turned to Lord Giovanni. "I am going with them." She flew to get her horse. "Gio," she thought. She had asked him to stay behind with her, not to go bury James . She didn't want him to be caught and suspected by the Inquisitor. "I'll find him when I return."

She raced to the courtyard where the army had assembled.

"Men!" the commander shouted. "Our queen is in danger. The funeral party left early this morning, but they will be travelling slowly. They have several hours lead on us, but we should be able to overtake them quickly. Be prepared and on alert for any signs of danger, we believe an ambush awaits our Queen and our Captain!"

Nearly sixty soldiers on horseback left the castle in the direction of the funeral party. With any luck they would overtake the party within a couple of hours. In a cloud of dust they departed.

Robert and his few men set up in the rocks.

"Majesty, we are under attack, but from whom I do not yet know," Robert reported. "Ercole is gone, and there is blood on his horse and saddle."

"Is there no sign of him?" Catherine asked.

"None...nor Marcus, his companion."

"It is a planned ambush, then."

"I am afraid so." Robert excused himself to have a word with some of his men. Catherine saw him pointing in the direction of the woods. He directed a few of them to keep watch from behind the rocks.

He returned to Catherine and Bella at a run. "I suspect the attack will come from the woods. For now I believe we are in a better position here, ready to fight." His eyes darted continually, scanning the tree line of the forest for any movement. "By now they know that we are aware of their presence, so they have lost the element of surprise. If there are only a few of them, they may decide to leave us be."

Catherine looked at Bella who seemed to have come back to herself a bit. Catherine did not want her to worry, but was relieved to see her responding to something other than her despair.

Catherine looked around at their small group. "Our biggest danger is in numbers, isn't it?" she asked Robert.

Solemnly Robert nodded. "If we are outnumbered, we have little chance of defeating them." He noticed that her hand gripped the handle of her sword. "I wish I had insisted that you return for your chain."

"I would have ignored you anyway," she said. "Bella has none, and I did not care to burden myself additionally. It will be fine, cousin."

He started to take his off his own chain to give to her. "Don't!" she commanded. "You will be at the forefront of whatever battle might ensue. I will not wear it!"

His look implored her, but he knew it was useless to insist. "Please, stay hidden. Do not engage the enemy except in defense."

"I will be careful," she said. She avoided his eyes.

He shook his head.

"You are always careful. I am asking for more. I am asking you to stay hidden unless directly engaged by the enemy."

Catherine heard his worry and didn't want to distract him with his concern for her. "Very well, cousin. I will do as you ask."

He called to one of his soldiers, "Cosimo, you are the best rider and have the fastest horse. How quickly can you return to the castle to bring reinforcements?"

"Two hours, Captain."

"Good, see that you gather a force of at least fifty men as quickly as possible and double back with them on a fresh horse," Robert commanded.

"The sun is high, I will return by mid afternoon. You have my word." And he was gone.

Catherine sat in the rocks next to Bella. She took Bella's hand and held it. "I am sorry, love. It seems my title has endangered you when I wish most to protect you."

Bella squeezed Catherine's hand and rested her head on her shoulder, but she said nothing.

"I don't know what to expect, but it is clear we are under attack. Take this and use it if you have to." She held out a dagger. Bella didn't touch it. "Bella, you must be armed. I could not bear to think of you totally helpless if--." She broke off. Bella met her eyes, nodded once and took the dagger. She placed it through her belt. "Stay hidden if we are attacked," said Catherine. "Only use the weapon if you have no choice." She sat next to Bella and watched the line of trees marking the edge of the forest. It was eerily quiet. Her eyes played many tricks on her.

The sun was directly overhead. It was very warm. Their shadows disappeared. It was an hour since Cosimo left.

The soldiers hiding on top of the rocks had the best vantage point, but saw nothing.

Robert again sought out Catherine and said, "The longer they wait, the better for us. If Cosimo can get back, we should have no problem defending ourselves no matter the size of our enemy. I would be surprised if the size of the lot numbered more than our own group, we would have heard some sound at the very least." Robert stood and looked around again. Catherine knew he did not like the waiting. If she were not with him, she knew he would have made a more offensive strategy.

"Captain," said one of the soldiers on top of the rocks. Robert looked at the soldier who jutted his chin toward the tree line.

Robert whirled and saw a rider. Instantly he tensed. "Majesty, please stay hidden," he hissed.

He mounted his horse and spoke just softly enough to be heard by his own soldiers, "Mount and be ready." As he spoke, twelve more riders moved out of the trees and into the open field. Without taking his eyes off of the approaching group he added, "Move away from the queen and servants. Engage the enemy as far away from them as possible." They rode forward at a slow walk.

Robert calculated in his head, "One soldier wounded, or dead. One missing. One hopefully on his way back with help. Thirteen to eight."

He did not like the odds, but his men were professional soldiers. The others looked ragged and undisciplined, but fearless.

When Robert was close enough to be heard he pulled his horse to a stop. "Identify yourselves!" he commanded.

The rider who originally emerged from the trees rode forward slightly. Robert could now see that he wore a large wooden cross around his neck. "It is you in need of identification, sir."

"We are a funeral party only."

"A funeral party happens to be just what we are looking for," the harsh man smiled. His riders laughed at his comment as if it were a great joke. "In fact, we are seeking the funeral party of the Queen," he went on. "Given that you are obviously soldiers of the Queen, I am guessing that we have found our party."

"State your business with us or let us continue on our way," Robert demanded.

"My business is with your heretic Queen," stated the leader. He drew his sword and spurred his horse toward the rocks where Catherine hid. His compatriots drew their swords and with a huge, single battle cry of "For Christ and Church!" they attacked Robert and his company.

Catherine watched all of this from her cover in the rocks. She saw the attack begin and saw the lone rider barreling toward the rocks with his sword drawn. Without hesitation she ordered Bella to stay hidden with the servants and she stepped out with her own sword drawn.

When the man on the horse reached her he burst into malicious laughter. "Ah, Your Majesty, I have heard that you fancy yourself quite the swordsman." He dismounted and made an exceedingly patronizing bow before her.

"Who are you and what do you want with us?" demanded the Queen.

"I am the one asking the questions, Majesty," he responded curtly.

"The swords of your men do not question, sir. And you have asked no questions. Again, what do you want of us?"

"I am following up on reports of heretics in your group. In particular, a crowned heretic and her companion," snarled the man.

Catherine did not wait for further information but lunged at the man with her sword. Her action took him by surprise, but he recovered quickly and engaged his own sword. His smile left his face quickly once she attacked. She knew he was surprised by her strength and skill. But he was stronger.

Catherine was able to ward off many of his blows and strike enough of her own to throw him off balance. She was making the majority of the offensive moves, lunging and faking, then striking where he did not expect. Because of his strength and expertise, Catherine knew her best strategy was to continue to surprise him. At one point his sword tip became caught up in the twist of metal that served as her loop guard. She twisted her forearm up and away and nearly disarmed him, but he managed to hold onto his sword and with a curse, he pulled it free. He was a moderately built man, so he did not possess the reach of most men. This gave her a slight advantage as her sword was longer, but she knew she would have to dispatch him quickly or her strength would give out.

Each clash of her sword against his, echoed off the rocks. She was aware of the battle raging in the field, as well, but knew better than to lose her focus. She continued to ward off his blows and strike some of her own well placed ones, but still he came at her, his teeth bared and his grin unnerving.

As Robert had taught her, she made a move toward the man's face, causing him to raise his sword to protect himself. But she was not after his face. She made her move and reached down to cut his femoral artery. She managed a deep gash that caught him unaware, but she missed the artery and did not stop him. He was furious and came after her with more power than she could handle. He was backing her into the rocks. Her arms were growing heavy, and her hands were cramping, but she did not let up and continued to attack him, trying to keep her edge.

Catherine had both hands on her sword, her throat issuing grunts and cries as she swung at him. She was on the defensive, warding off his attacks and deflecting his lunges. She knew she was doomed if she was forced against the rocks. She needed to move to his side to maneuver herself back out into the open. The rocks were right behind her. As she engaged his blade from underneath and twisted upward with all her might she managed a turn than brought her to the side of the rock so that he was next to the huge boulder, but easily beginning to push her again.

A sickening thud dropped him to his knees. His head split down the center. Catherine stared at his body lying on the ground before her, his brains spilling out of his skull. The surprise of his end took a moment to register.

Catherine looked up. Bella stood on top of the huge boulder. She had lifted as large a rock as she could and dropped it on his head.

Catherine stared at her in awe, then, slowly, a smile spread across her face. "Thank you, my love!" she shouted up at her. Then she turned and made for the field where her soldiers battled.

"Catherine, no, please," Bella begged. But Catherine was already too far away to hear her.

Several men on both sides were already felled. She counted only six of her own soldiers, Robert one of them, still fighting. There were eight of the others. "We could win this." She thought.

Knowing her best strategy was surprise, she held back until she saw an opportunity to strike at the back of one of two men who had engaged one of her guard. Her man was fighting well, and holding his own, but she wanted this fight finished sooner rather than later. When both of the enemies were positioned so that their backs were to her, she moved swiftly forward and slashed at hamstrings of one of the men. He collapsed instantly. Then she impaled the other man from the back through his heart.

Now the battle was more even.

Robert saw her out of the corner of his eye. "Majesty, back to the rocks!" he shouted.

"Robert, watch--!" she yelled back. But in the split second of his distraction to order her out of danger, his opponent took his opportunity and put his blade through Robert's neck.

"Nooooo!" Catherine was on the enemy in a flash. Her horror, her anguish, her fear and rage gave her strength she did not know she possessed. Against all practical swordsmanship, she grasped the grip of her sword with both hands, raised it over her head and with a deep, powerful yell smashed the blade down on the man who stabbed Robert, splitting his head in two. All of the other men were engaged with each other. Catherine turned to find Robert looking up at her. She dropped down next to him and lifted his head onto her lap. He was still alive, but the life was ebbing quickly out of him.

"Robert, cousin,' she cried, "please don't leave me." She rocked his head and cried out to God. "Please, please let him live." Her heart tore in two, the pain as excruciating as if she had been run through by a sword.

Catherine bent low, cradling his head next to hers. "My Queen, I am sorry. I have failed you," he whispered.

"You have done no such thing!" she said as her tears splashed upon his face. "I beg you, cousin, hold on."

"I am lost..." his face held a multitude of pains, "be safe...tell my wife...my Gio...I love them..."

"They will know," she sobbed, "and all of Montalcino will know that you died protecting your queen.

Robert fisted his right hand. With his last ounce of strength he drew his fist up over his chest where it stopped and fell over his heart.

Bella was making her way to them when Robert died. When she was nearly to them she saw the man that Catherine lamed crawling on his belly, pulling himself on his elbows, to where Catherine was holding Robert.

"Catherine!" she called out. "Catherine...." But as Catherine looked up at Bella, her face streaming with tears, the lamed man used all of his strength to thrust his sword up and into Catherine's back. Robert's head fell from her arms. She looked up at Bella running toward them.

"For Christ, you heretic!" cried the man who plunged his sword into her.

Catherine still not believing that Robert lay dead in her arms did not, at first, realize what happened. Then the pain shot threw her. She looked down at the point of the sword sticking out of her chest. It was covered in blood; her blood. With horror she looked back up at Bella and her thoughts were only of the woman she loved more than life itself. She had not intended to die.

Bella was running toward her, her face a mask of fear, agony and rage. "Nooooo!" Her scream pierced the air, but Catherine didn't hear it. The only sound she heard was a deafening silence. Gone were the sounds of metal on metal, the swords clashing and the grunting of the battle.

She watched Bella, almost as if in slow motion, running toward her, her mouth open wide, her face fierce.

As Bella rushed toward her, she momentarily wanted to order her back to the safety of the rocks, but all she could do was watch as Bella neared the battleground.

That was when she realized that all of the pain had left her body. She felt an overwhelming sense of peace. It filled her and she was no longer afraid.

She closed her eyes, and as she did her mind filled with her life's loveliest visions. She was a child on horseback, racing through the flower fields with Robert, laughing, her hair flying behind her. She saw James's newborn face looking up at her from her own arms, and felt the rush of love for him. Sofia's little arms wrapped around her neck as she heard her daughter whisper, "Te amo, mama," for the very first time. She was transported to the cave behind the waterfall at Ribolla, resting back against Bella, hearing and feeling the water splash all around her. Then, she was in the flower fields again, kissing Bella for the very first time. As she gave herself, again, to that kiss, she found herself sitting in the chapel at Montalcino, her parents on either side of her. They smiled and wrapped her in their protective and loving arms, and that was when she was consumed, surrounded, filled with a force of Love so powerful that she knew all was well.

There were still four men fighting. Robert's soldiers, realizing what had happened increased the ferocity of their battle.

Bella reached them and picked up Robert's sword. She stood over the man who had run Catherine through. He looked up into her eyes. The smug look he held quickly vanished when he saw her face. No man could see her expression and not feel his blood run cold.

Bella hoisted Robert's sword with both hands, the point aimed at the man's neck. She plunged it with such force into his neck that she nearly severed his head. She left the sword standing upright and went to

Catherine. Her stomach clenched when she saw where the sword protruded from Catherine's body. She fell to her knees.

Catherine had collapsed onto Robert. She was still breathing, still alive, but barely. Bella positioned her on her side with her head supported in her lap.

"Don't you dare..." she sobbed, "don't you dare die!"

"Bella...my love..." Catherine managed weakly. "Can you," she struggled for breath, "forgive me?"

"What am I to do without you?" Bella wept. She held her forehead to Catherine's as if she could will the life back into her. "No, no, no...please," Bella pleaded as she held her love's head, cradling it gently.

"Bella..." Catherine whispered as she looked into Bella's eyes. Blood and breath seeped from her body onto Bella. "I...am...sorry," she managed with great effort.

Bella moaned and rocked as she buried her face in Catherine's neck. As she felt the life ebbing out of Catherine she began to shake violently.

It was then she heard the horses. She looked up to see Sofia and her army riding into the field. The fighting was over. Two of Robert's soldiers were still standing.

Sofia saw her mother lying on the ground and ran her horse close to them, leaping off before the horse was stopped. She ran to her mother.

"No! God, no!" she cried. "Mother, no, oh God," she wept as she bent and covered her mother's face with tears and kisses.

"Sofia..." Catherine could barely breathe and her speech came at great cost. Catherine tried to reach her hand up to her daughter's face, but lacked the strength. Sofia grasped her mother's hand and pressed it to her heart.

"I have been a fool," she sobbed, "I am so sorry."

Catherine closed her eyes and shook her head slightly. "Don't," was all she managed. Then she turned back to look one last time into the face of her beloved. She placed her daughter's hand into Bella's and held her own there momentarily. Blood gurgled from Catherine's throat and spilled out over her lips. Though her eyes never closed, and never stopped looking at Bella, she was gone. Her hand slipped from both of theirs.

As the small army made its way back through the Borgo to the castle, villagers saw their queen lying dead and followed the procession. By the time the troop entered the outer wall near the guard house, some two hundred townspeople brought up the rear crying and lamenting the death of their queen.

The bodies of Robert and his dead companions were draped over their horses, arms swinging to the slow, steady clomp of each hoof. Remy, tears streaming from his eyes, held the reins of Robert's horse at the head of the procession. Other soldiers, each leading a horse with a dead man followed slowly. Behind them came Sofia, her face unreadable. Then came the wagon that had left just that morning with the coffin of James. The coffin was still in the wagon. Bella sat in the back leaning against her son's coffin. In her lap she cradled the body of the queen. Bella's face was stained with blood, dirt...and the tracks of her tears. The rest of the army followed, surrounded by the townspeople.

As they made their way through the second wall, the castle residents were filling the courtyard. King Ambrose and Lord Giovanni waited on the steps.

Apart from the occasional sound of a snorting horse, no one spoke until Sofia said, "Take the Queen's body to her quarters."

"Yes, Majesty," answered one of the soldiers.

Bella reluctantly gave up Catherine's body to the soldiers who carried it to her quarters on a litter draped in the colors of Montalcino. Once the weight of Catherine's body was lifted from her Bella, sat leaning against her son's coffin. She was cold. So cold.

For the second time in her life, she was utterly alone. She realized no one was going to assist her down from the wagon, so she stood and climbed over the side. When her feet touched the ground, and she let go of the side of the wagon, her hand brushed against the dagger still in her belt. As she walked into the castle, her hand grasped the hilt and she was comforted by the thought of having it.

Sofia stayed astride her horse until the bodies of all of the dead were gone from the courtyard. Lord Giovanni made his way haltingly to Robert's horse. He reached for Robert's swinging hand, grasping it as he walked, not holding back his tears. Sofia found herself wanting his gentle reassurance, but he would not meet her gaze.

After what seemed like an eternity, only Sofia remained. A stable boy came to take the reins of her horse. King Ambrose went to his daughter and held out his hand to help her dismount. She looked into his eyes and saw his love, in spite of everything, and fell to weeping in his arms. He walked her inside, his arm protectively around her.

The bishop was peeking out of a window in the Chapel when Sofia returned with the army. He knew that Sofia had raced off with the army to intercept the funeral party. He also knew that whether or not the Princess found her mother in time, it did not bode well for him. But, he did not expect this. When he saw Lady Isabella in the back of the wagon, the queen dead in her arms, his legs began to shake. Bile rose in the back of his throat. He sneaked out of the side entrance of the church and made his way to his private quarters.

Thomas Capshaw slipped into his quarters unnoticed by anyone and went to his bedroom. He could barely stand, his entire body shook with the knowledge that he was doomed. He went to the window and looked out on the courtyard. He did not cry. He did not pray. He went to fetch a bottle of wine and returned to his bedroom.

He pulled a wooden box out of the little chest next to his bed, opened it and slipped a small vial out of a velvet bag. He poured the contents of the vial into his cup of wine and downed it in a few swallows, then poured himself another cup. He climbed onto his bed and sipped at his wine.

When the soldiers arrived to arrest him under orders from Queen Sofia he was dead.

Chapter Fifty Three

Father Timothy came to conduct the funeral Mass for both Robert and the Queen. Bella insisted that Catherine and Robert be honored together.

The night before the Mass, Sofia and Bella sat in the chapel. The light of the moon filtered through the stained glass window, painting Catherine's coffin with a soft blanket of muted color. Robert's coffin stood guard beside hers, vigilant even in death.

Father Tim found the women when he went to the Chapel around one in the morning. Unable to sleep, he decided to spend one last night with his Queen and her Captain.

Bella sat. Sofia knelt. They were on opposite sides of the Chapel. When the doors to the Chapel clanked, Sofia turned. She went to meet Father Tim as he made his way up the center aisle.

"Queen Sofia," he smiled gently, "you must be tired. I'll stay. Go and rest."

Sofia looked at him only briefly before her shame and sorrow brought her to her knees. She cried out. Bella turned in time to see Father Tim catch her.

"I cannot live with what I have done!" she wept. "I cannot live…"

Father Tim knelt and enfolded her in his arms, holding her body as it heaved with sobs, his own tears blurring the flames of the candlelight surrounding them.

When her weeping subsided, he held her face between his hands and said, "You are so like her."

"How can you say such a thing after what I have done…what I have caused?" Sofia cried.

"Because, my child, it is true." He smiled at her and looked over at Bella. She looked on from her seat in the front pew, but made no move to join them.

"Your mother," he continued, "saw how fiercely you defended your faith and your Bishop." He helped Sofia to her feet and led her up to where Bella sat. Bella and Sofia had not spoken, except in need, since they had returned from the battlefield.

379

"Catherine was just as fierce in her convictions," he said. "And, like you, she was just as pained and full of sorrow when she discovered that her beliefs inflicted pain, sorrow, and even death."

Sofia looked at him with considerable confusion. She was unaccustomed to thinking about her mother as anything but a recalcitrant heretic. The new feelings and information she continued to absorb about her mother in the past few days relentlessly wounded her with regret for the woman she never allowed herself to know.

"As Queen, your mother continually dealt with conflicting information and emotions." He went to grab the small, ornate, chair behind the pulpit. He brought it down to place before Sofia and Bella, so that he could sit facing them both.

"Your grief, and your remorse, will always be with you." He reached to take Sofia's hands in his. "I am afraid that is now a fact of your life." He paused and inhaled deeply before continuing. "I remember once, years ago, having a similar conversation with your mother." He closed his eyes as if remembering. When he opened them he looked at Sofia so tenderly that she felt the threat of a new wave of grief. "I told her, as I tell you now, it is not the knowledge of what we have done, but rather, what we do with that knowledge that makes us who we are…that transforms us."

He let the echo of the last words fade before he went on. "How will you, as queen, use what happened to guide you as you rule your kingdom? How will both of you," he reached to take Bella's hand in one of his, "find a way to help one another, heal one another…forgive?"

Bella didn't look up while he was talking, but finally raised her head to reveal the anger in her eyes. It threatened to consume the Chapel. He held her gaze, lovingly, tenderly, until slowly the sharp edges of her fury began to soften, to drift and float outward mingling with the glow of soft light surrounding them.

For the second time in as many days Sofia and Bella felt their hands joined together by someone who loved them both, unconditionally. Sofia looked at Father Tim, then slowly turned to look at Bella and with her tears streaming down her cheeks said, "I do not deserve your forgiveness." She fell on her knees before Bella, grabbing her hands, "But, I beg you for it," she wailed. "I beg you!" Sofia buried her face in Bella's lap releasing, fresh torrent of unrestrained grief.

Bella looked once more into the eyes of Father Tim, then down at the weeping body of Catherine's daughter, her daughter. Ever so slowly, her face softened, and she placed her hands on either side of Sofia's head and fell beside her, allowing her sorrow to split the seams of her soul.

Father Tim held a small, private service for James. He was buried in the family cemetery just outside the walls of the castle. It was where Catherine had wanted him buried all along.

The local boy's choir sang at the Funeral Mass for Catherine and Robert. Originally, a full scale Requiem Mass was planned, but everyone agreed the requiem music originally selected, did not really reflect the spirits of Catherine and Robert. Catherine always commented on the boy choir when she heard them on special occasions, so they seemed the perfect choice.

Ambrose stayed next to Sofia during the Mass. At times, her shoulders slumped and it looked as though she might collapse. Ambrose held his arm around her waist, supporting her throughout the service.

Bella was next to Sofia. Occasionally, Sofia slipped her arm through Bella's. A few times, when the voices of the choir filled the chapel with sounds so sweet and tender, they could not hold back their tears, Sofia reached her arm around Bella and they rested their heads together, weeping and clinging to one another.

When it was time, Father Tim made his way to the pulpit. For a long time before he spoke his first words, he gazed at the coffins of Catherine and Robert. He stepped down from the pulpit and walked toward the coffins. He stood between them and placed one hand on each.

"Montalcino," he began, "has lost a brave and loyal servant, a soldier who died giving his life to his queen, his kingdom. You have lost a precious man in Captain Robert. He was a husband, a son, a father, a leader, a protector and a defender of justice. He was a friend. But I wonder if you know how much more he was? Captain Robert was not just a soldier in your queen's guard, I believe he was a soldier in God's own army. These are perilous times. As a Church, we have suffered and struggled to figure out the difference between what we should fight against and what we should defend. Captain Robert fought that battle within his own soul. When that battle was over, he was, I believe, one of the greatest defenders of truth and justice I have known. He heard Christ call to him and he answered. He answered when he stood side by side with your queen in her fight against injustice.

"Captain Robert's was a gentle spirit, cloaked in the armor of a warrior. He showed us both sides. I was proud to call him my friend."

Father Tim paused briefly, and turned to lay both hands lovingly on Catherine's coffin.

"And you have lost a queen," he said softly. "But Catherine was not just any queen, she was a magnificent human being. She risked, and eventually lost, her life because she believed that no one but God has the right to judge the faith of others. She fought for her people, her kingdom, using everything in her power to try to protect her subjects from unjust and unfair cruelties. She was a wife, a daughter, a mother," he looked at Bella, "and a companion who loved fully and with her whole being. She was a leader. She, too, was a friend."

He walked a bit away from the coffins toward the congregation. "A queen holds great power. Your queen was aware of the power she held, but she used that power to touch and strengthen those she served. That power humbled her. That, I believe, made her a great monarch.

"Queen Catherine was not afraid to know her subjects, because she was unafraid to look deeply into her own soul. She was an uncommon queen because she allowed God to illuminate her fears, her doubts, her darkness, her light, her strengths and her power. And she allowed God to guide her as she strove to be a good leader. This was not always easy for her, but it was necessary. She saw it as necessary in her role of queen."

Father Tim walked over to a section of the chapel where a close knit group sat, tears streaming down their faces. He smiled at them.

"I want to tell you a story. It was one I did not hear until just last night, but it is one that I believe tells of the pureness of heart of the woman who was your queen.

"Several years ago, your queen took it upon herself to visit Radicondoli. You know what she found there. It is the stuff of legends. Your queen, finding abuse of power, injustice, and murder, among other hideous acts, eliminated the sources of the abuse in a single night, restoring peace and justice to a town that had been terrorized for years.

"But there is more to the story of Radicondoli, to any story really, than just the larger event. Last night I had the pleasure of meeting the Guilia children. Both Guilia parents lost their lives in the course of the doings in Radicondoli. The children were shunned, broken and living as best they could on their own. Queen Catherine came into their lives in the middle of the night. She listened to their story. She rectified, as best she could, the injustice done to the children. That could be the end of the story. For most of us it would be…and it would be a fine end. But it wasn't enough for Queen Catherine. The Guilia children, not really children so much anymore," he smiled as he looked at them, "told me that Queen Catherine never forgot them. She kept in contact with them. They, along with several others from Radicondoli, discovered that their queen had instructed each of them who had been injured, to contact the others. The result, as we discovered last night when so many of us met, was that the queen, quite surreptitiously, created families where none had existed before. Without realizing it, each person contacted by Queen Catherine, found healing, comfort, and solace in ways that helped them grow stronger as individuals and as a community.

"So, you see, she was more than a queen. She was a mother to us all, in ways that, I suspect, we will continue to learn as we mourn and celebrate her life.

He returned to the coffins, again stepping between them and placing a hand on either side. "And so it seems right that these two beautiful souls should be here together. Catherine and Robert. They spent their lives together, first growing up as cousins, then serving the kingdom of Montalcino. He, always vigilant, always striving to keep her and her kingdom from harm, always protecting her; she, always working to make things better for her kingdom, her subjects…her family and friends, and able to do so because he was watching over her.

"It is my duty to try to comfort you today, to reassure you that they are with God and at peace." He looked out at the congregation assembled and smiled. "They are with God, and I have no doubt that they are at peace. In fact, I believe that God may have taken them because He needed a little reassurance that He did not make a horrible mistake when He created us. I believe that God looked down at all the misery and pain on the earth and saw these two souls and recognized in them two of his creation that He might call friends.

"He chose well from among us. But in doing so, he left a tremendous hole here. Montalcino will not be the same without Queen Catherine and Captain Robert. I know because I feel the loss here." Father Tim placed his hand over his heart. "They were my friends. The world will be a sadder place without them. It is a lesser place without them. It will be a more frightening place without them. But, it is a better place because of them. And for that, we must be grateful. No matter how much I will miss them, I will remember how they fought to make this a better place…and I will honor them by continuing to follow their example, no matter how much I miss them. Let us pray."

Sofia knew that her grief would be with her until her dying breath. Too soon she was forced to take up her mantle and assume her role as Queen. Her first official act was to have James' murderer brought before her for sentencing. While it was customary for the lower courts to deal with such criminals, Sofia wanted, needed, to see the face of the man who initiated the events that had changed her world forever.

The prisoner was brought before her in chains. His head and face were covered with matted hair. He was filthy and insolent. He stunk. He demanded to see the Bishop.

"You were found searching the body of James Mariani. He was killed by a single shot through the heart and you were in possession of the pistol. What have you to say for yourself?" asked the Queen.

"I was defending myself. The boy attacked me."

"His weapons were not drawn. They were still in their scabbards when he was found. With what did he attack you?"

"With his fists."

Sofia knew that James would never attack anyone unprovoked. She found herself seething as she looked on this man. "Why did he attack you?"

The prisoner shrugged and did not reply.

"Why do you wish to see the bishop?" she asked as she leaned back in her chair.

"I am known to him. He will remember me." The prisoner answered insolently.

"In what capacity do you claim to know him?" She leaned forward, staring into the man's eyes suspiciously.

"It is my business, and his only."

"Your business only," she corrected him as she sat back in her chair. "The bishop is dead."

Fear flashed in his eyes. She saw it, but it didn't matter anymore.

She had seen him, and his person did not, in any way, soothe the loss she felt. James's murder seemed even more senseless now that she had met with his killer. With something close to indifference she ordered him removed and executed by hanging.

As he was being led out of the chamber he looked back over his shoulder and shouted, "Hah, you think you can hold me...I escaped your prison once, I do not need your bishop's help to do it a second time! Your own mother could not hold me...I will escape your punishments as well!"

"Stop!" Sofia ordered. "Return him."

He stood before her again. Feelings stirred within her...memories of something. What? She looked at him and tried to recall, tried to brace herself for words that were forming and fighting to surface.

"So, you have been here before. When?" she asked.

"Long ago. And for a matter of such insignificance that even the queen's own guards, and her bishop, thought to help me escape," he laughed.

The words arrived tumbling into her like rain pouring off a roof into a cistern. The voice of Lord Giovanni flooded her. "The rapist was marked, branded on his cheek with a hot iron. Robert was so incensed at his treatment of Lady Isabella that he actually used an iron with the queen's mark, a crown with a sword...the only time it was ever used."

Sofia's heart was racing. It could not be. "Guard, bring scissors and a blade. Shave his face." She stood and paced as she waited.

The prisoner fought as his beard was cut. The blade was painful on his cheek and in his struggle it cut him several times. When enough of the beard had been shaved away she could see it there, the crown and the sword, symbol of Queen Catherine. Lady Isabella's rapist. James was murdered by his own father.

Sofia collapsed back on her throne and stared at the prisoner before her. The knowledge of who this man really was overwhelmed her, numbed her. All his life James believed that his father was the Lord Daniel Mariani. That is what Bella told him. Sofia understood now why Bella and her own mother wanted to protect him from the identity of this... this inhuman animal that stood now before her.

Lord Giovanni was the only other person alive to know that Lady Isabella's rapist was branded with the queen's mark. Sofia did not want James' memory tarnished with the knowledge that this hideous creature standing before her was his father.

"I have changed my mind about this man's sentence," Sofia informed the guards. "I want him beheaded....before day's end. When all is ready I wish to be called. I will have a final word with the prisoner before his execution."

Sofia left her throne without another word.

She went in search of Lord Giovanni and confided her discovery and her plan. Together they vowed that the secret of James' birth would die with them. She asked if he would be with her when she went to see the prisoner and when he was executed. He agreed.

When the block and the executioner were ready, Queen Sofia was called. Together, she and Lord Giovanni went to the cell where the prisoner was being held. He was chained to the wall by both his feet and his hands. She ordered the chains be shortened in such a way that he would not be able to move. He spat curses at her.

"Gag him," she ordered the guards.

He fought with his teeth and his head, twisting and turning it, making it almost impossible to gag him. Finally, one of the guards grabbed a fistful of his hair and held it firmly while the other guard gagged him. He would never speak another word.

When the guards finished, Sofia asked them to wait outside the cell. She and Lord Giovanni were alone with the prisoner. Her heart raced and she did not know if her legs would hold her up. She was afraid and infuriated. She wanted to rip this man apart with her bare hands.

She did not touch him, but moved close enough that his stench pierced her nostrils. Sofia stood in front of him and spoke softly, so that only he and Lord Giovanni could hear.

"Seventeen years ago you were found by Queen Catherine in the forest near the granite cliffs. You held a woman prisoner whom you had been brutalizing for days. The queen and her guards brought that woman back here where she eventually recovered." She paused briefly before continuing, "You were branded with the Queen's own mark…the one you hid beneath your beard. You did escape, with help. You will not escape this time. You will be dead within the hour. But you will die with this knowledge; the woman you raped bore a child, a son, nine months later."

The prisoner watched as Sofia spoke to him. His eyes did not reveal that he cared about her or the story she told. They, like his life, reflected the hate and bitterness that were his heart and soul.

As Sofia looked into those eyes now, she wondered if he would feel anything when she spoke her next words. She considered leaving and not telling him, but she had come this far.

"It was he that you murdered."

It was slow to come, but come the realization did, just a subtle change in his eyes as he glared at her. Powerful, horrifying awareness. He turned away and shrugged as if the information was meaningless. But it was too late. She had seen it.

The guards were called to escort the prisoner to the execution block. Sofia and Lord Giovanni left the cell and rode in a covered carriage to where the execution would take place. The prisoner was led up the steps to the block. Before he was forced to his knees he looked up and saw the shade raised in the royal carriage. His eyes met Queen Sofia's. Hatred spilled out of them. She was glad she had thought to gag him. The gag was still in place as his head was placed on the block. It took two swings to sever his head. As the head rolled off the block Sofia drew the shade.

Queen Sofia and Lord Giovanni never said a word to Lady Isabella.

Chapter Fifty Three

Queen Sofia, Lady Isabella and Father Tim continued to fight against the persecutions of the Inquisition. None of them saw its end.

Although Isabella participated as she could, she never recovered from losing James and Catherine. She was prone to bouts of melancholy and unable to leave her bed for long periods of time. She finally succumbed to pneumonia in August of 1584, thirty years from the day Catherine had found her near death. She had been in and out of consciousness for days, but came fully awake that August morning while Father Tim was administering Last Rites. She smiled at Father Tim, whom she grew to love so well over the years, and thanked him for being with her. Queen Sofia was at her side. In fact, Sofia never left Bella's side from moment she became ill.

Sofia wept openly. She had come to love the woman who shared such a rich history with her mother, and who loved her in spite of everything. She took Bella's hand in both of hers, kissed it and clasped it to her heart. Bella looked up at her with tenderness and smiled, but then her gaze was drawn beyond Sofia, to something else. Her eyes widened and her face filled with joy.

"Catherine," she whispered as she reached into the air. Her spirit left her in that moment.

Epilogue

November 2008

The story of Catherine and Bella stands alone. I know that. Still, there are a number of events that occurred during its revelation that may give the reader pause when reflecting upon the *fictional* aspects of the novel. Call it my overzealous need for honesty if you like, but the following are facts which I feel would be unfair to keep from the reader.

Early in the process of writing the book I was introduced to a local editor, Terry Cutler. At the point we first met, she had arrived at my home to pick up my original outline of the story. When I brought her back to my office I had a large table set up with a map of Italy.

"Is your story set in Italy?" she inquired. I had not mentioned that when we talked on the phone.

"Yes," I acknowledged. Although I was still struggling with the exact location of the story, I had a very strong sense of where it happened. The visual impressions were vivid in my mind. Interestingly, as I studied the map, I was continually drawn to a specific area.

"Have you ever been there?" Terry asked.

"No, but it feels like I'll need to go there at some point to finish the story. I can't explain it, but that feels vital to me."

It was May, and I'd been working on the story since the end of February.

"I am doing a writer's workshop in Italy in October," she offered. "Part of our itinerary will be touring various places." She continued to look at the map.

"Where is the workshop being held?" I hadn't indicated where I thought my queen lived, but she leaned over the map to study it closely. My heart began to beat wildly.

"Here," she pointed. "Here is where we are staying."

The little town she indicated was on a small lake just south of where I had continually been drawn since I first started looking at maps of Italy. I had only just gotten the detailed map the day prior.

I looked at her, and without any knowledge of how I would make it all happen, financially or otherwise, said, "I'll be coming."

As the summer progressed, Catherine and Isabella wreaked havoc with my sleep and emotions. The more immersed I became in their fight, their relationships with others, their intense love for one another, the more I began to think I had lost my mind. I did not know if this was what all writers went through with their characters, but I felt that in some strange way I was losing myself.

Characters I thought I was inventing turned out to have actually existed. Sometimes, I would write about a character and think, this guy needs to be a pope. The next thing I knew I found a pope that fit my character, in the time frame set out by the story, whose activities closely resembled the ones of my stories. Other times, I would simply be researching a certain aspect of the Inquisition and find a character too perfect to resist adding to the story.

Summer flew by and suddenly it was October. A few days before we were to leave for Italy, Terry emailed me that one of her speakers cancelled. She had a contact that might be able to set us up with another one, but some of the workshop plans had to be rearranged. Before we left, a new speaker was set.

The day just prior to his presentation, the speaker contacted us. He preferred we come to him, about an hour and a half north of where we were staying.

His home, it turned out, was an ancient hermitage on the grounds of one of a multitude of sixteenth century Italian castles. This particular castle was situated in an area known as Vivo d' Orcia. The hermitage, or rather the entire Vivo d' Orcia, was given to Saint Romualdo by Emperor Arrigo in 1003. Saint Romualdo founded the hermitage for the Camoldolese monks, but in 1328 the hermitage was ransacked by the inhabitants of, believe it or not… Castiglione d' Orcia.

The hermitage sat in ruins by 1460, although a handful of monks still lived there. By 1534 there were no monks living there at all and Pope Paul III sold the property for next to nothing to one Cardinal Cervini for services he had rendered to the Church.

Cardinal Cervini, it turns out, became Pope Marcellus II. No, I am not kidding.

So, there I was in Italy, on the second day of a writer's conference, poised to visit a place that may or may not turn out to be directly connected to my story. A year ago my life could not have looked more different. If anyone had suggested this might be my life a year ago, I would have thought them quite mad. But, there I was. And I can't say if the anxiety I felt was more related to finding out if this place we were going *was* connected to my story, or concerned that there was no connection at all. One interesting note is that the moment I arrived in Italy every battery and electrical powered device I brought with me began to malfunction. These included; my brand new watch battery (replaced before I left the states and twice in Italy), my cell phone, my camera and my computer. None of the others in our group had any trouble with their electronics. They all wisely refused to allow me near their devices.

I don't remember much of the ride up to the Vivo d' Orcia, but when we finally reached the little village surrounding the castle of the Countess Cervini, descendent of Cardinal Cervini/Pope Marcellus, I thought I might leap from my seat I was wound so tight.

At first, the narrow road led us down an old cobblestone street. There were old buildings, lots of people there for a festival of some sort. The buildings disappeared and were replaced by tall trees. I didn't know what kind of trees, but we were definitely surrounded by lush forest. Scant light filtered through the trees. I rolled down my window and inhaled the deep, dark smells. Scents of centuries, moistened earth and woodlands, poured into me, submerging me until I thought I might drown.

There was no way to breathe without inhaling the past. There was no way to speak without voicing a cry. There was no way to see without facing the fear. Then, just in front of us, an old stone bridge, big enough for one small car.

We crossed the bridge, and as we did I left my insignificant self on the other side, dropping my fears like breadcrumbs, hoping they might be gobbled up by the birds and animals inhabiting the woods. I gave myself over to whatever might happen without thought to how it might impact my life.

When we reached the other side of the bridge we faced a stone wall and turned. The path veered left and before I could brace myself, there it was. I knew it as well as I knew my own home. It was Catherine's castle.

Two stone walls surrounded the palace. The inner of the two was identical to the very one I had tried to draw, unsuccessfully, several months ago. It, and the entire right front side of the castle, blazed in crimson vines. It was autumn and the hills were awash in a thousand tones of greens and golds.

Jonathan, our speaker, awaited us in the front courtyard. He was tall and rugged-looking, but his bearded face softened when he smiled. He wore a hunting outfit and could have stepped right out of a Chaucer novel. When he spoke, his English accent completed the image.

He connected, instantly, warmly and without pretense. He introduced us to Countess Cervini, current owner of the castle. Equally as warm and welcoming, she also exuded an air of comfort. She genuinely seemed happy for us to be in her home.

I had never met a Countess and didn't know what to expect. She was casual and charming. She wore tight, brown slacks with brown leather boots, a simple shirt and sweater. (I had clearly overdressed.) Her hair hung to her shoulders, straight, flat. I liked her face. It was rather no nonsense and classically Italian – beautifully Italian.

The introductions made on the sun soaked terrace, we walked through the large double, wooden doors. I was struck by an impulse to stop and caress them, but resisted. The room we entered was large and covered with portraits—mostly of Marcellus II, the Pope who was not only the Countess's ancestor, but was also responsible for the design and construction of the palace early in the 16th century.

Jonathan suggested we walk down to the village where an ancient festival was being held. The "Funghi Festival" was in full swing, celebrating the porcini mushroom.

The festival was fun. The food was good, the wine even better. I loved watching the villagers roast chestnuts over a fire in a huge, circular metal pan that hung from the top of a six foot tall tripod. Periodically, the chestnuts were shifted around with a long-handled hoe, and wine from an old jug was tossed on the fire to give them a unique smoky flavor. As a child I had not appreciated that the chestnut custom was Italian. I have long missed my grandfather's role of cross cutting a bag full of chestnuts and roasting them on Christmas day. Now, of course, when it's too late, I wish I could ask him about it.

As delightful as the mushroom festival was, I was anxious to get back up to the castle. When, finally, we made our way back, I realized that every time I crossed the stone bridge I felt caressed by the smells, swaddled by the rich, textured gifts of the wood. It was odd, but I felt strangely at home.

As we strolled back across the bridge, Jonathan talked about the trees in the surrounding forest. Some of them were rare, but most of them were chestnut trees. He talked about the critical importance of chestnuts to the survival of the village in ancient times.

"Without chestnuts the inhabitants of this village would have died," Jonathan explained. "They ground chestnuts to make breads and flours. Chestnuts were often the only form of protein available during the many harsh winters." As he talked he had an interesting habit of placing his hand inside the breast of his jacket. It was a small gesture, and clearly he was adjusting his scarf, but I found it endearing. It reminded me of someone, or something.

By the time we sat to listen to Jonathan speak in the large room inside the entrance, I found myself wishing he would be brief. I really wanted to get to the tour of the castle. Just sitting became an act of will power.

Terry introduced Jonathan, and he gave a slight bow, adjusted his scarf again, or was it an ascot? Whatever it was, he began and it was not long before I welled up listening to this sensitive, quite attractive man, tell his story. Clearly he was a romantic, but more than that, he was drawn to the Palazzo and just knew he was supposed to be there. He believed his destiny was linked to the Palazzo. No sooner did he land in the hermitage than he found himself writing for the first time in his life. He is now the author of several books.

When Jonathan finished, the Countess invited us to enjoy refreshments, and we did so, but she wanted to show us around before the light began to fade. Just as she started talking about the portraits in the room, a little girl came running in from outside. Her face startled me and I did a double take. She had dark hair, blue eyes and the most mischievous expression I'd ever seen. She laughed her way into the room, a bundle of what I guessed to be about seven year old energy. As she chattered away in Italian, oblivious to the fact that adults were engaged, the Countess admonished her, "Sofia!"

Countess Cervini went on to say something to the child in Italian, but I was no longer listening. Terry had the same startled look on her face that I felt on my own. But all she had to do was chuckle and shake her head. I knew I wasn't alone. It was a good thing, too. For this Sofia's face so resembled the one of my story, the face I had been seeing all this time, that had I any artistic ability, I could have painted it months ago, before I ever knew this child existed.

The Countess began the tour with an explanation of her ancestral uncle, Cardinal Cervini. "He was very humble and cared deeply about people." The Countess struggled a little with the English language, but did a beautiful job telling us everything she could. "His progressive thinking and interest in a variety of subjects made him unique at a time when learning, and so many books, had been banned.

"He became Pope Marcellus II in April of 1559," she said. "He died little less than a month later."

I couldn't help but ask, "Countess," I interrupted, "the articles written about him all say that he died of a weak constitution. Is that true?"

We had just entered a small sitting room on which hung a hand-painted detail of the family tree back to around 1063. She had just located "Pope Marcellus" on the tree. She stopped and looked at me. "You know about him?" She seemed surprised.

"A little, yes," I replied.

"He did not," she said with some considerable pride, "have a weak constitution. He was physically active and," she paused for emphasis, "watched what he ate very carefully. Nonetheless, my family is convinced that he was poisoned."

I found myself nodding, as I thought back to the conversation I'd had with Terry about this Pope. I wondered if she remembered my emphatic insistence that it just didn't feel right to me that he "simply died". I remember telling her about my strong feeling he was poisoned.

When I looked at her this time she wasn't smiling. In fact, she had turned a tad pale.

I stayed behind in the little room with the family tree and hunted for Catherine on it, but the light in the room was sparse and the tree was in dark colors and difficult to read. I leaned heavily onto the small table in front of me trying to steady myself, I felt a little shaky. As much as I wanted to just sit and be alone for awhile, I gave up and followed the rest of the group.

The Countess was pointing out details in yet another room. It was a small guest room, but with one important addition. Behind a bookcase was a small, undersized door that led to a secret passageway. As the Countess opened the door I found myself looking down a narrow, stairwell.

"Where does the secret passage lead?" I asked.

"To the kitchen," she said. "I will take you there and show you where the passageway comes out."

A medieval kitchen is not a place I would want to learn to cook. It was dark and dusty. The ceilings were low, hanging with the tools of the times. A large step took you up to the great stone fireplace where pots of endless soups and stews were undoubtedly prepared. There were a few stuffed animals on a ledge near the only other door to the kitchen. The door appeared to go outside, but the Countess led us in the opposite direction, down a very narrow passageway on the other side of the kitchen.

"This is where the secret passageway comes out." She indicated a small circular stairway with an iron railing.

With the Countess's permission I climbed the stairs a short way up. I couldn't even see where the passageway led because of the way it curved and disappeared into blackness. As I turned back to face the group I noticed that the passageway did not end at the kitchen, but took off in yet another direction.

"Countess," I called, for she was already leading us back to the kitchen, "where does this hall lead?"

"Oh," she stopped to explain, "It follows along and comes out near the church."

I didn't even bother to look in Terry's direction "Church?" I asked. "Can we see it?"

"I am sorry, no," she shook her head apologetically. "It is unsafe. We are planning to have it restored, but there is a large crack in the tower and it is not safe to enter."

My disappointment must have registered on my face because she quickly added, "We can go look at the outside, however."

As we made our way back to the kitchen I stole a look back at the secret passageway. I could almost see Robert following Mary and Sofia as they secretly went to meet the bishop.

I hung back from the group, needing a little space from the chatter. I let them get a bit ahead of me, but following the voices, I moved through yet another small sitting room and into what I heard the Countess describing as the library. The room was dim. There were no windows, but that was the only surprise as I surveyed the environment I had practically been living in all year. Directly across from me loomed a great, wooden bookcase. It filled the wall, and although it did not sit adjacent to a pallet, there was a small lounging sofa where I had placed the pallet. The sofa, and two large chairs were arranged in front of a huge fireplace, the top of which held the Cervini coat of arms. As I drifted toward the sofa, I felt myself filled with such a sense of longing that it took everything I had to hold myself upright. I sat. It probably was not appropriate, but I couldn't help myself. I guess I could have snapped more photos. Perhaps that would have been the wisest course of action, for in retrospect, I wish I could attach more details to the experience. But this was no tourist activity for me. This was a reality so anticipated and yet so unexpected, that I was content to just sit and take a few moments for myself. This place, this room, like Italy, knew me, and was glad to see me. This was the room where Catherine and Bella fell in love.

The only other noticeable difference between this room and the one in my Catherine's quarters was that there was no dining table. I always saw a large dining table, separated from everything. I didn't have a real chance to examine the room before the Countess led us into an adjoining room. I followed the group through the door to the next room...a private dining room, with its own fireplace. The coved ceiling, of the dining room, was ornately carved and painted with light green, frescoes. The whole of the ceiling was made of carved wood separated into sections. Every other section contained a small oval into which was painted, or perhaps carved, a scene. Along the edge of each section was a smaller carving of a creature...a swan, a spider, a lion, a snail. It was quite the most intricate ceiling I had ever seen. (Of course I had not yet been to the map room in the Vatican!)

The dining table was long, rectangular and seated twelve. The table I envisioned for Catherine was large and round, reflecting my feminist nature, but that seemed a petty detail. We went back into the 'library'.

I wanted everyone else to go away. I willed them away. As if on command, the Countess led them through another of the many doors out of the library.

I stayed behind and walked over to the two chairs in front of a massive fireplace, a small table between them. How many days and nights did I sit in those chairs hearing their conversations, feeling the sexual tension grow and bloom between Catherine and Bella? I could almost hear them whispering, "Here we are."

I don't know how long I sat before I heard the voices of the group again. They emerged from the room they entered, what, ten minutes ago? My sense of time, and even space, seemed to be warping. When they all left the library to head off through yet another door, I went into the room they just left.

Sunlight poured in through a single, large window directly across from the door and I was temporarily blinded. I looked down, away from the window, allowing my eyes to adjust. When I looked up Terry was standing, leaning on the broad windowsill, looking out. The double windows were swung fully opened to the inside of the room.

I swore Terry left with the others. I was wrong. She stood silhouetted against the window, and didn't hear me enter. As I stood watching, she pulled the clip from her hair and bent to shake it loose, briskly rubbing her scalp. When she straightened again she ran her fingers through her soft waves to fluff it up, and then leaned against the open windowsill again, resting her chin in her hand. Almost dreamily, she looked out. I walked over to the window. It did not surprise me to see that even though we hadn't left the first floor, the view from the window was high up, three stories up, in fact, and overlooked a garden. Beyond the garden was a view of the entire valley surrounding the palazzo.

"This is it, you know," I whispered as I stepped up to the window and looked out over the scene before us.

"I know," she said softly. Only Terry had read my manuscript and knew the details of the castle, the name of Catherine's daughter, and the suspicions I expressed about the pope who had been poisoned. I wasn't crazy. It was all here.

I turned and looked back into the room. To my left was a magnificent bed. Catherine's bed. The canopy was pulled back, but the draperies were the rich, velvet green I had always seen. I resisted the urge to climb up and lay on the bed. I knew that would cross a boundary, even if I could explain everything away by simply handing over a copy of my manuscript.

I turned back to Terry. She was staring at me with a look I did not, at first, understand. We stood silently for a few moments as understanding burrowed its way into my heart.

Her hair shimmered, and the words, "all the colors of the sunlight" rushed at me. They were the words Catherine said to Bella. I was instantly filled with so many emotions I didn't know who I was or what to do. Longing, relief, sadness, joy and surrender engulfed me. I fought the urge to pull her into my arms, but I wasn't sure who *she* was anymore. I didn't trust myself with everything I felt; didn't know what was real, so I forced myself to turn from her. I leaned on the windowsill and looked out at the valley, the church steeple, the gardens, and waited for the intense ache in my chest to subside.

When I felt Terry's hand on my shoulder, I pulled myself together. We caught up with the group and made our way outdoors to wander around the grounds. At the front of the church I was seized by a force of incomprehensible power. It took all of my strength not to fall to my knees as they threatened to buckle beneath me. I took several long, slow breaths and attempted to act normally. Again, I pulled out my camera. Again, it refused to function.

The sun was settling toward the horizon and the colors in the valley glowed. I moved toward a low, ancient rock wall and leaned against it.

As I watched, the last sunlight set the castle shimmering above me. The trees, the hermitage and the church descended into shadows.

It was then that the grief struck. I knew in an instant that I was alone. Catherine and Bella, my constant companions for these past many months, were gone.

Perhaps you will think me mad. Perhaps I am. But I felt their leaving like a shot through my chest. The pain was real. The grief was overwhelming. It was all I could do not to begin weeping. I was suddenly exhausted…physically, emotionally and spiritually exhausted.

The remainder of my time in Italy passed as, apparently, only time in Italy can pass. The days were over before I knew it, but the weeks seemed to move slowly. I developed a routine of writing, of wandering, of drinking wine and of thinking about all that had happened to me in the past eight months. I did enjoy every bit of Italy, although my last night there, as I wandered the streets of Rome, was painful. I'm not sure if it was because it was my last night, or because I chose to spend it alone, wandering aimlessly, looking for heaven knows what.

I know I was lonesome, lonelier than I remembered feeling in quite some time. But, even now, I can't say if the loneliness was carved from my loss of Catherine and Bella, or the kind of emptiness one feels when a dream fades. My dreams of Italy were drawing to a close. Maybe it was the realization that the story of Catherine and Bella was nearing its end in my life. Perhaps it was because I was missing my family acutely. Wherever my sadness came from, I could not shake it, so I let it accompany me as I went back to the Borgo. I wandered in and out of shops, sat at an outdoor café to enjoy my last meal and carafe of wine, and strolled into St. Peter's Square.

A group of singers was in the square. The harmony of their voices soared over the sounds of the water fountain and I was drawn toward them. As if to emphasize my desolation, they turned, in unison, leaving as I approached. So I went back to the tiered water fountain for the sheer comfort of her sounds. When I realized that the splashing of the water into itself only echoed the emptiness I felt, I went back to my room.

It was time to go home.

December 2008

It is finished. Less than a year in the making. I know that is a very short time to work on a book. But I did have help, lots of help.

Catherine and Bella were key, of course. My family, in their infinite patience and support gave me time, sending me off to Italy when we could not afford it, to help me fulfill a dream.

Whether or not Catherine and Bella lived real lives in sixteenth century Italy, I am convinced that this story came from outside of me and on some level is true. There are stories out there in the universe that just need to be told. I may never know why I was picked to tell this one. But this much I do know; the experience of writing this story, of researching everything I could about the Inquisition and sixteenth century life, of meeting new people and finding out about long gone ones, of falling in love with another time, another place, another culture, and, especially, the coincidence of being led to a place that I had spent the better part of eight months seeing in my mind, all of it transformed me in the most marvelous way.

Initially, I did experience a profound grief over the loss of Catherine and Bella. They have not returned since I left the Palazzo. My sadness ebbed slowly away and the empty space miraculously filled with an abundance of appreciation and joy of life's mysteries.

I still can't explain it, and I'm not sure I'll ever be able to. I confess I am left wondering about the confines of linear time and space.

But maybe, just maybe, the universe has a way of making certain that none of us are forgotten...even after almost five hundred years.

Fine

Sources

Estimates of the Number Killed by the Papacy in the Middle Ages and Later ©2006
David A. Plaisted
A great deal of information about the Inquisition came from this paper. The accounts of atrocities throughout Europe and the Americas, as presented by Father Tim's brother, Thomas, borrowed liberally from it.

Life In The Middle Ages: The Castle ©2001
Kathryn Hinds
Benchmark Books/Marshall Cavendish Corporation

Knight ©1993
Christopher Gravett
Eyewitness Books
Dorling Kindersley Limited

Historic Civilizations: Medieval Europe ©1960
Susie Hodge
Gareth Stevens Publishing

Daily Life in Elizabethan England ©1995
Jeffrey L. Singman
Greenwood Press

The 1500s: Headlines in History ©2001
Stephen Currie, Editor
Greenhaven Press, Inc.

The Encyclopedia of the Sword ©1995
Nick Evangelista
Greenwood Press

The Inner Game of Fencing: Excellence in Form, Technique, Strategy, and Spirit ©2000
Nick Evangelista
Masters Press

The Oxford History of Italy ©1997
George Holmes, Editor
Oxford University Press

Stephen Biesty's Castles ©2004
Meredith Hooper
Enchanted Lion Books

The Writer's Guide to Everyday Life in Renaissance England (1485-1649) ©1996
Kathy Lynn Emerson
Writer's Digest Books

Web Sources:

http://www.answers.com/topic/inquisition

http://www.alleanzacattolica.org/idis_dpf/english/i_medieval_inquisition.htm

http://womenshistory.about.com/od/medieval/Medieval_and_Renaissance_Womens_History.htm

http://www.middle-ages.org.uk/middle-ages-sitemap.htm

http://www.answers.com/topic/roman-inquisition

http://www.thenazareneway.com/inquisition.htm

http://www.medievalacademy.org/

http://atheism.about.com/od/christianityviolence/ig/Christian-Persecution-Witches/Witches-Satan-Court.htm

Wikipedia.com